A royal robber

by
Heribert Rau

TRANSLATED BY AGNES A. E. BLAKE

© 2015 NELVerlag
ISBN 978-2-914789-35-6

Dépôt Légal: Juin 2016

A royal robber

Part I.

A royal robber

A royal robber

I.
Louis XIV and his court

The peace of Nymwegen had strengthened anew the power of Louis XIV, King of France. He now stood before the world victorious and more powerful and greater than ever, while on the one hand his century greeted him with acclamations, and on the other curses and imprecations followed him. For more than half a century the predominating influence of this powerful and ambitious king was felt in European affairs. Louis XIV succeeded in crushing the opposition of the nobility, which had been the bane of the whole kingdom; in breaking the power of Parliament, and treading into the dust, with iron heel, every attempt made by the people for freedom. The nation obeyed; Parliament received laws from the monarch who did not hesitate to appear before it in a hunting-jacket, muddy boots, and riding-whip in hand. Even the leaders and heroes of the Fronde sunk to flattering, hypocritical courtiers. Louis had brought his kingdom to submit to the most absolute and unlimited sovereignty, and his bold motto, *«L'état c'est moi»* rolled over a world trembling with astonishment and excitement. But above all the king knew, understood and comprehended France and the French. Civil war had nourished and increased the energy of the French people; now the crafty prince used this strength, for his chosen ends. Bold plans wake the ambition of the nation; conquests – just or unjust – strengthened it; heroes like Condé and Turenne excited the volatile and war-loving people to an almost fanatical desire for battle; while the brilliancy and magnificence of the court, the growth of giant buildings, the protection and support of the arts and sciences, filled the French nation with the contagious poetical intoxication of greatness. What was more natural than that the warlike, vain, easily excited French should now rush into the pathway of fame and greatness, which had been opened to them by their beloved monarch At that time the stars of the first magnitude in France were Mazarin[1], Colbert[2],

---

[1] Giulio Mazarini (1602-1661), chief minister of the French king from 1642 until his death.

[2] Jean-Baptiste Colbert (1619-1683), minister of Finances of France from 1665 until his

A royal robber

Louvois[3] – Condé, Turenne[4], Luxemburg[5], Catinat[6], Vandonie – Corneille[7], Racine[8], Molière[9], Bayle[10], La Fontaine[11], Boileau[12], Fénelon[13], Bourdaloue[14], Bossuet[15], Saurin[16], Massilon – Mansart[17], Claude Lorrain[18], Poussin[19], Lebrun[20] and many others.

Three things worked together to give to France an age of brilliancy such as she has never since seen; and these were: the increasing Intellectual activity of the whole people- the rare individuality of the prominent men just mentioned – and the great interest and co-operation of the government. A new era dawned for France, an era which in many respects reminds one of the time of a Pericles, an Augustus, and the Medicis. And this brilliancy was so much the greater because the formerly dreaded rivals of France had fallen into inactivity and weakness.

The sun of Spain had gone down. The strength of Germany had long since faded, and the Emperor Leopold I, son of the Emperor Ferdinand III and the Spanish Infanta Maria Anna, was not the man to rescue the German

---

death.

[3] François-Michel le Tellier, Marquis de Louvois (1641-1691), secretary of State for war under Louis XIV.

[4] Henri de la Tour d'Auvergne, Vicomte de Turenne (1611-1675), marschal of France.

[5] François Henri de Montmorency-Bouteville, Duke of Piney-Luxembourg (1628-1695), marshal of France.

[6] Nicolas Catinat (1637-1712), marshall of France.

[7] Pierre Corneille (1606-1684), French dramatist.

[8] Jean Racine (1639-1699), French dramatist.

[9] Jean-Baptiste Poquelin (1622-1673), French playwright.

[10] Pierre Bayle (1647-1706), French philosopher.

[11] Jean de La Fontaine (1621-1695), French fabulist.

[12] Nicolas Boileau-Despréaux (1636-1711), French poet.

[13] François Fénelon (1651-1715), French writer.

[14] Louis Bourdaloue (1632-1704), French philosopher.

[15] Jacques-Bénigne Bossuet (1627-1704), French theologian.

[16] Joseph Saurin (1659-1737), French mathematician.

[17] François Mansart (1598-1666), French architect.

[18] Claude Gellée (1600-1682), French painter, born in Lorraine.

[19] Nicolas Poussin (1594-1665), French painter.

[20] Charles Le Brun (1619-1690), French painter.

A royal robber

Empire from its disunion, lethargy and perversity. Managing the helm of state with a weak hand, he saw the Empire threatened by the Turks, Hungary in rebellion, his capital, Vienna, besieged, France at war with Germany, and the north of the Empire growing strong as an independent government under Frederic Wilhelm, Elector of Brandenburg. The hopes of the once proud and dictatorial imperial crown now rested in the support of Holland and England. Denmark and Sweden, however, one or the other alternately allied to France or her enemy, annulled their influence, while at that period the voice of Russia was heard but little, and the Sultan was a friend to Louis the Fourteenth.

So, in two great wars against half Europe, Louis gained, through costly conquests, a brilliant, and richly rewarded victory.

Nothing would have been wiser and more natural than for all the allied European powers with the German Emperor at their head to oppose Louis in his plans for conquest, but the Elector Frederic of Brandenburg was almost the only one who recognized the importance of doing so.

He entered into an offensive and defensive alliance with Spain, the Emperor of Germany and Holland against France.

Louis, in consequence of this, was obliged to withdraw a portion of his troops under Turenne from Holland. Although there had been no great battles in the Netherlands, the French army had been very much reduced by skirmishes, sickness, etc.; while an attempt of the new general to invade the interior of Holland on the ice utterly failed.

The French were so luxurious that they would eat nothing but the tongues of cows, and buried the rest of the animal to avoid the stench. As soon as misfortune overtook them their wantonness quickly changed into wild vandalism; they commited so many frightful crimes, plundering, levying, burning etc., that the worst days of the Thirty Years War seemed to have returned.

The troops of Louis the Fourteenth, were obliged to withdraw, but this retreat was graced by 3.000 wagons laden with plunder and booty.

The king of France had now, as before no further cause to continue the war or commence a new one, east of all with Germany which really wished for peace. But since Louis XIV was convinced that his seizure of Holland had been a mis-step, his pride and insatiate desire for new conquest sought another means of bringing the conflict he had commenced to a victorious close.

The idea of a universal monarchy, which at a later day, intoxicated and led astray Napoléon I, haunted the mind of Louis. But as he was never accustomed to take justice into consideration with his desires, he now turned against the German Empire.

Under a mere pretext the Rhine-bridge near Strassburg, this pearl in the chain of German cities, was burnt; the other imperial cities in Alsace were captured, soldiers took possession of German provinces, taxes were unjustly levied, and within the boundaries of Germany the French committed many arbitrary acts which even their own rulers – the Emperor and Empire – would not have been justified in doing. But all this, so said Louis XIV, was in no way a violation of peace, but only kindly interference against the dangerous and powerful Emperor, although no one had asked for this assistance. Louis declared that the welfare of the German Empire was very dear to him, and his troops, under Turenne, had only invaded it to keep peace and order. Still he, with his whole army, was ready to withdraw from Germany, if the German Emperor would do the same.

Thus stood political affairs at the time of the beginning of this story. At the same time the brilliancy and magnificence of the court at Versailles and the apparent greatness of Louis XIV dazzled France and the whole world. Louis stood at the height of his power; he was possessed of the best armies, the greatest generals, a fine navy and still retained the affection of his subjects. Throughout France, arts, sciences, and commerce flourished better than ever before – the most brilliant society existed in Paris – nothing could be prouder and more magnificent than the court of Louis XIV. The most beautiful and intellectual women of France surrounded the throne of the king like a magnificent diadem of flowers. But Louis XIV knew how to appreciate this great charm of his court as his motto proves: «A court without women is a year without spring, and a spring without roses», and verily; he

A royal robber

plucked enough of these roses to sumptuously adorn his life.

II.

Louis XIV.

The scene in the great gallery in the palace of Versailles was a very animated one. Servants in glittering liveries, cavaliers in still more gorgeous court costumes, ladies dressed in satin, silk, or velvet, glistening in the colored rays of costly jewels, but still brighter in their own loveliness, filled the spacious room which Mansart had adorned with a wealth of mirrors, marble and gold bronzes, and Lebrun had decorated with his noble pictures. The palace of Versailles was then considered one of the new wonders of the world; as it will remain for all time one of the most remarkable monuments of the history of Art. At one time only a priory, a farm-house and a wind-mill stood on the eminence which now bears the crown of palaces. In the days of Louis XIII the farm house had disappeared, but the wind-mill still existed and often the sad and thoughtful monarch, returning from the chase, had slept in this miserable hut. He built a pavilion. Three years later the pavilion was converted into a small castle. Louis XIII made this little palace his toy. He passed the winter of 1632, the carnival of 1633 and the whole autumn of the same year there. One morning when he was wandering about this residence – the only one which he regarded as his own property – he said in a moment of enthusiasm to the Duke of Grammont[21]: «Marshal! do you remember having seen a wind-mill here?» «Yes, Sire» – answered the marshal –» the mill has disappeared, but the wind is still here.»

At last – in the year 1683 – Louis XIV determined to make a royal residence of Versailles. Mansart designed the plan, Lebrun sketched it, and now arose the magnificent building, which swallowed no less than one hundred and sixty-five million livres, and which by the unfortunate desire to imitate Louis XIV, for a long time – to the misery of nations and subjects – gave the example and pattern for a multitude of castles to European princes.

The courtiers and dignitaries of the kingdom were gathered together in the

---

[21] Antoine III Agénor de Gramont, Duke of Gramont (1604-1678), marshall of France.

great gallery of this castle, to attend His Majesty according to their rank and title at «*les grandes ou secondes entrées*» of the «*Lever*»; for Louis XIV was surrounded by a strict, almost incredible ceremony which reminded one of Eastern potentates. Louis XIV liked it to be so,... but Louis XIV was cunning enough to unite therewith diplomatic strategy. For him everything depended upon making an end of the feudal system in his kingdom, bending the once proud and independent French nobility under the yoke of his scepter, and reducing them to an absolute dependence upon the crown. Two things materially aided him; the innate French vanity and extravagance, and the ambition of the nobility. Charmed and attracted by the splendor and magnificence of the court, the noblest families rushed into a rivalry in expenditure which only too soon, led them to bankruptcy, and thus to the most entire dependence upon the crown. But the crafty wearer of this crown gave them a good example of pompous show: for example, the value of the crown jewels, which at the death of King Louis XIII, amounted to 700.000 francs, in 1696, under Louis XIV, had increased to 11.330.000 francs: At the same time, satin, silk, velvet, costly laces, jewels, gold and silver brocades, leathers and trinkets of all kinds decked the ladies and gentlemen of the court to excess; but if this was usually the case, how much more so to day,... the day on which the Persian ambassadors had been granted a ceremonious audience – in which they had begged to lay at the feet of the King of France the homage of their ruler. Everything therefore exhibited the greatest magnificence, which reached its summit in the toilettes of the Duchesses de Chatillon, de Rohan, de Montbazon, and de Beaufort, who passed through the gallery with the ladies of honor to the «*entrée du cabinet*». As the resplendent suns of this court, they were surrounded and followed by other stars; and a long line of ladies and gentlemen of high rank. Merry conversation enlivened all, but the merriest among the crowd of courtiers was the Duc de Saint Aignan[22], the favorite of the King, who, inexhaustible in spirit and wit, had won an important influence over Louis XIV. This Duc de Saint Aignan was a handsome man, the perfect representative of a true Frenchman, joyous as the day, changeable as quicksilver, slippery as an eel,

---

[22] Paul de Beauvilliers, 2nd duc de Saint-Aignan.

and yet proud and chivalric in all his ways. His pale, rather thin, face, had fine features, intellect shone from his black eyes; the small delicate moustache, and beard à la Henri IV were finely traced. Boldly arched eyebrows, with the slightly aquiline nose, evinced courage and decision; while his black waving hair and a delicate allongenperuke, such as the King was accustomed to wear, harmonized admirably with the rest of his appearance.

The slight figure was very conspicuous in the dress of dark red velvet, whose texture was almost hidden under its gold embroidery, while the vest of gold brocade covered the body almost to the knees, like a glittering coat of mail. His handsomely formed legs were clothed in white silk stockings, fastened by ruby clasps to the red velvet small clothes. Buttons and shoe-buckles were set with the same stones: a large ostrich feather- white as new fallen snow – waved lightly from the small three-cornered hat, while the sword hung with a defiant air, by the side of the cavalier, and pert and defiant, merry and easy – as was then the custom of Louis XIV's Court – were the words of the Duc. The Duc's frivolity in matters of religion was well known, but as the report had been spread among the courtier's that Saint Aignan had taken off his hat before a crucifix, the Duchesse de Chatillon had just asked him if he had been converted and turned to the Lord.

Saint Aignan smiled and answered: – «We bow to each other, but are not on speaking terms.»

«He is a perfect heathen!» – exclaimed Saint Fargeau – «Do you know, ladies, what a heretical answer the Duc lately gave me?»

«No!» exclaimed all.

«What was it Prince?» replied St. Aignan, laughing – «I have forgotten that crime.»

«A few evenings since, as I was rising from the gaming table with the Duc, he was polite enough to offer me his equipage.»

«He is always a perfect gentleman,» said the Duchesse de Montbazon.

«As I knew,» continued St. Fargeau – «that his horses had been in use all day, I refused his offer. What do you think he answered?»

A royal robber

«Well!» cried all laughing.

«*Morbleu!*» said he – «if God had created my horses to rest, he would have made them chaplains to the sacred chapel.»

General hilarity followed this remark; but the Duc received many delicate taps of the fan from the ladies, accompanied by «godless man!»

«I don't really know whether I am godless,» exclaimed the Duc – «but it was certainly godless that the Prince should have won three thousand pistols from me on that same evening.»

«Why, what is that?» said the Duc de Hacqueville – «the Duchesse de Bourgoyne lost 12.000 Louis d'or last evening.»

«Pah! 12.000 Louis d'or!» exclaimed Monsieur de Brissac scornfully – «a mere bagatelle, the Montespan[23] understands that better. She lost four million livres at Bassette at one sitting, but compelled the bankers to continue playing till she won all back. The gentlemen hoped to compensate them-selves another time, but they were bitterly deceived, for the next morning the Montespan wisely forbade the game of Bassette.»

«That she could easily do,» said the Duchesse de Sevigne merrily – «for the *jeu d'amour* still remained.»

«And with it the six prizes[24],» said Prince Condé laughing.

«And yet she has been supplanted by Madame de Soubise!» exclaimed St. Aignan carelessly.

«And how long will that color hold?» asked the Duc de Caumartin ironically;

«What is that to us,» said St. Aignan – «For my part I agree in this case with Her Majesty the Queen. A short time since, when the report was spread that Madame de Ludre was the King's mistress, one of the queen's ladies had the audacity to inform Her Majesty, and added: ‹Your Majesty must oppose this new love!› The Queen said quietly, «It is nothing to me; that concerns Ma-

---

[23] Françoise Athénaïs de Rochechouart de Mortemart, Marquise of Montespan (1640-1707), maitresse of Louis XIV.
[24] The six children she bore to Louis XIV.

A royal robber

dame de Montespan.»

At this moment the voice of the first chamberlain called: «*L'entrée du cabinet!*»

The faces of the noble company were immediately drawn into the lines demanded by etiquette; the Duchesse, ordered their brocade skirts to be smoothed out by their ladies in waiting; the gentlemen took off their hats, and the whole group entered the royal apartments. Those who remained in the large gallery replaced their hats for their hour... the hour of the great audience, or the passing of His Majesty on the way to mass, had not yet struck.

There were about sixty; gentlemen and ladies, court and state officers, cavaliers, marquises, counts, barons, and officials of all grades. Many of them – who perhaps had not a sou in their pockets – gleamed, and sparkled in magnificent costumes, costing more than their whole property. One fine looking young man, who stood modestly, almost with an air of embarrassment, in a window-niche, formed an exception, by his simple dress, which marked him as a country nobleman. But how could the modesty of the youth and his plain costume escape the notice of the cortiers of Louis XIV? They whispered and jested about the youth, and were highly delighted to shorten, the «*entre temps,*» the tedious hour of waiting in the great gallery of Versailles, by witticisms about the newcomer. The young man, however, noticed nothing of this. The splendor and magnificence of the court at which he found himself to-day for the first time – the impression made by the palace and his present surroundings – the crowd of noisy courtiers, who moved about as easily and as much at home as if they were in their own chambers – the ardent glances of the ladies, who notwithstanding his old fashionned, plain dress, looked with pleasure at the handsome young man – the levity of their appearance, which allowed all their charms to be seen, so that there was scarcely anything to conceal. .. .all this perplexed the youth so much that he was incapable of quiet observation. But there were still more important things which made him thoughtful and depressed in heart and mind. Young Gauthier de Montferrand stood at one of the most important turning points of his life – for it was the intention of his uncle, – the worthy old captain of the royal guard, Monsieur de Torcy – to present his nephew to the King, and introduce him to the celebrated Court of Versailles. This was no trifle to do. Gauthier, who was only twenty-one years old, had lived till now in the most perfect retirement in the country, and had been brought up with the strictest principles.

Conflicting feelings raged in the breast of the youth. Once enrolled in the King's body-guard, what a brilliant pathway might perhaps be opened to him! Generals and statesmen had gone forth from this body guard, which stood so near the monarch. Gauthier was Frenchman enough to place his aim high – young enough to dream of the easiest fulfillment of the boldest desires.

Gauthier felt that this was for him the birthday of a new man and a new world. He felt that in this, hour, he took the first step out of the boundaries of his childhood; but, he felt, too, that in this same hour the paradise of his childhood closed behind him, and yet the youth understood that he must break, through the flowery chains of childhood, if he would be a   man and gain a future. And yet in this decisive hour, the thoughts of the young man turned again with pain to the past. Who can bid adieu to an Eden without a last look of love, of sadness, and painful renunciation? And in this Eden still wandered for Gauthier, a lovely angel who had shared with him the plays of his childhood, the simple, but pure and noble joys of his youth. She was indeed a lovely maiden – a distant relation – Marie Angeline Scoraille de Rousille, Mademoiselle de Fontanges; – a vision of beauty, whose auburn hair, mild eyes, and dazzling whiteness of skin, gave an idea of the Madonna.

What joyous, happy hours Gauthier had passed with her where her little ancestral castle stood in charming Limagne[25], on the banks of the Allier[26].

The youth was lost in these sweet dreams, forgetful of his surroundings, thinking of this picture of his loved home, of the ancestral castle, of the faithful old mother, who now occupied it alone and of Angeline, when a well-known voice fell upon his ear. It was that of his uncle, Captain de Tor-

---

[25] Large plain in Auvergne, in Southern France.
[26] A river in Southern France.

cy, just coming from the royal apartments into the gallery, who now. Approached his nephew:

«It is even so, Prince,» said de Torcey at this moment – «the Fontanges are connections of ours, but only a single brand of this old family remains. It is a very pretty and charming one, however.»

«And that is Mademoiselle Scoraille de Rousille?»

«At your service.»

«But how did you learn that the child is so beautiful. Monsieur de Torcy? You have not left the court these twenty years, and yet you say that Mademoiselle Angeline is only sixteen years old.»

«Where did I learn that?» – answered the captain with a proud, pleased smile – «I know it from yonder young fellow!» and he pointed toward his nephew, who still stood in the window niche, and at the approach of the Prince and his uncle, bowed respectfully, though rather awkwardly.

A scornful expression played round the corners of St. Aignan's mouth; then he shrugged his shoulders and said: «The heart of a youth is a partial painter in such matters.»

«And you. Prince» – interrupted the captain – «are a doubting Thomas. Look here!»

Torcy drew a miniature from his breast-pocket. But the Prince had scarcely cast a glance at the picture, when he exclaimed with astonishment. «That is indeed a charming creature! How did you get such a treasure, old swash-buckler?»

«Gautier brought it to me,» – answered de Torcy with ill-concealed vanity, and at the same time introduced his nephew as Angeline's young friend and playmate.

What thoughts rose in the mind of the Prince at this moment, neither the new-comer nor the old soldier could guess. Only one thing was plain; the Prince suddenly welcomed young Gauthier to the Court of Versailles, with great warmth and kindness. Indeed at parting he even offered his hand to

A royal robber

him and said: «We shall be friends!»

But how this scene had suddenly changed the manner of all present towards the young man. The Duc de St. Aignan, though a much younger man than the king, was one of his favorites. In a moment all jests, witticisms, and bon mots upon the new-comer ceased, and the scornful manner of the courtiers instantly became respectful now that the Prince, a favorite of the king, had honored him with so friendly a reception.

«You are a lucky fellow,» cried the Captain, as the Prince withdrew. «If he speaks a good word for you, you are secure! He is, to be sure, one of the wildest and most extravagant men at court, but certainly one of the most influential!»

«One of the wildest and most extravagant?» repeated Gauthier with astonishment – «and I must depend upon him?»

Monsieur de Torcy would have answered, but at that moment came the announcement that the great audience of ceremony was about to begin. The whole gallery was in motion, as if by magic, and all streamed toward the Audience Hall. Torcy and his nephew followed. Gautier's heart beat audibly; now for the first time he was to see Louis XIV, surnamed «the great.» Grand and imposing was the Hall of Audience, upon which Mansard[27] and Lebrun had lavished all the resources of art. Grand and imposing was the company collected here, for it comprised the high birth, intellect, and beauty of France. But what was all this in comparison to the moment in which the doors flew open and the grand-master of ceremonies appeared among them with the announcement – «the King» – all heads were uncovered, and the Sun of France, Louis XIV, followed by the Queen, the royal Prince, the Marquise de Montespan, Madame de Soubise, Madame de Ludre, the whole Court and the ministers and officers, entered amid a flourish of trumpets. Every one bowed to the dust and a deathlike silence followed the sound of the music. The king alone was covered. Slowly, proudly, and gravely he inclined his head and the bended backs dared to straighten themselves.

---

[27] Jules Hardouin-Mansart (1646-1708), a French architect.

A royal robber

Louis XIV wore a dress ornamented with gold and precious stones worth twelve and a half million francs; his tall, noble, and powerful figure could scarcely stand upright beneath its weight.

And yet Gauthier did not see this dress, but only the king, only Louis XIV, whom the world called the Great and who indeed stood before him like a demi-god among men. Louis XIV throughout his long reign, knew how to represent in a masterly manner, the king. With him, everything, down to the slightest movement, the slightest word, was measured, majestic, grand, and yet unstudied and natural.

No man ever accomplished- so much, or produced so profound an impression by such means. A glance from his eye, a«gesture of his hand was sought and noticed, caused happiness or misery. And was he not at the same time one of the handsomest men in France? Though not tall, he was of good height, and knew how to place himself on a par with the tallest by his perfect bearing, as well as his high heels. His mouth was beautiful, his aquiline nose indicated firmness, there was an imperious expression in the glance of his blue eyes, while his slow, sharply accented manner of speech, lent a commanding earnestness to his words. In his whole bearing appeared the Spanish gravity, an inheritance from his mother, a gravity, however, most agreeably tempered by French grace. Gauthier was overpowered and enchanted, as every Frenchman must have been by such a king; but the formality almost depressed him, so that he breathed more freely and easily when the sovereign, and, following him, the Persian ambassadors, had retired. For him, there yet remained the most important moment, that of his own presentation. But the hour had not yet struck; for at the Court of Louis XIV, everything moved according to the laws of an immutable, all-controlling etiquette. Gauthier's presentation could only take place in the great gallery at the king's progress to holy mass.

III.
A day from the life of a king

When Gauthier had returned to the gallery with his uncle – the whole court, with the exception of the princes and princesses of royal blood, did the same – Captain de Torcy asked his nephew what impression he had received. The youth, full of enthusiasm, disclosed his whole heart. He was, as is the custom of youth – fire and flame. Only this tedious ceremony; the fetters of etiquette were disagreeable to one who was accustomed to a free, happy life in the midst of nature. Torcy listened to him with smiles; but when Gauthier had finished, exclaimed: «O, ho, my young man! I see you think it is the same here as in Limagne! You cannot forget the beautiful mountains of Puy de Dôme[28] and Mont d'Or; but Paris and Versailles, St. Germain and Marly are not on the charming banks of the Allier, and at the court of a great king things are different from the life in your ancestral castle. But that you may understand the manners of our court, I will describe a day from the life of the king, and thereby pass away the tedious hour of waiting.»

«How will that help me, uncle!» said Gauthier, «surely each day brings its own affairs, its own changes!»

«Scarcely, my young friend!» answered the uncle; «one passes like another, at least so far as etiquette is concerned; and to this His Majesty clings, as to a sacred thing. So listen and impress what I say upon your mind, for any misstep upon this smooth floor may deprive you of position and future prosperity.»

The young man had not expected such constraint at the court of so powerful a king. His joyousness, youthful courage, and ideas of freedom, rose strongly against the yoke which was about to be laid upon him; but he could not turn back. He therefore yielded quietly, and – suppressing a deep sigh – lent an ear to his uncle, who stepping with his nephew into the win-

---

[28] Volcano in Auvergne, in Southern France.

dow, continued: «At eight o'clock in the morning, if the king still sleeps the *garçons de chambre* enter, if it is cold, make a fire, or if warm gently open the windows. Then they take the *l'en-cas*, the *mortier*, and *lit de veille* away.»

«*L'en-cas, mortier, lit de veille?*» repeated Gauthier, «what are they?»

«*Ventre-saint-gris!*» exclaimed the captain, «it is very evident that Limagne is far away from here, otherwise, young man, you would know things which are daily used by our great king. *L'en-cas* is a meal which is always ready at night in case the king should become hungry. The *mortier* is a silver dish in the form of a mortar which is filled with water, and upon which floats apiece of yellow wax.»

«And its use?»

«It serves His Majesty for a night lamp.»

«And the *lit de veille?*»

«Is the bed which is prepared every evening in the king's room for the first groom of the chamber.»

«Well, and when all these things have been taken away?» asked the young man, with a slightly ironical smile.

«Then,» continued the captain gravely, «the first chamberlain waits till the clock strikes half past eight, and then wakes the king before the last stroke dies away. Thereupon the head surgeon and physician rub the king, and if he has perspired help him change his linen. Now comes the entrance of those who have free access to the *Lever* or *les grandes entrées*. The first courtier opens the curtains of the bed, and offers His Majesty the consecrated water out of the bowl which has been brought to the head of the bed.»

«And those who are present at the *Lever?*» asked Gauthier.

«They remain a few moments, in which they have the right to lay before the king any petitions. When no one has anything more to request, the cavalier who drew aside the curtains and offered the holy water, gives him the prayer-book. Five minutes later His Majesty closes the book, and the chamberlain hands him his dressing-gown, when the *secondes entrées* takes place.»

A royal robber

«And who are admitted to this *secondes entrées?*»

«Only those of the highest rank.»

«Poor king!» exclaimed the youth, «he never has a moment to himself.»

«O!» said his uncle, «there is more to come. A few moments after the recaption of these persons, all of great distinction are admitted, and finally those in the gallery enter.»

«And the king?»

«He, in the meantime, busies himself in gracefully putting on his shoes, which the first groom of the chambers hands him, after clothing the royal legs in silk stockings. Every other day the Court is present while His Majesty is shaved, when a cavalier is allowed to hold his mirror.»

«Allowed! Allowed!» repeated the youth, and a dark flush crimsoned his noble face. «Is that an honor for a cavalier?»

«*Ventre saint gris!*» exclaimed Monsieur de Torcy, «a great honor!»

Gauthier was perplexed and silenced; but the captain gravely continued, and explained that as soon as the king was dressed he knelt in prayer. Then all present, the clergy, the court, and even the cardinals, knelt about him. Only the lackeys remained standing, and the Captain of the Guard on duty stood by the door with drawn sword. «After that,» continued M. de Torcy, «comes the *entrée du cabinet*, The king is followed into his cabinet by all the officers, who here receive their orders for the day. So the whole court knows in the morning what His Majesty intends to do.»

«But cannot the king make some change afterwards?» said Gauthier.

Torcy shook his head. «What Louis XIV has once ordered,» he answered, «is never opposed or changed, unless some important, unforeseen circumstance occurs.»

«Good heavens!» exclaimed the youth in an undertone, «then the king is no better than a slave.»

«Imprudent boy,» said the captain with an angry glance, «can you never forget your Limagne! Here even the walls have ears,» and twisting his moustache, the captain looked cautiously around, fortunately they were unheard and unnoticed.

«I will be more careful!» said the youth soothingly, but he blushed like a girl, and his heart became more despondent at what he heard.

The captain took up the thread of his discourse again: «After giving the orders for the day, the king, by a slight nod, grants all permission to retire; he then converses with the young princess and their tutors for about half an hour. Next follows the time for the state audience and the *entre temps*, which is the present time, and in which the whole court waits here in the gallery.»

«Then almost every minute has its particular name!» said the youth smiling sadly.

«And its duties!» added the captain, «In a quarter of an hour, for instance, the king will pass us on his way to mass, and at that time it is allowable to speak to him, and present strangers. Collect yourself, young man.»

Gauthier trembled. The great, decisive moment, in which he should stand face to face with Louis XIV, was approaching. He scarcely heard his uncle's further description of the subsequent council of ministers, and the visits of the king to his different mistresses, the Marquise de Montespan, whose star was now paling – Madame de Soubise, and Madame de Ludre.

Of this Gauthier had already heard. France had long been accustomed to see her kings languishing in the rosy chains of love and beautiful women, and the fact was now scarcely repulsive to a Frenchman. He listened more earnestly to the further description, when Torcy said: «His Majesty's dinner is almost always *au petit couvert*, that is, the king dines alone.»

«Alone?» exclaimed the youth with astonishment, «and the queen and princes?»

«Alone,» repeated M. de Torcy with an emphasis which cut short all farther questions. «*Tel est notre bon plaisir*, the king says. When the table is laid, the court appears with the princes at their head, and the first chevalier informs the king that dinner is served. The king appears, sits down, and is attended by the first chamberlain and the princes – often even Monseigneur his brother, while every one else stands silently in the background with uncovered head. But, what is the matter?» exclaimed Captain de Torcy suddenly. «*Ventre saint gris*, you are blushing like a girl!»

«It is nothing!» answered Gauthier with embarrassment. «I only wondered at Monseigneur –and the other nobles.»

«For what reason?» broke in de Torcy, «the king is the state; all others are his servants.»

«But his own brother.»

«The king never offers him a chair during the meal. Standing with uncoverred heads and napkins under their arms, the princes of the blood serve him and consider it an honor.»

«The young man bit his lips. With what different conceptions of honor he had come to court! What different ideas, too, of the one whom the world called the *greatest of kings*, whom since his earliest childhood he had revered as the finest and proudest of chivalry.

«After dinner,» continued de Torcy, finishing his picture with rapid strokes of the pencil, «the king sometimes receives Monseigneur alone, and at the same time feeds his setters. A second toilette in the presence of the favorites then follows, and then – fine weather or foul – they drive out, to chase a stag in the park, to shoot, or to look at the different buildings. Sometimes His Majesty orders a promenade with the ladies, or a collation in the woods at Marly or Fontainebleau.»

«And his family?» asked Gauthier anxiously.

«An hour after the return belongs to them; then comes the Montespan or Madame de Ludre, in whose apartments the rest of the evening is passed.»

«And supper?»

«Takes place about ten o'clock. The master of ceremonies on duty then appears with staff in hand, accompanied by the captain of the guard, who has kept watch in the ante-chamber of the lady whom the king visits. Only the captain,» said Torcy proudly, «is allowed to open the door and say *Le roi est*

A royal robber

servi. A quarter of an hour after, the king comes to supper. During this quarter of an hour the officers of the household have made les *prets*.»

«*Les prets?*»

«That is they have examined the bread, the salt, the plate, the napkins, the knives, forks, etc.»

«For what purpose?»

«To see if they are poisoned.»

«Poisoned?» repeated the youth with astonishment and his brow darkened.

«This takes place at the dinner also,» said his uncle. «But the dishes are always prepared by this rule: under surveillance of two guards, a doorkeeper, one of the first chevaliers, the controller general and the overseer of the kitchen, while two guards must see that no one approaches the king's food.»

«Poor king,» sighed Gauthier.

«Why poor king?» asked Torcy with astonishment.

«How can a man have an appetite with such precautions?» said the young man.

His uncle laughed heartily «*Ventre-saint-gris,* –»said he merrily. «You can be at rest on that subject. His Majesty wields an admirable blade in the field and at the table.»

«And does the king eat alone here also?»

«Yes, and the court stand at a distance. Six noblemen serve him. The princes and princesses of the blood may now seat themselves at a little distance. A circle of the fairest women of France stand behind them, while during the supper soft music, sounding from a distance, by no means disturbs conversation. After the king has taken supper in this manner, he rises and with him, of course, all who were seated. Two guards and a doorkeeper now precede him, and he enters his bedchamber. Thereupon begins the *petit coucher*, to which the *grandes* and *secondes entrées* as well as the favorites, remain.»

«Again,» exclaimed the youth with astonishment.

A royal robber

«Again,» repeated the uncle, «until the first stroke of midnight, and till then the privilege of being in the presence of the greatest and most powerful monarch of the world is made the most of. Requests and petitions are presented, flatteries and calumnies uttered, marks of favor sought for, and enemies overthrown. When the king speaks to one of those present, all the others withdraw. The clock strikes, the ladies bow low and retire, and the king goes to bed.»

«Freedom at last then.»

«Not so fast. The valet now receives His Majesty's watch, and the relics which he always wears for protection against daggers and poisons, and his orders; – two chevaliers then unfasten his garters, two valets, one on each side, draw off his small clothes, shoes, and stockings, two pages from the oldest families hand him his slippers. At that moment the dauphin approaches and offers the king his night shirt, which the, master of the wardrobe has warmed. And now –»

«Well?»

«Now comes the moment for the greatest favors.»

«Now? I should think the tormented man would get into bed?»

«The monarch now selects from the gentlemen the fortunate one who is permitted to light him to bed with the well-known silver candlesticks and two lighted candles. The doorkeeper calls: *Retire, gentlemen.* Those present withdraw, the favored one precedes the king with the lights and the king goes to bed, the royal physician then inquires concerning His Majesty's health and one day of the king's life is over.»

«And this is repeated daily?» asked the youth despondently.

«Daily, one is like another,» replied Captain de Torcy.

«Then,» exclaimed the youth with a sad smile – then I would not wish to be a king!»

IV.
«Nec pluribus impar.»

At this moment the folding doors opened, and the king came into the galle-ry. Every head was immediately barred, the ladies curtsied deeply, the gentle-men bowed almost to the ground. Louis, his covered head proudly raised, advanced gravely and solemnly. He no longer wore the dress overloaded with gold and precious stones, which had adorned him in the audience at which he received the Persian ambassadors, but instead a plain, blue frock coat – the blue coat which has become historical. For in order, according to his opinion, to reward personal services rendered to him, Louis XIV had instituted a strange privilege at his court; this privilege consisted in the dis-tinction of being allowed to wear a blue frock coat) such as the king himself wore. The permission was conferred by a diploma,, and was the more sought, because those who wore the blue coat had the right to accompany the king to the chase and in his promenades. But what services were some-times rewarded by this privilege? Condé, the victor of Rocroy, Sens and Nördlingen, begged for this favor. He received it; but not because he had won four great battles, and was victorious in twenty smaller engagements, but because he had humbly waited upon the king, with his napkin over his arm, on the canal at Fontainebleau![29]

The king now approached de Torcy. The uncle presented his nephew to the monarch, he had wisely first obtained a position for him in the body-guard. The king graciously exchanged a few words with both; then passed on, and after a few similar presentations which lasted for a moment, disappeared within the doors leading to the Royal chapel. Fame is a strange thing. This was nowhere more true than at the court of Louis XIV, whom flatterers cal-led the «Great.» Did not the whole court, princes and princesses at its head, bow before the king's mistresses? Did not the queen even ride in the same carriage with la Valliere and Madame de Montespan, till at last the people shouted, «We want to see the *three* queens?» Did not the queen consider her-

---

[29] Louis XIV and his Century, iv. 186.

self fortunate if she was received and invited to play cards by Mme de Montespan, who retained her home toilette. Were not the Montespan's six children; the Duc de Maine, the Comte de Vexin, the Mademoiselles de Nantes, Tour, and Blois, and the Comte de Toulouse, made legitimate, in defiance of the French laws, and did not the whole court treat them as princes and princesses of the royal family? Did not the Marquis de Villerceaux offer to win his nieces for the king, and were not these nieces sorely disappointed because the king refused the proposal? These were the ideas of honor and greatness at the Court of Louis XIV!

To the credit of Gauthier it must be said, that his heart and mind were still free from these sad errors.

The inexperienced young Frenchman was overpowered by the intoxication of fame, and glory which the nation drew from the bewildering appearance of the king. Gauthier was young, warm blooded, and ambitious, like every Frenchman – how could this *tête-à-tête* with the most powerful monarch of his time fail to excite him? His face glowed -with color – his eyes sparkled; resolution beamed from his features – while within him a voice cried: «To be sure, I stand alone, and walk without fame among men; but cannot one who is a perfect man do more than hundreds who are only parts of men?» And with an air of boldness and determination he assured his uncle, that no aim should be too high for him to strive after!

At this the captain smilingly stroked his beard. «*Ventre-saint-gris!*» he exclaimmed, – «you are right; I like to see such a spirit in youths, though… there is nevertheless a *but*.»

«A but?» asked Gauthier,

«Yes! and when we have left the palace and are sitting over a bottle of wine in the wine-room at the 'Cardinal Richelieu' – I am not on duty to-day; – I will make this 'but' clear to you by a little story of the past, or have you already heard in your ancestral ratnest at Limagne of the king's device *'nec pluribus impar!'* and the fate of the minister Fouquet?[30]»

---

[30] Nicolas Fouquet (1615-1680), superintendent of Finances in France 1653-1661.

A royal robber

«In our quiet little ancestral castle,» answered the youth smiling, though with a significant emphasis, there are certainly many rats, but they have never told me anything of the device '*nec pluribus impar*'.»

«Well, come along then, my lad,» exclaimed the captain, much pleased. «To-day is your day of honor, and while we are sitting over our wine, you shall hear the story, which must serve as a warning for your whole life.»

Half an hour after, the two were sitting at a large oaken table in the drinking room of the 'Cardinal Richelieu' with an enormous bottle of wine before them. The captain filled a glass, emptied it to Gauthier's health, and then commenced.

«Now attention, young man! We are alone, and so you shall hear the story of '*nec pluribus impar*' as a warning! The omnipotent minister of Louis XIV, Cardinal Mazarin, died. As soon as the king received the news, he summon-ned the men who had been recommended to him by Mazarin as his success-sors, Le Tellier Lyonne and Fouquet, and told them that from this time he would reign himself.»

«I like that in the king,» exclaimed Gauthier enthusiastically, «whoever wi-shes fame in this world must stand upon his own feet.»

«Yes,» added the captain, – «and firmly too, that! he may not fall at the first storm. But now do not interrupt me, if I am to tell the story.»

«I will be silent.»

«Very well,» said the captain, emptied another glass, and continued: «The men recommended by the cardinal were wise – Fouquet was an excellent minister of finance who always knew how to open new sources of supply under the most untoward circumstances.»

«You jest, uncle!» exclaimed Gauthier merrily, forgetting his newly made promise. «A Louis XIV cannot be in want of money?»

«*Ventre saint gris!*» exclaimed the captain, «not the king, but the country!»

«But this splendid court?»

«Young man! all that only glitters on the surface. You will soon learn the proverb, 'all is not gold that glitters!'»

«But France, France,» cried the youth, «its resources must still be inexhaustible.»

«Yes,» said the captain gloomily, «if the good Cardinal Mazarin had not been its leech for twenty years.»

«The great Mazarin?»

«Oh! innocence!» exclaimed M. de Torcy, with an ironical laugh, «the great Cardinal Mazarin was a great rascal. To satisfy his ambition Mazarin betrayed France, to satisfy his avarice he ruined it. He left fifty millions at his death, and he had buried fifteen millions in addition.»

«But uncle,» whispered Gauthier, «I thought the walls had ears here!»

«Pah!» exclaimed the captain, «Mazarin is dead, the king hated him, and the country curses him! But we have wandered from Fouquet again. Fouquet was an able financier; he had an admirable intellect, was considered an excellent jurist, was finely educated, and of noble manners. He also understood how to listen and to reply, two qualities one seldom meets in a minister. He knew how to answer people who came begging so pleasantly that he could dismiss them almost satisfied, without opening his own or the state treasury. Generous towards scholars whom he knew how to criticise and reward according to their deserts, he was the friend of Racine[31], La Fontaine[32] and Molière[33], the Macacnas of Lebrun and le Notre. Unfortunately, Fouquet flattered himself that he could lead the young king as Mazarin had done, while at the same time, he would diminish his work, care for his pleasures, and help him in his love affairs. See, my lad, this was the stumbling block of his ambition. The king wanted no second Mazarin, and so hatred towards Fouquet became rooted in his heart.»

The captain took a long draught and then continued. «But Fouquet suffered not only from the hatred of the king, but also from the envy of the princes

---

[31] Jean Racine (1639-1699), a French dramatist.
[32] Jean de La Fontaine (1621-1695), a French fabulist.
[33] Jean-Baptiste Poquelin (1622-1673), a French playwright and actor.

and the court, for he was enormously rich and his influence in the country grew from day to day. Then the unfortunate idea of surprising the king occurred to the minister; he would exceed the little festivals at Fontainebleau, would show Louis XIV what splendor, taste and luxury could do. So Fouquet invited the king and his whole court to his castle of Vaux.»

«Then the castle of Vaux was very large and beautiful?» asked Gauthier.

«Well, young man!» said the captain, «you can judge of that by what it cost.»

«And how much did it cost?»

«It cost Fouquet fifteen million livres.»

«Fifteen millions!» exclaimed the youth, staring with astonishment.

«Fifteen millions,» answered the captain quietly. «The king went. He was accompanied by a company of musketeers, under command of Monsieur d'Artagnan. The court followed, as all were invited who could make claim to any distinction. La Fontaine was appointed to describe the festival, Benserade[34] to celebrate it by song. A prologue was to be recited by Pelisson, and a comedy by Molière to be performed, for Fouquet discovered the talents of Molière and La Fontaine before Louis XIV did. The king was received at the gates of the palace by its owner. He entered; the whole court followed him. In a moment the magnificent alleys, the lawn, steps and windows were covered and filled by young nobles, delicate and beautiful women and maidens. It was a delightful panorama – which I shall never forget, for I was with the king's escort – it was a delightful panorama of trees and glistening fountains; a charming, sunny horizon of blooming, flowery life – as one of the poets present said – and yet in the midst of all this joy, a great hatred, a great revenge brooded in the rustling of the wind which moved the leaves. If Fouquet's fall had not already been determined upon by the king, the decision would have been made at Vaux; for Louis XIV, whose device is '*nec pluribus impar*', could not brook that a man of lower origin should outshine him in splendor. According to the will of Louis XIV no one in the whole kingdom must dare to equal him in splendor, fame and love. As there is only

---

[34] Isaac de Benserade (1613-1691), a French poet.

one sun in heaven, so there must be only one king in France. *Ventre saint gris,*» exclaimed the captain, «there His Majesty was right. Long live Louis XIV!»

The glasses clinked, and uncle and nephew drank to the king's health.

«And Fouquet?» asked the youth, not without sympathy.

«If any one could have looked into the monarch's heart,» continued Monsieur de Torcy, «he would have read fearful wrath towards the subject who dared to receive the king more magnificently than the king could have received him in any part of his kingdom. The king's wrath was increased by other aid; the hatred and envy of the minister Colbert fanned the monarch's anger as a breath of wind kindles a flame.

«But mark further. The fountains began to play. Fouquet had bought and destroyed three villages merely to enable him to lead the water from a circuit of five miles, into the marble basins of the castle of Vaux. Every one was enchanted, carried away with delight. The king ground his teeth.

«At the appearance of the first star, a bell sounded. All the water ceased to play; the tritons, the dolphins, the gods of Olympus, as well as those of the sea, the nymphs of the woods, ceased their noisy respirations; the falling waterdrops once more disturbed the clearness of the surface, and then followed a rest which was to last forever, for the breath of the king's anger was wafted over it. One enchantment now followed another.»

«Enchantment?» asked the youth holding his breath.

«Yes!» said his uncle, «at least so it appeared. We entered the castle, covered tables came down from the ceiling; a subterranean, mysterious music was heard, and when the dessert appeared, the company were more than ever delighted by a movable mountain of confectionary which – by some mechanism, which to this day I cannot comprehend – passed from one guest to another.»

Gauthier stared, but the captain continued: «The king now allowed Fouquet to show him the apartments of the castle, which by its splendid illumination rivaled the brightness of noonday. Louis – and that is saying a great deal –

had never seen anything to equal it. He perceived pictures from a master hand which he did not know; gardens, the work of a man who made pictures from trees and flowers, and whose name had never come to his ear till now. But Fouquet drew the king's attention to all this in hopes to excite his admiration – to impress him and render him pliant,... but... the thoughtless man only aroused the envy and hatred of the monarch more and more.»

«I tremble for him!» said the youth.

«Learn rather from this imprudence of the wisest man in France, to be wiser than he!» said the captain. «But listen to the rest. Now comes the point.»

«What is the name of your architect?» asked the king.

«Levau, Sire,» replied the minister of finance.

«Your painter?»

«Lebrun.»

«Your gardener?»

«Le Notre, your Majesty.»

«Louis XIV remembered these three names, at that time still unknown to him, now so celebrated, and went on. He was dreaming of Versailles.

«Then came the moment when the consequences of a too great and bold ambition drew the lightning of revenge upon the head of the unfortunate man.

«They had entered a magnificent, broad gallery – the one in the castle which we were in to-day is copied from it. The king – accidentally looking up to the ceiling – noticed the Fouquet arms, which were in the four corners; a squirrel with the device *'Que non ascendom.'*[35]

«Louis XIV turned pale. An angry glance shot from his eyes. He made a gesture to me, and ordered me to call Monsieur d'Artagnan, the commander of the musketeers. But the queen mother and Mademoiselle de la Vallière, then the favorite ladylove of the king, both of whom were close behind the

---

[35] Where can I not ascend?

monarch, perceived the coming storm. They separated the king from the minister in some clever way, and begged him so earnestly to remember the ingratitude which would lie in repaying such a grand reception by such a course, that Louis deferred his revenge.

«Fouquet suspected nothing. The court now went to the theater in which Molière's 'Les Facheux' was brought out for the first time. The king was highly amused. After the theater there were fireworks, and after the fireworks a ball. Louis XIV himself danced often with Mademoiselle de la Vallière, who beamed like a fairy rose in the fullness of her beauty, and in the thought of having restrained her royal lover from an unworthy action really resembled an angel.

«Yes, yes!» exclaimed the captain. «*Ventre saint gris*, the picture of the charming La Vallière, and the memories of my youth made me forget the rest of my story. At three o'clock in the morning the court departed. Fouquet accompanied the king to the gates at which he had received him. 'My lord,' said the king to his host as he left him, 'I shall never dare to invite you to be my guest again; you would be too poorly lodged,' and Louis XIV returned to Fontainebleau. He could only console himself for the humiliation to which the minister had subjected him, by the firm resolve to ruin the inso*-lent man.»

«And did the king carry out this resolve?» asked the young man almost breathless.

«In a few days the Bastille lodged another unfortunate prisoner to die in solitary confinement. It was – Fouquet.»

The captain was silent, and hastily emptied the last beaker. Gauthier, too, was silent.

«Come, my boy,» said the captain at last, as he threw the money for the wine on the table, «and observe two things, first, that a strong healthful aspiration is seemly in youth. Without this aspiration a man is a coward, and a despicable nothing. Second, that precipitation makes flaws, and pride comes before a fall. '*Nec pluribus impar*' is the king's device, and this motto perfectly describes him and his character.

A royal robber

Gauthier gazed gloomily into vacancy. «How differently I pictured many things at this court,» he said softly.

M. de Torcy smiled. «Ah! my lad!" he exclaimed, «you will find many things in life different from what you thought them to be,» and therewith uncle and nephew left the drinking-room of the 'Cardinal Richelieu'.»

V.
The Marquise de Montespan and Louvois

The Maquise de Montespan, Françoise Athenais, de Rochechouart – till now the omnipotent mistress of King Louis XIV – sat at a window in Marly le Roi, bowed in sorrow and lost in thought, gazing sadly at the setting sun. Was she thinking of the past… of the instability and decay of all earthly grandeur? Was she wondering what would become of this proud Marly le Roi at the end of another half century?

At the left the road leads toward Versailles, at the right lies the village of Marly, which stretches out to the Belvedere, while the base of the triangle is bounded by the beautiful wood which that lovely morning more than a hundred and fifty years ago, was brought hither fresh and full grown from Compiègne. The pavilions of the twelve signs of the zodiac were connected by magnificent arbors and walks, through .which the beams of the sun could not penetrate. Nearest to the sun (the pavilion of the, king) were those for the princes of the royal family and the ministers; the others were for the officers of the court and persons invited to Marly. The frescoes which decorated the walls were painted by the most celebrated artists of the time Louis XIV pictures which represented the joys of the immortal inhabitants of Olympus, and heightened the happiness of earthly divinities. On the opposite side, was the great fountain whose stream ascended to the height of a hundred and fifty feet. Fouquet languished in prison, but Louis XIV had learned something from his visit to Vaux. In the middle of the triangle, at the right and left of the king's pavilion, were the rooms of the hundred Swiss and the kitchen and apartments for the numberless retinue. Statues, fountains, parterres of flowers, and cascades, were found on every hand. Louis XIV, who had changed the simple palace of Saint Germain for magnificent Versailles, the sweet illusions of youth for the ambitious dreams of a riper age, and the delicate La Vallière for the proud Montespan, began one day to be wearied of the world and its bustle, and convinced himself, as Saint Simon says, that he sometimes longed for solitude. The buildings with their pure, colossal lines, the large gardens with their stiff, angular paths and

A royal robber

clipped trees, among which an army of courtiers, pages and lackeys incessantly wandered, had in a great measure lost their charms for him, since the lovely Vallière no longer enlivened them.

On the day when the king awoke for the first time full of these thoughts, the usually proud, haughty expression of his face was softened by a slight touch of sadness. On this day the chase was countermanded, and contrary to his habit, Louis XIV entered his carriage without inviting any of the beautiful ladies, who were his daily escort. Only accompanied by some of his confidential friends, he left Versailles, after giving directions to drive to the most sequestered environs of Paris. The carriage stopped at the pleasant chain of hills of Luciennes[36], and the king alighted. One of the courtiers, who had probably been made aware of the intention of this ride, approached and said respectfully : «Sire, your Majesty would scarcely find a better position for the erection of a palace.»

«That is very true,» answered the king, «but it is not what I seek – I have already spent too much in building, and this beautiful situation would demand expenditures which would be ruinous. We will go farther, gentlemen. Do you see that valley with the little village on the brow of the hill? Ah! what repose – how quietly life must flow here! I feel that this place would satisfy me!»

«Sire,» said the courtier, «your Majesty has not probably noticed that this valley is very narrow, and on account of the surrounding hills, entirely without a prospect, at the same time the approaches are so rugged that it would be very hard to reach it.»

«All of which I seek!» answered Louis, «I wish for a place where it is impossible to build anything but a hermitage, which I may occasionally visit in order to leave the world and the court. A nothing would satisfy me. What is the name of this village?»

«Marly, Sire.»

«Well, gentlemen, once or twice a year we will visit the hermitage of Marly in

[36] Today Louveciennes, near Paris.

atonement for our sins.»

That evening, immediately after his return from the drive, the king sent for Mansard and commanded him to go to work at once and draw up the plan for his hermitage. But this hermitage this – nothing – cost over a thousand millions.

A thousand millions, as Saint Simon says, to beautify the refuge of snakes, toads, and frogs, and make it accessible to the distinguished world. But what is a thousand millions to the caprice of a king!

The Marquise de Montespan sat bowed in sorrow and lost in thought at one of the windows of Marly de Roi. gazing sadly at the setting sun. Was she thinking of the past – of the instability and decay of all earthly grandeur, or was it the sad change which now threatened her own fate, that occupied her thoughts? The glory of the gentle, affectionate La Vallière, so passionately loved by the king, had faded. Louis XIV had wearied of her likewise, and sent the mother of his children – Maria de Bourbon and the Comte de Vermandis – in the thirtieth year of her age to the cloister of the Carmelites in the suburb of Saint Germain, where the poor, loving heart of Sister Louise de la Miséricorde was now slowly bleeding.

Did not such a fate now stand before the Marquise de Montespan, notwithstanding her six children, who shone at the court of Versailles as legitimate princes and princesses? The marquise was, to be sure, thirty-nine years old, but these years had not effaced the traces of her once exquisite beauty, and moreover her former vigor of mind still remained, but the natural merriment and joyousness which had characterized Françoise, when she was introduced to the king by the Duchesse de la Vallière had, with time, given place to excessive love of money, moodiness, obstinacy, and desire to rule – attributes which gradually, without her knowledge, made her wearisome to the king. The Duchesse d'Orleans had lately said «the Montespan is a living devil, but so droll and amusing that time does not hang heavily in her company.»

The most perishable thing on earth is the favor of kings and princes. She herself, though married to the Marquis de Montespan, had overthrown La

A royal robber

Vallière, and must she not expect her own fall, for Louis XIV, the most glowing and passionate, but also the most inconstant of lovers, began to neglect her.

She felt only too well that her influence was decreasing, that the sun of her happiness, like the earthly sun, was sinking. But she could not bear the thought of parting with her power, of stepping back from the dizzy height of a mistress of Louis XIV. The victories of Madame de Soubise and Madame de Ludre did not annoy her. The marquise had long been accustomed to occasional, passing unfaithfulness, in her royal lover. And the short reign of Madame de Soubise had already reached its end. A petty court scandal – such as at that time often occurred – had soon shattered it. One evening the queen awaited her husband at an appointed hour in vain. Very uneasy at his non-appearance, she sent everywhere in the palace and the city for His Majesty, but in vain. His Majesty was not found till the next morning. This insult to the queen made a great sensation. Everyone was talking about it; Madame de Soubise among others. The latter even went further, and in the presence of the queen, mentioned a lady with whom the interview had taken place. The queen, who was very indignant told His Majesty the name. Louis denied it, the queen assured him that she had been well informed, as Madame de Soubise had told her.

«Well then, if that is the case,» answered His Majesty quietly, «I will tell you with whom I was.; No other than Madame de Soubise herself. If I wish to speak to her, I place a diamond ring on my little finger; if she will permit it she puts on emerald earrings.» In consequence of this petty court scandal Madame de Soubise was dismissed.

From her, therefore, the marquise had nothing further to fear, and equally little from Madame de Ludre, who was now in favor. She possessed beauty, butj neither intellect nor the talent to fascinate permanently.

Very different would be the case if chance, or any intrigue, should throw into the hands of Louis XIV a woman who understood how to fasten the king to herself by strong bands, and to rule him by her intellect and wit. In such a case the marquise would be lost, and it would be but too easily with her as with those whom she had overthrown; the gloomy walls of a cloister might yet be her living grave. It is no trifle to lay down a scepter. One who is accustomed to rule cannot so easily step down into the obscurity of common life – the grave of oblivion.

And then – was not Louvois, the ambitious minister, secretly working to accomplish her fall, because he wished to rule the king alone? True, no one as yet ruled Louis XIV, but many were constantly striving to attain this end: the marquise, Madame de Ludre, Louvois and the Duc de Saint Aignan, the king's favorite. And had not the crafty Louvois partially obtained control over the king?

François Michel le Tellier, Marquis de Louvois, the son of Chancellor le Tellier, was in his youth so completely given up to the gratification of his passions and dissipation, that his bwn father considered him incapable of entering upon public life with success. But Louvois reflected upon his position, and unexpectedly developed the most distinguished talents. It was one of those many changes which often occur in prominent persons. The faults of youth had passed – in their stead appeared an unbounded desire for fame and respect And he had, in truth, the talents to attain them. To the most intense activity and a fine memory were added even when a youth, and much more when the man approached maturity, a quick glance, a piercing sagacity, and a firm will. But this will was only the effluence of a still greater ambition, and to it he sacrificed everything; the happiness of millions, his honor, and even himself.

So long as Louis XIV held the rudder of state with an iron hand, the young secretary of state did not dare to overstep the bounds of a pupil; but the crafty man knew how to gain the full confidence of his monarch by wise counsels, mostly advantageous to himself, though retaining the appearance of a courtier. He felt that the talent of a general rested in him; he perceived that the king was his as soon as he could involve him in a continued war. Thus the Marquis de Louvois knew how to gradually extend his power over the army and its ruler. Good fortune and the will of Louis XIV made him minister of war, which was what the ambitious man had in view. Into every department of military affairs Louvois now brought order and unity. The wise Colbert had saved the state treasury millions, Louvois gave France the

A royal robber

largest and best army. He was certain of victory, the power of Louis and the pride of the whole nation would be flattered. Two campaigns in Flanders and Franche-Comté, gave the signal for a series of bloody combats, which soon made the French name universally feared. France was victorious in both cases; Louvois had the means ready, and his influence with the king increased. The minister had craftily calculated that these two years of war would be the prologue of an extended struggle, and therefore involved the king in plans from which he could not easily recede, especially without the assistance of the minister of war.

From this moment Louvois was necessary to Louis XIV. A new war with the States of Holland followed.

The peace of Nymwegen, dictated by Louis XIV, ended it after a struggle of six years, during which Louvois had led France to the summit of its power and almost the half of Europe had been called to arms. What mattered it that thousands were beggared and that the blooming Pfalz – that rich and beautiful garden of Germany – had been barbarously desolated and burnt, and changed into a smoking waste dripping with blood,

Upon Louvois fell the curses of numberless unfortunates for if one could pardon the severity with which the marquis had treated all who were defeated, still the ineffaceable stigma rested upon him, not only that he suffered the horrible crimes, but even, with inhuman coldness and cruelty, commanded them in the Netherlands at Trier, in Savoy, and especially in the Pfalz. The Pfalz should, according to his shameful policy, be changed into an eternal desert and waste, in order to secure the boundaries of France against Germany.

Since Louvois, as well as his king, mistook false fame for the true, he was obliged to resort to contemptible measures to serve bad ends, and justice, laws, treaties and oaths, appeared to him as trifles, which a great ruler might trample upon at pleasure.

Such was the situation of affairs at the time of our story – the time at which the star of the Marquise de Montespan began to pale. By her downfall Louvois hoped to obtain the sole command of the king, especially as the latter was becoming wearied of the personal control of the helm of state, and preferred to seek rest in the arms of a beautiful woman. On the one side a war had commenced between the Montespan and Louvois, a secret, but therefore all the more bitter one, and on the other the crafty minister was involving the ambitious king in new plans against Germany and Alsace, in order to hold him firmly and safely in his hands for the rest of his life. In order to hold the king and keep him dependant upon him, Louvois had persuaded him that France must possess Alsace, till now a part of Germany. The safety of the kingdom and the greatness and honor of the French crown required it. Let the upper Rhine once become the boundary between France and Germany, and the lower Rhine must in consequence become so too.

Was anything more required to awake and inflame the ambition of a prince so eager to acquire territory as Louis XIV? The only question was; how this robbery should be effected? The answer to it was not difficult for Louvois: by force, but under the appearance and veil of justice.

Louis XIV and Louvois soon came to an understanding, and the minister of war wept to work. It was in this very apartment at Marly, in which the Marquise de Montespan, lost in sad and serious thoughts, sat watching the setting sun, that Louis XIV had held a secret council with Louvois a few days before.

The king and the minister met for that purpose in His Majesty's pavilion. They were alone, Captain de Torcy guarded the door. Louis, with his head covered, sat upon a costly seat, Le Tellier, Marquis de Louvois, stood with uncovered heads a little on one side. Etiquette did not permit the ministers to sit at any council at which Louis was present.

«And what is to be done next?» said Louis in his slow, sharply accented speech, concealing one hand under the gold brocade vest, and fixing his piercing glance upon the marquis, who stood before His Majesty in an humble attitude, and with an expression of the deepest submission.

«Sire,» answered Louvois solemnly, «I am sure of my cause.»

«And you think the hour has come, marquis?» asked the king.

A royal robber

«Yes, your Majesty,» continued the minister, «the fruit is ripe, Louis XIV, whom the world justly calls the 'great,' Has only to put out his hand for it to fall.»

«And the German Empire, and Spain?"

«Were never weaker than now; your Majesty is thoroughly aware of the discord prevailing in Germany.»

«Yes, yes, we know it!» said the king. «We know this foolish division right well, and truly we have not failed to feed the envy of the German princes towards their emperor by bribery and diplomatic arts.'

«And this bribery and these diplomatic arts have worked excellently everywhere,» continued Louvois, in a tone of bitter scorn, while the royal smile at the same time found a faint reflection in his usually stern, strong features. «At every step which he may attempt, the hands of the German emperor are bound. He cannot reckon with safety on three of the Imperial princes. First of all Swabia and Bavaria are ours, Brandenburg causes him anxiety, and Leopold himself –»

«Is weak,» exclaimed the king with a proud flash of his eyes. «Leopold I, is born to be a good father, but not an emperor. He has a gentle, mild, Industrious nature, great memory, and much knowledge – but not the unity and strength of character required by a ruler.»

«Sire,» said Le Tellier, with a low bow, «rulers like Louis XIV, are shining and flaming 'Flowers of Peru' in the garden of History. It requires not a century, but hundreds of centuries to produce one.»

«You are a flatterer, marquis,» said the king well pleased, «we intend indeed to do honor to our motto *'nec pluribus impar.'* We consider the moment favorable to the carrying out of our great plans for the honor and fame of France. The impotency of Germany and Spain is visible, and England is weakened by the foolish quarrel of her king with his own subjects. Well then, we will boldly confront this divided, weakened and timorous people. First of all we will occupy the good credulous Germans with some diplomatic affair, a congress perhaps. Then, while they are discussing for months in what order of rank the delegates shall sit at table or in what chairs we will act.»

«Sire!» exclaimed Louvois, affecting to be astonished at the king's words, to which he had himself in a former consultation given the impulse. «Sire, what an excellent thought! Prove to the world by its execution, that a great monarch has not to question trifling scruples when his enlightened mind shows him the way to make the people prosper.»

«Marquis!» said Louis after a few moments and a cloud darkened his brow, «the way we intend to take cannot be that of strict justice.»

«The welfare of the state is the justice of the king,» answered Louvois significantly.

Again there was a short pause, then the king repeated slowly and with a sharp emphasis, «The welfare of the state is the justice of the king!» and Louis bowed his head with joyous assent, then a beaming glance met the minister of war, and the king said:

«Marquis! you solicited us for the privilege of the coat; we graciously grant it to you the decree shall be issued to-morrow.»

«Your Majesty,» exclaimed the delighted Louvois, and bending his knee before the king, he kissed the monarch's hand with overflowing gratitude.

«But,» now continued Louis, «we must at least have a semblance of justice in the eyes of the world, in order to tear Alsace from the German Empire and incorporate it in France.»

«Your Majesty has the best army Europe can produce,» said Louvois.

«Yes,» answered the king, «and the blessing of the church is also something, Alsace must become Catholic again.»

«The admiration of the world cannot therefore escape your Majesty!» continued the minister. «Whoever has the power of arms and the church upon his side is in the right with the majority of people. The broader and higher claims will content a diplomatic sophist.»

«The Westphalian treaty,» said the king slowly, seeming to ponder over every word he spoke, «has, to be sure, given the bishoprics of Metz, Toul and

A royal robber

Verdun[37], the district of Hagenau[38], and the sovereignty of Pignerol[39], the Sundgau[40] and Breisach[41] to the crown of France, with the condition, however, that the bishops of Strassburg, the city of Strassburg itself, the ten other noted imperial cities of Alsace, four abbeys, as well as the counts and gentlemen of Lützelstein, Hanau, Fleckenstein and Oberstein[42], together with the knights of the empire, should remain firm in their allegiance to the German Empire. The treaty of Nymwegen has made no change!»

«Because France wisely left the question of Alsace open,» replied Louvois with light scorn. «Your Majesty's penetration had the present day then in view, as before, in the marriage of the Spanish Infanta, her inheritance.»

«Hush, marquis!» said the king with a cunning look at the minister, «hush, betray nothing before the time. Procure for us rather a plausible pretence of justice under which we could incorporate Alsace into our good France.»

«I have one your Majesty,» answered the marquis.

«Louvois!» exclaimed the king joyously. «You are a man of the pattern we like!»

«Then I am the happiest of mortals.»

«But the pretext?»

«It is as good as the right itself.»

«Speak.»

«Well then. Sire,» continued the marquis, «as your Majesty knows the weakness of the German and Spanish Empires, the dissensions of the former, and the envy of the German princes towards their emperor, which has been excellently nourished by bribery and diplomatic skill, your Majesty will not be obliged to abstain from taking unconditionally, and notwithstanding the

---

[37] Former German imperial cities in Western Lorraine.
[38] City in Northern Alsace.
[39] Pinerolo, city in Piemont.
[40] The Southern part of Alsace.
[41] City on the East-bank of the Rhine.
[42] Places in Northern Alsace.

treaty of Nymwegen, all places and regions of the German and Spanish boundaries which you desire. Your Majesty in so doing will be entirely in the right.»

«Excellent! and the proof?»

«I have intrusted an old pettifogger of the council of Parliament, Roland Ravaulx in Metz, with the discovery.»

«We are curious.»

«Ravaulx by my direction, rummaged over some old documents, and discovered that much land which lies far and wide beyond the bishoprics of Metz, Toul and Verdun, which have been ceded to France – formerly belonged to her.»

A crafty smile of assent passed over the king's features.

«*And therefore,*» continued Louvois, «are included as fiefs of the same.»

«Excellent, marquis, excellent!» exclaimed the king joyously. «Your Ravaulx may reckon upon a princely reward. And what shall we call this recovery of the former rights, and the seizure of the respective cities and provinces?»

«I would humbly propose to your Majesty,» said the minister with a low bow, «to call this righteous and perfectly lawful recovery, the 'Reunion.'»

«Reunion,» repeated Louis with a gentle inclination of the head. «Reunion! yes, that is good! But how shall we accomplish this 'Reunion' and take legal posession?»

«By your Majesty's sovereign will. Be pleased, Sire, to accept this elaborate plan, which I herewith lay at the feet of my great king. Separate courts of justice, under the name of *Chambres de Reunions* will be established, which will hold their sessions at Metz and Breisach.»

«And these?»

These *Chambres de Reunions* led by Ravaulx, will then prove to the world that eighty of our fiefs are liying in foreign countries, to which among others, belong Homburg, Pont à Mousson, Salm, Saarburg, Saarbrücken, Vaudemont, Hagenau and Weissenburg[43], and the ten Alsatian imperial cities – that all these are dependencies of the French possessions.»

«*Diable!*» cried the king, «that is strong, the treaty of Westphalia reserves most of them to the German Empire!»

«If your Majesty accepts my plan!» answered the Marquis de Louvois, bowing respectfully, «The *Chambres de Reunion* and your Majesty's humble minister of war will so forcibly impress upon the world the right of the French crown to these dependencies, that in a short time all these cities will, without opposition, sparkle and glisten as precious brilliants in the crown of Louis XIV.»

«And if the inhabitants deny the claim?»

«Then remember. Sire, that you possess the greatest, most powerful, and bravest army that Europe has to show.»

«And if the Emperor and Kingdom and those concerned cry out against us, and assail our throne with complaints?»

«Then will your Majesty's minister, Colbert de Croissy, give answer to the bawlers that their grievances are no cabinet affairs, but a matter of justice, therefore they must not turn to the government, but to the congress at Metz and Breisach,» – and here a truly diabolical mockery beamed from Louvois' eyes, – «which the king has instituted to prove to his neighbors that he wishes to do no one an injustice!»

«Good, very good!» said Louis with great satisfaction. «And the Duchy of Zweibrücken?[44] It is the property of the king of Sweden.»

«Will be occupied as a French fief by your Majesty's faithful troops.»

«And King Charles XI?»

«Invite him to appear before the *Chambres de Réunions.*»

«He will not come!»

«Then they will dispossess him of his Duchy.»

---

[43] Places in Lorraine and Alsace.
[44] City in Pfalz, at the border to Lorraine.

A royal robber

«And the king of Spain, to whom the Principality of Chimay[45], the city of Cortryk[46], and the Duchy of Luxemburg belong?»

«He, too, will be summoned to the congress – of course will not appear... and will consequently be deprived of his possessions.»

«And *Strassburg*» continued the king, after a few moments, «Upon Strassburg, this pearl of the German cities – this important possession for Emperor and Empire – this true German city, which is, moreover, a little republic in itself – have you found a claim for us upon this Strassburg? We confess that its acquisition appears to us the most important and desirable of the whole undertaking.»

«Your Majesty,» answered Louvois shrugging his shoulders, «with infinite regret I must confess: even Ravaulx has not found the slightest claim upon Strassburg.»

The king knit his brows gloomily. «Then the whole plan is worth nothing,» said he angrily, «Strassburg, above all, must belong to us. It is our will.»

«And it will belong to your Majesty,» added the marquis firmly and decidedly. «Will your Majesty have the grace to entrust to me the incorporation of this beautiful city into the kingdom of the great Louis?»

«Be it so!» enclaimed the king rising. «But how to begin?»

«As if there were no traitors, no bribery, no stratagem,» said the minister, smiling craftily.

«Traitors?» asked the king, «who are they?»

«Prince Franz Egon of Fürstenberg, bishop of Strassburg!» announced Captain de Torcy at this moment.

Louis XIV looked at his minister with astonishment.

«We commanded that this private council in Marly le Roi should be held secretly,» said he angrily.

---

[45] City in Hainaut.
[46] Kortrijk, city in West Flanders.

A royal robber

«The will of Louis XIV is the law of the world, replied Louvois with a low bow.

«But it appears to have no restraining power for our minister of war,» answered the king with a haughty, angry glance.

«Your Majesty,» said Louvois quietly, «to open a locked door a key is required!»

The king started. «I understand,» he then added, and the dark clouds on his brow gave way to a crafty smile.

«And Sire, if the key must be gilded?» asked Louvois forcing his hard features at the same time into a sarcastic smile.

«Then gild it!» exclaimed the king, «provided it is the right key.»

«It is,» said the marquis.

The king sat down again, and at a gesture from the minister, M. de Torcy admitted the German prince, Franz Egon von Fürstenberg, bishop of Strassburg, to the presence of His Majesty, the king of France.

VI.
An intrigue

The day was dying. The last beams of the setting sun steeped the walls of Marly le Roi in a reddish, golden light. The royal hermitage lay in a strange magical radiance which surrounded with its glowing splendor her who hitherto had ruled France like a queen, and was now a recluse in Marly le Roi.

«My day is fading also! – so sinks my sun,» exclaimed the Marquise de Montespan, as the door of her chamber softly opened and the first waiting-maid announced the Duc de Saint Aignan. The features of the marquise expressed astonishment. What had Saint Aignan to do with one who was threatened with the loss of the royal favor? The court rendered homage not to the setting but to the rising sun. She however admitted the nobleman. He came in with the chivalric manner peculiar, to him, and greeted her with a respectful bow.

«M. le Duc,» said the marquise gravely, «what do you seek from me? Do you wish to take leave of me, and thereby procure the pleasure of watching the pangs of a bleeding heart?»

«Noble lady,» answered Saint Aignan with a second bow, «you do not know me.»

«You are a *roué*,» said the marquise quietly.

«There you are right!» exclaimed the Duc. «But what has that to do with it?»

«For a man like yourself,» continued Mme. de Montespan seriously, «close upon the edge of an abyss, there is no greater, but, also, no more diabolical pleasure than – to venture either alone or with others to sound the gulf of wickedness or misery, to feel its cold breath and then – to draw back.»

«I can never cease to admire the wit and penetration of the Marquise de Montespan,» replied the Duc, «even though I might complain of a slight injustice. It is true that this approach to the abyss of the wicked can delight me – it fills me with a diabolical pleasure which nothing on earth can equal –

what other pleasures are there for us? But enjoyment of the misery of others? I do not understand what you can mean, noble lady!»

«Oh!» cried the marquise bitterly, «what innocence in the heart of a Saint Aignan! It will create even greater delight for your wicked heart, if the victim who writhes under the lion's claws herself relates the history of her disgrace and suffering. Well then, M. le Duc, lookout of yonder window! There stands my fate written on the heavens in blood-red characters.»

«What can a hand accustomed to wield the scepter do? Hold your position firmly, Madame la Marquise!»

«This too!» exclaimed the marquise bitterly, «this thrust also! Go! go! M. le Duc! What do you desire of me, the degraded one? Go and pay your homage to the star which will soon rise to announce the new day!»

«Marly le Roi has inclined you to be sad, madame!» said the Duc. «Persuade the king to return to Versailles. It is your due, as the most beautiful woman in all France, to reside there.»

«It is my due?» exclaimed Mme. de Montespan sorrowfully. «Does not the noble Duc, who is always overflowing with witty anecdotes, know the king's reply to the Duchesse de la Vallière?»

«No, madame, to my shame be it said – no,» answered the diplomatic courtier.

«Well then – when matters had gone as far with la Vallière as they now have with me, she spoke of something to His Majesty which was her due. The king, in a fit of temper, which he often has, took his little Spanish dog, Malice, threw it into her lap, and said, 'Take it, madame, that is your due.'»

St. Aignan was also silent for a moment and it seemed as if something like seriousness shaded the eternally smiling face. Then he took the hand of the marquise and imprinting a light kiss upon it, said:

«Do you know why I am come?»

«Well?»

«To avert such a result, and we shall succeed… if we go hand in hand.»

A royal robber

«I am astonished!»

«But I need one thing: your friendship. Do you know what friendship means?»

«I think so.»

«Do you know the story about Madame de Rambouillet?»

«Ah! another of your stories. I believe, if your father lay dying in your arms, you would have a witticism or anecdote on dying ready.»

«They are instructive, dear madame. For example, there was no truer friend than Madame de Rambouillet. Monsieur Arnauld d'Audilly who called himself a 'professor of friendship' once offered to give her instructions in this science, and began with the question: 'what do you understand by friendship?' 'A perfect subordination of my own interests to those of my friend!' answered Madame de Rambouillet. 'Then would you consent,' continued Monsieur d'Audilly, 'to suffer a great loss for the benefit of one of your friends?'

«'Not only for one of my friends,' she answered, 'but of any worthy man.' 'If you know so much, madame,' replied d'Audilly, 'all instruction is superfluous, and you have nothing to learn!'»

The marquise had grown rather pale. She knew at what a low ebb the treasury of the young nobleman, who was extravagant above all bounds, usually was, and avarice was one of her chief faults. But Madame de Montespan quickly comprehended that an alliance with the confidential favorite of the king might possibly save her from the threatened ruin. Her decision was therefore quickly made. Like the drowning man, who in his despair grasps at every means of rescue, she seized the offered hand and the alliance – the word «friendship» she naturally omitted in her thoughts – was concluded. Both saw clearly enough what each intended. St Aignan was striving for power over the king. If he succeeded in securing to the mistress of Louis XIV her position, if not the monarch's heart, her influence would be strong enough to support him – whom the envy and intrigues of the all-powerful Louvois constantly threatened. He therefore promised to risk everything to overthrow Madame de Ludre. In return Madame de Montespan was to in-

A royal robber

form St. Aignan of the intrigues of Louvois. The reciprocal conditions were made and agreed upon. Yet each of them hid a secret desire which concerned their especial interest. It made no difference that both were perfectly aware of this perfidy. Perfidy, or acting with diplomacy, in their society signified the same thing. The downfall of Madame de Ludre was not enough for the marquise; she needed, now that her fading beauty was no longer sufficient to enchain the king, another subject for the heart of the monarch. This new subject must neither be a match for her or the king while she must on the contrary be and remain her tool. This thought was the fruit of to--day's painful reflections. If she were once in condition to work upon the king by a new mistress, who was intellectually her inferior, she would have no further need of St. Aignan. Madame de Montespan was already thinking how, if her plan succeeded, she would revenge herself upon him for all the sacrifices which the present alliance demanded of her avarice. But no eagle's eye is as sharp as the inner glance of a courtier, when it is necessary to penetrate the by-paths of another of the same stamp. St. Aignan knew what plans Madame de Montespan was brooding over. He knew, because in her position he would have thought and done the same. But the affair could also serve him, though irf exactly the contrary manner, to the fall of the marquise and his sole monarchy over the king, possibly even to the overthrow of Louvois, only then the new-found mistress of the king must be his creation, and not that of the marquise. Still, to give Madame de Montespan a rival was difficult. She must therefore assist him. But let the new one be once firmly fixed in her position, and the old one could and should fall. Close calculations are everything at court. Here, those of the marquise and her companion had one and the same sum. St Aignan knew that he should hit upon the right tone ... he therefore resigned his own aim and aided the marquise to give herself a rival inferior to her in intellect. Such a delicate attention to the monarch must, moreover, win his favor for her again.

«And the passions yet be affected in His Majesty!» said the courtier, with a frivolous laugh. «The passions are the most fearful when they break forth in a riper age, where weakness already mingles with them. Then to them is added the sweet, despairing joy of the gambler who is making his last throw.»

«Hush, hush!» cried the marquise, «when you give me a glimpse of your soul, a chill runs through me.»

«Ho! Ho!» exclaimed St. Aignan merrily, «then, madame, I must at last cure you by Voiture's method.»

«Oh! dear,» sighed Mme. de Montespan, «another of his stories!»

«And do you know how Voiture, the clever friend of Rambouillet, cured his wife of fever?»

The marquise shook her head with a sigh; her whole soul was occupied with other things, and – this incorrigible man tormented her with his anecdotes. But she needed him!

St. Aignan did not allow himself to be disconcerted.

«Voiture had the strangest fancies in the world,» said he, stretching himself out comfortably in his armchair. «One day, when Mme. de Rambouillet had a fever, he remembered having heard that sudden great surprises often drove away such attacks. He was thinking how he could surprise Madame de Rambouillet in an original and effective manner, when he perceived two men leading bears. 'Excellent!' thought he, 'that is what I am looking for.' And he took the Savoyards and their animals to the Hotel Rambouillet. The marquise sat near the fire, surrounded by a screen. Voiture came softly into the room, put two chairs behind the screen, and made his actors get upon them. Madame de Rambouillet heard a snorting sound behind her, turned, and saw two bear's noses over her head. She thought she should die of terror; but as Voiture had rightly supposed, the fever yielded to the fright. However, it was a long time before she could pardon Voiture for the restoration of her health. He, on his part, told everywhere that it was the finest cure he had not only ever made, but had ever seen made.»

«Have you finished?» asked Madame de Montespan, awaking from a deep reverie.

«I have!» replied St. Aignan, «but the deuce – I believe you have not heard any of my pretty story.»

«Yes,» said the marquise, «I heard something about a bear!»

A royal robber

Her companion laughed, and then said: «Your bear, however, has something good, he has probably found the honey you seek.»

«M. le Duc,» exclaimed Madame de Montespan sorrowfully. «You know my heart is almost bursting, and you do not cease to jest!»

«Because the thought that I am carrying in my pocket what you vainly seek far and near, makes me merry.» And putting his hand in his breast-pocket, he drew from it a miniature which he held before Madame de Montespan.

«What an angel!» exclaimed the latter. «The bust of a Venus!»

«Yes,» said St. Aignan with the glowing eyes of a sensualist, «beautiful as a marble statue but cold as marble also. But to be sure! this appearance of frigidness charms and enchants doubly, like the singularity of such a quantity of deep-red hair!»

«The hair is wonderful!» said the marquise, «who could deny it a peculiar charm! what delicacy of skin! what a sweet expression of childish innocence.»

«Did you ever see anything more piquante?» asked St. Aignan enthusiastically, and his looks almost devoured the picture.

«Only one thing is wanting!» said Madame de Montespan, «intellect!»

«So much the better!» said her companion with a careless smile, «apparently prudish, without the exalting but often annoying wings of intellect, this wonderful girl will become a bond which you –»

«Heavens!» exclaimed the marquise, «you believe?»

«Madame,» said St. Aignan merrily, «between ourselves – I believe in nothing. But I am firmly convinced of three things: firstly, that if we bring this young girl to court, the king will immediately fall desperately in love with her; secondly, that this apparently frigid beauty is a woman, and like all others, cannot withstand the offers of a Louis XIV, and lastly that this beautiful marble bust lacks the intellectual element to rule the king, and to supplant a Marquise de Montespan – the most intellectual woman in France.»

«If she is an innocent child, as it appears by these features,» said Madame de

A royal robber

Montespan, «she will shrink from a man who has loved so many and crushed so many a heart.»

«Yes, if the man were not Louis XIV and king of France!» exclaimed St. Aignan. «Trust to me, I know women! With them love is always the cause for a perfect absolution. The man who really and strongly loves a woman can commit crimes, and she will still love him.»

A sigh escaped the lips of the marquise. The truth of these words cut too deeply into her soul. Then she asked quickly: «And who is the poor innocent creature, who is to fall a victim to us and the insatiate ardor of the king?»

St. Aignan laughed mockingly. «By all the saints, I should not have expected that this fatal hermitage of Marly le Roi would infect even the Marquise de Montespan with its sentimentality. What do you care for a young girl's innocence if it succeeds in retaining the favor of the king!»

«Monsieur le Duc!» said the marquise sadly, «my soul is heavy with many sins, but you are even worse than I!»

«And you are divinely naive!» exclaimed St. Aignan laughing and kissing her hand. «I should never have thought that we should have suited each other so well in, diplomatic affairs. I could tell you –»

«For heaven's sake, do not tell another anecdote,» cried the marquise imploringly. «Tell me rather who is this charming little red-head, whose picture you have just shown me.»

«She is the most innocent soul in the world!» replied St. Aignan, «a little country girl, wondrously beautiful, as you see, dazzlingly fair, with red hair–»

«Monsieur le Duc!»

«Slight, with deep blue eyes, delicate nose and mouth, dainty hands and feet, outwardly cold, and yet full of secret fire, of very limited intellect, and what especially suits us, excessively vain.»

«I am astonished!» said the lady, «you have surely become minister of the police of the kingdom, since you possess such a detailed description of your beauty. But you have forgotten to mention her name.»

A royal robber

«Our beauty is called: Marie Angeline Scoraille de Rousille, Mademoiselle de Fontanges!»

«Ah! Fontanges!»

«An ancient family from the valley of the Puy de Dome, and connected with the Montferrands and Torcys. Poor as a church mouse – but only sixteen years old.»

«So she is still a child!» said the marquise compassionately. «And how did the wolf find out this poor little lamb?»

«By a remarkable coincidence!» answered the nobleman, and then related how he had come on the track of this charming creature through Captain de Torcy. As he had long been interested in the fate of the noble lady whose happy influence upon the king was just now opposed by *his* enemy, Louvois, the first glance at this picture had inspired him with the thoughts which he now, in connection with the marquise, stood ready to carry out. Gauthier, in his innocence and enthusiasm for Angeline, had himself given the Duc, who had won his regard by his courtesy and assurances of friendship, the most minute particulars about Mademoiselle de Fontanges. Of course he had not said that he loved the young girl, but this did not escape a man of the world like St. Aignan. That she possessed small intellect did not, of course, come from Gauthier's lips – perhaps he was not even aware of it – but enchanted by the Duc's flattering confidences and fiery wine, he related so many traits of her disposition and character, that the Duc, skilled in all the infirmities of human nature, soon recognized the true nature of the enthusiastically praised lady. Upon this he. built his plan, and this, he now laid before his new ally. They agreed that Mademoiselle de Fontanges – the quiet blossom of charming Limagne, the gentle, innocent child from the paradisiacal valleys of the Allier – should play into the hands of Madame de Montespan. The nearest pretext for this was offered by the distant relationship of the marquise, as a born Rochechouart, to the Montferrands. It was only necessary that Françoise Athenais should hint to her relatives that it was in her power to give a young lady a position at court, and she could be certain of half a dozen offers.

A royal robber

Was there at that time any higher ideal for the country nobility than the court of Versailles? And was not the silent affection of Gauthier and Angeline the best thing for St. Aignan and the marquise? The innocent love of the young people springing up in secret, was counted upon by the two allies as a lever for their intrigue. St. Aignan, under the pretext of sincere friendship, was to attach Gauthier more and more to himself, so that he should at last belong entirely to him. False love letters should then first fill Angeline with desires for her absent beloved playmate, then for the place where he now was, and at last for the court itself. They could then arouse the vanity of the little one, until no doubt could exist of a happy and free acceptance of a decided summons to Paris on the part of Mademoiselle de Fontanges. The rest was committed to the care of the marquise and the clever machinetions of St Aignan, to whom as a friend and especial favorite of the king, it must be a trifle to lead the monarch's easily moved heart to the desired goal.

The Duc and Marquise were now agreed on their plans and only the latter feared as often as she glanced at the picture of the beautiful Fontanges... that this pure, angel face concealed in its bosom a marble heart. The Duc de St. Aignan laughed scornfully.

«Ho you know, madame, how this conquest will be made by us and the king?»

«How?» asked the marquise.

«Like the capture of Candia by Achmet Pacha.»

«And how did that proceed?»

«When Achmet Pacha landed on the island which then belonged to the Christians, he foretold the subsequent capture by a smile. He threw his saber into the middle of a broad carpet, and said: 'Which of you will take my sabre without stepping on the carpet?' As the sabre lay in the center, and could in no way be reached with the hands, all present declared it impossible. Then Achmet Pacha began to roll up the carpet till he came to the saber, so that he could take it without stepping on the carpet; seized it and cried: 'Thus in time I will take possession of Candia, foot by foot.' And,» added the Duc gayly, rising, «so will we and the king take possession this beau-

59

A royal robber

tiful marble statue!»

The sun had long since set, and deep night lay over the earth, when St. Aignan and the marquise separated.

VII.
The conjuration

It was «Friday»… and this Friday fell on «the thirteenth of the month!» The day, which had been very warm, was declining as a strangely mixed company found themselves on the way to *Saint Denis en France*[47], situated on the Croult, which united with the Seine at a little distance, in those days a small city of about five thousand inhabitants. The holy Dionysius, who preached the gospel in Gaul, and was nominally the first Bishop of Paris, by his martyr's death converted a heathen, who buried his body and built a chapel over the grave of the martyr. This chapel was afterwards enlarged, and in the year 636 raised to an abbey by Dagobert I. Pictures of the saint and frankish kings decorated the inner walls, and the bones of more than thirty kings and queens, and about eighty princes and princesses rested there. The above mentioned party were going towards their[48] resting place. There were two Savoyards, of whom the older – a fine-looking, well-preserved man – did not seem to feel at home in his dress. His body was too well rounded for a poor Savoyard, and one might swear that his head suited a distinguished prelate better than that of a man of the people. His younger companion could better be what he appeared, although a certain refinement, blended with marked carelessness and ease, appeared in his bearing. He was moreover a handsome man, notwithstanding his wasted features – and possessed an unusually bright black eye. The Savoyards did not travel alone; there were in their party two old discharged soldiers, while in the rear followed a negro and two old women, the first of whom carried a strange apparatus, partly covered with a cloth. Still the negro and the women undoubtedly belonged to the Savoyards; for where the road was quiet and lonely one could see the younger one linger behind and exchange some mysterious words with one

---

[47] City northern of Paris.
[48] Napoleon had the church rebuilt and decorated, and appointed it as a resting place for all the royal family. The remains of the old kings were collected by Louis XVIII and buried here: but the protection of them was transferred to the newly appointed canons who from that time held the first rank among the clergy of France.

of the women.

Night soon closed in; the sultriness which had reigned until now did not lessen, but rather increased. Not a leaf stirred, and not an animal was to be seen. Storm clouds lay on the distant horizon like tired prostrate giants. The wanderers must have experienced a painful feeling of oppression, for not one of them spoke a word. They walked silently on, only now and then the younger Savoyard urged on the older one, to whom the walk was apparently toilsome, by telling him they must move quickly, in order to arrive at St. Denis before the closing of the gates.

It was already dark when this strange company passed through the gates of St. Denis. Here they parted, and – without wasting a word – the Savoyards, the soldiers, and the women with the negro struck into different paths. But many different paths can all lead to one point. After the lapse of a short half-hour, the party met again in an insignificant looking house, which stood not very far from the Abbey of St. Denis – that huge tomb of so many royal sleepers.

They were silently greeted by the owner of the little house – the sacristan of the neighboring church. He bowed very low to the two Savoyards, particularly to the elder. No light burned in the little narrow room – all was dark as night. When all had entered, the younger of the Savoyards said in the purest French to the gray-headed old sacristan, who stood timidly in one corner of the room with a large bunch of keys in his hands: «Well, how is it? Are you prepared to render obedience to the will of the right reverend Cardinal?»

«I am ready to do so!» said the man in a trembling voice.

«Well then,» continued the former, handing the old man a purse and a roll of paper, «here are the promised hundred pistoles, and this document contains the decree which secures you a good position at St-Pierre-le-jeune.»

The sacristan of St. Denis took the proffered papers so timidly, that it seemed as if the extended arm was not in perfect understanding with his own conscience. «And the most reverend Cardinal,» – said he with an embarrassed air.

«We assure you upon our honor,» answered the now steady voice of the old

A royal robber

Savoyard, «that a sacred vow obliges us to pass the whole night in the church of the abbey.»

«Well, make no longer delay!» continued the younger man, «and lead us through the underground passage to the place known only to you.»

«Only one word first!» interrupted the musical voice of a woman.

«Why now?» asked the younger Savoyard angrily. «Can not the matter wait till morning?»

«No,» answered the female voice decidedly. «Every article of the agreement must be accurately kept, otherwise –»

«Be silent,» said the other as he turned to the sacristan and whispered a few words in his ear.

A few moments later the old man with the soldiers, the negro, and one of the women left the apartment. The outer blinds were closed, and when he came back with a dimly burning oil lamp, he found the two Savoyards with a lady in a black dress of fine material, but cut in a strange fashion. Her features were not beautiful – one might almost call her expression unearthly – but it was by no means repulsive. The figure of the woman – she was perhaps about forty years old – on the other hand, was faultless, and revealed firm, graceful outlines. The loose garment she had worn as a disguise lay on the ground.

At the first ray that streamed from the dim oil lamp the sacristan shrank back; still it would be noticed by every close observer that the old man was no longer astonished at the appearance.

«And what do you wish now, madame?» asked the younger Savoyard, after they were left alone.

«You know, M. le Duc,» answered the lady, «the agreement. If all these articles are not entirely fulfilled the conjuration will come to nothing.»

«Do her will!» whispered the cardinal in the Savoyard's dress, «you know what depends upon it.»

«Uncle!» said the Duc de St. Aignan, in a scarcely audible voice, bending down to the cardinal's ear.

«Uncle! have you considered sufficiently? – the sum is enormous!»

«Count it out,» replied the distinguished prelate in a whisper, «true, the demand of La Voisin[49] is enormous, but – the property which Marshal Turenne (whose heir I am as you know) left, must be a thousand times greater.»

«But, uncle, are you certain that the marshal had property? It has been disputed.»

«With such a name, such dignities, and the thousand opportunities for becoming rich which such a general has, would a man die without leaving a sou behind? I tell you he has buried his wealth, and to-night the place where the treasure is hidden shall be specified. La Voisin will summon the spirit of Turenne out of his grave to-night, so that he may tell us where and how we can find his property.

«You are still convinced of the witch's magical power?»

«Certainly,» replied the Duc and there was an expression of perfect conviction in the tone with which he said this «certainly.»

«Then court out the appointed sum!» continued the cardinal.»

«Well, gentlemen?» said the lady, tired of the long delay.

«Accept it, madame!» answered St. Aignan. «Here, according to the agreement, are the twenty-five thousand livres in gold; the other twenty-five thousand are, according to agreement, deposited with a third person, whom you yourself proposed, the pious Père St. Etienne, from whom you are certain to receive them after the conjuration has taken place!»

«Very well,» replied La Voisin as she pocketed the offered sum. «But now let us go to work – it is high time.»

A distant peal of thunder answered these words. The storm was approaching. St. Aignan called the sacristan. The old man came in with a lantern

---

[49] Catherine Monvoisin (1640-1680), a French fortune teller and poisoner.

and bunch of keys in his hand – the horror of the day of judgement was expressed in all his features. The others waited in the dark little vestibule. At a gesture from the trembling hand of the old man, all followed and soon disappeared In a gloomy, cellar-like arch that led to the underground passage known only to the sacristan of St. Denis.

Those were strange times, and strange people lived in them! While on the one hand the greatest levity, immorality and frivolity reigned at the court of Louis XIV, on the other there was a still more rigid apparent observance of religion, priests and churches played a great role; confessions and masses were attended with incredible punctuality, if only to see and be seen, or even to carry on the most frivolous love adventures. It was the fashion under the «great king» to trifle with everything, with hearts, with the people, with cards, with the welfare of millions, with virtue and crime, with religion, with finances, with poison and dagger, and… with the devil himself.

Men of the church, like Cardinal Richelieu and Mazarin, were at that time powerful ministers of state. The state was under them ecclesiastically also – but men did not become better and more pious, but only more hypocritical and evil. Neither populace nor priesthood, nobles nor king, were imbued with the knowledge of true religion. In a word, religion at that time consisted only of superstition and superficial rites. People were anxious and childish about trifles, and incredibly hardened in regard to the most terrible evil. All sins in the world, after all, were pardoned at the last confession. But where could such a practise lead save to disgraceful hypocrisy and corruption, which naturally go hand in hand with superstitions of which our century has no conception. Louis XIV and his whole court served as an example of levity, corruption, and immorality, to the people. Since the sudden death of the wife of the Duc d'Orleans – the brother of Louis XIV – which, as was whispered, was caused by poison, to the horror of all the world a number of deaths occurred whose cause remained un-ascertained. Prophesies, exorcism of spirits, and similar things were the order of the day. Indeed at court and among the people a magic and enchantment bureau was spoken of, as well as a secret manufactory of the horrible poison, which the Parisians, in their desire to jest at everything, called «Succession powder» – *poudre de succession*. Two Italians, Exili and Destinelli, while searching for the philosopher's stone had, it was said, discovered the preparation of this poison, which left no trace. The terrible poisoner Brinvilliers[50] had first tried it on Lieutenant General d'Aubray, who died and was buried without raising the least suspicion against the guilty woman.

Soon after this, a certain La Voisin, a celebrated fortune-teller, who was sought in the very highest Parisian society, saw what an advantage she would gain if she could extend her branch of industry in this manner. From this time she therefore not only prophesied the death of a rich relation to an heir, but also helped to carry out her prophecy so that her fame became extraordinary.

Two priests, Le Sage and d'Auvaux assisted her and the result of this frightful union was such an excess of crimes that all France trembled, and Louis XIV saw himself at last obliged to create an especial court of justice, the *Chambre-ardente*, for such crimes, because the highest people of the court might perhaps be concerned in the intended investigations.

Even Monseigneur, the king's brother, visited La Voisin many times, and though disguised, was accompanied by the Sieur de Lorraine, Comte de Beuvron, and the Marquis d'Effiat. The first time he came to learn what had become of a son of his wife, Madame Henriette, born in 1668, and of whom he declared he was not the father. According to his assertion, the child was born in England where the report of his death was spread. He wished to be certain upon this important point. This could be ascertained without magic. La Voisin therefore determined to explain it by natural means, and with the prince's consent sent her cousin, Beauvillard, to London. After the lapse of a month, Beauvillard returned and gave the following account, true or false. Madame really had a child, born in England in the year 1668, which was not dead, but given up to the guardianship of his uncle, King Charles II, who loaded him with every token of love and tenderness. It was thought that Louis XIV was himself the father of this child.

Monseigneur paid 4000 pistoles and a diamond to La Voisin for the disco-

---

[50] Marie-Madeleine-Marguerite d'Aubray, Marquise de Brinvilliers (1630-1676), a French poisoner.

very, and 250 louis d'or to Beauvillard. The second time that Monseigneur visited La Voisin was at Mendon. He wished to summon ga the devil, from whom he would demand Turpin's ring, or some such means to rule the king. La Voisin caused a spirit to appear whom Monselgneur, who was very courageous, recognized as Satan. Monseigneur demanded the before mentioned ring or talisman, but the phantom answered that the king possessed a charm which protected him from any control.

The queen, too, wished to see the celebrated fortune teller. La Voisin placed the cards for her, and offered to prepare a love potion which should procure her the undivided love of the king; but the queen answered she would rather, as before, lament her husband's faithlessness, than administer any potion to him which might injure his health. The queen never saw the poisoner again. Not so with the Countess de Soissons, Olympia Mancini, she visited La Voisin more than thirty times, and perhaps received her still oftener. Her aim was to secure for herself the possession of the enormous property of Cardinal Mazarin, her uncle to the neglect of all other relation, and to regain her former influence over the king, which she had allowed to escape her. Less conscientious than the queen, she vehemently demanded an elixir of love which should turn Louis' entire affection and devotion to her, and in order to prepare it had given to the poisoner hair, nails, shirts, several stockings and a collar of the king's from which to make a love-puppet like the one which had attracted so much attention about a hundred years before at the trial of La Môte. It was said she had also procured, for La Voisin a few drops of the king's blood in a little crystal flask. The conjuration had taken place, however, without the slightest result.

Fouquet, at the height of his good fortune, had been connected with the fortune teller, and had even given her an annual stipend. Bussy Rabutin[51] came to her to receive something which should procure him the love of his cousin, Madame de Sévigné[52], and a talisman to make him the sole favorite of the king. The Duc de Lauzun desired to always be loved by the sovereign's mistresses; and to obtain some certainty about his marriage with ma-

---

[51] Roger de Rabutin, Comte de Bussy (1618-1693), a French memoirist.
[52] Marie de Rabutin-Chantal, marquise de Sévigné (1626-1696), a French writer.

demoiselle, and learn whether he should receive a certain order. In relation to the latter point, La Voisin answered that he should have the blue ribbon. The prophecy was fulfilled; but it was not the order of the Holy Spirit, of which he was thinking, but the order of the Garter which he obtained.

The Duke of Luxembourg had desired to see the devil upon whom he wished to make a claim: namely that Satan should, by his power, demand his appointment as Duke of Pinez.

Such were the spiritual, religious, and moral relations, at the court of Louis XIV, when even the heir of Marshal Turenne, the reverend abbot of Auvergne, Emanuel Theodosius de la Tour, Prince and Cardinal de Bouillon, High Almoner of France, in company with his nephew, the Duc de St. Aignan, La Voisin and her waiting-maid, the two priests, disguised as soldiers, and a negro to carry the magical apparatus, went to St. Denis in order to conjure up, by a «devil's mass» the spirit of Turenne from his grave, that he might tell the avaricious souls where Marshal Turenne had buried his property.

Night brooded over the earth. It was Friday and this Friday fell exactly on the thirteenth of the month. So, according to the statement of La Voisin, it must be, and the conjuration could only take place in the church of St. Denis, and then only at the midnight hour.

It was about eleven. Thanks to the corruptibility of the old sacristan, they had passed through the underground passage to the abbey. An arch of the bell-tower now concealed the sacrilegious group.

Still it seemed as if, at the last hour, the voice of eternity sought to warn them, for the thunder of the approaching storm rolled, the wind howled round the tower, the lightning gleamed through the little windows of the building illuminating its darkness for a moment, and making the pale, unearthly faces of the participants in the ceremony look like spirits.

The clock struck eleven, and with the last stroke, a key turned in the lock of the little iron door which led out of the arch of the bell-tower into the interior of the church. A small faint ray of light streamed in from the dark lantern of the sacristan.

A death-like stillness reigned in the wide apartment. Silently – like warning giant fingers – rose the mighty columns – the pious thoughts embodied in stone of a century long since dead. Softly the party moved through the empty space to the back part of the church, for here only – aside from the abbey – was the glimmer of light securely shielded from any eyes which might still be open.

They had now reached the place where the «devils' mass,» that is, the service read backward, was to be repeated. Quickly and noiselessly, Lesage and d'Auvaux erected a kind of altar, the negro, like a dark demon risen from hell, assisting them, spread a black cloth over It, and lighted five black wax candles. Then the sacred books were placed upon it upside down, the crucifix head downward, and the priests put on their vestments wrong side out.

Even the heart of the reverend abbot of Auvergne, trembled at this moment. A death like pallor covered his face... his limbs shook.

«Nephew!» he whispered softly to the Duc de St. Aignan, who was standing near him, and around whose lips, though a little pale, the perpetual smile played, «nephew! I fear Satan.»

«Wherefore?» asked the Due, with difficulty concealing his own agitation, for so deeply in those times was superstition implanted in every soul, that even the most frivolous believed In magic and the possibility of raising spirits from the grave.

«Wherefore?» repeated the Cardinal, whose conscience – notwithstanding his insatiable avarice – began to cry out in his soul: «Because, after all, his horrible appearance might kill us!»

«Do not fear, most worthy uncle,» answered St, Aignan softly, while with great effort he put on an air of easy unconstraint. «Do you know how the devil looks?»

«No,» replied the bewildered abbot.

«You know the trial of Madame Brinvilliers?»

«Yes! The Duc de La Reynie was presiding at the trial.»

«Yes!»

A royal robber

«Well, the Duchess de Bouillon was summoned on account of a devil's conjuration. When La Reynie asked: 'Did you see the devil Madame? And if you saw him, tell me how he looked!' she answered quietly: 'No, my Lord, I have not seen him; but I see him at this moment: he is ugly and dressed like a councilor!'»

«Do not jest!» answered the cardinal sternly. «How can you at this hour?»

A fearful peal of thunder at this moment shook the old building to its foundation. A sea of fire flamed in at all the windows of the church. Hell seemed, in fact, to have opened its gates. Everyone stood affrighted, every ear listened to hear a cry of fire. But all remained quiet and only the storm continued to rage.

«Let us begin,» said La Voisin at last, «and you, my Lords, be composed, in all probability the spirit will appear during the consecration.»

The mass began. But the storm grew fiercer and fiercer. Heaven and earth were continually bathed in fire and flame while one peal followed another, the earth trembled and – rocked by the storm, the bells of the tower called anxiously for help.

Then d'Auvaux, the infamous priest, raised the Host, calling upon the devil instead of God. But at this moment a piercing scream resounded, a flag stone in the choir rose and a figure enveloped in a shroud appeared. La Voisin and the priest sank on the floor; the cardinal and even St. Aignan staggered back. But the figure cried with a hollow, sepulchral voice: «Wretch, you have degraded ray house, made famous by many heroes. It will fall! My name will be extinguished before a century has passed. Know! – the treasure which I left – is – *my fame – my victories!* Worthless man, seek for no other.»

With these words the figure sank back. Another fearful peal of thunder rolled over the church. A blast of wind destroyed one of the decaying windows, and the candles went out.

VIII.
The dream

Charming Limagne is like an Eden surrounded by laurels and myrtles, ever-greens, oaks, orange and lemon trees, while above arches a soft, almost eter-nally clear sky!

Yes, charming Limagne is like an Eden! and above the vineyards and the olive-groves and the golden fruit-fields rise the summits of the Puy de Dome and the grand Mont d'Or.

And yet another thing in Limagne in those days reminded one of the Eden of man; the simplicity and unspoiled condition of manners, which – in con-trast to Paris and the court – reigned in that neighborhood.

Here was where Marie Angeline Scoraille de Rousille, the lovely sixteen year old daughter of the house of Fontanges grew up upon the banks of the Al-lier like a beautiful flower hidden from the world. Left to the care of an in-valid mother, upon whose shoulders still heavier cares rested, for the family of Fontanges – like so many of the provincial nobility – had long since de-clined and been impoverished, Angeline had not the benefit of any especial education, but her intellect was not of the kind to feel the need or to strive independently for a special cultivation. Childishly pious and good by nature, she enjoyed the little knowledge which her confessor brought her, and this was confined to instruction in religious matters, a little reading and writing, a hasty glance at the history of her native country, and the more accurate knowledge of the departed greatness of the house of Fontanges and the family of the Comté de Montferrand.

But in those times the daughters of the provincial nobility seldom learned more – with the exception of the art of needlework – and so this simple education would have done no particular harm to the charming Angeline, if the only thing which was taught her thoroughly, the history of her house and its former splendor, had not strengthened and advanced that weak point in her character, which must be designated as the most prominent.

This weakness was – vanity. But could Angeline be otherwise than vain?

A royal robber

Even as a child, she was beautiful as a little angel and every one took pains to tell her so.

Goethe said: «Women are vain by nature; but it is becoming to them, and we like them the better for it.» Still this might have passed away in the case of Mademoiselle de Fontanges as with so many other young ladies, if this vanity had not found new nourishment in the faded greatness of her house, which awakened in the young girl's breast a silent longing for the recovery of such splendor. The consequence was that, with all innocence and childishness – a secret, vague ambition consumed her. But the lovely Angeline was, in fact, still too immature to give any other than a childish expression to this ambition. She found it in sweet reveries, for which the loneliness of her quiet life in poetic Limagne afforded her plenty of time. Then she dreamed herself back in former centuries, as the daughter of the once famous and powerful Rueil Charles de Fontanges, who rose to a high rank, and was the friend of Philip VII of Valois; or as the niece of Laurent de Fontanges, the Abbot of Notre-Dame de-Bon-Port, who under King Charles VII, with Agnès Sorel[53], was one of the most prominent characters at court.

Amid such visions had Angeline grown up and with her – as a near relative – the little Gauthier de Montferrand. The children had but one heart and soul; their natures in time almost blended into one. In the common childish plays Gauthier usually took the part of the knight of the Lady of Fontanges or even Charles VII himself, who not only paid homage in every way to the niece of the Abbot of Notre-Damede- Bon-Port, but also made her his queen.

Thus a childish affection between Gauthier and Angeline developed, and increased, although it scarcely gave token of being anything more than the love between a. brother and sister. Only when both had grown up, and Gauthier – to open a career for himself – was summoned by his uncle. Captain de Torcy, to Paris and the court – only then, agitated by the thought of parting, both became aware that an affection had grown in their hearts which was something more than fraternal love.

---

[53] Agnès Sorel (1422-1450), favourite mistress of Charles VII.

72

A royal robber

Thus it happened that, from this moment, Angeline's thoughts were directed towards Versailles. There lived the one for whom her heart beat, and this youthful heart was passionate enough, notwithstanding her frigid exterior. Thither turned her quiet reveries.

The first letter of the youth – directed to his mother and also to Angeline had not been very enthusiastic about the court of Versailles. The heart of the young man seemed to be depressed and saddened. In how many expectations he had been disappointed! How his pure, child-like soul shuddered at the unrestrained frivolity and immorality which met him here! How he wished himself back in his quiet Limagne! Only one thing according to his first letter comforted him: the cordiality with which his uncle received him; and – the astonishing complaisance with which the noble, intellectual Duc de St. Aignan, the especial favorite of the king, had tendered him his friendship. What visions of the future he could build upon it; what hopes for his mother and Angeline Gauthier suggested.

This first letter was soon followed by others. Angeline trembled with delight for they were directed to her – and how differently everything at court now appeared to her cousin, how constantly he thought of her! Oh! what a glowing, longing love could be read in these words, a love which drew her with magic power, to the court.

Oh! what a life it must be there! People appeared in dresses so costly and beautiful, that one could have – no idea of them in poor Limagne. And the festivals the king gave! And what homage he, the great king, the handsomest and most chivalric man in France, paid to women. Like a sweet, intoxicating poison, the lovely Mademoiselle de Fontanges drank in these alluring words. They flattered her vanity too much for her to weigh their meaning quietly, and compare them with Gauthier's former turn of mind, so well known to her. Already in imagination she saw herself among all these high-born noble ladies – outshining them – envied by them – admired and honored by Louis XIV!

At this time a new impulse and excitement was stirred in her heart by the news; that the Marquise de Montespan, the mistress of the king, had expressed a wish to one of her distant relatives, living in Clermont, that she should send her one of the young ladies from the nobility of Limagne to occupy a position at court, as lady of honor to the queen.

The marquise had requested her to propose several of the young ladies belonging to the nobility.

Among those proposed – so much Angeline had learned from the friend through whom Gauthier's letters had lately come – was her name, although her mother, as well as her confessor and teacher, had at first very decidedly opposed it. The urgency of the family, a letter from Gauthier, and the entreaties of Angelina had won the victory.

How the hearts of all the young girls whose names had been sent to Versailles beat with anxiety – how quickly and passionately that of the charming Marie Angeline throbbed in her bosom. But no answer had as yet arrived. The uncertainty and expectation almost overpowered little Mademoiselle de Fontanges, and she sought solitude more than ever.

And with this memory, Angeline's waking dreams and thoughts change. A full hour might have passed when Père Hilaire, the confessor of the lovely Mademoiselle de Fontanges, came down the path. He was a plain, somewhat narrow-minded, but worthy man, who without questioning, submissively believed what the church commanded, but at the same time intended to be honest with men, especially with the souls intrusted to his care. Therefore he loved Angeline like a father, for since her childhood she had been to him the type by which he imagined the angels in heaven.

The idea that there was a possibility of the removal of his pupil to court, made him very anxious, and while coming-from the sick bed of a poor woman at the other end of the valley, he was again meditating upon this vexatious subject, when he found his darling sleeping at the edge of the wood.

Oh! how charmingly the lovely girl lay there, like a beautiful flower among her sisters, resting so lightly on the swelling turf, and in fact a thousand charms exerted so powerful an attraction, that Père Hilaire could not resist pressing a soft kiss upon her dress. Suddenly she breathed quicker and more heavily, the smile which had just played around her lips disappeared, terror was expressed in her features, and a low groan indicated an anxious,

A royal robber

troubled dream.

«Poor child,» thought the priest, «life will bring you still more troubled dreams.» and he gently awoke his pupil. Angeline de Fontanges started up in terror. She needed time to think where she was, and how she had come there.

Père Hilaire smiled at her with fatherly kindness, and then said: «You have had a troubled and anxious dream, my dear child.»

«Yes, father,» answered the young girl, still half bewildered and frightened. «And it was strange enough.»

«Strange?» – repeated the priest, – «what was it that my lovely child dreamed in the open air?»

Angeline hesitated, pressed her hand upon her brow, and after a little pause said, as if speaking to herself:

«Oh! – it was beautiful, and at the same time horrible, but strangely mysterious also. But,» she continued eagerly, «you know how to explain dreams, Père Hilaire.»

«Dreams?» replied the priest gravely, «dreams come from God, and in this way He often warns his poor, weak human children of evil and destruction!»

«Strange!» said the girl bending her beautiful head thoughtfully, «but you are my confessor and teacher, so I will relate my dream to you – and you may interpret it.»

The priest sat down by Angeline and she began:

«I thought I had climbed to the summit of a very high mountain, around me lay the world, but just as I reached the top I was so much dazzled by a purple and gold cloud that I could not find my way. The cloud seemed to rise – and I was inspired with courage – but I suddenly began to sink, deep darkness enveloped me, and my soul was so agitated by anxiety and fear that I awoke.»

Angeline was silent – the priest's expression had become grave and sad.

«And the interpretation?» asked Mademoiselle de Fontanges anxiously.

A royal robber

«The interpretation,» repeated the priest, «is a warning to you in your path of life. Take care, my daughter, the mountain is the court, where you, if you go, which I hope will not be the case, will excite great attention. But this attention will not be of long duration if you forsake your God; for in that case God will forsake you, and you will perish in eternal night.»

Angeline was terrified. She went home beside the pious priest, absorbed in her own thoughts, and speaking only in monosyllables.

On her arrival she found every one in excitement; the Marquise de Montespan had made her selection from among the young ladies of Limagne and her choice had fallen upon Marie Angeline Scoraille de Rousille, Mademoiselle de Fontanges.

IX.
A noble friend

Gauthier sat alone in his room. It was a small apartment, – and in these days, with our ideas of comfort and ease, would be considered a very poorly furnished one, – near that of his uncle's, who as an unmarried man, and a soldier, thought very little of the luxuries of life. To him, a good glass of wine and a game of cards after the performance of his toilsome duty, were the greatest enjoyments earth could offer, and he troubled himself very little about anything else.

He was now on duty and Gauthier alone, so the young man could give himself up to his sad thoughts, though the youth, only a short time before,- had arrived at the court of Versailles so full of life and courage.

Gauthier was by no means a hypocrite, but his pure heart could not fail to be filled with uneasiness, nay with fear and aversion, at the life of the court of Versailles.

What a horrible contrast this excess of immorality and corruption, outward splendor, and inward poverty, hypocrisy and wickedness, frivolity and superstition, insatiable desire for every refined pleasure of life, and utter corruption of the soul – made to the simplicity and worthy, honest life of his home.

And did not his pure, ardent love for her, the deaf playmate of his childhood, attract him? Ah, he had not written to her yet, writing was a difficult task, for it was an art seldom taught young nobles in those days, but still in the two letters to his mother which he had entrusted to a friend of St. Aignan's, he had sent a loving message to her – nevertheless no answer, either from his mother or Angeline, had as yet arrived.

How isolated Gauthier felt in the whirl of court life, for his military position in the king's guard was not much more than a place of honor. The young, strong man, thirsting for activity, would have preferred service in the army, the constant alternations of fate in the field while opposing the enemy – to his monotonous duties in Versailles.

A royal robber

Gauthier expressed this to his uncle and the Duc de St. Aignan; but only the latter thought the young man's wish natural, and promised to remember his desire at a suitable time. Captain de Torcy, on the contrary, with the quiet experience of riper age, exhorted him to be patient.

Gauthier thanked heaven that he had at least found one warm, true friend at court – for such, the Duc de St. Aignan had become. And was he not in the youth's eyes, a pattern of a courtier, a polished man of the world?

St. Aignan was amiability itself. Always merry, he bubbled over with witticisms and anecdotes, while his attention and readiness to serve the poor insignificant novice, filled him with true emotion and the most sincere gratitude.

Gauthier therefore greeted the entrance of his noble patron and friend with joy, especially as he was just now very sad again.

And indeed, anyone who saw St. Aignan enter with his handsome face, upon which the eternal smile rested like eternal sunshine, beaming with good nature – must have been influenced by the charm which surrounded him and banished all sadness and sorrowful thoughts. Even though the Duc had no money, which was often the case on account of his lavish expenditures, he was always gay! Now, too, the fright and thunder of Saint Denis was long since forgotten, and sunshine and merriment reigned in this frivolous heart.

«*Ventre-saint-gris!*» exclaimed the nobleman at his entrance with a beaming face, while he imitated old Captain de Torcy most excellently. «*Ventre-saint-gris!* We come, it seems, just in time to help our friend catch the blues; or is Gauthier de Montferrand thinking of his celebrity after death?»

«How would that help me. Monsieur le Duc?» answered Gauthier, but. St. Aignan laughingly interrupted him.

«Monsieur le Duc!» said he scornfully, «how often, my friend, have I already forbidden you to call me that when we are alone together. You might say, my friend or St. Aignan, that sounds much more in harmony with my friendship. But, my young friend, you have really been thinking of your future fame, so I will tell you how it may be gained here!»

«For me it would bloom earliest on the battlefield,» said the youth with a sad smile.

«What battlefield!» exclaimed St. Aignan laughing. «One must make it, like Mazarin. To satisfy his ambition, he betrayed France – to satisfy his avarice, he ruined her, and yet he has obtained at this court gratitude and immortality.»

«How?»

«By the *Pâtés à la Mazarin*, which he invented, and which are still a favorite dish with the king and all his courtiers.»

«You are and always will be a jester,» answered Gauthier laughing. «Still, Cardinal Mazarin did a great deal for the welfare of the country of his adoption.»

«In which, however, he forgot his own welfare as little as he denied his descent,» exclaimed the Duc sitting down upon a common leather chair which constituted the principal portion of the furniture. «My young friend, do you know the story of the cardinal and the pamphlet speculation?»

Gauthier answered in the negative.

«Listen then, and learn something from the old gentleman: Cardinal Mazarin was once informed of a shocking pamphlet against him, which had appeared at a book-store. It was immediately confiscated. As the dealer naturally doubled the price of the pamphlet, the speculative cardinal sold it again secretly on – his own account, at an enormous price. By this commercial intrigue, which he often related with delight, he made a thousand pistoles.»

«Clever,» said Gauthier and his brow darkened again, «but surely not worthy of a man like Cardinal Mazarin. Ought he not, with his position at court and in the country, to give an example of virtue?»

St. Aignan laughed loudly.

«Virtue!» he exclaimed, stroking his handsome beard. «Virtue! and here at court? My young friend, if you wish to make your fortune at court, you must be excessively liberal in your ideas! You know the pretty little story of Mademoiselle *La séductrice plénipotentiaire?* But now, how should you know it and still believe that virtue breathes in this region!»

«Unfortunately,» began Gauthier; but St. Aignan interrupted him, and exclaimed with an ironical smile.

«Hush, my little friend! As I feel drawn towards you as if by magic, and we have concluded a friendship, r consider it my duty as a friend to open the lungs of your conscience so wide, that you will be in a condition to breathe and bear the air of the court. So listen, and draw a conclusion for yourself.»

«When the last war with the Netherlands had been decided upon in the noble head of Louvois, the minister of war, It was resolved upon in council. But it was no child's play. England and Spain were to be feared; it was necessary therefore to take precautionary measures. One of the first measures was to be assured of the neutrality of Spain and the alliance of England. The Marquis de Villars was sent to Madrid to make the Spanish Cabinet understand what an interest it had in weakening its natural enemy, the United Netherlands. But an ambassador of an entirely different sort must be sent to King Charles II of England.»

«And what kind?» asked Gauthier.

St. Aignan compressed his lips, smiled, and elevated his eyebrows in so strange a fashion, that for a moment his usually handsome face resembled that of a faun. His glance was so diabolically significant that, for the first time, Gauthier really shrank from his noble friend.

With a burning blush, the youth again asked in an embarrassed tone, «who was sent as ambassador to England?»

St. Aignan smiled and continued: «His Majesty Louis XIV announced that he intended to take a journey to Dunkirk and invited the courtiers to accompany him. All the magnificence and splendor the king could display was paraded on this occasion; thirty thousand men preceded or followed him. His whole court, that is, the richest and noblest of the nobility of Europe, the most graceful and most intellectual ladies in the world accompanied him.»

«Ladies?» asked Gauthier with astonishment.

A royal robber

«Louis XIV is never without women,» answered St. Aignan laughing. «Neither in the field nor the drive. His motto in this respect was and is: a court without ladies is a year without spring and a spring without roses! But to the point! – the queen and madame, who was alive at that time – possessed nearly equal rank, but, and here the satyr-like expression again appeared on his face – but unprecedented sight, then followed in one carriage the two mistresses of the king: Madame de la Vallière, – and well, you know, Gauthier!»

«Madame de Montespan?»

«Right, who at that time often sat in the same large English carriage with the king and queen.»

«Monsieur le Duc!» exclaimed Gauthier.

But St. Aignan motioned to him to keep silence, while he said laughing: «The best is yet to come. Madame was accompanied by a charming person, who had her secret instructions, by Louise Rencè de Panankoët, Mademoiselle de Queronaille, she was the *séductrice plenipotentiaire!*»

«But, it is not possible.»

«The commission was important,» continued St. Aignan quietly, with a pleasant smile, «and the rôle was difficult.»

«How – I don't understand.»

«She must take precedence of seven well-known mistresses of King Charles II, who at that time, all at once enjoyed the high privilege, so much sought, for in England, of driving away the vexation caused by His Majesty's financial embarrassments, the murmurs of his people, and the opposition of parliament.»

«Monsieur le Duc!» exclaimed Gauthier, flushing and paling by turns, «I cannot believe what you say. One must despair of any virtue, any morality.»

St. Aignan laughed again, and said so quietly that Gauthier was horrified.

«These seven mistresses were: Countess Castlemaine – Miss Stewart – Miss Wells, lady of honor to the Duchess of York – Nell Gwyn, one of the gayest courtesans of the time – Miss d'Avis, a celebrated actress – the dancer Belle Orkay, and finally, a Moorish girl named Zinga.»

The young man looked at the Duc in amazement; while the eyes of the latter, as he perceived the increasing effect produced by his story, gleamed with an expression, that resembled the triumph of a fiend, though he retained the same stereotyped smile, while he continued as quietly as though reading a passage from the Bible:

«The treaty succeeded far better than was expected. King Charles II found Mademoiselle de Queronaille charming, and upon the promise of a few millions and madame's consent to leave Louise de Queronaille in England; King Charles II of England, agreed to everything that France required.»

«I am bewildered!» exclaimed the young man, pressing his hand upon his brow.

«I am not,» answered St. Aignan gayly. «But I will have to relate the end.»

«Was the crime not yet complete?» exclaimed Gauthier with the noble indignation of a youthful heart that still believes in God and virtue.

«Why no,» replied the Duc with amiable irony, «Mademoiselle de Queronaille remained in England, where King Charles made her Duchess of Portsmouth. Our gracious Lord and King, the great Louis XIV, presented her in the same year with the manorial estate of d'Aubigny; – that estate which Charles VII in 1622 gave to Johann Stuart as a reward for the great and important services which he rendered the crown of France in the war against England.»

St, Aignan was silent. A longer pause ensued.

«Monsieur le Duc!" began Gauthier at last in a very grave tone, «you have had the kindness to bestow upon me the honor of your friendship. I know not, in truth, how I shall ever thank you for it ; but your affection is deeply engraved upon my heart. Who else at court would have instructed me so kindly, who would have distinguished m^; an insignificant youth, from among the crowd, and with truly princely kindness introduced me to the most brilliant entertainments? To you – to you alone I am indebted for this advantage, and for so much besides.»

«Friend,» exclaimed St. Aignan laughing, «I beg you to say no more.»

«Let me speak, my noble friend!» continued the youth eagerly, «for it is time – I *must*!»

«Well, then, go on, Gauthier, what troubles you?»

«I cannot remain here.»

«Oh – ho!»

«Procure me a place in the army, whatever it may be, or let me return to my beloved Limagne.»

«Gauthier!» exclaimed the Duc with an expression of astonishment, which, however, was contradicted by a lurking glance of triumph.

«Call my conduct either presumption or childish homesickness, it is neither the one nor the other. But by heaven – there is a heavy weight upon my heart; I cannot breathe this air. Perhaps I am a fool in your eyes – as my uncle says – but something urges me away – into the free world, – if possible to the field of honor. You, Monsieur le Duc, can do what you will with His Majesty, procure me a place in the army, – even though it be that of a lieutenant – I will do honor to you, to my native country, and to His Majesty.»

The young man was silent, but his eyes flashed, and his heart beat almost audibly.

St. Aignan remained perfectly unmoved. The strange smile still hovered round his lips; but he took pains to conceal the ironical expression which generally rested upon them.

«And if, my young friend, I: were prepared, to give you a proof that my friendship is the truest and most tender?»

«Monsieur le Duc!» exclaimed Gauthier with joyful astonishment.

«Friendship must be capable of every sacrifice,» continued St. Aignan. «To part from you, Gauthier, will be hard for me, still I respect your pure, noble heart, the impulse which inspires you to flee from this Sodom and Gomorrah, and seek on the battlefield a glorious future, I have –»

«Oh, what? what?» impetuously cried Gauthier.

«A place for you in the army!» replied the Duc, drawing the commission from his pocket.

«My friend.»

«But –»

«But, what?»

«It requires you to leave Versailles to-morrow and repair to the frontier.»

«Anywhere, so that it is away from here,» cried Gauthier.

«Good,» said the Due. «Then we will have a gay night.»

«But my mother? And Angeline?»

«Write to them both, and give the letters to me. I will send them by the next royal messenger.»

«Oh, thanks, a thousand, thousand thanks,» cried the delighted Gauthier shaking the Duc's hand vehemently in the excess of his joy, «how shall I repay you for all this love and kindness?»

«Preserve your friendship for me, Gauthier, and return a hero from the battles which await you in the immediate future. But now write your letters and make the necessary preparations.»

«But my uncle,» cried the young man, suddenly turning pale.

«It is an order from Monseigneur Louvois, who summonses you to Arras. You must obey your commander.»

«And I do it with joy,» cried Gauthier, his face radiant with delight.

«Well then, adieu till we meet again this evening at my hotel, for a farewell supper,» said the Due, offering his hand to the overjoyed youth.

But when the door had closed behind him, he burst into a fiendish laugh: «Won,» he murmured, «he will leave Paris forever on the day that Angeline de Fontanges arrives here.»

X.
The chase and the deer

A hunt was announced to take place in the woods of Marly. The whole court was invited; and the Master of the Hunt, the Duc de St. Aignan, as well as Madame de Montespan, had exhausted themselves in preparing for the festival, the former in his official position, the latter as hostess to the king and court.

It was necessary for her to lay hold of every opportunity to warm the heart and enchain the fancy of her royal lover, by acts of consideration, novelties, and gayety. To-day a strategy was to be executed upon whose success or non-success rested the whole future of the marquise.

The intrigue with Gauthier de Montferrand and Mademoiselle de Fontanges, conducted by these cunning and practised allies, had succeeded perfectly up to this point.

Mademoiselle de Fontanges had, in fact, arrived at Versailles on the very day on which Gauthier left Paris. The youth, in a former letter to his mother and playmate, had described with indignation the state of affairs at the court, excused the change in his position by the impossibility of his living in such a sphere, and lastly entreated both to preserve their love for him.

Angeline, especially, he ardently implored to keep the affection which had bound their hearts to each other from earliest childhood. Her image would ever rise before his soul like a guardian angel and soon, soon – he hoped to greet her and lovely Limagne again as a man, and a brave soldier.

To be sure this letter did not arrive, nor were those received by the lovely Marie de Fontanges written by Gauthier. But, in their inexperience and innocence, neither party saw the threads of the net which had been set for them, and in which they were already ensnared.

Gauthier, happy at escaping from the court of Versailles – hastened to Arras and his new path of life the more joyfully, that youthful courage and vigor pointed to the field of honor as his only true position.

A royal robber

Mademoiselle de Fontanges, on her arrival at Versailles, was very much surprised not to find her cousin. But he had only – as she learned – gone to the army for a short time, honored with a high and important commission.

He would return within two or three weeks. Besides, Angeline soon felt that she would make herself ridiculous if she particularly noticed this short absence of her former playmate. To be sure, she grieved in secret; but the splendor and magnificence which met her on every side, confused and filled her mind with intoxicating delight. Did not the usually haughty Marquise de Montespan treat her exactly like a loving mother, for she could not immediately enter upon her position at court with the queen. Was there not a little court of charming young men about her, at whose head stood Gauthier's noble friend, of whom he had spoken so highly in his letters, the Duc de St. Aignan, the principal favorite of the king. Her cousin, so said the Duc, had especially recommended her to his care. And what flattery, what praises of her beauty, poured into her ears, and found a joyful echo In the vain little heart.»

How the marquise overwhelmed her with presents of every kind – how the noble lady hastened to have new and beautiful dresses made for her on the spot, for she could not allow her to be seen at court in her country clothes.

Angeline was intoxicated with delight, and when the relative from Clermont, who had brought her to Versailles, – it was the same one who had secretly brought Gauthier's letters to her – returned, Angeline could not sufficiently praise her cordial reception and happiness In the letter to her mother, which she entrusted to her care.

And yet the greatest joy was still before her for she had not seen the king,… Louis XIV, the greatest monarch on earth. How many times the thought of the joy of being preferred by such a king had made the simple child from Limagne strangely happy. At these moments, delight, blended with a sweet tremor, thrilled her whole being; and such moments occurred more and more frequently, for what Mademoiselle de Fontanges now heard and saw of the universal enthusiastic adoration of the king, far surpassed all she had learned from her relative on the journey.

A royal robber

The result of all this, as well as the numberless new and powerful impress-sions which rushed upon her mind and excited her nervous system in the highest degree, was that the old dreams awoke, and transported the dazzled bewildered child into a kind of fairy world, whose shining central point was the great king.

Angeline thought of no evil in all this; but to be distinguished or even loved by such a prince and knight, to see him at her feet, to outshine all others – such a fortune was scarcely to be thought of and comprehended. And did she not have that wonderful dream, only a short time before her summons to the court? The dream of the mountain and the golden, purple cloud on which she floated in such blessedness? And had not Père Hilaire – who was so celebrated for the interpretation of dreams – said: «she would obtain a distinguished position at court?».

And «dreams come from God» – said the priest. Suppose she had been des-tined by God and fate; even from her birth, to please the king by her beau-ty? Must God therefore desert her. Oh, certainly not, Louis was so good, so noble!

Only one thing Angeline did not observe, that she had already forsaken one person, forsaken and almost forgotten her cousin and playmate, poor Gauthier.

The marquise always had some new pleasure or surprise, so that Angeline had no time for reflection. Then, too, she had many things to learn; court etiquette, how one must deport oneself, and many such things – in which, however, Madame de Montespan was very careful not to disturb the expres-sion of childish innocence and country simplicity which she found in the good child; for it was on this very charm of novelty that she depended to ensnare the king.

Marie Angeline knew not how she could prove to the noble lady the over-flowing gratitude of her heart. She vowed a thousand times – she would al-ways remember the marquise with filial affection, and the marquise seemed to listen to the assurance with pleasure.

At last the day approached on which Mademoiselle de Fontanges was to see

A royal robber

Louis XIV for the first time. It was the day of the great hunting party in the woods of Marly. The marquise, in honor of the occasion, had presented Angeline with a very tasteful dress which the young girl had already put on, and indeed she looked enchantingly beautiful in it! Her tall figure was clad in a riding habit of royal-blue velvet, trimmed on the arms and waist with rich, white lace. The front, falling slightly apart, disclosed a closely fitting vest of white satin and a skirt of the same material. A royal blue velvet cap, from which nodded a blue and white feather, rested coquettishly upon her luxuriant hair. A costly pearl necklace, the only inheritance of the Fontanges family, rose and fell upon the matchless bosom, whose exquisite outlines were fully revealed.

Even the Marquise de Montespan herself was astonished when Mademoiselle de Fontanges entered the room in this costume. The young girl was indeed a dazzling beauty, and moreover, by her wealth of auburn hair and her unusually white complexion, whose effect was heightened by the dress she wore – a beauty of no common order. A single glance at that face and figure could not fail to recall one of the exquisite white marble statues which the old masters of antiquity have bequeathed us.

Was it any marvel, that in the first moment of astonishment a feeling of envy and jealousy, a doubt of the wisdom of her purpose, arose in the mind of Madame de Montespan? But these emotions soon vanished in the proud consciousness of being a thousand times superior to her chosen rival in intellect, wit, and the art of influencing and guiding. Angeline was beautiful, but she was only to be looked upon as a charming, insipid doll for a great royal child. And the one thing necessary,' the prudent woman had already secured: the most absolute gratitude and dependence on the part of her protégée.

Angeline, delighted at the praise lavished upon her from the lips of the aristocratic lady, and at the thought of being presented to the king, once more poured forth her tender, child-like love and gratitude for Madame de Montespan. «Only be happy, dear child,» said the latter, gazing kindly at the beautiful girl and drawing her towards her, «arid promise me one thing!»

«Everything, everything,» said the young girl, covering Madame de Montespan's little hands with kisses, «how can I thank you enough for your kindness?»

«Only promise me,» continued the elder lady, «under every circumstance to do nothing without the true and loving counsel of your maternal friend.»

«I swear it!» exclaimed the girl, in the exuberance of her gratitude.

«You are still young, still inexperienced,» continued the marquise, «how should you know how to conduct yourself towards the court, the king, and the intrigues of the wicked. Promise me therefore – whatever way your fate may shape itself – in every secret of your heart to confide in me as your true friend, and always to act according to my advice.»

«Oh how gladly I promise it,» said Angeline, «I feel deeply how far I, a poor awkward girl from the country, am wanting in everything, and how greatly you surpass me in intellect and amiability. All I am I have become through you, whom I call with pride my second mother. To you, therefore, as to my mother, shall belong the fullest confidence of my heart in the future.» And Angeline laid her hand in that of the marquise to seal the promise.

At this moment the signal of the approach of His Majesty, and the court echoed on the air, for Françoise Athenais, Marquise de Montespan, expected him at Marly as her guest.

Angeline de Fontanges trembled, for a moment her cheek flushed and paled by turns, but she soon regained her composure and apparent coldness.

«Come, my child!» said the marquise. «We will receive His Majesty in the most cordial manner, as befits so great a king and gracious a gentleman.»

And motioning to the rest of the ladies of her suite, who were in the anteroom, Madame de Montespan advanced to meet the hunting party, consisting of numberless horsemen and carriages.

They were to partake of a little breakfast at Marly, and then proceed to the chase.

The notes of the horn, the baying of dogs, cracking of whips, and trampling of horses, sounded like the roar of a tempest. Such a tumult might well have overpowered the lamentations of a whole nation; at least it drowned the voices of many a conscience, while it reminded the distant listeners of the legend of the wild huntsman.

The royal coach now came in sight. The master of the hounds, M. le Duc de St. Aignan, who rode beside it himself, sprang from his foam-covered horse and opened the door for His Majesty. Louis XIV alighted and stepped under the portals, decorated with flowers and foliage, which welcomed him with their flattering inscription, as pleasantly as the woman who had so long been the mistress of his heart greeted him in words.

But the marquise needed only one glance to be assured that His Majesty was far from being in the mood she had desired. Louis XIV, so fickle in his love, was weary of Madame de Montespan and therefore her kindness and flattering attentions troubled him much more than her former caprices, her obstinacy, and the desire to rule she had often manifested.

As yet he had not dared publicly to break with one who had borne him six children, legitimate princes and princesses, and therefore accepted for to-day an invitation, which annoyed and put him out of humor.

The penetration of the marquise observed all this; while her royal lover's manner plunged a thousand daggers into her heart, which she multiplied a hundred fold by the observation that the cowardly, cringing world of the court, already began to be cooler toward her.

At this moment she could have rent the father of her children in pieces like an-enraged lioness, and yet she loved him, and could not give him up – him and the thought of being the joint ruler vof France. For this reason she now played her *va banque!* and the last trump had. slipped from her hand. The king must remain hers, and if her own power was no longer sufficient, then, (with the aid of hell) by the help of a stranger! How divinely beautiful the lovely Mademoiselle de Fontanges appeared, as she stood among the other ladies in the train of the Marquise de Montespan, lovelier than ever in the sweet confusion into which her approaching presentation to the king had thrown the still inexperienced child of Limagne. But poor child, the king in his ill-humor scarcely sees you. The red hair only brings an expression of scorn upon his lips, and turning indifferently away, he says to St. Aignan with a mocking laugh.

«That wolf will not eat us!»

Madame de Montespan was fairly crushed.

«To the chase!» cried the king, and without even touching the luxurious breakfast that was prepared the party withdrew into the dense woods of Marly.

With tears in her eyes and despair in her heart Madame de Montespan – as was customary on such occasions – entered the king's hunting carriage and sat down beside His Majesty. But Louis neither saw the tears, nor heard the soft reproaches of the lady. He was thinking to-day of very different things of Louvois and his military plans and of the latest disagreeable intelligence from the Netherlands, from Spain, and especially from Alsace, which had informed him that the free German imperial city of Strassburg would not submit to French government, nor respond to the eager desires of the king. Every contradiction was an abomination to Louis XIV and now came that of the one miserable city toward which he cherished the best intentions.

The chase would divert his thoughts – but nothing else. On reaching the appointed spot he fired with fierce delight at the game which was driven past. But this murder soon became tedious. He pressed farther into the forest, leaving the carriages, ladies, and suite far behind, till at last he entirely disappeared. The master of the hounds, who never left his side in a hunt, must, however, according to His Majesty's express command, continued the chase, and make the court believe that the king was still at the head of the gay, blood-thirsty horde.

The trampling of hundreds of horses resounded from the distance, the wild boars, red deer, and does, broke through the bushes and hedges in herds, the horns sounded merrily through the dark aisles of the leafy dome while the flourishes of the trumpets quickly alternated from «*à la mente*» to «*à la vue*»… the hounds bayed as if mad; a magnificent young stag dashed by. But all this left the king unmoved.

His trusty gun-bearer – old Moustache, who had taught the young Dauphin to load his gun when a child – might walk close behind him with the loaded weapon ready to hand it to the royal hunter but Louis did not take it. With deep and gloomy clouds upon his brow, he thought over all the political embarrassments into which Louvois had drawn him; of those into which his connection with Madame de Montespan had brought him, and how he could break the last threads with which the marquise, who had become wearisome, still bound him.

«I am tired of women,» said he to himself, «and will never again wear the chain of love. Pride, ambition, and desire to rule are the only reasons which make them yield their charms to princes. I will be free, perfectly free!»

At this moment a loud scream fell upon his ear, and a strange vision appeared in the distance.

A horse, white as new fallen snow, which seemed to have become wild with fright, dashed along the path at furious speed. It bore, she could scarcely keep in the saddle, a beautiful, slender form in a white satin dress; the royal-blue velvet hunting dress floated over the back of the animal. The plumes on her little hat waved proudly in the air, as if nodding a merry greeting to the green woods.

A smile of bitter scorn played round the corners of the king's handsome mouth.

At the first glance he had recognized the red-haired country beauty, who had been presented to him an hour before. She was probably still inexperienced in riding and hunting, for the horse had apparently runway with her. The king, with a certain amount of malice, was really anticipating the moment in which the horse would throw her.

A still more piercing cry was heard.

A powerful wild boar had forced its way through the hedge opposite to the horse – the terrified animal reared, and the rider fell.

The bristly monster now rushed toward her. All this was the occurrence of a single moment; but in this same moment Louis XIV was again the chivalric prince, that – apart from his political conduct – he was rightly considered.

A royal robber

With the quickness of thought he had seized the proffered gun from the hands of Moustache... a shot... and the wild boar fell dead upon the ground.

Louis XIV was the best shot in France.

The animal fell and covered the surrounding grass with blood. The horse had fled, hut his rider still lay motionless upon the ground.

«Let us go to her assistance,» said the king to Moustache, as soon as the smoke had dispersed and his quick glance had surveyed the position of things, – «To be sure it is only a fox, but we are sorry for it!»

And Louis XIV, followed by his gun-bearer, approached the place where Mademoiselle de Fontanges had fallen insensible.

But what new surprise awaited the king.

Impossible! that could not be the maiden, whom only an hour before, and even at this moment he had so harshly scorned? the little girl from the country, whom in his angry mood he had found so ugly?

By all the saints and the Virgin of Saint Germain en Laye this was not she, this was a charming creature who lay stretched before him. What bewitching yet childlike features! what a dazzlingly fair complexion! what a magnificent figure!

Oh! how fortunate, that the branches of a thick bush bad lessened the force with which she was thrown from the horse and broken her fall. Insensible from fright, by this fortunate circumstance she had slipped softly to the earth upon a mound thickly overgrown with grass and moss, upon whose upper edge rested the pale, little head as if sleeping, while the delicate limbs and feet scarcely touched the lower portion.

And what a peculiar, strange, novel charm the hitherto despised auburn hair produced upon him. Its luxuriance, and the harmony between the unusual coloring and the whiteness and delicacy of the skin, through which the smallest blue veins gleamed softly.

Louis XIV stood enchanted, entranced! He, whose whole nature was so thoroughly sensual, glowed with delight. He, who only a few moments before had wished to renounce all women, was intoxicated, a charm hitherto unknown, enthralled him.

He knelt by the side of the fainting girl, took a little, golden flask from his pocket, put his arm under the beautiful head, and let her inhale its invigorating contents.

Angeline's bosom heaved, the stiffness of death disappeared from her limbs, her breath came more and more quickly, and in a few moments the beautiful blue eyes opened with an expression as enchanting as if the rosy finger-tips of Aurora had drawn aside the last morning clouds from the rising sun.

And into what a sun she gazed! Into what wonderful deep eyes, full of a dark, passionate fire, full of strong, deep love, and at the same time nobleness and greatness. Angeline did not know what had happened to her. Where was she, was this all a dream, was it truth, was she living, or just awakening into another world? And upon whose breast did her head rest so softly?

A dim remembrance of the last few moments dawned upon her, the horse's running away, her fear, the horror then a wild boar bursting through the bushes and the horse's rearing, her fall, and the loss of consciousness. And there lay the monster dead on the ground, bathed in his blood. But who had killed him? and who embraced her now so gently, and tenderly? Angeline started up and her eyes opened wide, she gazed in astonishment, questionningly, into the face of her deliverer.

And she almost lost consciousness again!

Just heaven! was it not the king, to whom she had been presented that morning? the king, of whom she heard so much that was noble? The great Louis XIV, the sun of France and the world?

«Sire!» she exclaimed, growing deadly pale, while a heaven of delight beamed from her face.

But the king laid her head gently upon his breast, pressed a burning kiss upon her brow, and said:

A royal robber

«Rest forever upon this heart, it is the greatest and most loving one that beats in all France.»

He then motioned to Moustache to withdraw and bring a hunting coach to take the unfortunate girl to Marly.

XI.
A distinguished rascal

Louis XIV was alone with his favorite, the Duc de St. Aignan. After enduring the daily torture of an endless tedium at the «*Lever,*» the «*grandes entrées*» the «*secondes entrées*» and the «*entrée du cabinet*» with the heroic courage necessary to a monarch, he had made use of the *entre-temps* to be alone with the Duc at least for a few moments. The king was now often in the mood to seek solitude, if in fact there had been such a thing for him. And yet who in all his broad, beautiful kingdom was more exposed to intellectual solitude than he?

Can there be a greater solitude than that which surrounds the wearer of a crown? and does not this very solitude generate pride. The less one is surrounded by mankind, the more superior he considers himself.

To-day the ill-humor of Louis XIV had exalted his unbounded pride to the uttermost. It was bad weather at court, and every one trembled at the appearance of the monarch.

But what was the cause of the anger? Perhaps even the king was not himself aware of the reason.

The position of Louis XIV in regard to Madame de Montespan became more and more uncomfortable. Since the last hunting party in the woods of Marly she had lost all charm, for the king's mind was filled with but one image which should not be disturbed by the shadow of a Montespan and yet it did so every moment.

«Heaven and Hell!» cried Louis, stamping his foot angrily, and casting a dark, proud glance towards heaven as if he would demand its obedient co-operation. «We will yet be able to banish the shadow of a woman who has become wearisome to us.»

St. Aignan stood at a little distance. With the inborn craftiness of a true courtier, he suspected what was gnawing in the breast of his royal friend, and quietly enjoyed his approaching triumph over his hated rival in the favor of the sovereign.

A royal robber

But neither he, the marquise, nor the court knew anything of the affair of Mademoiselle de Fontanges, excepting that Moustache had rescued her. To be sure, everyone also knew that Moustache, the king's gun-bearer, was His Majesty's shadow in the chase, and never left him. Still he alone had arrived at Marly with the young girl. The king said nothing about it, and Mademoiselle de Fontanges, it was supposed, had not seen the king on this occasion. She must be silent, because it was the king's will; and is it not in many cases much more blessed to be silent than to speak? Besides, Angeline was secretly astonished at herself; she had never thought she possessed so much talent for the court and could govern herself so, well. But she was very glad that fate had removed her cousin Gauthier for the present. He was a good, dear boy, but, what was he to do at court. Angeline now liked to think of him as a hero, a brave general on the field of honor. Outside of this she thought but little of her old playmate, in fact, she could not, for she was now so much occupied with her toilette, and no delight can compare with triumphant vanity.

Unobserved she drew from her bosom a ring, in which a large, wonderfully brilliant diamond sparkled, but what was its lustre and brilliancy in compareson to her eyes? And, how she covered it with hot glowing kisses; and when she glanced up, how like a queen she looked!

Louis XIV was alone with St. Aignan, but he was gloomy, something was gnawing at his heart. St. Aignan vainly exhausted himself in witticisms and anecdotes. Louis XIV was philosophically inclined, and looked scornfully down upon the court and men.

«You all try to rule me,» he cried angrily. «All who surround me, but especially Colbert, Louvois, and Madame de Montespan.»

St. Aignan silently triumphed; but he was a courtier, striving for his own advancement.

He therefore first thought, by flattering words, to present the absurdity of such a project; how could common mortals dare to desire to aspire to a son of the Gods, to a Louis XIV, whom the world called *Dieu-Donné*. In a masterly and innocent manner he recalled the most amusing anecdotes from the lives of Richelieu, Mazarin, and the most celebrated mistresses of present and former times, letting the king plainly feel the yoke which Louvois and Madame de Montespan wished to lay upon him.

With delight he watched the veins of the king's brow swelling with anger, for he was more jealous of his power and authority than any former sovereign of France.

St. Aignan, however, like a clever courtier, did not let this anger come to a second outbreak, while he slyly – lamenting the dizzy height of a throne – pointed out the happiness of common men, 'who were allowed to love according to the free choice of their hearts.

The king sighed... St. Aignan knew enough; like a skillful artist he sketched a picture of happy love in the most glowing and life-like colors, and touched so skillfully upon the picture of the beautiful Mademoiselle de Fontanges, that the king rose and stepped to the window to hide his emotion.

«Ah, yes,» said the king, and then remained lost in thought for some time. «Ah, yes, that was a delightful age, when we, almost a boy, felt the first sensations of love, and were free to follow our own heart's choice; where is she now, the sweet Frontenac?... and that enchanting time, when the fiery Olympia Mazarin, the niece of the proud cardinal, almost died from love of us oh! we can still see the charming little dimple in her cheek; – the large, beautiful Sicilian eyes, which flashed like lightning – full of the wild delicious fire of love – and then – the tender La Vallière, with her golden hair, sparkling brown eyes, and rosy mouth – oh! heaven, how we loved her, almost timidly and with reverent affection.»

But St. Aignan was too adroit a man of the world and too crafty a representative of his own affairs to allow disagreeable thoughts to again spring up in the king's mind. He flatteringly alluded to the still youthful feelings of the monarch's heart, his handsome person, his chivalry, and the eagerness with which all the most beautiful and noble ladies of France solicited his favor. The last hunting party had shown this again. So long as the charming horsewomen thought the king was at the head of his train, their zeal for slaying the game had no end. St. Aignan was well aware why he struck this note;

A royal robber

with the remembrance of the chase, the image of the lovely Mademoiselle de Fontanges was recalled to his royal friend – and, in fact, Louis' expression was transfigured, and a strange happy smile rested upon his face.

At this moment, Laporte, the first valet and confidant of the king, announced His Excellency, Monsieur le Tellier, Marquis de Louvois, and His Eminence, Prince Franz Egon von Fürstenberg, Bishop of Strassburg.

«Insufferable» – exclaimed the king – «they do not leave us a single moment in peace!» But unconsciously yielding to the usual influence Louvois exerted over him, he ordered the gentlemen to be admitted. A few moments later the minister and bishop entered with the customary three profound bows.

Franz Egon, Prince of Fürstenberg, Bishop of Strassburg, was a handsome man in the very prime of life. His tall, slender figure displayed to the best advantage the violet clerical dress, gold chain, and cross set with splendid diamonds which he wore. His head was beautifully formed, and showed that superficial dignity which so easily becomes natural to the holders of ecclesiastical offices, but which nevertheless could not wholly cover an expression of sensuality. His features were sharply cut, his hands small and of an aristocratic delicacy and whiteness. There was intellect in his eyes, but also an expression of deep cunning. The bishop remained standing opposite the king – with his head bent, waiting for the monarch to accost him.

Louis XIV, indignant at the resistance of Alsace and Strassburg, loaded the reverend gentleman, who as we know, had formerly been recommended by Louvois as a gilded key to that greatly desired portion of Germany, with the bitterest reproaches.

Waiting in his humble attitude, holding the violet velvet cap in his folded hands, the German prince, this distinguished servant of the church, listened patiently with an air of the deepest submission to the thunders of the King of France. And a thunder clap it was, when Louis XIV now cried: «We certainly ought to have considered that, though the Lord Bishop of Strassburg is connected with France by many of his offices, he is still a German prince and as such remains our enemy!»

The king was silent; but the reverend gentleman, scarcely daring, in his humility to raise his head, said, while his features assumed an expression of the most profound submission. «Your Majesty must graciously pardon me! Louis XIV, the noblest of living monarchs, cannot find a more sincere admirer of his greatness and power, a truer and more loyal servant than I.»

«Silence, my Lord Bishop,» cried the king sternly. «You might fail signally if you sought to produce the proofs.»

«Sire» – replied Prince Egon, with a satisfaction which would have incensed to the uttermost every German heart. «Sire, I believe that I shall not have to go far to prove to your Majesty, in the most striking manner, the loyalty and the true, French sympathies of the house of Fürstenberg although it is certainly a German house.»

«We are curious!» said the king coldly.

«Your Majesty will perhaps be graciously pleased to recall the time» – continued Fürstenberg with a mild, insinuating voice – «in which Mars, the warrior god of our age, Louis XIV, at the peace of Aix-la-Chapelle, devised the plan to capture Holland.»

«To the point!» cried the king.

«We are at the point,» continued the bishop with a touch of pride: «at that time there were in Germany three brothers of the House of Fürstenberg, who proved themselves most active in toiling for your Majesty and France. One of them, Wilhelm Egon von Fürstenberg – the right hand of the elector Maximilian, Heinrich of Cologne, persuaded the latter to enter into an offensive and defensive alliance with your Majesty against Germany.»

«In which he sold his country to France!» thought the Duc de St. Aignan, who stood behind the king's chair, and cast a scornful glance at the German prince.

«Such is the case» – said Louvois, and added with an expression of scorn – «Your Majesty surely remembers the sacred clause.»

«Yes» – replied the king haughtily. «Besides three public articles, the document of the treaty contained one other, which alone was valuable, while the three were only made for the sake of appearances.»

A royal robber

«And by virtue of this secret article,» added Fürstenberg – «the Elector consigned the fortress of Nuys[54] to your Majesty.»

«In other words,» thought St. Aignan – «he delivered his country and subjects up to the enemy.»

«And the secret clause,» interposed Louvois mockingly – «was by no means bad, it brought his Highness, the Prince von Fürstenberg, four hundred thousand livres.»

Prince Egon looked as if he had not heard the last words. Considering the treachery of his family to their native land as an honor, he continued in a fawning tone, still maintaining the same humble attitude.

«Your Majesty will also remember a similar proceeding on the part of Wilhelm's two brothers. And is not the fourth a colonel in your Majesty's service? Has he not, although a German Prince, renounced the service of the Emperor for the honor of serving under the flag of Louis XIV? Did he not, when ambassador at Cologne, intrigue against his own country in order, if possible, to prevent the declaration of war?»

Here Prince von Fürstenberg paused, as if to observe the impression his information had upon the king. A disagreeable smile, the expression of his servile soul, played about his lips.

«But you, my Lord Bishop» – exclaimed the king impatiently – «what have you done? Where are the fulfillments of the promises you made me in regard to Alsace and Strassburg?»

«Sire» – replied the bishop quietly, but with an humble, crafty manner – «my weak hands have sown in the name of the Lord, that Louis, XIV, whom the voice of the people so beautifully and truly calls *Dieu-Donné*, can at some time reap.»

«By our dear Lady of Saint Germain!» cried the king – «the seed must be very small, at least our eyes cannot discover it.»

«You rest in the hearts and minds of thousands.»

---

[54] Neuss, a city in Rhenania.

A royal robber

«How so?»

«Your Majesty knows that since the accursed time of the Reformation, Alsace has been almost entirely in the hands of heretics. Odious Lutheranism, like a poisonous weed, has taken root there, and even the proud and holy temple of the Lord, the magnificent cathedral of Strassburg, which created pious enthusiasm for the holy mother church, is in the hands of the fallen ones.»

«And did you not promise us to lead the wandering sheep back to the fold?»

«Yes, Sire.»

«And —»

«Upon this field, with the blessing of the Lord, I have industriously labored. To be sure, my work was met by a strong opposition»...

«What is opposition!» exclaimed the king. «The arrogant seek occupation, and the people oppose them if it goes too far; as young lambs butt each other when they are satisfied with their mother's milk. But a good shepherd nevertheless drives them in pairs.»

«Pardon me your Majesty» – answered the bishop, with a still more humble bow – «nothing can be done here by force, here we must use the mild means of persuasion, deceit, and where they do not suffice, bribery.»

«And what have you accomplished by these mild means, as you call them, ray Lord Bishop?»

«Much, Sire! and I came to Versailles to lay the report at your Majesty's feet.»

The bishop now related in detail how he had sent a number of distinguished priests into Alsace, and through them had secretly worked upon the people, partly in the spirit of the only, blessed, holy, catholic church, partly in the interest of France. His emissaries, disguised as traveling merchants, soldiers, and wandering handicraftsmen, were especially commissioned to work upon women, as their influence upon the obstinate men might be of the greatest importance. Louvois had assisted him not a little in the cities and provinces which had already been incorporated into France, by sending to some a number of catholic troops and officers, and in others. by the passage of new laws and ordinances, by which only catholics were permitted to fill vacant offices and positions. Moreover Louvois and Fürstenberg now labored together so well, that in the portion of Alsace already incorporated with France, no one could obtain preferment unless he belonged to the Catholic Church. Only in Strassburg itself were the endeavors of the pious bishop still unsuccessful; although his plans were naturally, first of all directed to this city and the recovery of the noble cathedral. But here, in the free German city, raised by commerce and manufacture, dwelt a well to do middle class, plain and of true German feeling. Here, where since the Reformation Lutheranism had found a eeaterj where a Gutenberg and many other brave men had worked and spread education; where there were scarcely a hundred catholic families; here, the secret intrigues of the bishop had as yet effected but little.

With single families, the emissaries of the bishop had already succeeded so far that they only awaited the proper time to become openly catholic. To be sure they were still few in numbers; but these secretly treacherous families belonged to the higher and more influential class.

The bishop explained all this to His Majesty fluently and in detail. Louis himself was more than once astonished at the expedients and treacheries so pious a man knew how to employ to attain his end.

But the principal point was, that Prince Egon now proved to Louis XIV, that he could probably never win and incorporate into France this beautiful piece of German earth, – Strassburg, the fortress on the road to Germany – the key to the German empire, unless at least a portion of the population was drawn over to the one holy church by his endeavors. He, Prince von Fürstenberg, glowed with an ardent desire to take Louis XIV into Strassburg, as its Lord and King, and have its cathedral given back toffee mother church!

The German prince urged this – which was in fact nothing but that he wished to become a traitor to his country – so zealously before the king, that the latter could not forbear to praise him.

A royal robber

Louvois, too, commended the bishop's zeal to his master, and both recognized only too well what an excellent instrument for their plans they had found in this man, though, in the depths of their souls, they despised him as a traitor to his own country.

The conversation next turned upon the essential point for the common business; that of the money to be given to the prince. His Majesty at this audience promised the bishop a brevet, according to which he was to receive 60.000 livres yearly; while the bishop promised on the other hand, not only to continue to proselyte Alsace and Strassburg to the utmost of his ability – but also, to tear away Strassburg from the German Empire and incorporate it into France.

After the conclusion of this treaty, Prince Franz Egon, with a radiant face and the dignity of a holy man of the church, left the palace accompanied by Louvois.

XII.
«The catastrophe»

A peculiar atmosphere, apainfully depressing sultriness reigned in those days at the court of Versailles, and especially in the narrow circle which surrounded the king.

Day by day, Louis XIV became more inaccessible, gloomy, and morose, and yet the Duc de St. Aignan often, surprised him in an almost extraordinary excitement. His keen eye saw plainly the true state of affairs; the king loved and was fortunate in his love, and who other than the charming Mademoiselle de Fontanges could be the object of his passion, although His Majesty had not as yet spoken a word on the subject.

But did this clever 'courtier require a confession from the monarch's mouth? He, who from the first arrival of little Mademoiselle de Fontanges, in which he bad substantially assisted, had approached the simple innocent child from the Limagne as a friend, , and surrounded her with his almost irresistible kindness – could easily discover in the young heart, so little used to court customs, a secret which was hidden even from the marquise.

The Duc used every means in his power to come upon the right track, to rule the king through the new mistress, and at the same time overthrow and supplant her, who till now had possessed the king's heart and been foolish and blind enough to make common cause with St. Aignan, in order to enchain it still longer.

Courtiers think only of themselves and their own interests. Who would seek among their ranks for friendship, confidence, gratitude, or any other childish offspring of a sentimental heart.

St. Aignan now courted – where he could do so unobserved – the favor of the beautiful Mademoiselle de Fontanges, as he would have done that of a queen.

And the king? Was it only a caprice,… or from the dislike of causing a public rupture with Madame de Montespan?... that he still restrained himself, though his heart beat with passionate throbs for this new object of his affection.

In this state of mind, it would have been easier for Louis to declare war against half of Europe, than to take a decided step. A hundred times he had determined to speak his will, as usual, with absolute decision, and require the most implicit obedience, but again a hundred times a vague something checked the outburst of his passion.

It was a little remnant of honorable feeling, a spark of attachment to the mother of his six children – which, to the real annoyance of the king, still lingered in his breast. His Majesty was indignant at this childish emotion, which was probably all very well for common people, but surely not for a crowned head. He felt injured and this put him out of humor and made him irresolute.

But the bitterest way in which injuries affect us, is by obliging us to hate. Thus Louis began to hate the one whom he had formerly loved.

And Angelina de Fontanges?

The poor child did not comprehend where she was!

How could she explain the king's manner, his reserve, his silence towards her? – after he had thrown himself at her feet in that happy hour, had entreated her, in a storm of the wildest passion, for her love – which Angeline could not withhold from her king, the ideal of her soul, so long adored in dreams.

And now, did Louis regret what he had confessed, and sworn to the blushing, delighted child!

The king at her feet – the earth had no longer any value for her. The boldest dreams of her vain little heart were surpassed – And what visions for the future? If the king, Louis XIV, bowed into the dust before her beauty, who of the whole world remained that must not follow the first of mortals?

And now? Could all this have been but a dream? Why this reserve? To be sure, now and then a glance from the king threw Heaven and Paradise into her lap. Then her heart would cry out; «Yes, yes, he loves me still. Only wait, be patient till it is possible for him to raise you like a queen before the whole world. He will do it, and then everything the heart can desire or strive for will be fulfilled.»

And she thought of the cloud, which she had once seen glistening in purple and gold and which had enveloped her and raised her to a height of bliss.

The position of Madame de Montespan was a desperate one. The usually clever woman, who knew Louis so thoroughly, seemed this time to have made a mistake. The king had said, «That is a wolf that will not eat us,» and as if by magic, he, who was usually fire and flame at the sight of every new beauty, remained perfectly cold and indifferent to this charming girl.

The anger of the marquise knew no bounds. What a sacrifice this intrigue had cost her avarice, what, a sum she had been obliged to pay St. Aignan alone, under the pretext that it was necessary for the demands of the intrigue; for the treasury of the genial, amiable spendthrift was bottomless, and nothing had come from the damnable conjuration of the devil.

The instrument was good for nothing, and she was determined to get rid of it at the first opportunity. Mademoiselle de Fontanges must return to Limagne. The friendliness the marquise had hitherto displayed towards Angeline, turned into coldness and severity and her conduct towards the poor child betrayed actual hatred and scorn.

But St. Aignan secretly flattered her all the more. How pleasantly and kindly he knew how to give her courage, to hint obscurely at a happy, brilliant future. Angeline did not understand him, but she saw that he alone still sought hey favor, and this flattered her. She felt that he wished her well, and this drew her towards him.

The Marquise de Montespan knew nothing of this. She was still too much occupied with her awn position, which was so perfectly unbearable that only a desperate stroke could save her.

The king was like ice. She trembled every moment in fear of the outbreak of his displeasure. Every anchor had lost its hold, her life boat was staggering like a wreck m the storm of the royal disfavor, the fear of going down almost broke her heart.

A royal robber

It was horrible to retreat from her position, which was more important than that of the queen. The thought of no longer ruling the king, – and through him France – no longer being sovereign herself, was unbearable.

But the ministers Louvois and Colbert, the Duc de St. Aignan, Monseigneur, and the king's confessor recognized that the moment had now come when they must gain the undivided favors of Louis, if they ever wished to rule him.

Each put forth all his strength to attain this end. Each secretly labored at his well-laid plan, which aimed at the overthrow and destruction of his rival. And yet outwardly there were only smooth, friendly faces, they, smiled In the most engaging manner and loaded each other with civilities.

The conflict between the different interest and passions at the court had now reached its highest point. Colbert depended upon the finances, Monseigneur sought to make the influence of his near relationship felt, Louvois urged war, the confessor a christian life, Madame de Montespan exhausted herself in assurances of affection all for one object and the keen eyes of Louis XIV read them all with the exception of St. Aignan, who craftily stood behind Angeline.

A little, unimportant occurrence sprung the mine, a grain of sand was the cause of a thundering, destroying avalanche.

Louis had just received the congratulations of his court upon a victory gained by his troops in one of the colonies. He was still in the large, golden salon but the crowd had retired, as the Marquise de Montespan apparently wished to exchange a few words alone with His Majesty.

The king, gloomy as ever, took his seat in one of the gilded arm-chairs, of which there were only two in every apartment, in case both their majesties wished to sit down.

When the king sat down – the queen with her suite had retired to her own apartments – the marquise stepped confidently forward. With almost superhuman exertion, she had crushed down all her cares and troubles, and given herself the appearance of the bright calmness, which, in happier times, had made her so dear to the king.

A royal robber

Louis did not observe it. With cold, gloomy politeness he asked what she wished.

He could not see how the coldness of his tone, the ceremonious politeness of his words, froze the blood in her veins. Her nerves, which were before excited to the uttermost, quivered almost convulsively, and only the strength of character of a de Montespan would have found it possible in such a position to repress tears.

But she would and she was mistress of herself. One learns at court, and as mistress to a king, to conquer oneself.

With a loving voice she personally offered her congratulations; but with the tact of a woman of intellect, before the king suspected It, she knew how to pass over to the happiness of former days.

She was probably once more reminded of the perishableness of such happiness, for Louis had never before allowed her to stand at his side. To-day there was no sign for a page to bring a stool. But this, now customary neglect, which in the presence of the court must have been doubly painful to the marquise, she forbore to notice.

«And does your Majesty no longer think of those bright days when Françoise Athenais was so happy as to drive away the dark clouds from the brow of her adored lord and king?» she said sadly.

«It was somewhat long ago,» said the king dryly. «We have become older and quieter, madame.»

The marquise bit her lip; the remark was malicious enough.

«True, earnest love never grows old,» she said – «How happy I should consider myself, if I might share the trouble which seems lately to have depressed my noble lord.»

«Affairs of state!» said the king. «We prefer to keep them to ourselves – firstly, because we wish to reign alone, and secondly, because thinking of such things is too wearing for ladies, and thereby makes them old before their time.»

A royal robber

«Age again!» thought the marquise.

«Pardon me, Sire!» she said in a trembling voice – «Louis XIV, the great, the shining star of his century, needs no helping hand to wield the scepter of France and the world; – so far my thoughts would never ascend; I only seek to cheer the heart of my king! But confess it yourself. Sire, matters are no longer on their old footing between us. How has your Athenais deserved this, Louis?»

«The old, unfounded reproaches,» he answered angrily.

«Unfounded?» repeated the marquise. «Could you but count. Sire, the nights I have spent in weeping.»

«You are nervous, madame!» replied the king. «Call in a physician and strengthen yourself by the fresh, country air.»

Madame de Montespan trembled! It had gone so far already. An idea of banishment? There were two great tears in her eyes. She intentionally let them roll slowly down, so that the king must perceive them, and then said:

«It would be too hard for me to part from the children which God and your Majesty have given me.»

But here Madame de Montespan had touched a sensitive spot. Precisely because she was the mother of his children – so unjust is man in his moods and his egotism – she was burdensome to the king, and till now she had restrained him from dismissing the burden.

«I think, madame,» replied Louis, even more indignant than before «the Duc de Maine and his brothers and sisters are legitimate princes and princesses, and provided for as such. You need take no farther trouble about their fate for they are the children of France.»

But what mother would let her children be taken from her without resistance? A feeling of bitter indignation arose in the soul of the marquise.

«Your Majesty,» she said sharply, though her voice trembled, «they are *my* children too.»

«Six,» answered the king courtly and sternly. «We fear that they have shattered your nervous system, nay – almost – your mind!»

«Your Majesty,» cried the marquise turning deadly pale.

«You are growing tiresome as usual lately» said the king.

But now the long repressed anger burst the fetters forged by despair.

«What!» she exclaimed in a smothered voice, while her bosom heaved passionately, «are these the thanks with which Your Majesty repays my faithful love, my self-sacrificing devotion? Have I exposed myself to the scorn of others to be insulted by you in such a manner?»

The king laughed aloud.

«A scene,» he said mockingly. «But, madame, you forget that fortunately we are not married like shop-keepers.»

«Fortunately?» repeated the marquise slowly.

«Remember where you are!» said the king angrily, «the court waits in the background.»

«And think. Sire, that not only the court is present,» cried the marquise violently, «but God,, whose justice I invoke.»

The king had heard enough. He made a movement to rise, saying:

«You are making yourself ridiculous, madame. Cease this farce. And if you wish for our well meant counsel, it is this: if you do not prefer the quiet of a country life, we would, if in your place, look about for a cloister. Court life is becoming too burdensome for one of your age.»

The marquise wished to answer, but her voice failed. The whole fury of her passion threatened to break forth – but recollecting herself, she pressed her fingers tightly together, stamping her left foot, as was her custom when angered.

A diamond buckle became loosened from the satin shoe.

Heaven be praised! there was now an escape for her anger.

With flaming eyes she gazed round the circle and her glance fell upon Mademoiselle de Fontanges, who was standing among the rest of her ladies.

«Mademoiselle de Fontanges!» she exclaimed.

The king flushed crimson, and then turned pale.

Angeline modestly approached although her heart almost refused service in the near presence of the king.

She now stood beside the marquise.

«What can I do for you, madame?» she asked in a whisper.

«Fasten the buckle of my shoe!» replied the Marquise de Montespan.

Angeline turned pale. Her pride rose against this unprecedented insolence especially in the presence of the king and court. She, a daughter of one of the oldest families in Limagne; she, the most beautiful of all these ladies; she, to whom the king had declared his love – was she to serve the marquise like a common waiting maid in the presence of this very king and his court?

Never.

«Be quick» cried Madame de Montespan with another stamp of her foot.

«I will call your waiting-maid,» answered Angeline, trembling in every limb.

But the anger of the marquise had overpowered her to such a degree that she forgot everything about her. No longer mistress of herself, she raised her hand and the next moment a slap resounded through the hall.

A long mark burned on Angeline's cheek. She staggered back with a loud cry. Two other ladies belonging to the suite of the marquise, hastened forword and supported her.

But the king had also started up with a thundering «hold!»

The whole court was agitated. A death-like stillness followed the first stormy outbreak of passion.

«Madame!» said Louis XIV, now standing erect, and in fact at this moment he resembled an angry god, «madame, you are ill,… we have already said so, your nervous system is shattered and requires rest. Within twenty-four hours

A royal robber

you will leave Versailles and repair to your country seat of Tonnay-Charente, where you will remain till it pleases us to issue other commands!»

«Louis!» faltered the marquise, and sank fainting upon the ground.

The king did not see her. Turning to Angeline he said so loud that the whole court might hear:

«Madame la Duchesse de Fontanges! From this day you will fill the position of first lady of honor to her majesty, the Queen!»

«Sire!» cried Angeline, confused and embarrassed.

But Louis XIV bent gently towards her, and whispered:

«Do you remember the hour in the woods of Marly? Will you reject the ardent love of your king?»

«No, no,» whispered Angeline.

«Then give me your hand, *Madame la Duchesse!*» said the king, once more aloud, as he gallantly extended his right hand to Angeline, who laid hers softly on the tips of his fingers.

«We will present you to Her Majesty, and install you in your office. After tomorrow, you will occupy the apartments in the palace, which till now, have belonged to the Marquise de Montespan.»

And with these words His Majesty, by the side of the beautiful Angeline, followed by the whole court, which had scarcely recovered from its astonishment, went towards the queen's apartments.

One person alone remained behind in the great hall. He was a young man, who stood pale, rigid, and motionless, like a marble statue.

The uniform he wore was in disorder and covered with dust, for he had just arrived as courier from Arras, with important dispatches for the Minister of War.

«Monsieur le Duc, what in the name of all the saints does what I have just seen, mean?» he asked of St. Aignan.

«How does my cousin, Angeline de Fontanges chance to be here? What is

113

there between her and the king?»

«What is it?» replied the courtier in a sorrowful tone, quickly recovering himself, «it means that Mademoiselle de Fontanges is now Madame la Duchesse de Fontanges, and the king's new mistress!»

«Monsieur le Duc!» cried Gauthler, laying his hand upon his sword, but the procession had passed. Gauthler stood as if benumbed.

In the evening, the rooms which the new Duchesse occupied in the palace of Versailles till the departure of the Marquise de Montespan, were brilliantly lighted, Louis XIV honored the charming Angeline de Fontanges with his presence.

Once only they were disturbed in their happiness by a shot. But it was only a momentary interruption. Nothing more was thought of the matter. It was only a young officer, who had shot himself under the window.

He threw away hope, like a cripple who is disgusted with his crutch. He was ashamed to weep, but also to live.

Part II.
A German city

A royal robber

XIII.
Strassburg

Who does not know, who does not love the beautiful, glorious Rhine whose name, as Schenkendorf happily says, rhymes so well with – wine?

The world debates as to whether the Rhine is, or is not a German river. The Rhine is a picture of the German as he is, his very self – a hapless Faust.

And Strassburg – If as a poet has described it, Alsace is «the heart of Germany torn out,» then the city of Strassburg, which lies upon the left side of the breast of the child, is the «heart of Alsace.» As all the arteries in man radiate from the heart and all the veins return to it, so that it promotes and regulates the whole circulation, so do the highways leading to all parts of Alsace radiate outwards from Strassburg.

The principal rivers, Rhine, 111, and Breusch, flow together here. This city forms the central point of Western Europe.

In those days Strassburg was a proud and beautiful city – a true pearl among the towns of the German empire and its banner ever floated in the van of the free cities, directly behind the Imperial eagle.

Even under the rule of the Romans, Strassburg was a municipal town, and as such, had the privilege of choosing its own magistrates and in a certain degree governing itself, which high and important right it retained under the dominion of the Franks, and also that of the German empire, for Strassburg and Alsace were and are of true German origin, as is proved by their very names: Strassburg – the «citadel of the roads» – and Elsass, the «seat of the Alemanni.»

The city made its own laws, coined its own money, maintained its own troops, and held the first place among the free cities in thie empire.

Kings, princes and republics solicited its friendship and concluded treaties with it; even the most powerful nobles in the vicinity considered it an honor to be enrolled among the citizens of Strassburg.

A royal robber

But, like everything else in the world, these flattering advances from the nobility had two sides. Towards the commencement of the twelfth century so many aristocratic families had become citizens of Strassburg, that their influence began to be paramount, and thus by degrees they obtained possession of all the higher city offices and in the course of time monopolized them so completely that they almost became hereditary.

The municipal goverment of the ancient, free city of Strassburg, rested upon the various guilds; its laws grew from this firm foundation, and only when the universal storm of the revolution of 1789 destroyed the government of Strassburg, did the powerful blows of the new spirit of freedom uproot the guilds.

XIV.
The tailor

One of the most important days m the city life of Strassburg had returned with the close of the year. It was called the Schwortag, the time when the citizens of the old *Argentorum* – the ancient free city – felt the full glory if their republican dignity. The citizens of Strassburg had sworn allegiance to the newly-elected Ammeister Rathsherren and the old «Schwörbrief» of 1482.

The same scene, that had been witnessed each year for centuries, had taken place that day, but on this day the glasses clinked with a doubly joyous ring to the welfare and prosperity of the sacred German Empire, the beautiful, beloved, native land and His Majesty, the Emperor Leopold I.

But the wildest mirth of all was undoubtedly in the drinking-room of the Schneider-zunft.[55] It was a large apartment for the Strassburg Schneider zunft in those days numbered more than four hundred members. The room was therefore necessarily a large one, although only intended to accommodate the masculine members of the guild; and it was not only large and lofty, but according to the ideas of the times, handsomely furnished.

But the whole room – now that the visit of the new Ammeister had been received – was filled with tables and benches, around and on which sat worthy comrades drinking and talking gayly to each othen At one table alone, close under the banner – sat four magistrates, distinguished by their black robes, whose cut recalled the Spanish costume: the Rathsherr Stosser, Dr. Obrecht, Dr. Ecker and the council and city clerk, Günzer.

These distinguished gentlemen drank their wine together, and their whole manner displayed a certain shade of anxiety, though they raised and touched their glasses with remarkable cordiality whenever any of the worthy tradesmen present drank their healths. Their conversation was principally conducted in whispers, while Günzer's sharp eyes kept a cautious watch that no

---

[55] Tailors guild hall.

one listened or approached them. If either of these things happened, he set down his glass in the middle of the table with a certain air of carelessness, and they relapsed into silence.

This now occurred, and the gentlemen exchanged glances, as a singular, almost comical figure appeared before them, glass in hand.

«The French-hater,» Günzer hastily whispered, «we must be cautious.»

«The old fool!» – muttered Stosser.

«The scoundrel!» added Dr. Obrecht.

At this moment, the man of whom the gentlemen had made such kindly mention came up to them.

It was the tailor Franz Blasius Wenck – assuredly a peculiar personage. The man was about sixty years old. His figure was small and bent, and as his head was somewhat sunk between his shoulders, and his whole body turned at every movement as if it were a part of the head; the strange being had a comical appearance, and there was something in the features, though it was difficult to define, which increased the impression.

Meister Wenck was really both kind and charitable, nay, one could conscientiously praise his strict observance of the Lutheran religion, while he expressed his unshaken trust In God in the saying: «Who knows what good it may do!» almost more than was needful.

Meister Wenck approached the four gentlemen who were seated around one of the best tables in the drinking hall of the tailor's guild, bowed, and said, holding out his glass:

«I greet the illustrious members of the council who honor the worthy Schneider-zunft with a visit on this great day; for the day is a great and important one to our good city of Strassburg, when the magistrates and citizens swear mutual fealty – on pain of banishment – and take a solemn oath never to enter into any alliance which might cause the ruin of the community and the free city itself.»

As he uttered these words, the little tailor's bold, twinkling eyes cast a strange, questioning glance at the group of black-robed gentlemen. There was something almost inquisitorial in the expression of the odd little man. Strange! The noble members of the council must have noticed it also, for it almost seemed sad if a momentary change of color was the consequence.

No one noticed this, it was true, except perhaps Meister Wenck, who raising his glass, exclaimed in a loud, distinct tone:

«I hereby pledge the most noble and learned magistrates of our city itself, and especially, our most gracious master and emperor, Leopold, the guardian and defender of the sacred German Empire.»

As he uttered the words, Wenck held out his- brimming glass to the members of the council and enthusiastically shouted, «Hurrah!» and «Hurrah, hurrah!,» echoed in thundering cheers through the spacious drinking hall.

The magistrates had also drunk the toast, though with some little constraint, but they quickly resumed their seats while the city clerk, Syndicus Günzer, turned to the tailor, saying:

«You are an honest man, Meister Wenck, whose heart and tongue are in the right place, and – and a patriot to boot, even your enemies must admit that. Your toast certainly had the right ripg. But,» and here the city clerk's long, slender figure bent almost familiarly towards the tailor, «but! you lack one thing, my worthy man, and that is – caution!»

«Caution?» repeated Wenck in astonishment, raising his bushy eye-brows inquiringly, while a faint smile flitted over the faces of the bystanders. «I don't understand how there can be any question of caution when we salute our learned magistrates, our good city, and our most gracious master, the German emperor, with a hearty cheer.»

«You don't understand, my worthy fellow,» Günzer continued with forced cordiality and great condescension, «because, being only a simple citizen, you know nothing about what is called policy and diplomacy,»

«No,» replied the tailor, shaking his head with a comical grimace, «I don't know anything about that, to be sure, but – who knows what good it may do!»

A royal robber

«A little policy, diplomacy and caution are useful in everything,» continued the city clerk, almost reprovingly, «but caution is doubly required of the citizens of Strassburg, since our little free state lies between the two powerful kingdoms of France and Germany.»

«But we belong to the kingdom of Germany,» observed Wenck.

Günzer made no definite reply to this; but bent his head, as if in assent and then said:

«But walls have ears! And surely His August Majesty, Louis XIV, the illustrious king of France, will not be very much edified if he learns that the people of Strassburg raise such thundering cheers, for the Emperor Leopold, his enemy.»

«O – ho!» cried the little tailor, advancing a little nearer to the city clerk. «Haven't we Germans a right to cheer for our emperor? What do we people of Strassburg care for the king of France? Let him hear that we nave true German hearts; – let him hear it, in spite of his *Chambres de Réunions* by which he got possession of Alsace and swallowed other peoples property under the pretense of a just claim; – let the king of France and his ministers hear that we are loyal Germans! Who knows what good it may do!»

The gentlemen of the council were actually embarrassed; the city clerk alone retained his calm bearing. Accustomed in every situation of life to control himself, feign, and dissemble, he smiled at the comic zeal of Meister Blasius.

«My dear friend,» said he, «you are perfectly right – only you seem to have misunderstood me. All honor to the German emperor and kingdom – but we men of Strassburg must be cautious and prudent. Vienna and Ratisbon are a long distance from here, and – what can the emperor and kingdom do for us? France, on the contrary, adjoins our little free state; its interests are ours – the armies of France can overrun us at any moment.»

«Only when the barriers of justice are broken down and we show ourselves cowards and poltroons!» exclaimed Meister Wenck, almost angrily.

«I only said: can!» continued the city clerk quietly with a most magisterial mine, «and I think it would be both wise and diplomatic not to irritate her.

A royal robber

Louis XIV is also our protector and friend.»

«Oh! indeed,» said Meister Blasius, whose eyebrows seemed to be trying to meet over his nose. «Then I will pray every morning and evening: 'Lord, deliver us from our friends, and we will take care of our enemies.'»

A shout of laughter echoed through the room.

«Yes,» continued Meister Wenck, «who knows what good it may do!»

«You have an evil tongue!» said Dr. Obrecht angrily. «King Louis means well by the people of Strassburg.»

«What is the learned Herr Doctor saying!» exclaimed Meister Blasius jeeringly. «Perhaps he means as well by us as he did by Hagenau, Homburg, Weissenburg and the ten free cities of Alsace, which have been incorporated into the dominions of France.»

«Meister Wenck is right!» cried many voices.

«Yes, he is right. We will remain free Germans. We men of Strassburg are proud of our German origin and independence.»

«We have always been free Germans and will so remain.»

«Hurrah for Germany!»

«Hurrah for the House of Austria!»

«Hurrah for the free German city of Strassburg!»

Such were the cries that resounded through the room, while glasses clinked and the joyous, enthusiastic cheers seemed as if they would never end.

When the noise at last subsided the city clerk also raised his glass, and casting a glance at his companions the whole party rose.

«Worthy Meisters of the honorable guild of tailors!» he said aloud, forcing his voice to assume the necessary tone of firmness and gentleness, and giving his keen eyes as kindly an expression as they could assume, «we, too, members of the council, will now propose a toast- long live the honest burghers of our dear, native city! May God protect and enlighten them, that in these difficult times they may find and walk in the right path to prosperity

123

and happiness. In the critical state of affairs at. the present day, the only means of safety is to once more assert the neutrality of Strassburg, and the city magistrates eagerly seized upon the well-meant proposal of the French government to again proclaim it. Thus the freedom and independence of our dear, native city is preserved, and as Louis XIV, the great king of France – the father of his people – lavishes his kindness also upon us, nay, has even promised peace and protection –»

«Cat's friendship,» muttered Wenck.

«We will, in addition to the health of the burghers of Strassburg – drink his also.»

At that moment, as if by accident, the little tailor let his tin goblet fall from his hand. It struck heavily on the floor, and as the wine bespattered the by-standers, there was a sudden crowding backward amid loud exclamations.

«What a shame!» said the little tailor, with wellfeigned vexation, «but – who knows what good it may do!»

The city clerk's toast was forgotten. Not a single cheer had been uttered.

A death-like pallor covered the faces of the four members of the council, and they silently resumed their seats, while Günzer whispered:

«For God's sake be cautious, gentlemen! So surely as there is a heaven above us, that damned tailor has caught a glimpse of our cards.»

«The scoundrel!» growled Dr. Obrecht.

«The fool!» muttered Strosser.

«I'll manage to stop his tongue,» said Herr Ecker.

The conversation now became general and the company eagerly discussed the political situation of the times and especially that of the city to which they belonged. The minds of all were still inflamed by the public display they had witnessed that very day – their self-importance was increased by the magnificent ceremony, by the pomp and splendor of the power of the Middle Ages, of which, however, only the appearance remained.

XV.
«Family joys.»

On the same evening upon which Meister Wenck had the little skirmish with the city clerk Günzer at the guild hall, Syndicus Frantz accompanied the newly chosen and ruling Ammeister upon his round among the twenty guilds.

It was truly a hard task, after the many solemnities of the day; and the worthy gentlemen had already been obliged to suffer much from the cold in their fine official costume, but now they shivered still more in the large, roomy councilor's coach.

None in the whole kindgom clung with greater obstinacy and stubbornness to such old traditions than the free cities.

Syndicus Frantz, a sensible man, cared very little for such things; but he alone could not change the custom, and on the other hand he knew that one could not take a single stone from an old and crumbling building without risking the destruction of the whole.

Moreover, the stormy days of the reign of Louis XIV were surely not fitted for a perfect transformation suitable to the times.

So the Syndicus patiently made the rounds by the side of the new Ammeister; but congratulated himself when the affair was over and the great coach set him down at his own house.

Syndicus Franz hastily descended from the coach, whose door the servant respectfully opened. He slipped in with a friendly nod, and was received on the stairs with warm and affectionate greetings from his wife and daughter. Both embraced and led him into the room.

Alma, the Syndicus' charming daughter and only child, ran for her father's dressing-gown, while her mother took off the black, helmet-like velvet cap, and assisted him to remove his state robe.

Syndicus Frantz, notwithstanding his sixty-five years, was a fine looking man, both in his home dress and state costume. Noble, open features revealed a similar character. The smoothly combed brown hair, now mixed with gray, betrayed an equally smooth disposition; the glance of the still beautiful eyes sparkling with intellect and thought, expressed kindliness and honor; while the firmly closed mouth showed firmness of character and energy of soul.

The wife and daughter had much to tell about what they, in company with the young and lovely Frau von Bernhold, an intimate friend of Alma, had seen on the cathedral square from the windows of the ancient nunnery; much to ask, and many things for the Syndicus, who had stood close beside the chief magistrate, to answer.

The old gentleman did so as readily and willingly as ever; but his wife soon perceived that some anxiety depressed and saddened her husband's usually cheerful temper.

They were not long in doubt as to the cause; Hedwig and Alma learned to their horror, that a secret and extraordinary session of the council had taken place before the festivities, in which it had been decided that Syndicus Frantz should immediately go secretly to Vienna to consult with the imperial court about the ways and means to be mutually adopted that Strassburg – exposed to the assaults of France – might retain its independence, and be held as one of the most important strongholds of the German Empire. This news affected Hedwig and Alma most painfully in more than one respect.

«And are matters really so bad with us?» asked the wife with an expression of the deepest concern.

«Alas! yes, my loved ones,» he said in a low tone, «the political horizon has grown very dark.»

«But why and how?» asked his wife. «You have never told me that affairs were considered serious.»

«There are things in political life which, unfortunately, must be dealt with in secret.»

«What?» said Frau Hedwig in a mournful tone. «We have been married more than five and twenty years and never had a secret, and now?»

«Hedwig!» cried the Syndicus, clasping his wife's hands warmly in his own. «Hedwig, dear, good, faithful wife, do not misjudge me.»

«In these sad times,» repeated the Sɒndicus mournfully, passing his hand gently over his child's fair hair, and pressing a kiss upon her brow with fatherly anxiety, «yes, yes, my loved ones, it may be that the coming days will be indeed grave and sad. There can no longer be a doubt, Louis XIV, the ambitious and grasping prince, has cast his eyes upon Strassburg.»

«How can he?» exclaimed Alma, alarmed and indignant. «Strassburg is German, and besides that, is a free, imperial city which – as the present day has brilliantly proved – has its own free government.»

«But the king of France has not even the semblance of a claim to Strassburg,» cried Alma, beaming with patriotic enthusiasm.

«They will seek for it.»

«But will not find it!»

«And is there not treachery, force, and bribery?»

«We will defend ourselves! Has not the ceremony of to-day reminded us of our former grandeur and power.»

«So our little republic,» continued the Syndicus, «resembles a ship robbed of its masts and rudder, given up to all that wind and sea can do. For this reason, my dear ones, the magistrates, in the secret session of to-day, resolved that I should immediately – to-morrow – quietly proceed to Vienna, repressent the condition of the city and its affairs to His Majesty, Emperor Leopold, and enteat him to send to our aid a sufficient army of allies.»

«Oh! he will grant it!» cried Alma, «for Strassburg is one of the most beautyful cities of the German Empire.»

«And one of its most important strongholds,» added her mother.

«The key to South Germany,» said the Syndicus seriously.

At this moment the door-bell rang.

A royal robber

All listened in surprise.

«Who can be coming here so late?» asked Frau Hedwig, whom, the excitement had made unusually anxious.

«Calm yourselves, children!» answered the Syndicus, «it is probably the messenger to bring me the necessary papers and letters of credit, for the court of Vienna. They had to be signed by the new Ammeister, who had only just returned home from his round.»

The old gentleman was not mistaken; it was really these papers, but he was the more astonished at their bearer. Instead of the usual messenger, the tall, slender figure of Herr Günzer entered.

After leaving the tailor's guild-hall--not in the best of humors – Günzer had gone to the chief magistrates, according to agreement, to have the papers which he had prepared signed and then, to the delight of the messenger, had relieved him from his duty, saying he would undertake it himself.

But the impressionhislatevisitmadeupon the Frantz' family seemed to be neither agreeable nor favorable.

«What!» exclaimed the Syndicus, with a slight frown upon his brow, as he slowly rose, «do you bring me the despatches yourself, sir?»

«Yes!» replied Günzer, bowing to the old gentleman and the ladies, and there was something servile in his manner and expression which affected them disagreeably. «Yes,» he repeated, «in my position, I did not wish to entrust these important documents to any other hands – you know what kind of men there are in these evil times, one cannot trust everyone.»

«But the old messenger, Andreas, is the most trusty and honest soul in the world.»

«Then ascribe it to my patriotism, that I undertook the walk myself!» exclaimed Günzer, as he handed the old gentleman the papers.

The frown upon the Syndicus' brow darkened. But he recollected himself and quietly thanked him in the name of the city.

Herr Günzer looked smiling at the ladies and said: «What need is there of thanks? Every one is more or less of an egotist, and I will confess that I was one here. The reward for my little trouble consists in being able to greet such estimable ladies again at the close of this beautiful and patriotic festival; may their pictures embellish my dreams.»

«The best pillow,» answered Hedwig, «is always a good conscience, and that every true and upright friend of our Fatherland has!»

As Syndicus Frantz and his family made no farther effort to detain Günzer – though they plainly perceived that he wished it – nothing was left for him but to take leave, especially as the night was already far advanced.

XVI.
Hans im Schnakenloch

In those days Strassburg was still provided with sixteen regular ramparts or bastions, the most important of which were the Ill, the St. Elizabeth, the Metzger, the Katherine, the Steinstrasser, the Heiden rampart, the bastion on the yellow corner and the watch tower.

Strassburg, which at that time contained thirty-two hundred houses, forty-five hundred families, and twenty-eight thousand inhabitants, therefore possessed defenses that inspired respect, especially as she did not lack guns and good ones.

Strassburg burghers were not a little proud of their guns, arsenals, and fortresses, and this pride gave most of them such a feeling of security, that – without being in the least disturbed – they looked quietly on the seizures of land made by Louis XIV In Alsace.

Skilled in commerce and business, firm in their Lutheran belief, a true German spirit imbued most of the community. Indeed one might say the Strassburg burghers of that time were true German patriots!

And yet a snake was creeping In the grass, whose coils descended from the higher strata of society – nay even from the highest – that of the government itself.

This snake was the little party of French partisans. The crafty Louvois had not failed to provide for the timely sowing of a poisonous seed, through whose gradual growth he hoped to sniotlier the germ of goodness, justice, and freedom in tlic German city. And did not the bishop of Strassburg, Prince Egon von Fürstenberg, give him faithful aid? To be sure the latter lived in Cologne; but his agents were numerous, and toiled secretly in Strassburg; and he too – often went there in disguise.

But Louvois' right hand was the French minister, Herr von Frischmann, whom Austria's ambassador, Baron von Mercy, steadily opposed. In the meantime, Prince Egon proselyted through his emissaries, and so the differrent factions toiled and worked for a long time in secret, before the simple, honest burghers imagined that the ground under their feet was becoming hollow and insecure.

And yet there were some individuals whose keener eyes obtained some idea of this unlawful action. To possess such eyes it was not neecessary to be of noble birth; more or less penetration is often given to the simplest and most humble men.

Such a man was honest Meister Wenck.

Franz Blasius Wenck had just opened the door of his house, which stood near the Hospital gate. It was a modest little building, painted red, and roofed with burnt tiles.

Evening had closed in, and Meister Wenck bad laid down his work to take a walk in the fresh cold air:

Wenck was a widower ,had no children, and always obtained so much work that, with his very modest desires, he could live without anxiety.

But the little tailor had other cares. He had much time for thought and reflection as he sat at his work, and moreover a heart full of patriotism, so he followed the political movements of his time with a watchful eye. Politics were his delight. But this love of politics had its painful side. It led to too much reflecting on the present. Who moved the world now? who but Louis XIV, the king of the hated Frenchmen, and his still worse minister, Louvois? And what political events were shaking the repose of Europe? No other than the alarming seizures made by France in Alsace, Holland, England, Spain, and above all, Germany and the German emperor, cried out to the world against this injustice, all these countries and their rulers solemnly protested against this violation of the treaties of Westphalia and Nymwegen! but – and this almost broke Meister Wenck's heart – it went no further than protesting; while Louvois took one part of Alsace after another and incurporated them into France.

Thus Meister Wenck had seen all the beautiful cities of Alsace fall into the hands of the hated Frenchmen – and now it seemed to him as if Louis was also stretching out his hands towards his beloved Strassburg. It cut Meister

A royal robber

Wenck to the soul, the mere thought of it made him wild. But he felt himself enough of a man to stake property and life, for her, and would not all the citizens of Strassburg think the same? His guild did, Wenck knew. And other members of the community, especially the guilds, were thoroughly patriotic.

But there was one thing which good Meister Wenck had long been unable to drive out of his mind, and that was the thought that things were not exactly right with the magistrates. Syndicus Frantz and his party were true patriots and honorable men: but the little tailor had many strange ideas about Herr Günzer and his friends.

Why, in such dangerous times, should a wise magistrate, from motives of petty economy, send home the imperial garrison placed in Strassburg for her security?

But Günzer and his friends prevailed, and the city was bereft of the troops. Meister Wenck shook his head, but did not say as usual, «Who knows what good it may do?» He only went about, humming the old Strassburg national song.

But when, soon after, the economical gentlemen also discharged two-thirds of the twelve hundred Swiss soldiers in the pay of the city – Meister Wenck ceased singing and humming, and became graver than ever.

He became more watchful of the course of things about him, and of certain persons. Herr Günzer was the first of these. Meister Wenck secretly watched him, and noticed that the clerk visited the French minister more than usual. To be sure, Günzer probably had a great deal of government business to transact with Herr von Frischmann, but it seemed to the little tailor that there could not be any necessity for such frequent visits, which were rendered more suspicious from the fact that they. were paid at night.

Wenck's suspicions increased, aijd were still farther heightened by the incident at the tailor's guild. Why had Günzer, who always showed himself in public and business life almost ostentatiously patriotic referred so craftily to the favors of the French and even cheered Louis XIV.

Meister Wenck was puzzled. He still kept silent to every one. He had been reflecting upon the matter today at his work till his head burned and throbbed. He determined to refesh himself by an evening walk, and went towards the so-called «Schnakenloch.»

The «Schnakenloch» was a low piece of ground by the water, covered with houses, which the snakes, the pest of that region, chose for a summer resort in such multitudes that they drove away every sensitive person. There, in the little tavern which bore the peculiar name just mentioned, once lived a host called Hans, an original fellow, who always pretended to be foolish, and was at the same time so sharp, that notwithstanding the snakes, he drew guests in crowds by his assumed simpHcity, so that he became quite a rich man.

The satirical songs made upon Hans im Schnakenloch are in the mouths of the common people and children to this day. At that time It was even more the case, although Hans was dead and the inn had sunk into a miserable tavern. Meister Wenck would have hardly visited it, if the present host had not been a distant relative of his and also a poor man and a widower, who with his seven children, needed assistance.

So Franz Blasius went there occasionally and drank and paid for his mug of wine, but almost always left a gold piece lying under his tin cup. To-day, too, this was to be the case, and the little tailor went merrily on his way.

Meister Wenck drew his fur-lined cloak closer round him, pressed the helmet-like cap more firmly upon his head, and inhaled tlie cold evening air in deep draughts. They were good for him, and refreshed both body and soul. Wenck, notwithstanding his small figure and advanced years, was a vigorous and healthy man. If, in former times, in the fatigues, privations and hardships that often fell to his lot in war, he had frequently exclaimed for his own consolatlon, «Who knows what good it may do!» the saying had really been verified.

His heart, too, was sound: the little tailor knew no fear, or he would not have so quietly passed the gallows, which In those days was erected in every neighborhood. Ravens, startled at his approach, fluttered - with hoarse cries around the fatal pillars, upon the cross-bar of which hung the body of a criminal swaying in the wind.

A royal robber

The inn of the «Schnakenloch» was only about a rifle shot distant. It was the first of the few poor, miserable housesin this unhealthy locality; scarcely anyone visited it at such an hour, and yet it seemed to him as if some one were following him along the road. He now heard very plainly steps and voices, but he could see nothing, for thick clouds covered the moon. Security at night and in the woods was not known at that time. Meister Wenck knew no fear, but he was by no means foolhardy. «*Before me is better than behind me*» thought he, and moved aside.

The steps came nearer. In the stillness of night words could be easily distinguished.

«What time is it?» asked a man's voice.

«Probably about eight o'clock,» answered another.

«Then we shall arrive at the right hour.»

Wenck's astonishment increased. He recognized the voices: he had heard them only a short time before. «Arrive at the right hour?» he said softly to himself, «where and for what? and who may the speakers be? I will, if possible, let them pass me, and then follow,» murmured the tailor. «Who knows what good it may do!»

At the same moment he noiselessly laid down on the frozen ground close to the road. The dark mass was scarcely to be distinguished from the earth.

The men came nearer. Wenck heard every word they said.

«And will our friends surely come?»

«Undoubtedly.»

«It is a long journey.»

«But the prospect is remunerative.»

«Who can know that?»

«Do you already doubt the result?»

«No.»

A royal robber

«Well then, don't let your courage fail.»

«Still, I am often anxious.»

«Are you a man?»

«Even a strong man may have scruples and hesitate.»

«Why?»

«What will our contemporaries and ensuing ages say?»

«Oh! faint heart! Shall we arrive at our end and aim by –»

Here the speaker's words were lost. A flight of ravens which, croaking and screaming, drew near the gallows, prevented Wenck from hearing more.

«That was Günzer!» he cried softly, starting up.

«So truly as God lives, that was that rogue of a clerk. I must know what is going on. Who knows what good it may do and this much is certain: important business is on foot. If the judgment of present and future ages is concerned, the point in question must be some great deed or great rascality.»

Meister Wenck softly hurried after the nocturnal wanderers.

Soon he Recognized them again in the darkness.

The tailor crept up to the house. The window shutters were tightly closed. Only the noise and cries of the children were heard in the inn.

Meister Wenck looked up. Above was another room, which in former and better times, had served as a parlor for city guests. But here, too, thick shutters closed every opening.

Suddenly the listener distinguished the tramp of several horses in the distance, and directly after steps approached.

Two men, wrapped in large, dark mantles, drew near the house. Both, from their manner, seemed to belong to the higher class, and one of them, especially, had a tall, stately figure.

They silently entered the doorway.

So they had come on horseback within a short distance, and then dismounted. A servant was probably holding their horses. Wenck was more perplexed than ever, but how the devil should he learn more of this secret meeting, about which he suspected no good?

He was still standing lost in thought, when a girl about fourteen years old stepped out of the door of the hut. It was Fränzchen, the host's eldest child, to whom Meister Franz Blasius had stood godfather.

The young girl started back as she saw a man standing in the shade.

«Who is there?» she cried.

«Hush, Fränzchen,» replied Wenck, «it is I, your godfather.»

«Oh! oh!» cried the child in delight. «My godfather – and so late?»

«Why,» said the tailor, «it does not seem to be so late with you, you have guests?»

«We?» asked the child, gazing at him in astonishment.

«Who else!»

«You are mistaken, godfather! no one is here but my brothers and sisters.»

«And your father?»

«He has gone to the city.»

«And you have no guests?»

«Oh! dear, they come seldom enough. Once in while a workman!»

«Come, Fränzchen,» said the tailor reproachfully, «tell your godfather the truth ... I saw –»

He stopped and corrected himself: «I thought I lieard some one talking in the dining room.»

«It was us.»

«You?»

«Yes, I and my brothers and sisters.»

«Well then, perhaps it was in the upper-room.»

A royal robber

«That is locked, and father has the key with him.»

Wenck shook his head. Could the child be telling an untruth?

Meister Wenck was reflecting upon this, when the young girl innocently exclaimed:

«But, godfather, how strange you are to-day, staying out here in the cold and darkness. Come in. I will put the little ones to bed, and then get your mug of wine!»

And with these words Fränzchen drew the alvays welcome guest to the door. Wenck followed without resistance, and found no one but the children in the room.

Loud cries of joy welcomed the tailor. The children eagerly ran up to him and clung around his knees. Franzchen pushed them away as well a she could, took the little ones to bed, and on her return placed a cup of wine before her godfather, who in the meantime, had sat down at the dirty old table.

Two boys were riding on his knees, but the tailor seemed to be thinking of other things. He pricked up his ears to hear if there were any noises above him. Everything remained quiet.

Suddenly a bright thought seemed to occur to him; he put his hand into his pocket and laid on the table as many copper pieces as there were children in the room with the exception of Franzchen. The little ones looked on with eyes and mouths wide open.

«Do you see this money?» said the tailor.

«Yes,» all exclaimed.

«Well,» continued Wenck, «whoever goes directly to bed shall have one of these pieces.»

«Hurrah!» in one moment money and children were gone.

Wenck and Fränzchen laughed heartily.

The girl's godfather now drew her towards him, and patting her cheek, said:

«I am making a new bodice for my little goddaughter.»

A royal robber

«For me!» cried the child, her eyes sparkling with pleasure.

«For you! and it is a Sunday bodice, ornamented with very pretty, bright braid.»

«Oh! godfather, you are so good –»

«Hush, my child!» said Wenck, kissing her on the forehead.

«How shall I thank you for it?»

«You can.»

«But how?»

«If you will do me a favor.»

«Anything, anything, godfather.»

«Give me your father's doublet, cap, and apron.»

The child looked at him in astonishment. Wenck smiled.

«It is for a joke,» said he. «I want to represent old Hans of Schnakenloch. You know the song.»

Fränzchen laughed. The little tailor, with his droll face, certainly looked comical enough.

«So, godfather,» said she smiling. «I am really to bring you father's doublet, cap, and apron?»

«Yes, child,» answered Wenck, pulling off his furlined coat.

The child brought him what he wished, and the little tailor dressed himself in the clothes. The little figure looked infinitely comical. Neither he nor Fränzchen could help laughing.

«And now,» said the tailor, placing some money upon the table, «now bring me a large can of your best wine.»

The little girl again obeyed.

When she had brought the wine, Wenck put the cap upon his head and took the can.

A royal robber

«I shall be back in a few moments,» said he, and left the house, to the increased astonishment of Fränzchen.

The child glided to the door after him… but her godfather soon disappeared in the darkness.

When Meister Wenck found himself alone, he stopped and listened.

All right! at a short distance horses were being led up and down.

Wenck followed the sound of the steps.

After about ten minutes, lie found a groom sitting in the saddle and leading two other horses up and dowm. The poor fellow was shaking with the cold and gave vent to his ill-humor by a soliloquy, which consisted principally of oaths and imprecations on his master.

«The devil take such service,» he growled. «I'll be damned if the horses and I don't freeze to-night.»

He stopped and breathed on the hand which held the horses' bridles. Wenck listened: that was no resident of Strassburg. To be sure he spoke German, but with the dialect of the Lower Rhine.

«What has the holy man to do in this rascally neighborhood at night?» growled the groom. «For I will be hanged if the place where those faint lights are shining isn't Strassburg.»

«Holy man?» repeated Wenck.

«Thunder and the devil! I wish we had stayed in Cologne,» grumbled the groom again, as he turned the horses. «The pious lord bishop treats us like dogs, to be sure, but one is at home, and here we creep about this heretic city like thieves and lodge in the rat's nest at Illkirch!»

«Hm! the bishop of Strassburg,» thought the tailor. «Oh! ho! what is the prince of Fürstenberg doing here at night, in the fog, and with the city clerk too?»

«I know what I'll do,» continued the groom, blowing on his hands again, «if there is another war I'll run away. It is quite a different life with the soldiers, drudgery enough there, but one has a good share of it here too.» The groom

139

stopped, he had noticed the dark figure approaching him.

«Who goes there?» he cried, in the tone of a sentinel.

«A good friend!» answered Wenck.

«What do you want?»

«To drive away the cold for you with a mug of wine.»

«Who are you?»

«The host of the Schnakenloch!»

«Of what kind of a loch?»

«Of Schnakenloch, that's the name of my inn there.»

«Is it a good tavern?»

«If the prince bishop of Strassburg goes therie, it can't be very poor.»

«I don't care!» exclaimed the groom, «if you have really got some wine, hand it to me. It's damnably cold. I'm shivering all over.»

Meister Wenck gave him the inug. One could see that the groom was at home on the Rhine, and had studied drinking with German soldiers; he emptied the enormous mug at three swallows.

«And who sent me the wine?» he asked, returning the empty mug.

«Your master!» answered Wenck, «the lord bishop, Prince Franz Egon von Fürstenberg.»

«Man!» cried the groom, «the devil put that lie in your mouth.»

«And isn't he your master?»

«To be sure he is… but he would never send wine to his servants, even if they were dying of thirst and cold; he's eaten up with avarice, and besides —»

«Well?»

«He'd rather drink the wine himself.»

«There was another gentleman with him,» said Wenck inquiringly.

A royal robber

«That's so.»

«He ordered me to bring you the wine.»

«He?»

«Who is he?»

«How should I know?»

«Didn't he come with you from Cologne?»

«No we met him, well muffled in his cloak, waiting for us un horseback near the great stone cross.»

«Where is that?»

«About half an hour's ride from here.»

«And you don't know him?»

«Thunder!» swore the groom. «Mr. Host of – what kind of a loch?»

«Schnakenloch!»

«Well; Mr. Host of Schnakenloch, you are deuced curious.»

«Well, well!» said Wenck, «who knows what good it may do! Everyone has his weak points. While the gentlemen are sitting up there at rny house, we can gossip a little down here. Were you ever a soldier?»

«Yes.»

«So was I. I fought with the Imperialists.»

«Really!»

«And have you no desire to worship the god of war again?»

«Yes»

«With the Imperialists?»

«No!»

Wenck perceived by the short, gruff answer, that the man was tired of his many questions. He vainly tried to induce him to speak of the bishop's companion, the groom stuck to his sullen «yes» and «no,» and would not give him any information.

He even refused another mug of wine, and at last relapsed into total silence.

«Well,» said Wenck with feigned friendliness, «no offense!» and retired.

Though he had got very little out of the man, that little was of great importance to him. This much was certain: Herr Günzer, with the bishop of Strassburg and some other disguised gentlemen, were holding a very suspicious meeting here, and in such times that was quite enough for a patriot like Meister Wenck.

But what was he to do with this discovery?

He thought of various things-- and at last determined to go very early the next morning to worthy Syndicus Frantz, and inform him of the history of this evening.

Fränzchen was waiting for him with the greatest impatience. The clothes were soon changed. Meister Wenck paid for the wine, pushed the customary present under the mug, told his little godchild to come next day for the new bodice, and departed with a paternal kiss.

All the way home he was absorbed in reflections about what had just occurred. It was strange that fate had led him to the Schnakenloch on this very evening.

«It is strange!» said he as he went to bed, «but who knows what good it may do!»

XVII.
Alma

How grand and majestic, yet how light and graceful, is the beautiful cathedral of Strassburg, the great work of the gifted Erwin von Steinbach, as it towers into the bhie sky a pure petrified prayer?

Yes, that is German architecture as Erwin von Steinbach was German – and Strassburg and Alsace also. The cathedral was steeped in beautiful sunlight, for it was a lovely Sunday morning, clear, bright and fresh as only January could bring. The bells in all the towers rang solemnly and gravely summonning the honest burghers to church with their iron tongues.

But in one heart they aroused no feelings of piety only hatred and envy… and that was the heart of Prince Fürstenberg, who with the early morning had come into the city in disguise. He who bore the title of Bishop of Strassburg now lived far from his diocese; for since the Reformation there had scarcely been a hundred Catholic families in Lutheran Strassburg and the Cathedral was in the hands of the Protestants. Lutheran preachers proclaimed within its sacred walls Lutheran doctrines. The Prince Bishop foamed with rage when he thought of it. The cathedral originally belonged to the true Church – the reformation had only robbed them of it – and the Bishop Egon should in justice and by right rule in this beautiful building.

Such were the bishop's thoughts while, the bells were ringing; and the hatred against the unbelievers who now possessed the minister swelled his heart with fury.

The Prince Bishop bit his lips his eyes flashed defiantly but a voice in the depths of his heart cried: «Patience, we will yet conquer. Let Strassburg but become French and then we shall return to it again. By all the saints!, I Prince Bishop of Strassburg, will yet lead Louis IV into the cathedral a victor."

Modest, austere and truly pious was Alma – the lovely daughter of the worthy Syndicus Frantz – as she walked to church' at her mother's side. Her eyes were cast down; her hands held the little black silver-clasped hymnbook. The long Journey which her father was obliged to take in the severe weather, and the long separation, was hard for the child who loved her parents so fondly; besides this, came fears for the beloved city, whose unhappy position the old gentleman had explained to her mother and herself in confidence, and finally anxiety for tlie love she bore in her heart, and which seemed to meet with more and more obstacles every day. Frau Hedwig walked along gravely and silently. She was thinking of her distant husband and of the storms which threatened the future.

But the bells rang on gravely and solemnly and called to every one needing consolation – come! come! come! come! And actually there came Herr Günzer. He never failed to be at church. How handsomely he was dressed, and how he held his prayer-book so that every one could see it. His manner was quiet and grave, and he saluted the respected Frau Frantz and her daughter with a low bow as they entered the church. The former returned his salutetion with dignity, but Alma did not notice it.

More burghers and their wives came streaming in. The little tailor Franz Blasius Wenck, came across the market-place and by the old «Pfalz,» the residence of the councilor. But he was not as merry as usual. There was a sorrowful expression in his little, sparkling eyes.

Meister Wenck had vainly sought for Syndicus Frantz to inform him of the suspicious meeting between Günzer and tlie bishop. The Syndicus – so he was told – had gone away on business. But the secret depressed and wore upon Wenck, who loved the welfare of his fatherland with his whole soul. To whom should he confess it? From whom might he hope forcounsel and consolation? Yes! there was one who could give comfort, and that was the One above, who surely knew how to protect Strassburg from treachery, and were not the bells ringing out solemnly: come! come! come! come!

Wenck entered. He had just reached his place when the organ sent forth its mighty waves of sound through the church, far above the heads of the worshipers.

Then the tones died away, and the worthy, old minister, with the snow-white hair and the mild, benevolent expression, entered the chancel.

A royal robber

All present devoutly followed the pious words of the worthy minister – with only one exception, though he tried to express in his manner the utmost attention and the greatest interest.

This person was Günzer, whose mind was occupied with very different thoughts. Hugo, the son of Stettmeister von Zedlitz, sat not far from him, and opposite him, in the ladies' seat, was the wife of Syndicus Frantz with her pretty daughter.

Herr Günzer, therefore, had plenty of opportunity to observe the two young people, and indeed did so all the more sharply because jealousy lent him her eyes.

Günzer sat with his tall, slender body bending forward, and his head on one side as if wholly engrossed in the sermon. His manner expressed interest and devotion, his eyes were cast down, but from under the eyelids constant glances wandered towards Hugo and Alma.

These looks had long since made him aware of an uncomfortable secret. There could be no doubt that the young people loved each other. The sudden blush when they saw each other on entering their pew betrayed it; it was confirmed by the joyous flash of their eyes if they chanced to meet during the singing. Günzer was convinced that the two hearts were not indifferent to each other. This would have made him very uneasy, now that he, too, was interested in Alma, if the rupture between the two families was not well known, a rupture which he secretly sought to nourish and increase in every possible manner. But Syndicus Frantz and Stettmeister Zedlitz both had strong wills and characters, that were not easily influenced. It was not possible that they would permit a serious love affair between their children. Günzer relied upon this; still he was too wise a man of the world to trust the awakening passion of love in two young hearts. He knew that love was a playful child, but often became a lion that would tear away all barriers.

Hugo had more than once put his hand to his left side, as if he wished to assure himself that he still had what was hidden in the breast pocket of his coat. At the same time this was probably a sign to the young girl.

«What could it be? A present for Alma? A poem addressed to her? – Hugo wrote poetry – or perhaps even a love-letter with a passionate declaration, and such a written offer the clerk feared very much; but it was to be expected, for how otherwise could Hugo approach her?»

Whatever it might be, it was to be given to the Syndicus' daughter secretly, for she would not leave her mother's side. The only possibility of approaching Alma was as the people streamed out of church, and it would then be necessary to watch closely.

The benediction was pronounced, the notes of the organ again pealed forth, and the mass of people surged towards the doors.

They were pressed and crushed so that it was scarcely possible to move hand or foot. In fact one would need to be as cat-like and slippery, a Günzer, to squeeze through and gain one's chosen position. He succeeded. He was now close behind Alma, who with eyes modestly cast down, left the church at her mother's side, as she had entered it, without looking at the crowd pressing behind and about her.

Günzer tried to stoop as if he had dropped something.

At the same moment a hand holding a letter, touched Alma's dress.

The young girl started, her book slipped from her hand, she tried to catch it, but Günzer had already grasped it and handed it to her again.

Hugo's eyes flashed, another hand had taken his letter.

But he was happy in the thought that she understood him.

She blushed crimson as she saw him.

They were in the street again, the crowd dispersed in every direction. Günzer was triumphant, the trophy was his, he held the note in his hand.

He hurried home, and tore it open with trembling fingers.

He had not been mistaken. It was a declaration of love in the form of a poem.

His head burned. Had it gone so far already?

There must be no time lost on his part, if the young girl's hand, together with her fine fortune, was not to be lost to him. He must know where he was. But how should he do this?

His position gave him admittance to the Syndicus' house at any hour. Suppose he should use the poem himself?

It was so fiery, so glowing, as passionate as it was beautiful But it must be done quickly, before the young girl could possibly learn the true author.

And could there be a better time to take Alma and her mother by surprise than now while the Syndicus was away.

«Fortune favors the brave!» exclaimed Günzer, and sat down to copy the poem as well as he could.

He succeeded admirably.

But how his heart beat when, in the afternoon, he handed it to the lovely Alma, and at the same time asked her mother for the heiress' hand.

Should he, who himself possessed a good fortune and whose position in the government was one of the best and most influential, should he sue in vain?

And yet! and yet it was so!

What he had thought impossible happened. Mother and daughter refused the offer, politely it is true, butwith almost masculine decision.

Günzer could scarcely control his rage as he left the house. Hatred filled his whole soul. Hatred against Frantz, his wife and daughter; hatred above all things, bitter, insatiable hatred towards Hugo, his rival.

And Günzer swore revenge upon all the Frantz family, revenge upon his fortunate rival!

XVIII
The traitors

Syndicus Frantz still remained in Vienna, where he sought to win freedom and independence for his native city, and enable the important, indispensable stronghold of Strassburg to be retained by the German empire, but without obtaining either from ministers or Emperor anything that met the hopes and wishes of the sorely threatened city. To be sure they talked of sending an auxiliary army of forty thousand men, but it was soon evident that they were to serve against the Turks, not against the French.

Thus, notwithstanding the superhuman efforts of the Syndicus and the cry of anguish from Strassburg, nothing was done in Vienna, while Louis XIV and Louvois advanced with a boldness that has not its equal in history.

A new and unheard-of step was taken by the French government. They suddenly adopted the measures arranged in regard to Alsace, to Landau, and the district lying between that city and Weissenburg. But in order to take away from this seizure the appearance of flagrant despotism, and at the same time to represent it as the just consequences of the Westphalian treaty, the decision of the case was referred to the «*Chambres de Réunions,*» the highest council in Breisach, and similar questions concerning Lorraine and Burgundy were given to the Parliament of Metz. At the same time the different nobles of the land received directions to prove their right to their estates and property before French courts.

In vain city, country, and nobles, as a portion of the German Empire and totally independent of France, protested against this measure. Louvois and his king treated them with contempt and violence. Without paying the slightest attention to their petitions, remonstrances and protestations, the *Chambres de Réunions* placed the whole ecclesiastical and civil property of the country under the supervision of the French government and, demanded that they should immediately take the oath of allegiance to Louis XIV, king of France, affix the French coat of arms to the city gates and public buildings, and in all legal matters, should obtain a final decision from no other court than the French one at Breisach.

To give this outrage the necessary show of authority, the French general, Montclar, marched forward, received the troops stationed in Alsace and established large store-houses at various points. The inhabitants vainly refused to take the oath of allegiance. The order was executed with military precision; if the land-owners made complaints to the French minister – Louvois and Colbert de Croissy – they were told that their injuries were no cabinet affairs, but a legal matter, they must not therefore turn to the government but to the *Chambres de Réunions* at Metz and Breisach which the glorious King Louis XIV had instituted, to prove to his neighbors that he would do no injustice!

Syndicus Frantz soon despaired of meeting with any success in Vienna. He assailed the ministers with entreaties, but nothing was done. The bishop of Strassburg had in the name, and by order of the French ruler, written palliating and mediating letters and made the proposition: to order the disputed points to be settled by special ambassadors to a congress at Frankfort on the Maine.

Vienna, the emperor, all Germany did nothing, while France continued to rob Germany and her other neighbors and aggrandize herself.

The whole Duchy of Zweibrücken, at that time a possession of the Swedish king, was claimed as a French fief. King Charles XI was invited before the *Chambres de Réunions* and as he did not appear, the Duchy was taken away from him. It was given to the Count Palatine Birkenfeld, and this German prince joyfully took the oath of allegiance to the king of France. The same thing was done to the king of Spain. He too, according to preconcerted plans, was summoned before the *Chambres de Réunions* and as he did not appear, was declared to have forfeited the Principality of Chimay, the city of Cortryk and the Duchy and fortress of Luxemburg, whereupon France took possession of all of these cities by military force.

Syndicus Frantz trembled at this injustice. He redoubled his efforts and staked everything on the attainment of his mission; health, rest, even the favor of the ministers, to whom his persistency became very annoying. Frantz persevered with the firmness and tenacity of a true German patriot. He spoke with glowing eloquence, showed in the most forcible manner how important Strassburg was to Germany, explained that it was the duty of the emperor to come to the assistance of his German subjects!... but all in vain!

At last they decided to send ambassadors to the congress at Frankfort. But during this time the enemy had been active. Louvois had entered into negotiations with Günzer through the Bishop of Strassburg, and the clerk promised to secretly further Louvois' plans with the magistrates and people as much as possible. A hundred thousand thalers were appropriated to bribe the members of the government. He also swore to return to the Catholic church, and promised his assistance in gaining to her proselytes. In return for this, the bishop, in the nameof Louvois, promised him thirty thousand thalers and – when Strassburg had become French and the cathedral been given back to the Catholic church, – one of the first, most lucrative, and influential positions.

This was certainly a pleasant prospect for Günzer. He had long since intentionally striven for such a bribe on the part of France; now it came, and the fall of Strassburg was doubly welcome to him. With such a catastrophe all his enemies, the German patriots and Syndicus Frantz at their head, must be ruined, together with their families.

Once in the hands of the cruel and unprincipled Louvois, they were, if Günzer wished, irrevocably lost.

The latter already thought triumphantly, of his revenge. But it was still too far away for his hated rival. An earlier blow must crush him; the more so because Hugo belonged to the patriots and would not only render the work of betrayal more difficult, but – if his wooing of Alma and the perfidious use of the poem came to Hugo's ears – might become personally dangerous to him.

Günzer, urged on by jealousy and hatred, did not require much reflection to invent a diabolical plan, and instantly set to work.

But if this were to succeed, Hugo must first be separated from his father, for he must receive no assistance from the Stettmeister. This was not so difficult a task, for a breach had long existed between Hugo and old Herr Zedlitz.

Hugo, the strong, resolute youth whose heart beat warmly for everything good and noble – who had educated his mind bj' the study of the classics, and the grandeur of the Greeks and Romans – was naturally a patriot.

His heart glowed with enthusiastic love for his native city and the beautiful German Fatherland. Louvois' base and insolent conduct enraged the youth's noble mind, and inspired him with the utmost contempt for Louis the «great» and his accomplices.

The noble youth recognized his sacred duty and fulfilled it in every act, especially by his beautiful and vigorous poems.

Hugo's patriotic poems made a great impression in those excited political times, but the Stettmeister condemned them in the harshest and most violent manner. Though old Herr Zedletz was no friend to the French government, he was a timid man, whom fear of the powerful enemy rendered half-hearted in politics and action. And in truth, he had companions in timidity and fear in the Ammeister Dominikus Dietrich, and many of the other members of the magistracy.

With such totally different views and characters, the father and son were soon at variance with each other. The old gentleman saw himself, the magistrates, and even the city itself, threatened and compromise by his son's action, while the son reproached the father and the city government for destroying the public by their indecision.

Thus a wide breach had arisen between father and son which Günzer in pursuit of his plan of revenge now rendered impassable. The scoundrel, under pretense of the warmest friendship and interest for the welfare and honor of the family, gave Herr Zedlitz his son's poetical love letter to Alma Frantz in the original handwriting.

The father immediately recognized it, and enraged at this love, called his son and there followed a scene, althohgh at Günzer's entreaties nothing was said of the poem, which entirely separated father and son, and embittered them the more, because, in the passionate outburst of anger from two men who entertained such different political views, they wounded each other with reckless severity. But this was Günzer's intention; the first step to the fulfillment of his revenge was taken.

The second was to make the magistrates keep Syndicus Frantz in Vienna. In this too, the persuasive and cunning man succeeded by the assistance of his party. But he knew that there was no danger for him. The hands of the Viennese court were tied by the Turks, and all anxiety in behalf of Strassburg was appeased by the false information of the prince of Fürstenberg.

But now it was necessary to deal the principal blow. The French bribes were already in Günzer's hands, so he had means to farther his plans by the potent aid of gold.

Alienated from his father's house, from Alma, who during Herr Frantz's absence, and in consequence of Günzer's offer, lived with her mother in almost nunlike seclusion, hearing nothing and seeing nothing in the outside world – Hugo was more than ever willing to join other young men. And strange! In a marvelously short time there were a great many who attracted him, because they shared his political opinions.

Enthusiastic and ardent, as youth ever is, they soon became united by the warmest ties of friendship, and formed a club where they could openly express their opinions.

How warmly the young hearts beat for the good cause, how they extolled their native city and country! With what noble patriotism they spoke of the ways and means by which Strassburg might possibly be saved from the hands of Louis and Louvois. A change in the magistrates and the introduction of a younger element seemed to be the most feasible plan.

They talked and wrote a great deal about it, and Hugo Zedlitz who had been nominated president of the little club was the most eloquent, open, and enthusiastic of them all.

He did not imagine that it was Herr Günzer who had brought these young people to him; it did not occur to him that he was caught in the snare of his deadly enemy, to whom every word was sent, for whom every document was copied; who had already given information to «the council of thirteen.»

A royal robber

The latter were horrified and enraged at the traitorous step of the thought-less youths. Suppose it should come to the ears of the French ambassador, of Monsieur Louvois, or His Majesty of France, would not the existence of the little republic be jeopardized?

Half of the anxious ones and time-servers, old Herr Zedlitz at their head, were in despair – Günzer had not as yet mentioned the names of the members of the club, but all were beside themselves with rage and horror when the news that a reorganization of the magistracy and the introduction of a younger and stronger element had been discussed, came to their ears. Ha! that was high treason! it was written in the *schwörbrief* of 1482 that «All alliances shall be punished by banishment,» and this was a secret covenant against the city government, and one that was laboring for its fall and dissolution.

So the imprisonment of the traitors was unanimously determined upon, and if everything was confirmed, sentence of banishment was pronounced in advance.

XIX.
A trying hour.

Quite near the so called «Cat's tower» on the Ill, which runs through the city in many streams, stood a little house, at that time called the «Crab,» in which an old fisherman kept a tavern. A crab carved in wood and painted red, and over it the figure of a man painted in many colors, was the sign, which no one could interpret. The tavern of the Crab was used only by common people; such as sailors, fishermen, workmen occupied on the water, or in the streets, and even these did not often visit it.

On the present evening there were only two men in the little room, whose walls, and ceiling were so black from smoke and dirt that it looked more like a prison than the parlor of an inn.

And indeed the old broken oil lamp, which burned dimly on the table, was as little suited to dispel this illusion on the part of a guest, as the table itself, whose rude, wooden top bore hundred of names and initials.

There was so much dirt and earth on the stone-paved floor, that one might easily have planted beets there. Only the old fishing implements, which hung on the wail, and the few cans and mugs standing upon the worm-eaten table, dispelled the fancy, and brought one back to reality.

There, on the evening In question, sat two guests: the little tailor Wcnck and an old constable, whose red, copper-colored face proved that he served Bacchus, the noble god of the vine, at least as faithfully as the wise magistrates of the free city of Strassburg.

And it was Meister Wenck who had brought the already somewhat intoxicated Trombert here. A strange report had been spreail tlirough the city that evening. They spoke ot the sudden arrest of Günzer; but the affair was so mysterious that no one could understand whether it was founded on fact or not.

That this report interested the little tailor very much was only natural. He asked and spied about, but had not learned anything definite when he met

A royal robber

Trombert near the «Cats' tower.»

Wenck knew that the constable had already taken more than sufficient to quench his thirst, for he was well acquainted with him. as they had served in the same regiment. «Who knows what good it may do!» thought the little tailor, and joined his old comrade.

«Good evening, Trombert,» said he, standing just in front of the servant of the law' and Bacchus, where did you come from?»

«Straight from the Pfalz!»

«Still on business?»

«I should think so!»

«You are an important man in the city.»

«May be so; old Trombert is wanted for a good many important things.»

«Indeed!» exclaimed Meister Wenck. «Is there any truth in that report?»

«What report?»

«Well… they say – it is whispered –»

«What?»

«That Herr Gtlnzer has been arrested!»

«Herr Günzer!» exclaimed Trombert, bursting into a hearty laugh, «gossips always have to invent and chatter. Herr Günzer in prison!» and he laughed again, till the air resounded with the shout.

«But there must be something»

«Yes! something, something!» said Trombert mysteriously, «but we don't tie that on the jackanapes' noses!»

The tailor listened in astonishment; there must be something going on.

«You are right, Trombert!» said he, «what is the use of letting foolish people know everything. I laughed at them too. Let the fools gossip and put their heads together. I go and drink my can of wine!»

A royal robber

«Indeed?» said the constable, who had the peculiarity not only of being glad to serve Bacchus, but if possible to do so at another's expense.

«Will you be my guest, Trombert?» Wenck asked.

«I don't care if I do! if it won't take more than an hour.»

«Not half an hour,» said the tailor, «we will step into the 'Crab' here!»

«Into the pig pen?»

«Hush, Trombert, there is some excellent wine in the dirty hole. And then we should have to go so far.»

«Well then, Meister Wenck, I follow you,» replied Trombert, smacking his lip.

But Wenck had still another reason. He knew that here he should be alone and over the wine could draw out the old man's secret. They were sitting over the second can, when made talkative by the liquor and the shrewd cross-questioning of the little tailor, Trombert, under the seal of the greatest secrecy, at last so far exposed his secret to his old comrade that Wenck learned with horror that: «A conspiracy, against the government had been discovered – at the head of which was young Zedlitz – that in an hour the traitors were to be taken unawares in their club room, delivered up to the magistrates, and punished for high treason.»

Wenck trembled with horror. Young Zedlitz, the author of the beautiful poems, whom he and all Strassburg honored – this noble, young man arrested! he, one of the most decided patriots, a traitor to the government, guilty of high treason!

No it was impossible! But might not the error prevail? Would it not be well to warn the young man?

«Yes, who knows what good it may do!» thought Wenck, ordered another can of wine, told Trombert to drink it quietly at his expense and went off, pleading weariness.

But Meister Wenck had scarcely left the «Crab» when he hastened as quickly as possible to the Zedlitz houfee. Since his last quarrel with his father, Hugo had lived in a room in the back building, entirely alone. Wenck soon reached the house, and hurried up the little staircase with a beating heart. Hugo was still sitting over his books and papers.

The information was quickly given. Hugo turned pale. He was he a traitor to his city? he, who had such honest intentions towards her, who only thought of her welfare, her happy future?

Wenck urged him to take a hasty flight; but the youth, in the full consciousness of his innocence, rejected the proposition with noble pride.

«No,» cried he boldly, raising his handsome head, «that would be cowardice! that would be acknowledging myself guilty where I am perfectly innocent.»

«But reflect that calumny may be at work here,» answered Wenck anxiously.

«Then my honor demands that I refute it.»

«You have a number of enemies in the magistracy, sir!»

«That is true, and unfortunately my father is among them!»

«My God! Be wise and prudent, sir, appearances are against you.»

«How so!»

«I, at least, cannot think otherwise: you have decided upon a total reorganization of the magistracy.»

Hugo smiled.

«Do you impute to me – or to our little club, such a foolish act? What could we young people do?»

«But for this very reason –»

«We only talked about the matter, discussed it.»

«Then you are all lost.»

«How so?»

«Because they will interpret every innocent word as treason.»

Hugo became more serious.

A royal robber

«Herr von Zedlitz!» cried the little tailor, looking imploringly at the young man, you know I am your friend, that I am a patriot and am not a coward!»

«I know it, my dear Wenck!»

«Well then, take my advice»

«And that is?»

«Follow me to my house without delay.»

«Flight... no!»

«You shall not flee.»

«What then?»

«Only conceal yourself for a few days, till we know how the magistrates take the matter... whether they consider it high treason.»

«That they cannot do.»

«Oh!» cried the little tailor in despair. «If the worthy Syndicus Frantz were only here. But as it is, the party of patriots have neither head nor support. They will succumb to Günzer and his adherents!»

Hugo started: the name of Frantz and Günzer had awakened an unexpected train of thought.

«Conceal yourself with me if only for two or three days!» repeated the tailor urgently. «Reflect, who knows what good it may do!»

«Very well! I will follow your advice, Meister Wenck. But only for a few days, till we know!»

«God be praised,» cried the delighted tailor. «And now there is not a moment to lose. Throw a cloak around you, take an old cap, and follow me through the side streets.»

The youth did as the worthy tailor advised, and a few moments later they left the Zedlitz mansion.

Two days had elapsed. Hugo was awaiting the little tailor's return in a small room which Wenck had prepared for his reception. The latter had gone into the city to learn how matters stood with Hugo and his friends. The sentence was to be given to-day, the proofs lay before them, and the magistrates wished to give a quick and decided proof that every conspiracy against France was disapproved, and at the same time to set forth an example that the government was strong enough to strike down its enemies at home.

Hugo had already waited three hours.

The door opened and Wenck entered, looking deadlypale.

«Lost!» cried Hugo, starting up.

«Lost!» replied Wenck, almost voiceless with emotion. «Oh! unhappy world! the true and honest friends of our native land are banished, and the traitors sit triumphant at the head of the government.»

«Explain, Wenck, explain!»

«The sentence is strange. I cannot understand it.»

«How so?»

«All the members, with the exception of the president –»

«There were only six.»

«Are set at liberty at the pressing intercession of Herr Günzer; but Hugo von Zedlitz, the president, is convicted of rousing ill-will towards France and stirring up the people against the magistrates of the city –»

«Well?»

«And, as a traitor, banished from her precincts forever.»

«Impossible,» cried Hugo almost beside himself. «Strassburg cannot so shamefully expel her most faithful son!»

«And yet she does it!» answered Wenck, forcing back his tears.

«But that is all a lie,» cried Hugo. «Who has stirred up the people to rebel? And did not the others do exactly the same as I? did they not speak even more boldly, so that it was often I who counseled moderation.»

«They all swore the contrary, and denounced Hugo von Zedlitz as their

A royal robber

leader!»

«They did that?»

«Swore it.»

A long, deep silence followed. Hugo stood as if petrified.

At last life seemed to return to him. He quietly and calmly held out his hand to Wenck, and said: «I will go. Invent some way to get me off secretly to-night. I can remain here no longer. May God forgive my enemies what they have done to me.»

«Go, dear sir!» said Wenck, and he could no longer restrain the tears that flowed down his cheeks. «Go! leave your unhappy and ungrateful city, at least for a time. Submit to the inevitable. Who knows what good it may do! Surely your innocence will be made known, and then . . . then you will come back justified.»

«I will go,» repeated Hugo gravely, «but you must do me one more favor.»

«You need money! The little I have saved –»

«Not that,» answered Hugo with deep emotion. «When I left my room with you day before yesterday, I hastily put in my pocket as much as I shall need for the present. I shall meet relatives in Mannheim and then but to the matter in hand.»

«What is that?»

«Try to speak to Syndicus Frantz's daughter immediately.»

«The lovely Alma?»

Hugo nodded – «but secretly.»

«And then?»

«Tell her what has happened – that I am innocent tell her what you know.»

«Willingly, dear sir, right willingly.»

«And implore her, by all that is dear and sacred, to give me a quarter of an hour in secret before my departure.»

A royal robber

«I will go immediately. I already have an errand to the house. I must speak to Frau Frantz – there are some things on my heart about which she must write to her husband. Who knows what good it may do!»

«Then you will –»

«I'll go at once.»

That same evening – while Frau Hedwig sat in her parlor writing to her husband about the important disclosures Meister Wenck had made, and the exciting incident about Hugo Zedlitz – Hugo saw his beloved. At first conscientious and maidenly scruples had opposed the step, but the power of the moment, the might of love and despair, which seized upon her, soon conquered.

Under the pretense of going to the evening service, she followed Wenck to his house, where she met Hugo, whom she had long loved in silence.

A royal robber

Part III.
Politics and passion

A royal robber

I.
The masquerade

Following the banks of the Loire and Indre[56] from Tours[57], we reach the beautiful spot which is rightly called the «Garden of France,» and which is crowned by the famous – or rather infamous – Castle Loches, about whose gloomy walls, battlements, and bulwarks the. ghost, of Louis XI and his hangmen still seem to hover.

It rises on a hill overlooking the town of Loches. From the tower the eye roves with delight over broad meadows and pastures, which resemble a beautiful, green carpet traversed by the silver thread of the Indre, and bounded by the dark border of dense woods. The foundation of Castle Loches must have been laid in the early times of the French monarchy, as is proved by its style of architecture.

The castle itself has since been surrounded by massive walls, and crowned with battlements. Outside of these are moats and dikes, flanked by round towers provided with cannon. The principal gate was also protected by four towers and a drawbridge , beyond -which were a second and third gate, both provided with huge portcullises – to oppose the steps of the bold intruder.

But the most interesting part of the castle was the donjon, a high, square building, which overtopped the whole fortress like a tower. It is difficult to fix the epoch at which this part of the castle was built. The donjon of Loches rises a hundred and twenty feet about the summit of the hill. It can be divided into two parts, namely, the chief tower, which forms an oblong square of about one hundred feet long by thirty feet wide, and a second tower, similar in appearance but much smaller, and which apparently only served as a species of outpost to the first. Passing into this little tower, we see the vestiges of a stair-case, whose steps rested upon a double wall in which arched vaults had been made. This staircase, which was lighted by numberless small windows, ended in the form of a tunnel at a door which opened

---

[56] Rivers in France.
[57] Town 240 km south of Paris

into the first story of the great donjon, and also served as an entrance to a very large apartment, whose paved door rested upon a stone arch. In the second story was a chapel with an altar on the eastern side, and over this chapel was still another story.

The Castle of Loches was one of the most formidable fortresses in France. Such fortresses were of importance in times when kings, as well as great and small feudal lords, always had something to do to defend themselves, either against foreign invasions, or the aggressions of neighboiing Seigneurs, who in the absence of the English, found time to quarrel with each other, in order to satisfy their hatred and love of plunder.

The beauties of the country, and the great forest full of deer had also attractted French kings to Loches. Saint Louis, Philip the Fair, John II, and Louis XI spent a great part of their lives here.

Louis XIV too had come here. The now omnipotent Duchesse de Fontanges had grown weary of Versailles. The bewitchingly beautiful marble statue – as she was called at court from her outward appearance – was well known there, and therefore her unbounded vanity no longer found the nourishment it desired. The king's charming mistress, whom even the endless flatteries of the court no longer satisfied wanted new admirers. The sun of beauty glittered in Paris and Versailles, Marly and St. Germain, in the zenith of her power and splendor but the rest of France must also admire her and sink adoringly at her feet. For this reason, she had persuaded the king to visit With her and the whole court, Orleans Belois, Tours, Angers and Nantes, so on his return Louis had stopped at Loches, and on account of the spleendid hunting, established himself and court in the castle for a long stay.

This stay was not exactly agreeable to the lovely Marie. What should she do at lonely Loches? Here there was little to be dazzled. The city and vicinity were soon seen, but the nobles were not numerous, and at the same time less smooth and flattering than those of the court; nay, when the latter, accustomed to see the king constantly languishing in the chains of a mistress, honored Angeline de Fontanges almost more than the queen, the ruder but less corrupt nobility of the country often held back coolly with forbidding reserve.

A royal robber

Of course the king gave festival upon festival in honor of his beautiful mistress; hunts, plays, theatrical representations and rural balls, at which he rejoiced to see Angeline shine; but to her the old fortress seemed empty and deserted. Fear and anxiety often took possession of her in the spacious, dreary rooms, whose gloomy magnificence was actually repellant. Were there not legends of many horrors which had been perpetrated within these walls; of spirits and ghosts that till appeared in the old towers and rooms.

It was fortunate that Angeline, in addition to her royal lover, had so gay a friend in the Duc de St. Aignan. Here in gloomy Loches he was doubly welcome witli his thousand and one stories and anecdotes, his wit and unfailing cheerfulness. In unguarded moments something still stirred in Angeline's breast that would not harmonize with the happy life she apparently led. It was the voice of conscience, which awoke in her, and though often stilled, awoke again and again, especially when, in dreams or waking hours, the images of her good mother, her faithful old teacher, Père Hilaire, or even the bloody ghost of Gauthier rose before her mind.

She could not forget Gauthier's frightful death, which she only heard of long after it occurred; she drowned herself in the waves of intoxicating pleasure, threw herself into the arms of frivolity, and deadened remorse by the proud feeling of satiated vanity, the love of a king, and the splendor and grandeur of a princess.

And these terrible thoughts, these horrible visions, recurred to Angeline more than ever in the dismal stronghold of Loches.

Gladly would she have left it: but the king enjoyed hunting in the neighborring woods so much, that she did not dare to urge his return to Versailles so quickly, particularly as she herself had been the cause of his leaving it.

To-day a masquerade had been arranged. The thought had pleased Louis XIV, in as much as being away from Paris and Versailles, he could on such occasions lay aside all ceremony. Perhaps the monarch had still other things in view.

He willingly agreed to the desire of his lovely favorite, with the sole condition; – that the country nobility, and the well to do inhabitants of the city of

A royal robber

Loches, should take a part in it.

In order not to resign any of his royal dignity, the invitations were given in the name of the Duchesse de Fontanges, His Majesty (so said report) would not attend the festival.

The evening approached. Two of the immense old halls were prepared to receive the disguised and masked company. One was panneled from floor to ceiling with wood, upon which was carved the staff of Bacchus wreathed with vine garlands, and other designs, all glittering with gilding. On the ceiling were beams adorned with exquisitely carved figures, and upborne by winged devils with hideous faces, whose heads served as cornices to support the clumsy mouldings of this Gothic architecture. The mantel-pieces rested upon the strong shoulders of two caryatides, horrible monsters, such as the bizarre fancy of the architects in the time of Louis XIV produced. Upon the outstretched tongues of these caryatides, as well as on the chandeliers, burned candles of yellow wax, whose pale light feebly illuminated the wide, dusky hall.

The other room, which was more richly ornamented than the first and panneled with black and white marble, was decorated with Flanders carpets and rich curtains. On the walls, in place of the wood carvings, hung large, finely embroidered tapestries.

The musicians were stationed in one of the adjoining apartments.

The halls were now opened, and hundreds of masks pressed in. The grotesque, variegated costumes resembled a huge mosaic of human figures combined by some magic spell.

All the gold, velvet, silk or – with the less wealthytinsel, velveteen, taffeta, and other bright materials, which taste, splendor and riches could offer, were lavished here. The crowd surged gayly to and fro, talking and laughing, and singing!

But the king had not returned from the chase, and Angeline would not enter the hall before greeting her royal lover.

So she sat, somewhat out of humor at the delay, clad in the costume of a

A royal robber

Juno, embroidered with gold and precious stones, in one of the old-fashioned chairs of which Loches had so many, and which perhaps Philip the Fair had once occupied.

Her suite, representing all the residents of Olympus, were in the waiting-room, one person alone stood, mask in hand, a few steps from her chair. It was the Duc de St. Aignan, to whom the costume of Mars was as becoming as that of the queen of the gods to Angeline. An expression of winning courtesy rested as usual on his handsome features – a smile, that apparently sought to cheer his lovely companion.

But the Duc did not succeed. Angeline de Fontanges was impatient. The king had not yet come, and she longed to be out of the dreary vaulted halls, which were her residence during her stay in Loches, and away into those in which the music already sounded. Angeline had hitherto only heard half of St. Aignan's flatteries. Her little hand toyed with the purple robe that fell lightly from her beautiful shoulders, and in whose wide borders a quantity of precious stones were' artistically embroidered.

«Monsieur le Duc,» said Angeline, «you always have plenty of stories and anecdotes, – I beg you to tell me one, I am dying of ennui in this gloomy old rat's nest.»

«With pleasure, queen of heaven and beauty,» replied St. Aignan, bowing, «and yet we can still remain in the dreary old castle.»

«How so?» asked Angeline absently.

«Because there was once a festival held St Loches, similar to the one given here to-day.»

«Indeed? you make me curious. Who gave it?»

«Louis XI.»

«Tell me about it!»

St. Aignan bowed and seated himself, then casting a strange, ardent glance at Angeline, said: «Then you command?»

«I entreat!» she replied, while a deep blush suffused her face as he met the

Duc's gaze. There must have been some strange expression in the glance.

St. Aignan continued:

«You know that Charles VII made the Castle of Loches a royal residence. The monument to the charming Agnes Sorel, the king's favorite, still remains, and is called the 'Agnes tower.'»

«I know it!» answered the Duchesse de Fontanges. «The canons of the cathedral of Loches sought at different times to gain permission to remove the mausoleum of the beautiful Agnes Sorel from the choir to another part of the church. His Majesty was speaking to me about it only yesterday.»

«It is so large that it interfered with the service. But none of the king's predecessors would consent, until Louis XIV gave his permission. And the removal took place.»

«But you surely do not intend to tell me about the monument here in Loches?»

«Certainly not. I will only dedicate memories of love to the goddess of love and beauty!» said the Duc, and again he cast a strange glance at Angeline.

The jewels at which she was gazing parried it. The Due continued:

«After the death of Charles VII, the Castle of Loches still continued to be a royal residence. But under Louis XI, very few pleasant and cheerful events occurred. Still he sometimes came here with his whole court, and then the festivals which were celebrated, such as for example, that of 1465 recalled, though interspersed with certain dark shadows, the merry times of former rulers.

«But never had the bells, the tramp of souliers, and the terrible thunder of the cannon on the castle walls, so excited the people of Loches as on the third of February in the year 1465. The good King Louis XI, who awoke in a particularly pleasant mood, called his trusty valet Doyat, and said to him: 'Go down to my burghers and peasants, and announce to them my will which is: that every one shall enjoy himself today as much as he can.' This was more than was necessary to put a people thirsty for enjoyment into motion. There was a cry, a shout of rejoicing, that almost shook the vaults of heaven, and exulting and cheering, they set to work without loss of time. They brought out their money-boxes and took the savings of a whole year now that carnival had come for once, and what was seldom enough under Louis XI, a time for rejoicing, it must be celebrated with bacchanalian revels, masks, and mysteries. Rich and poor, nobles and peasants, troubadours and scholars, vied with each other in obeying the king's command.»

«And that took place here, and under the gloomy Louis XI?» asked Angeline in astonishment.

«Yes,» replied St. Aignan, «does it surprise you, fair lady? Have we not a similar festival to-day, and does not the grave Louis XIV, who is so jealous of his royal dignity, give it?»

«At my request!» said the Duchesse, «and the king will not be present.»

«Who can be sure of that?» said St. Aignan. «Perhaps Louis XI told the charming Countess de Sassenages, the beloved of his heart, the same thing.»

The duchesse listened eagerly.

«Tell me more,» she entreated, but her hand let the purple robe fall, and her attention was evidently fixed upon the narrator. The Duc continued:

«So the whole day was passed in mummeries, in plays, pranks, moral representations. In the evening there was to be a ball at court, at which the beautiful Countess Elfride de Sassenages, the influential friend and favorite of the king, presided. But before this the following incident took place.

«The clock in the castle tower had just struck nine. Louis XI was lying comfortably on his long couch of state, when his trusty barber entered the room with the decorated bowl and Spanish soap.

«'Come, hurry,' said the king sternly, 'I wish to witness the pleasures of my beloved and faithful people.'

«The favorite, who was handling the razor, well knew his royal master's moods, and also the favorable moments when he might dare to ask a favor, so he went quickly to work to fulfill the duties of his office. After he had sufficiently soaped the king's thin face, he no longer feared to be interrupted in his petitions, and said timidly:

«'Sire, your majesty has already had the goodness to replace the nickname of Olivier le Diable by that of Olivier le Daim[58]. Now if I might venture –'

«'Hm, hm,' growled the king again, shaking his head, but he did not dare to open his lips for fear of getting a mouthful of soap suds.

«'If I might venture,' continued Olivier leDaim, 'I would beg your majesty to continue your favors towards me.'

«Louis XI cast an angry glance at him.

«But Olivier, without allowing himself to be disconcerted, seized His Majesty's nose with his left hand and with the right laid the razor on the king's upperlip, saying quietly: 'Sire, the Comte de Meulan has just died without heirs: the title is vacant –'

«'Plague take the oppressor!' cried Louis, as he freed himself from his barber's hands, 'will you stop tormenting me?'

«'The lands of Meulan are without any owner, repeated Olivier le Daim, while he put the razor to the royal throat; 'they would surely be in proper hands if they came into the possession of a person who stands in such close relation to your Majesty, and into whose care the most precious thing is daily intrusted, namely, this illustrious head.'

«These words made tlie king tremble; the barber noticed it, and passed the razor over the king's face as he continued: 'Sire, I dare to give the striking proof of being the most trusty subject of France in the service of your majesty. To prove this to you I am ready at any moment to sacrifice my life; but as a reward for my faithfulness and devotion I must humbly entreat your majesty to grant the favor I have just asked.'

«The king's chin was smooth, and the barber threw himseif at His Majesty's feet.

«Louis XI stood before the crafty and audacious barber with flashing eyes,

---

[58] Olivier le Daim, favourite of Louis XI.

and exclaimed:

«'What does this mean, you rascal, you deserve as punishment for this presumption, to be given over to my godfather Tristan and caressed by my little goddaughter![59] But no, rascal, I will not do that, for I need your services. So, I make you Comte de Meulan.'

«'I most humbly thank you, Sire.'

«'Yes, but I have one condition –'

«'Speak, Sire, I am your most obedient servant.'

«'You are no longer the subject of conversation.'

«'Who then?'

«'Listen, knave, come here! you know the pretty peasant maiden who lives at Jacobs gate?'

«'With the beautiful, blue eyes, noble bearing, and little velvet hands?'

«'The very one.'

«'It is sufficient, Sire; I understand your Majesty.'

«'See that you do not act on your owm account, you rascal!'

«'Oh! Sire, I am too well taugh to take precedence of my master.'

«'What do you say?' cried Louis XI, as he looked sharply at him.

«'I repeat my eternal devotion to your Majesty.'

«'One word more, fool of a count! You will see that the halls and large galleries are arranged for to-night's ball; Madame de Sassenages and the whole court will dance there this evening.'

«'Very well, Sire.'

«'That is not all. Do not forget to bring the young girl, whom I entrust to your care, here in disguise. Go now, and fulfill your duties well and quickly.'

---

[59] To be tortured by my executioners. Louis XI in his royal gibberish called the executors of his revenge «My little god-daughter little darling,» etc..

A royal robber

«Olivier le Daim bowed almost to the ground, and retired.

«The evening began with dancing and play; free conversation, and merry questions and answers, were – bandied to and fro; people crowded and jostled each other, and the gay throng wandered from hall to hall and room to room.

«In the meantime, two masks dressed as monks had withdrawn from the merry crowd into a window corner, and while looking at the surging multitude, amused themselves by a whispered conversation.

«'So you have fulfilled my commands?'

«'I have seen and spoken to her.'

«'Are you sure she will come?'

«'I am certain of it.'

«'What is her costume?'

«'She is dressed as a fisher-maiden, wears a green silk net, a black taffeta petticoat, and a little blue velvet cap with silver acorns.'

«'Very well What is the password?'

«'Love and faithfulness.'

«'All right! now go! stop, one word more, the Comte de Manlevrier will not come… you answer for it?'

«'Most devotedly –'

«'Say nothing about devotion, titles, and respect, you fool! Would you betray me? Speak plainly and briefly.'

«'Well, I have already told you that you wear the count's costume… she will take you for him.'

«'Then she loves him very much?'

«'She is infatuated with him.'

«'And she is very beautiful?'

A royal robber

«'Beautiful as an angel! Ah! you have good taste!'

"'Young?'

«'Scarcely eighteen.'

«'Go, devil, go! You will send me to eternal damnation! How many pater-nosters must I say for this!'

«One of the monks withdrew and disappeared in the crowd.

«Ten minutes later, two masks left the ball-room, and after hastening up a pair of stairs, reached a small apartment which looked like that of a page or valet, and was certainly the sm.allest and most solitary in the whole castle. The two masks immediately sat down upon a stuffed bench, and one of them said: – «'The Comte de Meulan has surely piromised you to be silent, Messire?'

«'On his soul, my fair one.'

«'Why do you disguise your voice?'

«'Prudence requires it.'

«'In so secret a place?'

«'Have we not a password?'

«'Certainly, it is 'love and faithfulness.'

«The monk and fisher-maiden now drew nearer, and conversed in low tones. Time passed: the clock in the castle tower would soon strike the hour of midnight, and the lovers still lingered… the beautiful fisher-girl noticed it and said entreatingly : 'But why do we keep on our masks, and disguise our voices? Do you fear that any one will surprise us in this lonely room?'

«'I do not fear it; but still, on such a night as this, another pair of lovers might be concealed In a neighboring apartment.'

«'Ah! it Is pleasant to see the face we love and hear the voice that moves our heart.'

«'Do you love me so fondly?'

A royal robber

«'Can you doubt it, after the proof I have given you?'

«'Oh! no, my angel, my little rogue, I do no,t doubt it in the least.'

«'If I take off my mask, if I appear before you as I am, will you not do the same?'

«'Yes,' replied the monk 'Can I refuse you any thing fair one.'

«'Gallant as ever, Monseigneur, I recognize you here.'

«'Well, dearest, why do you hesitate?'

«'Ah! monsieur, I would fain see your face. Grant me this request; let us unmask at the same time.'

«Both removed their masks.

«At this moment, the large lamp, whose oil was nearly exhausted, sent out one last bright ray before expiring. 'The king!' 'Treachery!' Instantly echoed from the lips of both.

«The mask disguised as a monk was Louis XI; the fisher-maiden, Madame de Sassenages, the king's mistress.

«'Madame Elfride de Sassenages,' cried Louis, 'I did not expect such a meeting.'

«The comtesse thought it best to faint, and Louis XI groped his way down the stairs, murmuring: 'That rascal of an Olivier has played me a bad joke. But no matter. My little peasant girl at Jacob's gate shall not be forgotten! and le Comte de Manlevrier shall learn that it is unwise to hunt upon the royal preserves.'

«A month had passed by. Louis XI still occupied the Castle of Loches making use of his maxim 'he who cannot dissemble, cannot rule.' He had omitted no effort to conceal his bad humor and deep displeasure.

The Comtesse de Sassenages again appeared at court and was treated with the same consideration and respect as before. Her royal lover even affected a greater admiration for her. If he spoke to her, the most friendly smile played upon his lips, while in his heart he cherished the deepest hatred towards her. One evening the arrival of the Comte de Manlevrier was announced. The face of Louis XI suddenly shone as if with unfeigned delight. He advanced a few steps towards thecomte. and offered him his dry, bony hand. After the audience was at an end, the comte rose and noticed that, accompanied by the king, he was led back through another passage than the one by which he had come. On reaching the threshold of the last door he turned and bowed low; the crafty monarch, following him with his eyes, said: 'May God take you under His care and the saints ever be with you, Monseigneur.'

«At this moment the floor opened, and the unfortunate nobleman, with a fearful shriek, disappeared in a deep, bottomless abyss.

«Louis XI went back to his room, laughing scornfully, and crossed himself.

«'Fortunately,' he muttered between his teeth, 'the trap door worked well, and the donjon cannot speak.'

«A year later, the report was circulated that the Comte de Manlevrier, Lord Seneschal of Normandy, had perished in Sicily in the service of the Duc d'Anjou →»

St. Aignan paused and rose. The trampling of many horses announced the arrival of the king.

The duchesse, too, hastily started up, looking somewhat pale and disturbed. She made a sign for her suite to approach.

«And what does the story mean?» she whispered to the Duc.

«It is a fact in history,» said the Duc.

«But has it no reference to anything?» asked Angeline quickly.

«Not exactly! There are still pretty peasant girls at Loches, still loving cavaliers, and also, still trap doors! Use caution, divine, beautiful being, caution in all things!»

At this moment the doors opened and Louis XIV entered. All present bowed low; but the king approached Angeline, who hastened towards him, and with a light bend of the head, took her hand and kissed it.

A royal robber

«Yes, yes,» said he, gazing at the enchantingly beautiful figure of his mistress with delight. «You are a worthy queen of Olympus, Jupiter has not chosen ill. The world will envy him; but they are awaiting you. Go, madame la duchesse, the evening which I cannot pass at your side will be a sad one.»

Angeline would have answered, but the king waved a farewell to herself and her train. She bowed low, the others followed her example, and all turned to leave the duchesse's apartments.

At the same moment the king touched St. Aignan.

«Is all prepared?» he whispered.

«Everything, Sire!»

«The blue domino?»

«The blue domino with the light yellow cross.»

«Very well!»

No one had noticed the king's whisper. He now quickly left the room by another door, followed by his attendants. St. Aignan and the rest of the suite put on their masks. The duchesse herself scorned to cover her face. The thought of concealing her radiant beauty by a mask was too painful to her.

A flourish of trumpets resounded through the room. Marie Angeline, the beautiful, proud hostess, Juno, the enchanting queen of heaven, entered, followed by all the gods and goddesses of Olympus.

The ball was now officially opened, the mad gayety increased. The sweetest flatteries, the most exaggerated compliments greeted Angeline on every side. But she did not understand how to separate the exaggeration – which often concealed a cutting sarcasm – from the true recognition of her beauty. She did not have enough quickness for that; her vanity too, since her exaltation to the rank of duchesse and her stay at court, was so unbounded that no flattery was too gross for her.

But there were two masks that disturbed Angeline incomprehensibly a white figure and a monk, who, always inseparable, were ever in her path.

It was evident that they were trying to approach the duchesse.

A royal robber

But Angeline evaded them; she did not exactly know why.

Ah! yonder came a little procession of masks! how fortunate, it separated the duchesse from her ghostly followers.

It was the seven deadly sins and the seven virtues.

The sins threw themselves in the dust before her, the seven virtues led her in triumph to a costly armchair standing ready for her. Then the fourteen masks grouped themselves before her and performed a mimic dance, in which the virtues struggled witti the sins, came to blows, and after ever increasing violence of gesture the virtues were victorious, overthrew the sins, and sank upon their knees in a beautiful group, worshiping the duchesse.

A dense crowd surrounded her arm chair and the disguised dancers; but hundreds of masks, who, on account of the throng; could not approach and could see nothing, still surged in the halls.

Two blue dominoes with light yellow crosses met.

It was a gentleman and lady. A brief whisper – and they disappeared.

The virtues, too, had left the hall, only the sins remained, and were now uttering jests which were not always very refined, and often inflicted deep wounds.

Angeline de Fontanges hastily rose. The mysterious, white, ghost-like figure with the monk behind him, again approached her.

A shudder ran through her limbs, the white garment involuntarily reminded her of a shroud. And, it was horrible, the figure awoke a memory!

«Queen of beauty and of heaven,» whispered a tall Spaniard, clothed in black, upon whose breast and cap glittered a quantity of great diamonds, «queen of beauty and of heaven, let me at last, in this hour, lay my heart at your feet.»

Angeline started. Who dared to address such words to her, the king's mistress?

If another ear should hear these words, if they should be conveyed to the king, Louis had spies everywhere.

A royal robber

Angeline looked around her in horror; but the deadly sins were of some use they were making such a noise that one could not hear his own voice.

«Angeline!» said the mask, «child of the gods, you know I love you madly.»

«Who dares?»

«Who dares to speak to you thus,» continued the mask, «there can be but one at court, except the king, and I hope, sweet lady, your heart guesses his name!»

«St. Aignan!» whispered Angeline in horror, while a deep flush crimsoned her face.

«It is I.»

«And you dare – .»

«Angeline! have I dared too much, has my heart deceived me?»

«Merciful God,» whispered the duchesse. «We shall be observed.»

«Only one word, beloved,, one word.»

«In heaven's name, remember Comte de Manlevrier, of whom you. have just told me.»

«My fate lies in your hands, Angeline Betray me, and I shall –»

«Monsieur le Duc! and you could think –»

«Let me think but one thing, Angeline, only one that I find acceptance.»

«And should I be so ungrateful as to betray the one who loves me so tenderly, who has raised me to his own height?»

«Remember Louis XI and Olivier le Daim!»

«You traduce him, Monsieur le Duc.»

«And it I produce proofs?»

«No, no, it is impossible,»

A fortune-teller, covered with precious stones, approached.

A royal robber

«Well, my friend,» said she, «'you have taken the role of a proud Spaniard. Take heed that you do not act out of character; here, as well as in Spain, people are confoundedly jealous.»

«Calm yourself, my pretty fortune-teller,» answered the Spaniard. «I play no role, but only with them.»

«God knows that,» said the fortune-teller, laughing, «with rolls of money.»

«They are the pleasantest and most acceptable.»

«And the ones with which you are most familiar.»

«Yes, unfortunately, for they all run off before I am aware of it.»

«Because you understand so well how to go through them.»

«I'm so much the more skillful in getting them.»

«That is surely no heavy task.»

«Heavy when they are light, and light when they are heavy.»

«You attempt the lightest and heaviest, and succeed in both.»

«Because I know their insignificant contents.»

«Which may yet, precisely because they are insignificant, be very painful to you.»

«My God, I love secret worth.»

«But just now you seem to be upon a wrong path.»

«Take care, take care,» cautioned the Spaniard, «do not burn your fingers. You think to take up a glowworm and may perhaps seize a fiery coal. What concerns me I recommend to the favor of the noble queen of Olympus.»

«That is a pretty rôle also!» said the fortune-teller. «Pity that it will be as short as it is brilliant.»

The duchesse had heard nothing. She was thinking of what the Spaniard had just said.

St. Aignan started.

A royal robber

«Was that a prophecy?» he asked the fortune-teller.

«I do not depart from my role,» answered the latter. «Take heed, noble Spaniard, for you measure your actions according to your own advantage.» With these words, the mask mingled among the crowd.

«And you could give me proofs of the king's unfaithfulness!» whispered the duchesse, in unmistakable agitation.

«I have proofs, yes.»

«And what are they?»

«In the Agnes Tower –»

«What have you to do with it? I wish to hear nothing about it. There are ghosts there. The old ghost of Loches, a white figure, has been seen there tor three days.»

At this moment, a half-smothered scream escaped the duchesse's lips, the white figure that had haunted her all the evening stood close beside her.

It raised its finger threateningly – the hand, too, was white as marble.

«What is it?» asked the Spaniard.

«Thaf mysterious mask,» replied the duchesse, pressing both hands to her throbbing heart, for out of the holes In the white mask sparkled a pair of eyes which she knew – which she had known – but which now –

«Cease this miserable joke,» said the Spaniard, steping between the mask and the duchesse, «who seeks to frighten ladies at such a ball?»

The figure stood motionless; but his eyes sparkled horribly in their deep eye-sockets.

The followers of Juno had pressed forward and surrounded her with a glittering circle. The Spaniard had disappeared – and ghost and monk' also vanished.

The duchesse sank into her chair exhausted.

She asked for some refreshment, and her attendants offered a beautiful gold

A royal robber

-beaker

The musicians now commenced a new piece. It was a march. The doors opened, and a long row of dwarfs with monstrous heads, appeared. But in the midst of the procession was a lovely fairy, surrounded by elfin maidens, the most beautiful of whom, preceding the fairy, bore some sparkling object on a purple cushion.

Slowly, wagging their thick, ugly heads, the dwarfs and gnomes approached. Amid the cheers of the multitude, the procession made its way round the great hall, till it paused before the hostess in such a position that the lovely fairy and her elfin maidens were directly opposite the duchesse.

The music ceased and the fairy advanced with her elfin train. It was a very pretty girl, the daughter of a prominent official in the city of Loches; and lovely as herself were the verses she now repeated, and which, gracefully composed, eulogized Angeline's beauty. To crown this beauty she had come with her gnomes and elves from the depths of the woods and mountains summoned by the city of Loches and its inhabitants; for the city of Loches, like Orleans, Blois, Tours, and Nantes, wished to offer the favorite of Louis XIV a token of their respect.

The lovely fairy motioned to the little elves with the purple cushion, who knelt before Angeline de Fontanges, but the fairy herself took the splendid diadem with the ducal coronet – the gift of the city of Loches – and amid the flourish of trumpets and enthusiastic cheers of the guests, placed it on Angeline's head.

But the beautiful duchesse was paler than usual, and could only express her thanks in a low, almost tremulous voice. The trumpets again resounded and amid shouts and merry nods from the dwarfs, the procession withdrew.

A! what different thoughts assailed Angeline at this moment; the king faithless to her? if it should be true! Jealousy began to burn and St. Aignan's love. Oh! he was handsome, his image had long secretly reigned in her heart. If the king were faithless to her!

A beggar approached and implored alms.

A royal robber

Angeline was so lost in thought that, for a moment, she forgot she was at a masquerade. Hearing only half of the beggar's request, she tore one of the emerald buttons from her dress, and threw it into his hat.

«Thanks! thanks!» whispered the latter, his voice trembling with joy, «green is the color of hope. But, sweet queen of beauty, when will hope be followed by fulfillment?»

Angeline trembled: it was St. Aignan again.

«Go!» said she in a suppressed voice, «go, old man, you make me a beggar, for you have roused causeless jealousy in my heart.»

«It is sad and dangerous to be blind,» said the beggar, «therefore I opened your eyes.»

«And yet it is often better to be blind than to see.»

«It is best to see – and act prudently.»

«And suppose one sees an abyss?»

«Then one can avoid it because they see it. Blind we should fall helplesly in.»

«Everything is at stake.»

«Nothing at all, if one is wise. Let the spoiled child have the toy with which he amuses himself for a moment; but revenge yourself in secret, divine Angeline. I offer you my hand and a heart full of ardent love.»

«*Memento mori!*» said a deep, stern voice.

Angelina and St. Aignan started.

Again the white figure stood before them, and behind him the monk, who had uttered the words.

Angeline was voiceless, the eyes of the white figure glowed like coals in their deep sockets,and his glance rested piercingly upon the duchesse.

«This is insufferable,» cried the beggar, putting his hand to his side, as if he wore a sword.

The figure raised its finger slowly and threateningly.

A royal robber

«Who are you?» asked the duchesse in a trembling voice.

«We are, what we seem,» replied the monk gravely.

«I command you to withdraw!» ordered the hostess, gasping for breath.

«When you have heard our message,» said the monk with immovable composure.

«I will hear nothing!» cried the duchesse. «Go! or I will command the guards.»

«Command yourself and your passions,» replied the monk.

Crowds of people now surrounded the group.

«That is going too far!» cried the beggar. «Off with your masks!... Ho! guard!» and before the white figure was aware of it, his mask was torn away.

A death's head was beneath.

A loud scream rang from every lip.

«The ghost of the Agnes Tower!» cried hundreds of voices. Every one drew back even the guards.

The trembling duchesse clung to the chair.

The beggar alone did not shrink.

«Away with this foolery!» he cried «off with this second mask!» and he grasped at it.

But a heavy blow dashed his arm aside. The hand of the white figure was slowly raised. «You have forsaken God,» the voice sounded as if it came from the depths of the grave, «therefore God has forsaken you. Woe betide you! If you do not repent, you will go down to eternal night.» At the same moment the white, ghostly figure removed the death's head; the pale, livid face of one newly risen from the grave appeared.

A still louder shriek rang on the air, and the Duchesse sank fainting into the arms of the terrified ladies who surrounded her.

The beggar, too, uttered a cry of surprise and horror, and started back as if from a spirit.

«The ghost of the Agnes Tower!» again echoed on all sides, and the horror-stricken crowd recoiled.

But the white figure and the monk walked slowly to the door and disappeared.

II.
The politics of France

Louis XIV was pacing up and down his room with rapid strides. It was a gloomy apartment, like all the chambers in Loches, and even its furniture was somewhat stiff and somber. Everything still remained just as it had been in the time of Louis XL Even the private altar of that crowned hypocrite was not wanting. It occupied one of the dark corners, and was surmounted by a massive silver crucifix.

Louis XIV had not yet prayed before it. He even averted his eyes whenever his quick steps brought him near it, not from want of religious feeling, for he frequently crossed himself, but because very different thoughts occupied his mind.

It was secretly rumored, and the report had reached the king's ears, that the ghost of the Agnes Tower was the spirit of Louis XI, who had perpetrated fearful crimes there. And in fact, that very night as he left the Agnes Tower, he had seen with his own eyes a white figure in one of the long passages leading to the donjon. But the strangest thing of all was, that it had apppeared in the great hall in the midst of the masquerade, and so frightened the Duchesse de Fontanges, that she had been taken to her room insensible.

Louis XIV was not indifferent to the affair. The remembrance of the fearful deeds which the walls of Loches had witnessed, weighed upon his, mind and spoiled the pleasure of his stay. The determination to leave Loches as soon as possible was settled, but a secret council had been appointed for this morning, to attend which the Marquis de Louvois and Colbert de Croissi had arrived the night before. Captain de Torcy, who was on guard before the room, had been ordered to admit the ministers without further announcement. Matters of the greatest importance, and which required the utmost despatch were to be discussed. Ambassadors from Prince Tokoli who, in connection with France, led the insurgent Hungarians against Austria, as well as deputies from the Turks had arrived, and must be answered as quickly as possible.

A royal robber

The ministers entered, and the king sat down with his hat on his head. The Marquis de Louvois and Colbert de Croissi, bowing reverentially, stood opposite, separated from His Majesty by the huge, round table.

The consultation began. Oh ! walls of Loches, into what a prefidious plot were you here initiated.

With what crafty skill Louis XIV and Louvois had ensnared Leopold I, the German Emperor. Occupied and harassed by the Hungarians and Turks, the moment was approaching when the emperor would be like a man bound hand and foot.

Oh long desired moment for Loais and Louvois when you come then will be the proper time to take Strassburg, with the whole left upper bank to the Rhine.

That was the old policy of Richelieu and Mazarin. And the wise crafty, ambitious Louvois had adopted it.

The royal ante-chamber remained the only field for parties, and the one aim was the gracious glance of the monarch. Despotism had taken up its abode in France, and revolution dug its mines. In the meantime Mazarin toiled unceasingly for the foreign greatness of his country, concluded the peace at Münster, and the treaty of peace with Spain, which brought both countries rich profits. When he died he surrendered to Louis XIV, then only twenty-three, a peaceful, victorious kingdom, which bore in itself strength for great things.

But Louis' penetrating glance knew how to choose the right man to take possession of the inheritance of Richelieu and Mazarin. This was Francois Michel le Tellier, Marquis de Louvois, whom Mazarin had himself recommended upon his death-bed. And Louvois, as we know, entered upon this inheritance with a firm hand. The old plans for conquest and extension were continued, and to the horror of all Europe, fell upon Alsace.

Now, as we have said, nothing remained to be seized except Strassburg, and the last part of the left, upper bank of the Rhine. Strassburg and the left bank of the Rhine must belong to France. What cared Louis XIV and Louvois, though wars arose, rivers of blood .flowed, countries were ravaged, and whole nations made miserable, if only their object were attained. So the «Most Christian King,» Louis XIV of France, formed an alliance not only with the rebellious Hungarians, at whose head was Prince Thököly[60], but also – to his and Louvois' eternal shame, be it said, – with the sworn enem-ies of Christianity and all civilization – the Turks.

The fearful and bloody war which at that time threatened the Austrian do-minions, and even Vienna itself, was in a great measure the result of French influence at the Porte. Louis XIV, since 1673, had kept an ambassador in Constantinople, whose duty it was to maintain a secret connection between France and the powerful Prince of the Crescent.

Hungary and the Turks were thus incited to make war upon Austria and Germany from the east so that France might tear one piece after another from Germany in the west.

The French interests in Hungarian affairs was represented by Christopher d'Allanday, Marquis de Boham. The latter had led the Poles to Hungary, re-newed the alliance between the insurgents and the French ministers and dis-tributed the monies received from Paris. And when at last the Turks wished to attack the emperor again and support the insurgents with an immense ar-my, the marquis forwarded the rebel's letters to the French cabinet. More-over, this was done in a very treacherous manner, which violated the rights of nations. The French government sent the letters and remittances of mo-ney for the insurgents to the French secretary of legation at Vienna, from whence they reached the marquis, and through him, the insurgents. The af-fair was discovered, and the French secretary of legation imprisoned, where-upon Louis arrested the Austrian ambassador.

The marquis de Boham, while the Hungarians were in possesssion of the mints, had two kinds of ducats struck off, one with the head of Louis XIV and the inscription «Protector of Hungary,» the other with the head of Tkököly as prince of the part of Hungary occupied by him., and the inscrip-tion «For religion and Freedom.» But the insurgents only maintained

---

[60] Count Imre Thököly de Késmárk (1657-1705), leader of a Hungarian uprising against Habsburg.

possession of these cities for a short time, because Thököly was soon after killed near Heilgenkreuz by Dünewald and Wurm. Leopold himself would gladly have restored peace, for the murdering, burning, and wasting of Hungary not only by the Hungarians themselves, but the Turkish Pachas continued in the cities, and many hundreds of villages were entirely destroyed, but with his Jesuit councilors nothing was to be done. Even when in 1680, a peace commissioner was appointed, nothing could be accomplished, because Louis sent money and rich presents to Thököly and Apaffy[61], and the Grand Vizier promised to aid the insurgents with the whole military power of Turkey. Thököly even sent Ambassadors to Paris and Constantinople, and continued his murder and arson at the very time he was negotiating with the emperor.

It was these ambassadors, who had occasioned the hasty and secret council; they demanded the Hungarian crown for Prince Thököly in return for which, Thököly and his insurgents promised to declare war anew against Austria.

These matters were reported to the king by Louvois, and discussed in the secret council. The result was that the crown and subsidies were granted, in return for the repeated promises of the Hungarians and Turks to attack Austria at once.

When this important and difficult matter was arranged, the king asked: «Is this all?»

Louvois bowed low and answered gravely.

«As your Majesty commands.»

«Is there nothing more to propose?»

«Yes, Sire, there is another important matter. If your Majesty would be gracious enough to prolong the council a few moments.»

«And what is it?»

«It concerns Strassburg!»

---

[61] Michael Apaffy (1632-1690), prince of Transylvania.

A royal robber

«Ah» cried the king, «then speak, Monsieur le Marquis. Is the fruit not yet ripe enough to shake down?»

«It ripens visibly and will soon lie at the feet of the incomparable Louis the Great,» answered the smiling minister, with a low bow.

«It ripens slowly,» said the king.

«But surely,» replied Louvois.

«And where and how do we stand?»

«Your Majesty's minister, Herr von Frischmann has seat new reports »

«Let us hear the most important ones – but only the most important. We are tired of the long conference, and it is time for the chase. So the most important.»

«Will your Majesty permit me to read Frischmann's dispatch?»

The king nodded, and Louvois read:

«Sire, since my last report, I have observed that several wagons laden with powder and balls, which have arrived in Alsace, have surprised the magistrates of Strassburg. The Stadtrichter, Herr von Zedlitz, one of the most earnest, wisest, and one of the most well disposed of the coouncil, has spoken to me about it, and that the people here can draw no other conclusion from these hostile preperations in the midst of peace, than that the city had been unfortunate enough to incur a diminution of your Majesty's favor. The acknowledgment of this fear was accompanied with expressions of the deepest devotion and respect for your Majesty, and the most emphatic assurances, that the magistrates had not the slightest intention of treating with the Imperial ambassador, Herr von Mercy, far less of accepting any Imperial troops. At the same time, Herr von Zedlitz assured me he was ready to enter into a closer intercourse with me than the other gentlemen. I thought it my duty, Sire, to express my special thanks for the service he had rendered France by the delivery of this news, and to give him the assurance that I would apprize your Majesty of his zeal, his submission, and his attachment to your interest.»

A royal robber

«Very well! said the king,» we have already granted money for bribes. Herr Günzer has recived 30.000 florins for himself, and 100.000 for the bribery of other members of the council, but...»

«Well?»

«He states that it will not suffice.»

«Is the man trustworthy, and zealous in our service?»

«Both, Sire. He has rendered us great services. Günzer is a trustworthy agent and an excellent spy. I have received a letter from him in which he exposes all the weak points of the city, especially the want of money, the insufficient garrison of the citadel, and the indifference and neglect of the Emperor and empire.»

«Then, Colbert,» cried the king, in an animated tone, «pay him 20.000 more for himself, and 200.000 for the magistrates. We will and must have Strassburg.»

Colbert bowed.

«There is still another mercenary soul among the magistrates, by the name of Stösser,» said Louvcis mockingly, «he has entreated the ambassador for your Majesty's picture!»

«It would be best to burn it on his forehead!» said the king with a contemptuous smile. «That is mere hypocrisy. If these venial rascals will serve us, we should be fools not to use them, but they still remain traitors to their country. Frischmann may throw this miserable wretch a sum of money, but he shall not have our portrait. Besides, the money will be more acceptable to him. But to business. We wish to go. What was that about the excitement, that is vexatious, how shall we soothe them?»

«If your Majesty will permit,» said Louvois with a scornful glance and smile, «we will deceive the very wise council of Strassburg, and the citizens of the good, old city.»

«Ah!» cried Louis laughing, «it is very evident that you arrived at Loches during a masquerade!»

A royal robber

«Masks, disguises and dominoes belong to the province of politics!» said the minister. After all, life is only a great masquerade, and the world the ball room.»

«Not bad!» said the king, «and Louvois, what kind of a mask are you wearing now?»

«That of the minister of a great king,» answered Louvois, with a low bow, «though in fact, I am nothing but the most obedient servant, the most devoted slave of the greatest of all princes and rulers, Louis XIV!»

The king smiled. «So we esteem in the faithful servant, the minister, and in the minister, the faithful servant,» said he. «But we are wandering from the subject! how shall the disturbance be quieted?»

«If your Majesty will graciously permit,» replied Louvois, «I will grant a leave of absence to all the officers stationed in Alsace who have requested one. That will soothe the people, and we shall not injure ourselves, for as soon as the right moment comes, your Majesty will order a change of garrison, and under this excellent pretext the troops will be consolidated, and the officers who have been granted leave of absence, again recalled to their regiments.»

The king was silent for a moment, then slowly bent his proud head and said: "Very well! but we fear the report of our military preparations in Alsace will also spread into foreign countries.»

«Then your Majesty will be gracious enough to send the order to our deputies at the imperial diet of Ratisbon and the Congress at Frankfort to disavow every military preparation in Alasace, with the statement that the crown of France will consider it an insult if such things are foisted upon it.»

«Those are strong words,» said the king.

«But they will frighten the brawlers and keep them quiet. Bold assumption and startling measures have accomplished much with the good Germans.»

«So be it then!»

«And now, one thing more, your Majesty,» said Louvois. «I entreat you, Sire, to empower me to order Marshal Vauban, our most famous strategist, to proceed to Alsace in the strictest incognito.»

«And could that remain concealed?»

«He can give out that he is going to Italy, take cross roads, and avoid the great cities and densely inhabited neighborhoods. We must know the country about Strassburg and be prepared.»

«Very well! We will grant this also,» said the king. «But in case of a war we have still something to consider; if it comes to fighting here or there, Protestant troops, if they can be obtained, are always to be preferred. We owe it to our holy mother church to spare her children, the heretic dogs are of no consequence!»

Louvois bowed; he knew this maxim of Turenne's, and shared it with him and the king.

He could, therefore, joyfully inform His Majesty, that bought over and influenced by the bishop of Strassburg and Günzer, already more than twenty noble families had declared themselves favorable to Catholicism and only awaited the fall of the city, to openly turn Roman Catholic. :

At this moment words were heard in the ante-room, in which Captain de Torcy's voice was distinctly audible.

«No one can see His Majesty now,» he said in a loud, resolute tone.

«And why not?» asked another voice.

«He is in council.»

«But I must tell His Majesty something.»

«I can admit no one.»

«The ghost...»

«Louvois,» cried the king, starting up in violent agitation.

«Sire.»

«Let whoever is there enter.»

Louvois went to the door and commanded de Torcy to admit the man.

A royal robber

It was a servant belonging to the suite of the Duchesse de Fontanges. The man was deadly pale and trembled in every limb.

«What is it?» asked the king.

«Oh I your Majesty!» cried the trembling wretch, – the ghost has appeared again. Your Majesty ordered me to inform you if it was seen.»

«And where was it?»

«Close to the apartment of the Duchesse de Fontanges.»

«*Mort de ma vie!*» cried the king angrily, stamping his foot. «What does this mean?»

«It was the terrible white figure again, they say – it is the ghost.»

«Have done with that!» cried the king quickly, with a clouded brow, «and what happened?»

«The guards ran away, crossing themselves.»

«Cowards,» muttered Louis.

«And the ghost went straight toward the apartment in which the duchesse was –»

«And? go on… go on…»

«But warned by the cries of the guard…»

«Well?»

«They locked the doors.»

«Locked them? and the ghost?»

«When he found that this was the case… turned round –»

«*Diable!*» cried the king, «he turned? Then there is treachery behind the mask! Up, my lords, follow us! We will yet see what rascal dares to play the ghost of Louis XI, and to terrify our little tender dove, the Duchesse de Fontanges. Where! where did the thing go?»

«To the Agnes tower!»

A royal robber

«And the guards did not detain it?» asked Louvois sternly.

«No one dared to do so.»

«Well!» cried Louvois, crimson with shame and anger. «I will teach them to deal with ghosts.»

The servant, in obedience to a nod from the king, withdrew.

«Did you hear of the affair on your arrival last night, Louvois?»

«Yes, your Majesty, I heard all; the whole castle was in an uproar.»

«What do you think of it?»

«What your Majesty's penetration has instantly perceived, that there is treachery here.»

«And what madman would venture to play this bold game.»

«Sire!»

«Well? Out with it.»

«Sire! —»

«We command you to tell your opinion.»

«If it should be confirmed,» said Louvois, «it might cost the traitor his head, for he is undoubtedly grasping at your Majesty's dearest treasure.»

«*Mort de ma vie!* Your meaning!»

«I was informed last evening that the Duc de St. Aignan was absent from the masquerade.»

The king turned pale, but said quickly: «No, there you have been misinformmed, Louvois. We saw him with our own eyes enter the hall dressed as Mars.»

«That is true. Sire, but Mars is said to have soon disappeared, become invisible.»

«What!» cried the king, with flashing eyes, «perhaps he was assisting us to —»

«Sire!» repeated Louvois craftily, but with scarcely suppressed scorn, «have

A royal robber

the grace to remember that what I say is only supposition.»

«The devil take such a supposition,» cried the king. «Yet, by Heavens, if it should be confirmed, there will be one head the less on earth. Follow us, gentlemen, we will face the ghost!»

And the king hurried, with flashing eyes, towards the Agnes tower. St. Aignan was his favorite, but, if he had really played the ghost – Louis would not follow out the train of thought that assailed him.

The guards were still standing in bewilderment, scarcely capable of making the proper salute on the approach of the king.

Louis XIV did not notice it; he turned hastily into the passage which led to the notorious tower, where, according to the statement of the guard, the ghost had disappeared.

He had just turned a corner, when the Duc de St. Aignan, dagger in hand, rushed down the corridor from the opposite direction.

The king stopped, horror stricken.

«Monsieur le Duc!» he cried. «What does this mean? It is high treason to carry a naked dagger in the king's house!»

«Sire» exclaimed the Duc, «I drew it for the king's house. Let me go, for God's sake, I must follow the ghost.»

«What?» cried the king sternly, «does the masquerade continue to-day?»

But the words died on the king's lips, for, involuntarily following St. Aignan's hand with his eyes, he plainly perceived the white figure in the passage that opened into the Agnes hall of the church of Loches.

«Ha!» exclaimed the king, much relieved, «so, St. Aignan, it is not you who play this rascally ghost?»

«I? Your Majesty?» said the Duc, as if utterly amazed, but a glance at Louvois put him on the right path. «Oh, no, Sire, I do not play the ghost, but it seems that someone else has played me a shabby trick.»

«Not a word now!» cried Louis XIV. «Draw your daggers and follow me, the sly ghost has caught himself. The wretch will not escape usi Down with him if he resists!»

Louvois' and Colbert's daggers flashed beside St. Aignan's, and all three, following the king, rushed to the end of the passage which opened into the church.

«There it is!» all exclaimed in the same breath, as they saw the white figure near the mausoleum erected to the memory of the beautiful Agnes Sorel.

«Down with him!» cried the king; and his three companions rushed forward.

Only a ponderous, gilded railing and some massive pillars, which supported the vaulted roof of the church, separated them from the figure.

They had now reached the mausoleum ; the beautiful, marble figure of the lovely sleeper rested peacefully upon the sarcophagus. Two angels held the pillow upon which the beautiful head rested, and two lambs, symbols of gentleness, were at her feet.

All was hushed, quiet, and solemn.

The king and his followers stood petrified with astonishment.

«Let us search everything thoroughly!» said Louvois, Jperhaps there is a recess or secret passage here.»

They made a strict search, but found nothing. All was stong, solid masonry, massive walls, immense columns, a mausoleum of marble, and behind it a huge oak confessional – nothing else.

There was no one to be seen; the figure had disappeared. The king crossed himself.

Louis XIV and his court left the castle of Loches that same afternoon.

III.
Storms

Syndicus Frantz returned fom Vienna with a heavy heart. The Emperor and his ministers had remained deaf to all his representations, enteaties and warnings. The storm that was approaching in Turkey kept Vienna and the court in constant fear and anxiety. There was no hurry about Strassburg ; the most satisfactory assurances had been received from Louvois and the Bishop of Strassburg, according to which the king of France had not the slightest idea of making any hostile demonstration towards Strassburg.

So the Syndicus left Vienna with a heavy heart, and hastened home, although the order had been sent to him to continue his efforts at the Imperial court.

The party of the patriots greeted their noble leader with delight; but Günzer's adherents were enraged that Syndicus Frantz should have left Vienna.

Herr Obrecht and Herr Hecker, urged on by Günzer made the motion: to indict Syndicus Frantz for disobeying the orders of the government. A fearful storm arose; the patriots fought for their leader with fiery eloquence; those in favor of France, Dr. Obrecht at their head, raged against Frantz and his party, whom they accused of having already urged the little republic to the edge of the abyss. But like all storms in human life and nature, this too subsided, and Syndicus Frantz began to speak.

Quietly and clearly, the worthy man laid his whole proceedings in Vienna before the meeting: proved by words and papers, that nothing was to be hoped for from the German Emperor, and that he was obliged to leave Vienna in order not to arouse a feeling of indignation against the city in the minds of the ministers and His Imperial Majesty himself.

Herr Günzer began to speak, and with a smiling manner, sought to prove that Strassburg had nothing to fear. In pompous language, Günzer dilated upon the great sevices rendered by Louis XVI, and how the king only wished for the welfare and freedom of Strassburg and of the German Empire, while Emperor and Empire had deserted the city.

A royal robber

But Syndicus Frantz could no longer keep silence. «What!» he cried, «folly to fear anything from France! Are we all blind here, or only Herr Günzer? Louvois is executing his king's commands with the greatest secrecy. Under the pretense of working at the fortresses, he is ordering numerous bodies of troops to march into Lorraine and Alsace. Do we not know this?»

«These are mere illusions, which may readily be pardoned in an over anxious patriot, like the Syndicus!» said Günzer,

«Illusions!» cried the Syndicus. «But see! What is this story about the broken meal-chest?»

«What is that?» asked the Ammeister, Dominikus Dietrich.

«This morning,» continued Syndicus Frantz, «before I came to the council, I received a written report of the great excitement in the surounding country.»

«Fairy tales!» cried Günzer.

The Syndicus did not allow himself to be interrupted.

«It has long been remarked, my friend writes,» continued Frantz, «that a quantity of chests, ostensibly filled with arms for Breisach and other strongholds have been sent here from France. But a few days since one of these chests was broken in transportation, and, to the astonishment of all, betrayed its true contents.»

«And what were they?» cried several voices.

«Meal!» answered Frantz.

«And what of that!» said Günzer. «Must not France provide for the maintenance of her garrisons?»

«She does that besides, and openly. Why, and for what purpose, are these provisions secretly brought into the country?»

«Probably to give the tattlers and busy-bodies no material for childish alarm.»

«No, Herr Günzer!» cried Syndicus Frantz; «Louvois has corn ground in distant places, and the meal, after being secretly packed, sent into Alsace in great quantities to have a store in readiness, in case of a certain possible occurrence.»

«If we make a few advances to France in a reasonable way, we shall have nothing to fear,» said Herr von Zedlitz, «Herr von Frischmann has told us of a diplomatic communication from his court.»

«And what does Louvois demand?»

«The king of France requires the oath of allegiance.»

«A German city cannot take the oath of allegiance to any foreign power,» cried several voices.

After a few grave words, the president again requested Syndicus Frantz to speak.

He did so, and quietly but plainly, showed that the proposition of France was the first direct blow against the political existence and independence of Strassburg.

When he paused, Günzer rose. He severely censured Obrecht's remarks, spoke long in beautifully chosen phrases, of the noble feeling of true patriotism, and said how necessary it was to keep friendly with the powerful country of France.

At this renewed praise of the government of Louis XIV, the Syndicus' heart beat with anger, his eyes flashed, the muscles of his face twitched, and when he rose, notwithstanding his years, he resembled a youth entering the arena, ready for battle.

«What?» he cried, «does any one dare, in the face of history, answer for Strassburg's safety from France? Does any one dare to speak of the French ruler as a protector of German freedom? Is it necessary for me to remind you of the theft of the bishoprics of Metz, Tull and Verdun?»[62]

Syndicus Frantz was silent; but his words had fired many a heart. Even those of many of the weak, undecided ones glowed, and when the loud

---

[62] The German bishoprics of Metz, Tull and Verdun in Western Lorraine were robbed by France in the year 1552.

cheers from the patriots greeted the noble speaker, their voices mingled in the shouts.

Günzer and his party were silent and gazed gloomily around them. But the clerk had no fears, for he knew his people.

To-morrow the momentary enthusiasm would die out of most hearts – and the rest were bought.

Günzer went up to the Ammeister, who, after a few moments, announced that on account of the great excitement the council would be closed.

A fiendish smile flitted over Günzer's features.

He knew that he had gained the victory.

IV.
The ghost

It was already very late, but although warm and beautiful, the night was one which kept not only half Paris and Versailles, but probably the greater part of the inhabitants of Europe on their feet, for the huge comet, for which the year 1680 was remarkable, hung in the sky like a vast, fiery rod.

This was the first time that it had been wholly visible, as hitherto clouds had partially concealed it; and its appearance terrified all. It was so large that, even when its head had set, a portion of the train which was more than seventy degrees long and very wide, could be seen all night above the horizon.

Men trembled, prayed, and crowded into the churches, for the destruction of the world, earthquakes, war, and pestilence, were prophesied; while all Germany resounded with the terrified cry: «The Turks, the Turks! it means the destruction of the empire by the Turks!»

Even in Versailles, at the court of Louis XIV, the excitement roused by this imposing sight was great; though, inconsequence of the incredible frivolity that prevailed, secret anxiety was expressed by jeers and scoffs at the fear experienced by all. The Duc de St. Aignan naturally set the example. Though secretly intimidated, and in reality painfully reminded of the legions of his sins, he was outwardly full of witticisms about the unbidden guest, while from his lips, ever ready with an anecdote, flowed a never-ceasing stream of tales about comets, ghosts, supernatural appearances, and similar stories. But the Duchesse de Fontanges was so deeply agitated that she had been unable to seek her couch.

She had undressed long before and was in a *negligé* costume.

She was a matchlessly beautiful vision, as she stood at the open window of her sleeping-room, gazing outhalf in terror, half in surprise and delight – at the night-heavens, in which the Eternal One had placed that great and terrible object, the fiery comet.

A thin white cambric dressing-gown, covered with delicate embroidery, scarcely veiled the wonderful outlines of her faultless figure, and through the lace that floated around her like clouds of mist, appeared her bare arms, beautiful neck, and matchless bust, for the light robe was only fastened by a girdle.

The king and the whole court had heard of the ghost; but it had been seen only by some of the guards and in the vicinity of the duchesse's apartments.

And the latter – had she not gazed at Loches, into its pale, livid face, the face of a dead man, that chilled the very marrow in her bones, and whose memory startled her soul like the trump of doom.

«Yes, it was his ghost,» cried a voice in Angeline's heart – and this ghost pursued her even here!

Angeline already repented what she had done. She was the worshiped favorite of the king; she had been raised to the rank of Duchesse de Fontanges, she was rich, powerful, almost a queen; she was radiant in youth and beauty, the boldest of her vain wishes had already been gratified and even surpassed, and she had hitherto felt unspeakably happy – but now?

Ever since she had gazed into the pale, livid face of the apparition at Loches, her composure had fled, her conscience cried out: «You have turned aside from the path of virtue, you have forgotten your poor mother, your faithful teacher; you have sent the man who loved you so truly and fondly to his death, you are Gauthier's murderer! – for the face of that unhappy ghost wore Gauthier's features.

The impression was a terrible one at the time, yet the next few days with their changes, intoxicating pleasures, homage, and mirth, majesty and splendor, utterly effaced it.

Angeline was still standing at the open window of her sleeping-room, and the picture she formed was indeed one of surpassing beauty. The fact that she was the king's favorite disturbed the charming Angeline de Fontanges very little. In those days – especially at the court of Louis XIV, – people were accustomed to such things. His Majesty had already had a succession of favorites, and moreover had been in love with all the beauties of the court, even his own sister-in-law. All the princes, princesses and nobles in

A royal robber

the kingdom – whether married or not – had their love affairs and intrigues. Therefore Angeline's relations toward the king would have disturbed her very little if she had not been haunted day and night, by fear of the ghostly apparition. It was Gauthier's ghost, of that she was sure, and the thought that she had sacrificed her early lover was the cause of the agitation of her soul, and of course the appearance of the comet increased her anxiety and terror.

There it was, the huge comet, and no one knew whence it came or whither it was going. The whole world trembled before the mysterious visitant that, perhaps the very next instant, might fall upon the earth and crush it into shapeless ruin.

Angelina trembled. Her mind had not strength to rise above the universal superstition, nor did she possess the blasphemous levity of St. Aignan, who, with fiendish joy, could think of perishing with a world, while yet in the act of draining the intoxicating cup of sin.

They closed the window and drew the heavy silk curtafns over it. A sigh escaped her lips; it was at the thought of the long hours of darkness which were still before her.

Then the secret door noiselessly opened by the pressure of a spring.

But at the same moment, a cry escaped Angellne's lips – the ghostly apparition stood on the threshold.

The ghost had entered – the ample, white robe fell off, and before the duchesse, who was trembling in every limb, stood – St. Aignan.

The duchesse stood in bewilderment, scarcely daring to trust her own eyes, as if turned to stone.

St. Aignan sank on one knee before her and said in his peculiar, caressing tone: «Pardon, divine Angeline, a double pardon. First, for having frightened you, wonderful creature, and secondly, for having dared –»

«Merciful God,» faltered Angeline in astonishment, glowing with blushes. «Merciful God! suppose the king –»

A royal robber

«We are safe from him,» replied St. Aignan smiling, as he still knelt before Angeline. «The king is ill and has gone to bed.»

«But who authorized you to enter here?»

«Who, Angeline?» cried St. Aignan, passionately, «who save my own ardent heart! Forgive me, heavenly creature, I cannot help it! The most passionate, fervent love consumes me. Let me be happy – or – perish at your feet!»

Angeline trembled like an aspen leaf. A mist came before her eyes.

«Angeline,» repeated St. Aignan imploringly, still kneeling at her feet.

«Rise!» said the latter, drawing back.

«Not until I know that you will pardon my presumption.»

«Oh! God! oh! God!» faltered the duchesse, «if any one should hear us – if the king should learn –»

«He will not. At the utmost, it will only be another appearance of the ghost.».

«And you?»

«Yes, I, I have played it this time; but it is no evil spirit that has come to you at this hour, fairest of the fair, but the spirit of love! Dearest, let us be happy, and the world and all else can crumble into ruin.»

«Do not blaspheme!» cried Angeline. «Let us think of our sins, not commit new ones. Rise!»

St. Aignan rose. Angeline drew her light robe close around her. The former eagerly extended his arms and was about to clasp the charming beauty in a fervent embrace, when boih started back as if a thunderbolt had fallen.

Again a low voice was heard.

«Merciful God!» murmured Angeline, turning deadly pale, «we are lost – the king!»

A livid pallor overspread the countenance of her companion. One moment more and their lives would be forfeited.

A royal robber

St. Aignan instantly thought of all this. His eyes moved swiftly around the room, and the next moment the heavy silk curtains that draped the nearest window concealed him.

Angeline clung trembling to the nearest chair.

Again the secret door opened, and again Angeline almost fainted – the white, ghostly apparition stood on the threshold.

But this time it was the right one – for Angeline gazed in horror at Gauthier's pale, livid face.

«Gauthier?» escaped her lips in a tone of mingled surprise and terror.

«Yes,» replied a hollow voice, slowly and solemnly – «I am Gauthier!»

Angeline passed her hand over her brow, on which thick drops of cold perspiration were standing. Then summoning all her courage, she cried, making the sign of the cross:

«In the name of God the Father. God the Son, and God the Holy Ghost, if thou art a spirit avaunt from me!»

But the figure remained quiet and motionless.

Angeline tried not to faint. She tottered, her arms fell by her side as if petrified.

«You are mistaken, Madame la Duchesse!» said the figure, in a trembling voice, but with a sharp, cutting emphasis. «It is no ghost, but a man that stands before you.»

«Impossible!»

«It may be wonderful; but that it is possible, you see!»

«Then I have been deceived. Gauthier de Montferrand did not –»

«When your faithlessness, your shame, Madame la Duchesse, broke his heart, he tried to put a bullet through his brain beneath your window.»

Angeline turned away and covered her face with her hands. The figure turned its back upon the door through which it had entered, and which still remained open.

No one in the room perceived that the king, Louis XIV, was now standing behind it.

The news that the ghost had again appeared in the palace had induced him, though ill, to leave his bed, in order, followed at a distance by several armed men, to examine the apparition in person.

«The bullet,» continued the figure quietly, «did not kill me, though I was supposed to be dead when carried from the spot – it did not kill me; but the wound was so dangerous that for months I hovered between life and death.»

«Oh! thank God, Gauthier,» cried Angeline, «your death was a terrible reproach to me!»

«Calm yourself, Madame la Duchesse,» continued the figure, «calm yourself – I shall not take the reproach from your heart. True, the wound has healed but the shot will still cost me my life – my health is destroyed – I am tottering towards the grave.»

«Do not talk so, Gauthier,» pleaded Angeline, «live for your mother.»

«My mother is dead!»

«Then think of yourself!»

«I, too, am dead to this world, although I still drag cut a miserable existence. What could the world have for me, while what was highest, most sacred, dearest to me, lies in the dust.»

«Gauthier?»

«I shall soon die – and willingly! But before my poor, crushed, weary heart can lie down to its last repose, I have undertaken one commission – and to perform this commission I now stand here. It is to appear before you, Madame la Duchesse!»

Gauthier paused, and then said in an inexpressibly sorrowful tone: «Before *you*, Angeline, to entreat you to turn back from the path of sin to the way of right and virtue. For this object I wore a mask; – for how else could I approach you?»

«Impossible! In Loches It was —»

«Gauthier de Montferrand, as well as here.»

«But the king himself followed the apparition to Agnes Sorel's monument, where the ghost —»

«Thanks to the precaution of the priests of the church of Loches, vanished without leaving a trace behind, through one of the confessionals behind the monument, which has a concealed entrance to the crypt.»

Angeline sank into a chair and covered lier face with both hands.

«But how was poor Gauthier to reach the proud, beautiful Duchesse de Fontanges, revelling in pleasure and gayety, pomp and splendor!»

«Gauthier!»

«The steps of the throne, where, — forgetting the admonition of her poor deserted mother, the holy lessons of her faithful, gray-haired teacher, God, virtue and her own salvation — Angeline de Fontanges, in the arms of a king —»

Louis XIV started, his eyes flashed witii anger, but he again forced himself to keep silence until he had heard all.

«I cannot utter the words!» continued Gauthier gloomily, «let your conscience speak instead. But I longed, I resolved to reach you, Madame la Duchesse, Money, so much I had already learned at court — money is the key to everything in the world. I therefore sold all I possessed, even our little ancestral castle, and in company with Père Hilaire, set about executing my last life-task.»

«Yes!» muttered Louis XIV, «it shall indeed be your last.»

«We tried for a long time in vain,» continued Gauthier, «then the court went to Loches, where Père Hilaire had an old acquaintance among the priests. All else that I needed to obtain the possibility of approaching you, Madame la Duchesse, I obtained there, as here, by lavish bribes. Men will do everything for money. They will betray God, and their king, nay, — sell themselves.»

«Gauthier, Gauthier!» cried Angeline in agony, still covering her face with her hands.

«Even the key to the secret passage that leads from the king's apartments hither, even this precious key – was to be bought.»

The king ground his teeth and then murmured:

«But the guilty ones will yet pay dearly for it. The price is – the Bastille!»

«But it was not only the key, I was also obliged to remove the guards. Here, however, it was useless to attempt bribery – and therefore I was obliged to pave my way by fear and superstition. Now, Madame la Duchesse, you know how and why I came to you as a ghost. Had any other way been possible, a man like me, who already has one foot in the grave would have scorned such mummery.»

Gauthier paused a moment. Angeline sobbed quietly – there was no movement behind the curtain – the king stood motionless before the door, anger and vengeance were throned on his brow.

«And now,» continued Gauthier, after a slight pause, «now, Madame la Duchesse, the dying man calls upon you to remember the vow you once made to God, your poor, deserted mother and Père Hilaire. He reminds you of the dream the Eternal One once sent you.»

Angeline' s head was bowed on her hands and she sobbed convulsively.

Gauthier fell on his knees at her feet. «Angeline!» he cried, in a tone trembling with agony. Hear the voice of a dying man! I ask nothing, nothing for myself – I only wish to save your soul, to rescue you from the horrors of the future. Turn back, Angeline, turn back to the path of virtue, back to the arms of your poor deserted mother, who is weeping herself blind for her lost child. You have fallen low, low indeed, but the mercy of God is infinite.»

Gauthier paused; Angeline still wept, but did not move.

«Angeline!» cried the youth again, while his voice trembled with secret emotion. «Angeline, cast your vain baubles from you! The king –»

«He loves me!» sobbed Angeline through her tears, «and I return his love!»

«But your love is sin, the king is married!»

«And even if it were a sin – it is still love.»

«No!» cried Gauthier rising, while his eye gleamed forth from his pallid face with a ghastly, supernatural brilliancy, "no, it is not love that binds you to the king, Madame la Duchesse, but base vanity. The king loves you? Oh! yes, to-day – to-morrow, perhaps even day after to-morrow! But he will soon grow weary of you, as he has of so many others and then, then, he will cast you aside, like them, to bewail your folly in perpetual misery and despair!»

«No! no!» cried Angeline, «the king is not capable of such conduct towards me.»

«No!» cried a loud voice at the same moment, «he is not capable of it!»

Angeline shrieked aloud, Gauthier started and turned – the king stood before them.

The king made a sign and Captain de Torcy entered with the guard.

«Arrest this man!» said the king, «and take him to the Bastille!»

«You will answer for his safety with your head,» continued the king sternly. «He has, as he says himself, one foot in the grave – so it will be easy for the other to follow.»

De Torcy moved forward, but the old warrior tottered.

Gauthier stood with his figure drawn up to its full height. He cast one grave, warning glance at Angeline, a look of admiration, of eternal farewell, then followed the guard with a firm, steady step.

«Angeline!» said the king gently, «I have heard all. You are innocent, my child; you love me truly and faithfully, and your king will be true and faithful to you. Forget the fanatic and go to rest. You need it after this agitating hour, and if you should ever have occasion to complain of me, remind me of it.»

He kissed Angeline on the forehead and left the room.

Part IV.
In exile

A royal robber

A royal robber

V.
The discovery

A wondrous summer night brooded over the earth. The air was soft and mild, the pine forests sent forth a delicious fragrance, at once balmy and spicy, and the moon shone so brightly that the magnificent landscape was plainly revealed to the eyes of the traveler, who descending from the heights, gazed thoughtfully at the scene.

It was a wildly romantic region; mountain peak rose above mountain peak, now covered with countless pines, crowded together like an army ready for battle, – now bare and barren, crowned by strangely formed masses of rock, that gazed like hostile spirits into the silent night. Ah! it was no marvel that the solitary traveler stood lost in reverie; the whole region seemed to dream of ancient times, of centuries that had vanished long ago.

Hugo von Zedlitz gazed over the wide plain towards the spot where flowed his beloved native river; the spot where Strassburg's ancient cathedral rose gravely and silently, and where lived the lovely, innocent girl, for whom his heart throbbed so warmly, so faithfully, so loyally.

Months had passed since he had seen Alma, and he had suffered during that time, both mentally and physically. He first went to Heidelberg, hoping to remain for a time with some relatives and work for his native city. But even this vague hope was instantly cut off, as his relatives – not crediting his statement and putting an evil construction on his flight – received him coldly and repellantly.

He could stay no longer in Heidelberg, as his slender means would not suffice, yet he did not wish to go far away from Strassburg. At last he remembered a school-friend, who lived in Breisgau.

Thus Hugo von Zedlitz set out, but as he wished to remain unknown, he wore the Alsatian peasant costume, with which Wenck had provided him at the time of his flight.

His disguise proved very necessary; for during the first days of his journey, a rumor reached his ears that French and Alsatian spies were on the track of a young citizen of Strassburg, who had preached high-treason and rebellion against France.

When he reached Freiburg and sought his friend, he learned that the latter had died a few weeks before. So this hope was destroyed.

Hugo found temporary shelter with a lawyer; but, though he did not mind frequent struggles with actual want, he could not endure the thought of being completely cut off from his native city and deprived of all opportunity to vindicate himself by some patriotic deed.

At last Hugo could no longer bear to remain so far from Strassburg, whose freedom and existence he knew were continually threatened. His resolution was quickly formed, quickly executed, and – this night he had already advanced so near his goal that, with a throbbing heart, he could recognize in the distance the spot where his beloved city stood.

Hugo von Zedlitz had already been on his feet two days and two nights, resting very little in the meantime. So it was natural that he was soon overpowered by fatigue, to which two worse companions, hunger and thirst, were now added. Just at that moment a miserable little inn appeared in the gray dawn as he turned a bend in the road, an inn before which a lazy, sleepy servant was feeding the horses of a wagon laden with goods.

«Good-morning, my friend,» said the young man, pale and weak with hunger, as he tottered wearily forward.

The servant looked at him with half-closed eyes, but was too sleepy to answer.

«Can I have something to eat?» continued Hugo.

«They're all asleep,» said the fellow sulkily.

Hugo collected the last small coins in his pocket and threw them on the stone table before the bouse, so that they rattled loudly.

«Will bread and cheese do?» asked the man.

«Very well!» replied the tired traveler, sitting down on the stone bench be-

A royal robber

side the table – «and a drink of water.»

Hugo was quickly served. The scanty meal refreshed him, only fatigue would scarcely let him enjoy it; his eyes almost closed.

Even the servant, who, meantime, had been attending to the carter and his wagon, noticed it.

«I suppose you are tired and would like to rest a while?» he asked.

«Yes,» replied Hugo, «but I suppose the whole house is locked.»

«But not the hay-mow close by,» said the man laconically, pulling his cap over his face and entering the inn.

This hint was enough for Hugo. He mounted the ladder leaning against the adjoining barn and threw himself, unheeding the cool morning air, upon the hay.

A few minutes after Hugo von Zedlitz was sound asleep.

But what a slumber it was. Nature demanded her rights and the young body gave them in fullest measure.

The servant had gone to the city to do some errands early in the morning, and as he had told nobody about the young man asleep in the barn, no one knew anything about him. Business had not been brisk during the day and not until afternoon did a few monks and soldiers arrive.

The sun was setting when Hugo was awakened from his deep slumber by loud singing. He opened his eyes in astonishment and at first could not understand where he was.

Soon memory returned, and with it, the recollection of what had occurred during the past night and morning.

Through a chink in the boards he perceived, close at hand, the miserable inn. There was the stone table where he had taken his frugal breakfast, and here he was lying on the hay-mow, where he had slept till sunset.

But what was going on below close by the barn?

To whom did the harsh voices, proceeding from throats somewhat too well moistened, belong? They were soldiers' and rogues' songs, sung amid peals of laughter and – sometimes in the French language.

He turned softly and moved nearer the old board wall of the barn.

Close beside the barn stood a huge linden, beneath which tables and benches had been placed, and around these universal gayety prevailed.

Monks and soldiers sat drinking and singing, while a red-cheeked girl, ruddy with health, brought them wine in huge mugs.

The girl was really pretty, only her beauty was somewhat coarse, like her whole nature. She laughingly gave still ruder answers to the rude jests of the monks and soldiers, and, when, in the universal hilarity, one of the friars pulled her into his lap, gayly submitted and even jestingly returned his kisses.

But a fresh shout rang out when one of the soldiers – evidently, as his French accent showed, an Alsatian from the French frontier – raised his mug and in a harsh voice began to sing.

One of the monks, who had apparently held aloof from the drinking as much as possible, made a sign to a soldier. After exchanging a few words, both moved noiselessly towards the place where the ladder rested against the barn.

Hugo was very much startled.

The monk pointed to the bay-loft where the exile was concealed, and the soldier nodded assent.

Had they heard of him? Had the servant betrayed him? He certainly had not been seen. Or did accident bring them to the spot?

He dared not show himself and then – there was but one way of getting down and this was by means of the ladder the two were just preparing to ascend.

Hugo heard one after another step on the ladder. There was not another moment to lose.

Quickly as a flash of lightning, he darted under the hay which was piled high in one corner, while only a few bundless lay In the others. He had scarcely time to roll two of them over to conceal his head, without running the risk of being suffocated when the monk entered, followed by the soldier.

«There,» said the former, «now we can talk over the other matters undisturbed.»

«Well, what's to be done now?» asked the soldier.

«You are ordered here?»

«Yes.»

«Well, you haven't been wanting in punctuality.»

«A soldier is accustomed to that.»

«And to obedience,» observed the monk. «So are we.»

«Obedience to our superiors.»

«That is our duty also. We too form an army.»

The soldier laughed scornfully, then replied: «Yes, an army of cowls.»

«We are the soldiers of God, the champions of the church.»

«Maybe so,» cried the soldier, «for my part, I prefer the sword to the cross.»

«The best way is: for sword and cross to fight with and beside each other, for one and the same good cause, our Holy Mother Church.»

The monk crossed himself devoutly, the soldier followed his example, but did not seem to fully agree with the remark.

«I think,» he said, «it is still better for each to keep his own place. We know how to strike with the sword, you, holy Father, understand prayers, masses and confessions; but – deuce take it, how would it look if I were put in a cowl and you in the king's coat.»

«Perhaps not so badly as you imagine.»

«You are jesting, Father.»

«It might be put to the test.»

«Devil take...»

A royal robber

«Calm yourself.»

«Speak plainly. What's the meaning of all the mystery with which we were sent here by secret roads?»

«Are you and your men good catholics?»

«Yes!»

«Do you serve His Majesty, the King of France?»

«Yes.»

«Well then, you will cheerfully, aside from your military duty, as good catholics, brave soldiers, and Frenchmen, do what the king, your commander and holy Mother Church desire!»

«But what's the use of these by-ways! Put us where blows are dealt and we'll know how to use our swords. We don't care for blood even if it flows in streams.»

The monk drew a parchment from his breast.

«Read!» he said, holding it out to the soldier.

«Let the devil read it,» replied the latter, «if he can make out the letters.»

«At least, you know the signature?»

«Who doesn't know the signature of the Minister of War, the Marquis de Louvois?»

«Then hear what the order says.»

And the monk read an order from Louvois, according to which the soldiers sent to this place were to render implicit obedience to Father René, a deputy of the Bishop of Strassburg.

«Calm yourself,» said Father René, perceiving the unpleasant impression this communication produced upon his companion – «I shall ask nothing of you which will conflict with your honor as a soldier. On the contrary, you and your comrades are to perform a service by which you will earn the thanks of your king and the church.»

A royal robber

«And that is?»

«You are to help His most Christian Majesty to conquer that nest of heretics, Strassburg.»

«I'm listening.»

«Do you know Strassburg?»

«No.»

«Well, that will do no harm – I'll guide you myself.»

«To Strassburg?»

«Yes, but first listen to me.»

«Speak.»

«We are bare-footed monks, as you see.»

The other nodded.

«Well, our monastery – one of the oldest in Strassburg and now the only one in the accursed nest of heretics – is in the heart of the city.»

«Well, and what's to be done with the monastery?»

«Why, I just told you; in the monastery of the bare-footed monks, which is under the bishops sole control, everything can be arranged as we please. So by degrees troops will be smuggled in, of which you have the honor of being the first. When there are enough – well, that you'll learn afterwards.»

«But will they allow us to pass the city gates?»

«Not as French troops certainly.»

«Then how are we to get in?»

«By stratagem. Down in the inn lies a large bag which we brought with us. Guess what is in it.»

«How can I?»

«Gowns for six bare-footed monks.»

A royal robber

«And what's to be done with them?»

«You will slip into them —»

«Never!» cried the other, starting up and pulling his beard defiantly. «Zounds do you suppose we're going to creep in in cowls? We are soldiers, not priests.»

«You are,» said the monk quietly, «good catholics, brave soldiers, and have sworn to obey your commander. Will you by resistance call down upon your heads the curse of the church? Will you refuse to obey the Minister of War, and also your master and king?»

The man was silent; but it was evident that he was passing through a severe mental struggle.

The monk said kindly:

«You see how your men are singing and carousing below. They are nothing, for — you are their soul. That is why I have applied to you. You must think for them and induce them to act. His Majesty and the bishop will value you accordingly. And if we succeed in throwing Strassburg into the king's hands you will be made men. Absolved from all the sins of your whole life — and that's saying a great deal.»

«Hm, hm!» muttered the soldier.

«And money and —»

«Will the city be plundered?»

«Of course! The inhabitants are heretics.»

«Be it so then,» cried the soldier. «We will put on the cursed cowls, but only until —»

«Until you are in the monastery.»

«And when do we set out?»

«This very night, when all are asleep.»

«Together?»

A royal robber

«God forbid! That would attract attention. They keep a sharp eye on us in the heretic's nest.»

«How then?»

«By twos. And in such a way that each of us real monks has one of you with him. We will approach the city by different roads and to-morrow, when it grows dark, enter by different gates and at various hours.»

«Done!» cried the soldier, clasping the hand the monk extended.

«Come down now,» said the latter, «and arrange the business with your men.»

The monks soon departed, one of them carrying large bag on his back.

Fifteen minutes after the soldiers marched away singing merrily.

But a young peasant also glided out of the hay-loft and followed the soldiers. He was pale and looked very much agitated.

Suddenly he paused.

In an opening in the forest, now illumined by the moonlight, a merry scene was taking place – it seemed as if people were preparing for a carnival. Monks' dresses were drawn from a bag, and amid jests and laughter, and smothered curses, put on by the soldiers.

The young peasant stood still some time, listening intently; then he too turned hastily towards Strassburg.

A royal robber

VI.
The superiors of the Franciscans.

Quiet and still as if lifeless, the Franciscan monastery stood in the heart of busy Strassburg. The crowds thronged around it, but the surging torrent broke against the gray old walls, gloomy as if mourning in sack cloth and ashes. like the fierce waves of the sea when they dash upon the stone surface of a huge cliff.

The walls rose high in the air, only pierced by a few small windows barred with iron, whose panes had long since grown dim, and behind which no human face ever appeared. The great iron-bound gate, with the figures of the apostles carved in oak, now black with age, scarcel}- permitted any human form to slip in or out during the day, and when this did happen it was a dirty, mendicant monk in haircloth gown with a rope around his waist and sandals on his bare feet – a Franciscan brother, who, according to the rules of his order, was going out to beg.

The dull sound of a bell echoed through the building and a few moments after a small window was cautiously opened. A monk's shaven crown appeared und a hoarse voice asked tiie visitor's wishes.

«Why!» said tlie boy wlio bad rimg the bell, looking at the porter with a by no means remarkably intelligent expression, «I'm to give this letter to the superior.»

«And from whom does it come?»

«You must see by that!» replied the youth, handing the letter to the porter and pointing to the seal.

The movement revealed a pair of muscular arms and hands that seemed formed to use the hammer and anvil – at any rate to deal blows.

The porter smiled with a well-satisfied air as he looked at him and the seal.

The little door beside the huge gate opened and the youth, at a sign from the porter, slipped through into the monastery.

A royal robber

He was now standing in a dark passage, leading through the front building, on either side of which stone saints frowned sternly upon him. A slight shiver ran through his limbs. He felt as if he were in a half church, half prison, and involuntarily made the sign of the cross on brow and breast. Holding his cap in his hand and glancing timidly around as if he feared at every step to jostle some monk, who half naked and bleeding, was scourging himself to death, he followed the porter.

The dark passage was passed. A second door at the end opened and the two entered a spacious court-yard, in the center of which stood the monastery. These buildings were formed of huge stones, weather beaten, and gray with age, and resembled a mediaeval fortress rather than a monastery.

When the principal building was reached, at a signal made by the porter with the latch, a heavy bolt was pushed back, the door half-opened, the porter gave his companion to the care of a second monk, exchanging a few words with him and then returned to his post in the front building, while the porter of the main edifice bolted the door behind the visitor and motioned to him to follow.

They walked through long, vaulted passages, up wide, stone steps, down dark corridors, on either side of which, on the right and left, appeared at regular distances the doors leading to the monks' cells.

At last the priest stopped before one of the doors, told the young man to wait, and entered.

The youth repeated a «Pater Noster.» Then the Franciscan returned and told him to enter the Right Reverend Superior's presence.

The superior of the Franciscan Monastery was the very ideal of a monk; not tall, but with a muscular frame, firm outlines and a round, fat face, in which a certain repulsive sensuality blended strangely with hypocritical piety, while the flabby, wrinkled cheeks as well as the drooping corners of the mouth gave his countenance the stamp of infinite weariness. Yet at times the lusterless, watery eyes flashed with a look which might be commonplace malice, or the echo of long-lost activity and energy.

He wore the coarse dress of the order, fastened around his waist with a

A royal robber

rope, and had on his bare feet old, dirty sandals.

«The Lord bless you, my son,» said the superior, unctuously.

The youth bowed with pious awe.

«And what do you bring us?» asked the Franciscan.

The young rnan handed the letter.

Father Bartolomeus took it; but instead of opening it, looked at the stout, vigorous youth with a well-satisfied smile.

«How old are you?» he asked.

«Twenty-six.»

«A peasant?»

«Yes.»

«Well,» said the monk, «your arms are strong enough for threshing.»

The young man smiled.

«Do you like to deal blows?»

«In case of need, yes!» said the young peasant, showing two rows of magnificent teeth.

«And what do you think while you beat the grain in the threshing season?»

The youth shook his head as if to repel the idea of thought while engaged in such an occupation.

«Well,» resumed the superior, patting him kindly on the shoulder, «I'll tell you what a good catholic must think. He must think that the stalks lying before him are thick-headed heretics and he is to crush them in the name of the holy Mother Church. Then he will put all his strength into the blows, and the piff, paff, puff – piff, paff, puff – will go on merrily.»

The youth grinned again and nodded a joyful assent.

Father Bartolomeus opened the letter, cast a hasty glance at its contents, and then thrust it into his pocket.

A royal robber

«What are you going to do now? » asked the Superior.

«Go back home, Reverend Sir.»

«Where?»

«To Illkirch.»

«And plow, sow and thresh again?»

«Yes.»

«Suppose the Lord had destined you for something greater?»

The young, man opened eyes and mouth He did not understand what the monk meant.

«If Holy Mother Church and your Reverend Bishop command you to return home to reap a harvest, that will make you acceptable to God above all His servants – will you obey like a true servant and pious Christian?»

«If it is harvest time and our crops are ready – why not?» replied the peasant.

«The Lord's harvest is always ready,» said the superior, in a grave, dignified tone, «but the Lord's harvest is the destruction of the heretics.»

«Yes, yes,» replied the youth, who, by dint of this fanning of the flame of in-bred fanaticism, began to dimly comprehend the other's meaning, and whose fist instantly clenched.

«So you will remain here now?»

«Here?» exclaimed the youth, evidently startled.

«Yes,» replied the superior, «your bishop, the pious Franz Egon, Prince of Fürstenberg, commands you to do so, in the name of God.»

«But –»

«You are not to become a monk, calm yourself. You are chosen by the Lord, with other faithful servants, to perform a great deed which will be pleasing in His sight. You will learn when the right time arrives in what it consists and how it is to be executed. Now God and the holy church, your bishop and I require from you unconditional obedience. Will you give it? Or

227

A royal robber

will you be cursed by the church and condemned forever?»

«Mercy, mercy!» cried the peasant, falling on his knees before the monk, while every feature expressed anxiety and terror.

«So you will obey?»

«Yes.»

«And will you swear unconditional obedience to me?»

«Yes.»

«Then swear!»

And the Franciscan with great solemnity and threat of every conceivable punishment, administered to the trembling peasant the required oath.

«There!» said Father Bartolomeus, turning to the monk, «now take him away with you, he is consecrated to the service of the Lord and must be strengthened for the great deed by the consolations of life.»

The monk beckoned and the peasant followed him. But the poor fellow felt by no means at ease in the gloomy monastery. If at hfs entrance it had seemed half church, half prison, now in his excited imagination it appeared wholly a dungeon.

And in fact the way by which he was led was not calculated to dispel these terrors. Once more he passed through long, gloomy passages, down dark, stone stairs as if descending into the depths of the earth.

And what was that? Was it not a distant cry? Perhaps the moans of some prisoner or – a monk scourging himself?

Yet no. What was it then? It sounded almost like a merry song.

The silent monk who led the way glanced at the astonished peasant with a smile of amusement. By Heavens! it sounded like a merry, drinking song, and the noise grew louder.

Suddenly a cheer rang out. At the same moment the Franciscan opened a heavy iron door and entered a vaulted cellar with his companion.

A royal robber

In a vast cellar, whose vaulted ceiling rested on short but thick stone pillars, and whose sides and ends were invisible to the new-com.er's eyes since the faint light of the few lamps burning left most of the wide space in perfect darkness – was a motley assembly of monks and soldiers.

There were few real monks; but many of the soldiers, as if for a jest, wore the Franciscan dress, carelessly thrown on so that here sturdy limbs clad in leathern hose and huge boots, there a soldier's doublet, a portion of a sword, or a broad shoulderbelt, peeped forth, while others had put on. above the monkish gown, the round military hat of the times.

At the moment the young peasant was ushered by his companion through the iron gate into this secret monk's paradise, and stood motionless with astonishment, a gigantic cask of wine formed the center of the scene. Before it, his eyes radiant with happiness, sat the monk in charge of the cellar. His face was suffused with a deep, purple hue, his little eyes were almost closed, but glistened with indescribable delight.

If, instead of the monk's robe, a tiger skin had been wrapped around his body, no finer ideal of Bacchus could have been found. And the worthy monk industriously filled his beakers, handing them to the other pious brothers or soldiers who were half sitting, half lying about on the floor and smaller casks. There were not a few thirsty throats here.

«Hurrah!» cried one of the soldiers, who seemed to be of higher rank than the rest, raising his mug – «Hurrah! Had I known the holy Francis was so good a host, by all the saints. I would have donned the cowl instead of taking the sword.»

«Or that he kept so good a cellar,» cried another, laughing.

«All honor to the holy Francis,» said one of the monks, pressing the mug of wine he held in his left hand to his heart.

«Laugh on –» said the Franciscan quietly. «We are accustomed to mockery, like our great model. What is taking place here to-day is only on account of your unwashed faces and thirsty throats.»

«Yes,» added another, «we usually strictly follow the example of our illus-

A royal robber

trious founder.»

«And how did he live?» asked one of the soldiers laughing, as he held out his mug to be filled again.

«He divided his property among the poor,» continued the monk, «wore like us a hair shirt next to his body, watched, prayed and fasted –»

Again the laugh burst forth.

«Often went out naked in the snow,» the monk went on, «to mortify his flesh, and scourged himself three times every night; once for himself, once for the sinful world, and once for the poor souls in purgatory.»

«The deuce!» cried the first speaker, «once would have been enough for me.»

«And I suppose you do all that?» asked another, in a jeering tone.

«Certainly!»

«But,» cried a voice from a corner – «do you call it poverty to have such cellars full of the best wine? By my sword, I don't understand how that is keeping the vow of poverty.»

«It's very simple!» said the monk who had charge of the wine, blinking happily, «each of us has taken the vow of poverty for himself and keeps it strictly – but, you simpleton, that doesn't prevent the monastery from having property for itself.»

«And so you, holy brothers, swallow all this magnificent wine not for yourselves, but for the monastery.»

«May the Lord be merciful to you sinners,» said the monk, with difficulty concealing his smile. «A drop of wine rarely touches our tongues. Only to-day, and in these times, we regale you sinful men in the name of the monastery and holy Mother Church, to whoso service you are consecrated.»

«Yes» – said the monk, in whose charge the superior had placed the peasant, and here is a new recruit. He must strengthen himself here to-day, and to-morrow be taught the military drill; he knows how to deal blows already.»

«Bravo!» cried all.

But the poor fellow was almost bewildered. Not until he had been almost compelled to swallow half a mug of wine did he awake from his stupor and feel a different spirit aroused within him.

The voices constantly grew harsher, the songs wilder the jests broader. It was nat only the newly arrived youth who now, with his back resting against a cask, and rigid limbs, sat motionless, gazing with staring eyes into vacancy, a victim of the excellent, wine the monk so lavishly poured into large mugs; older men – soldiers who had seen many lands and peoples, and won many battles with the wine-cup as well as the sword – bearded men inured to drink – had already been conquered by the wine-god.

But while the merry-making was going on in this subterranean paradise of monks, the pious father superior was engaged in very different affairs.

Not ten minutes had elapsed when the footsteps of a monk were heard coming down the long dark corridor.

The superior instantly threw himself on his knees before the picture, seized his rosary and began to pray aloud:

«Pater noster –»

Two minutes after the door opened and another priestly figure entered.

It was a tall, proud form that wore the Franciscan dress, a form which the first glance showed was not accustomed to the garb. The features were strongly marked; the shape and delicacy of the hands and feet betrayed aristocratic origin; the eyes sparkled with intellect, but also cunning, nay a certain gloomy expression.

When the new-comer saw the superior kneeling and praying so devoutly, he could not for the moment repress a scornful smile; but it was only a moment that the sarcastic expression rested upon the handsome countenance – it quickly regained its former grave dignity.

«Don't let me disturb you in the performance of your sacred duties, holy father,» said the new-comer. «I'll wait quietly till you have finished. Only I must remove this disguise which is no longer necessary and very oppressive.»

A royal robber

With these words, he threw back, with ill-concealed repugnance, the Franciscan robe and beside the kneeling superior stood Franz Egon, Prince of Fürstenberg, Bishop of Strassburg.

The superior finished his prayers, and rising, approached the bishop whom he greeted with great respect.

«Pardon me for keeping you waiting, your lordship,» said he, «but the rules of the Franciscan order are strict and severe.»

«But the men who obey it with so much faithfulness and punctuality as yourself are all the more holy and devout,» replied Franz Egon with a slight shade of sarcasm.

«That which is the ardent wish and desire of our hearts,» exclaimed the monk emphatically, «becomes a happy pastime.»

He kissed the scourge that hung by his side.

«And can we now finish our important consultations,» asked the bishop. «My secret residence of a week in your monastery will end to-morrow. I must return to France. The fruit is ripe, it must fall.»

«The most Reverend Lord Bishop has but to command!» replied the superior.

«Are we unheard?»

«As usual.»

«Well then the preparations for taking the city by surprise are all made.»

«Will the handful of men –»

«How many have you received into the monastery?»

«Sixty-five.»

«Very well, within the next few days, twice that number, clad in every conceivable disguise, will arrive.»

«But tne maintenance?»

«Has already been assured by France, and you know that while under the present heretical government your monastery is only a shadow, it will rise – when Strassburg is again a catholic city – to the first rank.»

«But what can this handful of men do in great German Strassburg?»

«Gently,» replied the bishop, with a proud, confident smile, «this handful of stout fellows, who do not fear, and would fight the devil himself, should we command, will not be alone. Günzer has an equal number. They are real fanatics, will not spare the babe at its mother's breast, and, if necessary, wade through seas of blood for holy Mother Church.»

«But the citizens and soldiers in the employ of the magistrates?»

«The citizens are poorly armed, badly disciplined, and partly ours. The soldiers are simply paid mercenaries, who have grown lazy and comfortable in peace.»

«But their commander?»

«Herr von Jenneggen?»

«Yes.»

«Has also been won over to our side. But that is not all; at the right hour, 30.000 men under General Montclar will appear before the city as if they had dropped from the clouds.»

«I don't understand.»

«Leave that to us, worthy father; to me, Louvois and the brave general I have just mentioned. You have to do as follows: Conceal the troops that have already arrived and receive those yet to come.»

«But what more? Ws have already provided for what you have just mentioned.»

«When the right time comes – when the hour has struck, the necessary leader for the troops will appear.»

«And how am I to know him?»

«By a letter and seal from my own hand.»

A royal robber

«Very well.»

«Then Günzer, who already has the majority of the magistrates under his control will manage some way to produce an outbreak at a meeting that has been prolonged until late at night. When this occurs our men will cry treason. The force Günzer has stationed in readiness will break in, arrest Frantz and his followers or cut them down if they resist. At the same time the resolute men concealed in your convent will rush out and take possession of the two principal gates of the city. Günzer has arranged to have fire break out in several houses to occupy the attention of the citizens and scatter them. Other signals will be made to the French cavalry; each man will take a foot soldier on the horse behind him; and before the citizens can assemble, before the city can recover from the surprise and terror, our men will be upon the walls of Strassburg.»

«God grant it,» said the superior. «But if the plan should fail, what will become of us and our monastery?»

«The Franciscan Order is not subject to any civil tribunal and – France is strong and grateful enough to reward brave allies for what they were ready to do for her.»

«Then let the affair take its own course as God wills!» exclaimed the superior. Our object is to tear Strassburg from the accursed heretics. The Eternal Trinity and the Holy Virgin will give us their blessing.»

«They will!» said the bishop solemnly, «they will, to that I say amen.»

VII.
The star of life.

The appreciation and longing for domestic happiness was nowhere deeper than in the family of Syndicus Frantz.

It was really beautiful to see how father, mother and daughter lived for and in each other.

But it was a pleasure to see how Hedwig and Alma vied with each other in the performance of household duties, the warm, sympathizing affection, with which both clung to the beloved husband and father.

Alma did not despair, though her heart was often very heavy. She had inherited the character of her father, who understood how, by firm principle, to keep what is unlovely, painful and confused in life within the narrowest limits, that space might be obtained for clear, free life.

But it required a firm, resolute character like hers not to lose courage; for affairs in Strassburg were becoming more and more confused, party strife more violent, attacks upon her father more bitter, the opposite party – with Günzer at its head – was incomprehensibly gaining more and more adherents among the magistrates.

Moreover the gulf between the Zedlitz family and her own constantly grew wider, as the old gentleman's time serving and leaning towards Catholicism became more and more marked.

Besides, of late – and this was the heaviest blow to Alma – Wenck had ceased to have any news of Hugo; nay, since yesterday, a mysterious rumor had spread through Strassburg, the news that Wenck had mysteriously disappeared.

The little man had been last seen at the meeting in the assembly-room of the tailor's guild, but he did not return home that night and had not been seen in Strassburg.

The excitement was great. Wenck had hated the Günzer faction, hated

A royal robber

France – at the assembly he had aided his fellow citizens to take a decided step – was it not possible that his enemies had puthimout of the way?

The matter made Syndicus Franz very uneasy; for he was sincerely attached to the comical and yet capable little man.

It was therefore no marvel that now – evening had closed in – he returned from his office and entered the room with a clouded brow.

The mother and daughter were startled on hearing the news that the little tailor, Wenck, was missing. Alma turned deadly pale. Wenck was the only person with whom Hugo maintained any communication, through Wenck alone had she sometimes received news of him.

The fears her father expressed about his disappearance alarmed her still more. It seemed as if the fate of both men were connected, and any misfortune that befell Wenck must be an evil omen for her absent lover.

If she could only have confessed her love to her parents and hoped for their kind consent, it would have relieved her tortured heart; for the anxiety of this poor little heart was increased by the conscientious scruples caused by the secret of her love.

Alma, dear, good child, had never before had a secret from her beloved parents. Her whole nature, her acts and movements were open to their eyes which were accustomed to look into the depths of her pure soul as if it were the bottom of a crystal lake.

But just for this very reason, this first concealment of anything, this first secret from her parents, seemed to Alma a heavy sin. And this burden increased in the same proportion as her rising anxiety for her lover.

Anxious as Hedwig was, it did not escape her maternal eye that some heavy grief was oppressing Alma. Alma's color varied rapidly from red to pale. Her self-command almost deserted her at the thought that her mother might have guessed, discovered her secret. She trembled from head to foot. Breath and speech failed and large tears filled her beautiful eyes. Hedwig' s eyes had also grown dim. Bending gently towards her daughter, she laid her hand on hers and said tenderly:

A royal robber

«Alma, my dear child, I have noticed for a long time that you were hiding some heavy sorrow in your heart.»

«Mother!» gasped the young girl, in great embarrassment.

«I know,» the mother continued, «that the fate which threatens your native city, whose existence, already numbered by centuries, is now imperiled, lies very near your heart, I know your faithful, loving nature, which grieves over the many hard trials your father is forced to undergo. My mother-heart tells me that there must be something else passing in your mind, something which of late has utterly robbed you of your former calmness, your unclouded cheerfulness. I know there is no room for aught of evil in your soul, so tell me, my child, what is it that so grieves you, causes so many secret struggles?»

«Mother!» faltered Alma, but a torrent of tears choked her voice, and weeping bitterly, she hid her face in Hedwig's lap.

Alma's sobs grew fainter and fainter. The mother stooped and tenderly kissed the daughter's luxuriant hair.

«Alma,» she began, in a low, tender tone, «my dear Alma, speak, speak freely. Candor is a great virtue. Usually only those rich in other virtues possess it. I am accustomed to find it in you.»

«Come,» Hedwig continued encouragingly, «many a misfortune might not have occurred, if people had had the courage to be frank – even when it was perhaps necessary to confess an error, a false step.»

Hedwig paused. A short silence ensued, then Alma said gently:

«Yes, dear mother, I have done something wrong and will throw myself down before you and confess it.»

Another silence followed. Hedwig was somewhat startled. She smiled through her tears; an inner voice said: «Your dear, good child cannot really have to accuse herself of any wrong.»

She gently stroked her daughter's soft hair and pressing a loving kiss upon her brow, whispered:

A royal robber

«Pour out your heart to your mother, my child; your grief and your cares are mine.»

Alma drew a long breath; the words inspired her with wonderful courage. And now, while she hid her blushing-face in her mother's lap, came the confession of her love for Hugo von Zedlitz and tine still harder one of her first and only meeting with him.

When the daughter, still hiding her blushing face in her hands and her mother's lap, had finished, the latter said after a short silence:

«Dear child, you have certainly committed a great error as well as a great imprudence. It was imprudent to give your heart to a man, with whose family we stand on an extremely doubtful footing, nay, one of almost positive enmity. But it was a great error not to sooner reveal your feelings to your parents – at least to your mother, whose love you well know.»

Amid tears and entreaties for forgiveness, Alma acknowledged both accusations; but could she help her love, the pure holy feeling of the warmest affection, which – without her will or knowledge – had gradually taken root unnoticed in her heart? Was she to blame because Hugo's patriotic feeling had produced so strong an impression upon her, that she was compelled to esteem a youth whose worth was universally acknowledged, that some strange emotion had drawn her with irrisistible power toward the noble, handsome young man, who as a boy – in the happier days when the Zedlitz and Frantz families were warm friends – had been her daily companion?

Embarrassed – yet secretly sustained by the consciousness of her innocence and the purity of her love – Alma now eloquently represented all this to her mother.

«And father?» asked Alma anxiously.

«Leave it to me, my child!» replied Hedwig, «to find a fitting moment to confide your secret to him. He must know it as well as I, then we will both discuss what is to be done.»

Alma sighed heavily, threw her arms around her mother's neck and whispered:

A royal robber

«And you forgive me?»

«Yes, my child, for I am sure my Alma will henceforth have no secrets from her mother.»

«And you don't condemn my love for Hugo?»

«I think it unwise that, under existing circumstances, you should have yielded to it – but I will not condemn it. The woman who has never felt the yearning of love, knows not the holy spirit of faith and virtue. Love is the strength and life of woman, her religion, her most sacred duty, her highest glory.»

«Mother, mother! How I thank you!» exclaimed Alma, with an eager embrace, «you have given me courage, strength, hope, you have restored the happiness of my life.»

«Then guard it in your pure, faithful heart,» said the mother, «and pray God to direct this affair to a happy issue for all.»

Alma followed her mother's advice.

VIII.
The deliverer

Günzer was at home. There was no meeting of the magistrates that morning, yet he sat in his private study engrossed in business.

The net in which Strassburg was to be imprisoned at a single pull grew smaller and smaller; but the nearer the day approached the more impatient and urgent became his French patrons, Louis XIV and his all powerful minister, Louvois.

Franz Egon, Prince of Fürstenberg and Bishop of Strassburg, could also hardly wait for the time, when he could enter Strassburg and its cathedral as their ecclesiastical master.

What a double victory – for Rome and France – he would then celebrate.

But a better part had been assigned to the Lord Bishop than to Günzer; while the latter was in the very crater of the conspiracy, Franz Egon remainned far away in his episcopal palace; while Günzer was exposed to all the changes of a capricious destiny, and had to use the utmost cunning to steer the ship of State through the countless rocks, surrounded by treason and peril – the bishop directed affairs at his ease from his arm-chair, while drawing the pleasures of life to the last drop.

Günzer possessed an unusual capacity for labor. His office as clerk occupied much of his time and yet he also had to maintain an extensive secret correspondence with Louvois and the Bishop of Strassburg, attend to the dangerous task of bribing the magistrates and influential citizens, manage the negotiations with the superior of the Franciscan monastery, in a word, direct the whole conspiracy.

Günzer only allowed himself three or four hours rest at night; during the day not a moment was unoccupied. He had but one recreation, the thought of the sums already obtained – the bribe money so lavishly sent by France – and the calculation of the honor and power to which he would rise by giving up his native city to the French king? Would he not instantly be given power

A royal robber

to crush his enemies – above all the Frantz family – and trample them in the dust?

But the pressure of business now left him little time for such pleasures – they were principally connected with Alma who had so coldly rejected his suit – the conspiracy was to break out in a few days. The Franciscan monastery was already filled with stout men, and his own soldiers had also been secretly admitted in disguise and placed in secure quarters.

Günzer was daily expecting the last decisive command from Louvois. A letter from the French general, Montclar, had just arrived. In it General Montclar announced that he was approaching Strassburg with a considerable force. Günzer and the superior must hold themselves in readiness. The surprise, however, must appear as if it had come from the citizens, since the Most Christian king wished to avoid any apparent deed of violence. His entrance into Strassburg after the work was done, must have the semblance of hastening to the aid of Strassburg in response to the summons of its worthy inhabitants.

Günzer was still occupied in deciphering this letter, when his servant announced the commandant of the city, Herr von Jenneggen.

He hastily concealed the despatch, while he sent word to the officer to enter.

«Welcome, Herr von Jenneggen!» he exclaimed, advancing to meet his visitor. «What gives me the pleasure of a visit from you at this unusual hour?»

«I think it my duty, Herr Günzer, to call your attention to an incident which has aroused my suspicions. You know my interest in the welfare of Strassburg,»

«You have given ample proofs of it.»

«Well, the times are difficult, the situation of the city is critical.»

«Certainly! Because foolish men, in their passion are blind to its real welfare.»

«But who can tell to what passion will lead, especially in politics?»

A royal robber

«Do we not see this in our so-called patriots?»

«We understand each other, Herr Günzer.»

Günzer smiled. He knew why Herr von Jenneggen had lately received through Frischmann – in consequence of Günzer's influence at the French court – a valuable snuff-box set with diamonds, and a commission for his son in the French army.

«I therefore think it my duty,» continued the officer, «to redouble my watchfulness in these dangerous times. The reports of the sentinels at the gates are suspicious.»

«How so?»

«An unusually large number of Franciscan monks and workmen are entering the city.»

Günzer could scarcely conceal his embarrassment. The disguised men were doubtless those concealed in the monastery and quarters selected by him and he dared not give even Jenneggen any information on this subject.

The officer's position was still doubtful. He was yet in the service of the city, and had sworn allegiance to her.

«And could there be anything suspicious in that,» he asked with apparent indifference. «It is probably mere accident.»

«That is scarcely possible!» observed the officer, dawing a package of papers from his breast pocket. «Here are the reports of the last week from the gates. Be kind enough to examine them yourself.»

Günzer, who was really not a little perplexed, bent over the papers to conceal the anxiety that could not fail to be expressed in his features.

«See,» continued the zealous officer, «everyday, at every gate, Franciscan monks entered, and the monastery contains only a few – while workmen –»

«Of what trade?»

«Principally tailors.»

«Tailors? And do they find work?»

A royal robber

«At once apparently; for none went out,»

«My dear Herr von Jenneggen,» said Günzer, who meantime had completely regained his self-command, «accept, in the name of our good city, the thanks due your zeal. But it seems to me that this is a mere accident. Nevertheless I will keep the reports and place them before the magistrates. You will, until then, have the kindness to maintain strict silence in regard to the affair.»

«Certainly,» replied Herr von Jenneggen, rising. «I merely came to do my duty.»

The two gentlemen bowed to each other and the officer left the room. Günzer accompanied him to the stairs; but when once more in his room, said angrily:

«Simpleton! That confounded snuff-box has made him so zealous that he was on the point of discovering and betraying our conspiracy. As if it were not my affair and that of the guardians of the people.» And he returned to General Montclar's letter.

But Syndicus Frantz was engaged at the same time with an extremely important missive which had reached his hands in a very mysterious way. He found it in his room, but no one in the house knew who had brought it.

But it was not how the paper had come there which principally surprised the Syndicus, its contents made his hair stand on end. In short, it revealed to his horror, a conspiracy against Strassburg.

The lines ran as follows:

«Treachery threatens Strassburg. The enemies of our native city have smuggled large numbers of soldiers into the Franciscan monastery where they are now concealed. The conspirators, who are in league with others outside, may break forth at any moment. The manner and time in which the plot is to be executed, the writer of these lines does not know. But the whole can and will be baffled if the monastery can be captured; this however must be speedily and secretly done. The writer of this letter, a true patriot, eager for the welfare of Strassburg, his native city, will therefore undertake the venture with a few trusted friends tomorrow night at eleven o'clock, and please God, execute the task, even if he should sacrifice his life. Prepare to keep an insurrection of the evil-disposed confined within the limits of the city. You will find armed allies at the assembly room of the tailor's guild at ten o'clock to-morrow evening. Take them to the monastery as noiselessly as possible, that they may afford us help in case of need. Love and our native land! is the countersign. Nothing must be done publicly, neither magistrates nor armed power called upon for aid, or all will be lost. May God strengthen and protect us.»

When Frantz had read these lines, he stood rigid with amazement and terror. Could it really be true, could treachery have approached so near hapless Strassburg? The affair looked probable, the monks were implicated, so doubtless was the Bishop of Strassburg.

But yet? Might not the letter be a snare to involve the Syndicus in some mad venture? Might not his enemies be trying to compromise him?

After a period of calm reflection, he no longer entertained a doubt of what was to be done.

The same hour the Syndicus hastened to a secret consultation with his most trusted friends and allies.

The evening of the following day closed in upon Strassburg. The day itself had passed like any other in the same routine of occupation and business.

«Watch!» said a little man wrapped in a dark cloak and with a broad-brimmed hat on his head, who stood at a street corner – directly opposite the Franciscan monastery – to another figure. «Watch! It's just striking nine, a couple come every evening at this hour. Are our men on the watch?»

The second figure pointed to another street corner, but It was too dark to see anything distinctly.

A death-like silence brooded over the street. Arising storm had driven people to their houses, and moreover, according to a good old custom, every respectable citizen sought his home before nine o'clock.

Suddenly both started in surprise.

A royal robber

It seemed as if they heard strange sounds from the monastery.

«What's that?» whispered the shorter of the two.

«Singing,» replied the other.

The sounds seemed to come from a long, long distance, almost as if out of a subterranean chamber.

«That is in the monastery,» the little man began.

«It almost seems so – and yet that is impossible.»

«Deuce take me,» whispered the the little man, «if that isn't one of our wildest drinking songs!»

«And yet it comes from the monastery?»

«Why not? They think the world is asleep and are celebrating a jolly revel with their comrades the soldiers, in the vaults below the building.»

«In the monastery?»

«Oh! innocence. As if the Evil One with all his crimes did not have his favorite abode in monasteries.»

«Oh! shame,» cried the younger, «these false saints unite all other vices to the crime of treason.»

«It is bad enough that such should be the case with the standard bearers of the Christian religion,» said the other.

«Who knows what good it may do!» rejoined the little man. «To us for instance this singing of dissolute, drinking songs can only be welcome.»

«Why so?»

«Because I am firmly convinced that we shall find the whole nest, monks and soldiers in the deepest intoxication.»

«That would certainly be well – it might spare much blood-shed.»

«I know that, I know soldiers and monks from the campaigns I have fought. With one it is blows and then robbery, burning, carousing – with the other prayers and then – the same thing only in a different way.»

A royal robber

«Hush!» said the other. «I think I hear footsteps.»

«Now is the time,» whispered the little man, giving a low whistle. At the same moment the two muffled figures moved forward, so that anyone who entered the monastery would be obliged to pass close by them.

Almost at the same instant two dark figures turned the corner of the street.

Not until they were close to the muffled forms did the latter perceive that they were two Franciscan monks.

«Blessed be the holy Francis,» said the younger.

«Amen!» replied two, deep, harsh voices.

«Are you going into the monastery, dear brother?»

The figures were silent, apparently perplexed.

«Aha!» said the young man, «the wolves are already in the trap.» He repeated his question in the French language.

It was now understood and answered in the affirmative.

«Then follow me,» said the muffled figure.

At the same instant a second low whistle was heard.

«What's that?» asked one of the monks in his native language. But he had not finished the question when he and his comrade were seized by powerful arms and at the same Instant gags were thrust into the mouths of both.

The result of the capture showed two well-armed Frenchmen concealed under the monks' cowls.

Far away as if from the depths of the earth rose the smothered notes of merry drinking songs. It was now pouring in torrents, and darkness, deep, silent night brooded over everything.

Hugo von Zedlitz and Wenck – for it was they who had captured the two French soldiers disguised as Franciscan monks – now went, followed by their prisoners and the armed citizens who guarded them, to a side street. Here stood an old, gloomy, dilapidated house, to which nothing could be more welcome than such a dark, rainy night as the present, since in the light of day it must have been ashamed of itself even among the modest houses in the neighborhood. The owner of the house was one of Wenck's friends, also a tailor and good patriot, and now a confederate. Hugo and Wenck had formed a conspiracy since the night they met at the Snake's Hole.

Wenck was surprised and perplexed at the danger threatening his native city, but like Hugo himself, quickly resolved at any cost and the exposure of his own life, to save Strassburg by prompt action.

Both men instantly perceived the difficulty of the task. All that was to be done must be performed without the knowledge and aid of the authorities for the greater portion of these magistrates were not to be trusted, nay it was even to be supposed that Günzer, together with the whole French party, belonged to the plot.

Thus poor Strassburg was robbed of her natural defenders; for though Syndicus Frantz and the patriots could be relied upon, it was to be anticipated that if the affair became known, the superior of the Franciscan monastery would instantly hear of it and be on his guard.

Thus the government must be left out of the question – the existence of the city was threatened and must be saved, so what remained save independent action.

Hugo von Zedlitz and Wenck were the right men for this.

But could they alone capture the nest of treason in which a large number of well-armed soldiers was concealed? Strong support was needed; the aid of a large number of patriotic men and also – stout arms.

This is why Wenck disappeared. But if he became invisible to the public he was by no means inactive. The little tailor worked in the darkness like a mole and soon almost tlie whole tailor's guild was in the couspiracy with him.

But Wenck did still more; as soon as he was sure of a number of patriots, he glided, supplied with all the money he could raise on his house and little property, into the country. Here he gained fresh allies whom he sent to

247

A royal robber

Strassburg under the pretext that they were tailors looking for work in the city.

Each one had the address of some tailor, who instantly set him to work, while secretly procuring the necessary weapons.

The plan formed by Hugo and Wenck did not require any regularly organized military force, only a number of strong, brave men.

This was the reason that the zealous commander of the city, Herr von Jenneggen, had noticed in the reports sent from the gates the large number of tailors seeking work.

So the plot had matured. Hugo undertook its execution. The monastery must be surprised, the monks and superior placed in custody, the French soldiers taken prisoners or slain.

Wenck's discovery that every evening at nine o'clock, two soldiers disguised as monks were smuggled into the monastery, was an important one. Hugo formed his whole plan upon this fact.

If these men – who undoubtedly possessed a password – fell into his hands, this password and the Franciscan dresses would procure him and a companion admittance. If he could once gain an entrance through the outer gate, the rest of the affair caused him no anxiety.

The disguised monks were in his hands. In their pockets papers were found among which was one containing the desired password.

They might now set out, especially as Syndicus Frantz had been informed of everything by the secret letter. Hugo and Wenck knew they could rely upon him.

By his mediation the patriotic magistrates were ready with their followers to take prompt measures in case their aid was needed. Almost the whole tailor's guild, well armed and ready for battle, was in the assembly-room with the Syndicus.

Yet nothing was seen or heard of all this. Strassburg seemed sunk in deep repose. Night and darkness, rest and silence, surrounded it.

A royal robber

Eleven o'clock struck. Noiselessly as If they had sprung from the earth, dark forms filled the streets near the monastery, the nooks and angles of the houses.

The bell at the convent gate rang.

It was sometime before the little square window, cut in the gate, slowly opened and a voice sleepily asked who was disturbing the rest of the monastery at so late an hour?

«Two sons of holy Francis.» was the stammering reply of a monk in the French language.

«At this hour?» was returned in a tone of angry surprise.

«*Mort de ma vie!*» retorted the other, «we got as wet as fish on our way to the city and stopped to refresh our inner man. *Parbleu!* The devil take this masquerading. Open the gate, reverend brother, that we may get rid of these cursed cowls. We're hungry and thirsty too!»

His voice was that of a drunken man.

«Speak lower!» said the monk with evident anxiety.

«Pshaw!» replied the mock Franciscan loudly, «it's dark, the dogs of citizens are asleep. What's the use? Open.»

The porter, scarcely aroused from a gentle shimber, angry and yet afraid that some nocturnal pedestrian or accidental passer-by might hear this more than suspicious conversation, was in the greatest perplexity.

He dared not turn the new-comers away, they were doubtless the men expected at nine o'clock, who had been belated by the rain and drunkenness. Everything was endangered by their condition.

«And yet, in the darkness, who could tell that they were the right ones?»

«Let me feel your sleeve!» said the porter, putting his hand out through the window.

He touched the rough, heavy cloth of the Franciscans.

«The pass-word?»

A royal robber

«St. Croix de Bejar!»

This was correct, the porter uttered a sigh of relief. He now had an undoubted right to admit them, and once in the monastery there was no longer any danger of treachery.

«Well? Will you be quick?» cried the drunken soldier.

The keys at the monk's belt rattled.

At the same moment there was a low, almost inaudible whistle.

Now the heavy bolt was pushed back, the key turned, the little door opened.

But the drunken man must have leaned awkwardly against it, he stumbled and fell upon the porter who, starting back a little, caught him in his arms.

«Brother!» murmured the soldier, embracing the monk with a strength that alarmed him.

But ere he could utter a word his terror was to be increased; for, with the speed of lightning, a gag was thrust into his mouth, and ropes bound arms and feet. He saw a throng of dark figures press through the door entrusted to his care, then was dragged into the inner court and laid face downward on the ground.

Soon a regular foot -fall showed that a sentinel was pacing up and down beside him.

But Hugo and Wenck were obliged to repeat their stratagem at the inner door.

Certain of success, they knocked; but to their terror found that they had made an error in calculation.

According to the regulations of the monastery, it was the duty of the porter at the outer door to announce all arrivals at the door of the building in the courtyard.

Besides the cunning brother stationed there knew that any little noises made by drunken men within the courtyard would cause no danger.

He therefore harshly repelled the expectation that lie would open the door at so late an hour with the words:

«Drunken vagabonds! Sleep off your carouse in the open air.»

The pretended monks raged. In vain, the porter made no answer.

Hugo and Wenck were in no little perplexity.

What was to be done now? Hugo had not thought of this.

He was discussing the matter with Wenck, when the singing heard before echoed on their ears again, only considerably nearer and more distinct.

Then Hugo, as if his patience were exhausted, exclaimed angrily: «*Mort de ma vie!*» and began to ring the bell as if the monastery were on fire.

This produced an effect. The startled monk not only opened the door, but the noise summoned the superior, who crimson with anger, was pouring forth a torrent of invectives when to his terror, he saw both wings of the door pressed open, himself and the porter surrounded and the wide space filled with armed men.

All this was the work of a few seconds.

The superior and porter were also bound and gagged.

The way was opened; but now cunning was at an end and the sword must speak.

A portion of the men, according to preconcerted arrangement, took possession of the entrances. All the others, sword in hand, followed Hugo and Wenck, who had thrown off their troublesome disguises and appeared armed to the teeth.

It was a motley throng, undisciplined, armed partly with swords, partly with pikes and guns; but men who had strong hands and brave hearts.

They moved quietly through the long, lonely corridors.

The doors of most of the cells stood open, but they were empty. From the distance, out of the depths of the earth, the faint notes of singing were heard.

A royal robber

Hugo and Wenck followed the sound.

It grew more and more distinct and the voices seemed hoarser and wilder; songs, laughter and curses, like some wild revel in a camp.

Words could now be clearly distinguished.

Hugo paused – they had only a flight of cellar stairs to descend.

«Brothers, friends,» he whispered, «all depends on this moment. We do not know how many there are; probably two to our one. But we do know that the majority are old, trained soldiers, who understand how to wield their blades, even when their heads are heated with wine. We are only simple citizens or plain workmen, but – we are fighting for a just cause, against treason and rascality – this must give us strength and courage. So forward, for God and our native land! Strike down all who resist, dead ,or alive, the whole troop must fall into our hands.»

With these words Hugo kicked open the iron door and, with the shout «For God and our native land,» he and his followers rushed upon the startled revelers.

But Hugo's anticipations had been correct; though Friend Bacchus was celebrating a great triumph, and heads were as heavy as throats were hoarse, the old warriors had scarcely perceived flashing swords and glittering weapons, than their own sabers flew from their sheaths and a desperate struggle began.

It was a wild, terrible scene. In the gloomy, vaulted apartment, scarcely lighted by the flaring torches, among huge casks, overthrown tuns and mugs, here, where the gayest mirth had just prevailed, a fierce conflict was now raging. Drunkenness and fury distorted the faces of the combatants – death-like pallor and terror were depicted on the countenance, of the monks, who had all taken refuge between and under the wine butts.

Already wounded and dying men lay on the floor. Hugo and Wenck fought like lions, but they and their party were forced to give way more and more.

Now they were pressed to the stairs, now, still fighting, were compelled to retreat towards the outer corridor.

A royal robber

Hugo and Wenck fought in front and gave way only step by step. Swords whizzed fiercely around their heads – they paid no heed. More of their followers fell wounded, they did not see it; death surrounded them in a thousand forms – they did not care. Yielding to superior numbers, they had now been forced out of the cellar, the long corridors of the monastery were already echoing with the clank of swords and the rattling of shots.

Then Hugo's ear caught the sound of bells ringing an alarm from the steeples of the city.

The decisive moment had come, and with it, Syndicus Frantz, at the head of the tailor's guild, that would no longer be restrained, rushed into the monastery.

Wild shouts of Joy greeted them. With redoubled strength Hugo now pressed forward. The soldiers gave way before his energy – a short resistance and the monastery with all its inmates – dead and alive – was in Hugo's hands.

IX.
The happiness of love.

Of course on the following morning all Strassburg knew what had occurred during the previous night. The excitement was terrible. The wrath of the people and their fury against the Franciscan monks knew no bounds.

The magistrates, to prevent an attack upon the monastery, were obliged to surround it with a guard of soldiers.

Even the bishop was bitterly cursed; for every one was morally certain that he had secretly formed and directed the whole conspiracy.

It was fortunate for Günzer that nobody suspected his connection with the intended treason; the excited citizens would surely have attacked his house and hacked to pieces or hung the already hated man.

Of course Günzer feigned the utmost indignation; nay the first motion he made the following morning, in the hastily convened session of the great council, was the immediate expulsion of the Franciscan monks from the city.

Günzer, who was the very embodiment of cunning, promised, as the city did not wish to be stripped of its few soldiers, to provide reliable people to serve as the priests' escort. He kept his word and in this way got rid of part of the men, whom in the bishop's name, he had smuggled into Strassburg to aid in surprising the city, and whose discovery now threatened to betray his baseness and thus entail upon him destruction and death.

All Strassburg rang with young Zedlitz's praise, his name ran from lip to lip. Every one now asserted that he had always known and declared that Hugo had been unjustly banished.

If the young man had appeared he would have been greeted everywhere with loud acclamations. The enthusiastic populace felt the utmost love for him and little Wenck. But both were too wise and modest to desire to celebrate such a triumph; nay Hugo, in his nice sense of honor, insisted upon presenting himself before the magistrates as a condemned man.

A royal robber

And he actually executed this design early the following morning.

The perplexity he thus caused the Günzer faction was very great, especially when, as the rumor spread abroad that the deliverer of the city, the innocent exile, had given himself up to his enemies – the guilds all assembled, and, led by the tailors, marched with banners flying to the Rathhaus, loudly and violently demanding the revocation of the sentence of banishment and the release of their hero and favorite.

No course was left the Günzer party except to put the best possible face on the matter, especially as Frantz and his adherents were on the side of the people.

Hugo vonZedlitz was brought forward and received permission to defend himself against the former accusation, which he did with all the power of truth. His words were plain and simple, but omnipotent by the weight of conviction, the fire of a holy enthusiasm, the ardor of a pure and noble patriotism which they expressed.

While the youth was defending himself with noble pride and his simple words rushed from his lips in a torrent, the mob outside the building, raging furiously, shouted with its thousand voices:

«Liberty for Hugo von Zedlitz! Freedom for the savior of the city! Down with traitors!»

Many of the council trembled, terrified by their own evil consciences and the danger threatening them.

The longer the session lasted; the more wildly and fiercely the mob raged and roared, like a surging sea in the streets.

At last the central window of the Rathhaus opened, the ruling Ammeister appeared at it and amid a deathlike stilless announced – that Hugo von Zedlitz had been found innocent, the sentence of banishment was revoked and he himself restored to liberty.

From thousands and thousands of throats rang a simultaneous:

«Hurrah! hurrah! hurrah!»

A royal robber

The leaders of the guilds passed into the Rathaus, and when they returned with Hugo the cheers seemed as if they would never end.

It was the finest triumphal procession Strassburg had ever witnessed.

When he passed the house occupied by Syndicus Frantz, two female figures were standing at one of the windows, waving white handkerchiefs – like the women and girls in almost all the houses – to greet the savior of the beloved city.

How Hugo's lieart thrilled with happiness, how overjoyed Alma was, she laughed, exulted, yet tears rolled down her cheeks. But when the procession had passed, she sank into her mother's arms, sobbing aloud.

«Dear, dear child!» said the mother, pressing a kiss upon her beloved daughter's hair. But she let her have her fill of weeping, for these were tears of the highest, purest, most sacred joy.

Two hours later the dinner-table in the Syndicus' house stood ready. But to-day instead of three plates as usual, there were five.

Who the guests were to be neither mother nor daughter knew, Syndicus Frantz had merely sent word to have seats ready for two guests and to set forth everything that the kitchen and cellar contained.

Now all the preparations were made; the table laid, the dishes cooked, the best wine placed on a side table – but the Syndicus and his guests did not appear. Alma was alone in the room. Yesterday a mountain of grief had oppressed her heart, yesterday she supposed her lover far away, trembled with the fear that no opportunity would offer itself by which he could prove to his enemies and all Strassburg the injustice they had done him and that he was no traitor, but on the contrary possessed a heart full of ardent love for his native country! And to-day?

Alma was so absorbed in her reverie that she did not hear the low knock at the door, which was now repeated for the third time.

Not until the door gently opened and a man's figure appeared, did she start from her dreams.

A royal robber

But! Good Hevens! What was this? Was she awake or asleep?

Alma passed her hand across her brow – the vision did not vanish, she was not dreaming, but awake and this, this – was…

«Hugo!» she joyously exclaimed and – «Alma, dear, dear Alma!» now escaped young Zedlitz's lips as he hurried towards her.

Alma, in her joy and surprise, could scarcely understand what had happened; it was her lover who stood before her – it was Hugo von Zedlitz who ventured to greet her in her parents' house.

«Thank God that you are back again!» said Alma with radiant eyes, as she eagerly clasped his proffered hand. Hugo shook it warmly.

«Yes, His name be praised!» he replied, «and I hope not to go away again without you!»

«And you have ventured,» she said, her heart throbbing with fear, «to come directly to this house without my father's –»

«No!» he feplied, «I should not have dared to do so, but when I left the Rathaus this' morning your father invited me to visit him at this hour.»

«My father!» exclaimed Alma in joyful surprise.

«Yes!»

«And he is no longer angry with you because you belong to the Zedlitz family?»

«Syndicus Frantz was and is a man of honor,» said Hugo gravely. «He felt that bitter injustice had been done me – he has convinced himself that my intentions towards Strassburg are honest and it seems to me as if he wishes»

«To atone for the wrong done you in his absence by the magistrates!» cried Alma joyously. «Oh! that is like my dear father!»

«And indeed,» said Hugo, his eyes sparkling with joy, «he can do so in the fullest measure. Do you know how?»

«Hugo, Hugo!» faltered the young girl, while deep blushes lent her sweet face the charm of girlish bashfulness.

A royal robber

«And how?» repeated the youth, taking her hands and drawing her gently towards him – «tell me?»

«By giving our love his blessing!»

«Yes, by giving our love his blessing,» exclaimed Hugo rapturously, and suddenly he pressed his lips to hers, clasping the lovely girl in his arms as if he would never release her again.

A few minutes after the doors at both ends of the room opened almost at the same instant, and while Hedwig entered at one, two men appeared on the threshold of the other.

It was Syndicus Frantz and the worthy tailor, Franz Blasius Wenck.

«Why Hugo! So the young fellow is here already!» exclaimed Syndicus Frantz, who to-day, after a long time, was once more radiant with happiness and joy.

Hedwig stood motionless with surprise.

«Yes, stare!» cried the Syndicus, turning to the mother and daughter, «stare because I have admitted the heir of the Zedlitz family to my house and invited him to dinner. But I will try to do all in my power to atone for the wrong Strassburg has inflicted upon Hugo. He is the preserver of our native city, the hero of the day; he has saved Strassburg at the peril of his life and I should despise myself if I extended the hatred that divides the fathers to my enemy's son.»

And holding out his hand to young Zedlitz, he added:

«Welcome, Hugo; I was your father's friend when you were still a child, before political feuds separated us. Take me once more as your paternal friend, and look upon my hou.se as your own. And now, he continued, turning to his wife and daughter, who were still standing speechless with joyful surprise – «welcome the old, yet new friend of our house.»

Hedwig and Alma did not need to be asked a second time, though Alma was so bewildered by all this that she could scarcely utter an intelligible word.

«But who is your second guest?» asked Hedwig.

A royal robber

«Who?» exclaimed the Syndicus, «the man to whom, next to Hugo, belongs the honor of the day! Our worthy Wenck!»

«Too much honor! Too much honor! Herr Syndicus!» cried the tailor and his short figure with the head sunk between the shoulders looked so comical as he bowed again and again, that none of those present could help laughing. «What I did was my duty. I am only glad that the affair turned out so well, and our brave young friend's honor was restored. Who knows what good it may do!»

The party now proceeded to dinner. It was not luxurious, but admirably arranged and accompanied with good wine.

The young people were perfectly happy, Hedwig alone seemed somewhat troubled. The Syndicus, in his own joy, did not notice it for a long time. Not until the meal was over and many a toast had been prosed: «The happiness and welfare of Strassburg! The German native land! The brave deliverer of the city,» and «the Frantz family,» did he notice his wife's grave face.

Bending towards his faithful companion he asked.

«What is the matter, Hedwig?»

She smiled. «Not much. Only a thought was passing through my mind.»

«And what thought?» asked the Syndicus gayly – «a good one I am sure. You have inspired many a good thought during my life.»

«Do you think so?»

«Certainly ! We men, in hastily pursuing things at a distance, often forget those which are close at hand. Therefore a good, sensible wife is a real blessing; if we seek to soar on the wings of our enthusiasm into the realms of infinite space, she seizes us by the feet and pulls us gently back, saying: 'see, my friend, there is still so much to be done here.' And we are obliged to confess that she is right. Many good things are required in our immediate neighborhood which we should have overlooked but for our wives. True, a man's thoughts often give depth and space to a woman's, but in return the wife's often inspire the man's with warmth and practical direction.»

A royal robber

Tears sparkled in the eyes of both. They looked at each other, bent forward and exchanged a loving kiss.

«But your thought! " exclaimed the Syndicus gayly.

«Why,» replied Hedwig, «with the best intentions we are always somewhat selfish.»

«Well?» exclaimed the Syndicus laughing – «what does that mean?»

«A petition.»

«Then speak, wife.»

«Well then, as a wise woman, I should like to profit by this favorable mood.»

The old gentleman laughed heartily, and then asked: «In what way?»

«Why,» replied Hedwig, «you might allow each of us to make some request which you must promise to grant.»

Hugo and Alma blushed scarlet as the smiling mother uttered these words.

«Very well,» said the Syndicus, «since God has given me so happy a day, I will gladly contribute to the joy of others. What do you think, Wenck?»

«Certainly, Herr Syndicus, who knows what good it may do!»

«Very well then,» cried Frantz gayly, «but who is to begin?»

«Mother! mother!» cried Alma in indescribable embarrassment, turning pale as death.

«Well then, begin,» said the Syndicus. «What petition shall I grant you?»

«To speak when our young friend the deliverer of our native city, has spoken.»

«Be it so. Well, Hugo, what is your request?»

Hugo rose from his seat; a noble, manly earnestness was depicted In his features, and his eyes sparkled with wondrous brilliancy.

«Yes,» he said, «I have a request to make, noble man, to you who in my childhood and now once more have received me with fatherly kindness; but,

A royal robber

Herr Syndicus, this is no light jest, as you perhaps suppose, but a grave, important petition on which the happiness of my whole life depends. In one word, my friend» – here Hugo extended his hand to the old man – «make me the happiest of mortals, make me your son, give me your daughter, my dear, beloved Alma?»

Syndicus Frantz looked as if a thunderbolt had struck him. He would have expected the heavens co fall sooner than this request. It was really impossible for him to regain his self control immediately. But what most perplexed the usually calm man was the very singular conduct of those who surrounded him.

Hedwig did not seem at all surprised, but smiled at her husband quietly and confidently as if to say: Come, consent; they love each other so tenderly, this is all that was wanting to our domestic happiness.

Wenck's face also clearly expressed: «Yes, who knows what good it may do.»

And Alma?

The lovely girl had started up, thrown herself at her father's feet and was now gazing into his face with such radiant, yet imploring eyes that the old gentleman felt a strange emotion – an emotion like that experienced when he had first looked deep down in Hedwig's eyes.

«But you, you!» cried the Syndicus to his wife, «are not you at all surprised?»

«No,» replied Hedwig, pressing a kiss upon her husband's brow. «Alma confessed her love to me a few days ago amid bitter tears. I was only waiting for a suitable opportunity to tell you the secret of her little heart, but could find none, until to-day a happy fate so unexpectedly unites us, that I cannot help seeing God's hand in the work. So my request is: give them to each other.»

«And mine too, Herr Syndicus» exclaimed Wenck with innimitable pathos; «give them to each other; who knows what good it may do!»

All laughed heartily, but Syndicus Franz remarked:

«So your requests have melted into one,» and the tender look granted what the lips had not yet uttered.

A royal robber

«Yes,» they all exclaimed, «and our request is granted!»

«Ah!» sighed the Syndicus, «last night I, with the little ship of State, escaped a political conspiracy, to succumb to-day in my own house. Well, be it so! I give my blessing to your love. But the blessing of the church and the marriage must be deferred until the fate of our dear native city is decided. This is no time for love-making and festivity, it is the hour of watching and conflict. On the day that makes us free again, you, my children, shall become man and wife.»

Hugo did not take his leave until evening. Alma accompanied him to the door, but before she opened it, they again bade each other farewell.

«Do you know how I feel at this instant?» asked Alma gently.

«How?» replied Hugo.

«I feel,» continued Alma, as if in a dream, «as though I were pressing towards the light, like the seed that has Iain concealed in the earth during long, long winter, and is now kissed by the spring sun.»

«Your soul breathes immortality,» replied Hugo, «because you love.»

He pressed an ardent kiss upon the lips of his betrothed bride and hurried away.

He hastened out into the darkness – but the darkness was light to him, the tempest a gentle zephyr; for spring is the life of love, and love the spring of life. If you dwell in love, light and eternal spring will dwell in you!

A royal robber

Part V.
Dark paths

A royal robber

A royal robber

X.
The suitor.

The conspiracy centered in the monastery at Strassburg had indeed been an alarm to the citizens. Those who had hitherto remained blind to the designs of France were compelled to see the truth. The victory of the German party, the pariotic magistrates, was – at least for the moment – complete. Günzer went as the saying goes, up to his neck in water. He and his party had not only strongly compromised themselves by the banishment of Hugo von Zedlitz, but Günzer himself had barely, as if by a miracle, escaped the discovery of his treason. This consciousness oppressed the usually daring man, as the consciousness of their own guilt weighed upon many of the other magistrates, who through his influence had been bribed and bought by France.

The opposition to Syndicus Frantz and the patriotic party therefore died away during the first few days after the discovery of the conspiracy, nay the influence of the latter suddenly became predominant. They were backed by almost the entire population of the city.

What Hugo von Zedlitz had accomplished with his few followers, each individual soon attributed to his own energy, and this consciousness of heroic courage increased till it reached an open defiance of France.

The work of arming the guilds was prosecuted with great zeal. Their rooms were transformed into a military bureau. Contributions of money to procure weapons were taken, and certain Iionrs designated for drill. The citizens undertook the daiy of mounting guard three days out of the week.

All was fire and flame, only nothing was conducted in the right way, because everything was managed hastily and without reflection.

Little attention was paid to whether the weapons obtained were suitable or not, if they were only secured.

Whether the characters of many men afforded a guarantee that they could be relied on – in case of any serious struggle – was not asked, if only the ranks were well filled. There was little subordination too, as was natural. Ci-

A royal robber

tizen stood beside citizen, and – was not all voluntary service?

Besides each guild managed its own affairs; there was no thought of a firm bond between them, the subjection of all to one commander. Now and then, it is true, Hugo von Zedlitz's name was mentioned. But no steps were taken to make him their leader. One thought him too young, another too impetuous; some objected to his father, others to his noble name.

Strassburg, at least in name, was a little republic – but, where were the real republicans?

Günzer was clever enough to perceive this. So when the first surprise and alarm were over, he quickly regained his self-command. His diplomatic genius did not desert him and – accommodating himself to the situation and the moment – he looked on with a smile at the excited activity of his fellow citizens.

He well knew that the flickering light of this torch of popular excitement, that rises almost to the sky to sink again all the more speedily.

He was less at ease about the influence Hugo von Zedlitz had obtained over the populace, and which the young man – though, preparing for his legal examination, he led a very secluded life – knew how to maintain.

As soon as Günzer was certain that he had not been cornpi'omised, he softly and imperceptibly took the reins in his hands again. At first this was accomplished without opposition, nay even with the semblance of achange in his views. But the crafty man was only giving the people time to rave away their patriotic intoxication.

Of course Günzer's creatures, as well as himself, were not inactive. Money flowed into the pockets of the people and when were men inaccessible to bribes?

But having advanced so far, Günzer stood forth again with the old, nay even with redoubled energy to recover the lost ground. Frantz and his party struggled against this new attack with all their strength; but the period of bewilderment on the part of the undecided faction was over, and the old instinct as well as secret obligations led them to cling to their old leader.

266

A royal robber

And now ah event occurred which greatly strengthened the courage of the adherents of France and correspondingly depressed their opponents. The court of France, with the king at its head, while on a pleasure tour, suddenly appeared at the neighboring city of Colmar, settled there to make a prolonged stay, and overwhelmed Strassburg with tokens of friendship.

Frantz and his followers, Hugo von Zedlitz, Wenck, and many other honorable men, saw through the maneuver and warned their fellow citizens, but the cries of the Günzer faction and the vanity of the flattered burghers made their voices die away without avail.

Ere it could be foreseen, affairs in Strassburg were precisely in the same state that they had been before the conspiracy in the monastery. Günzer was again master of the magistrates.

Meantime, however, another drama which was confined within the limits of family life, had been secretly arranged under Günzer's eyes,

Günzer was of humble origin. When a child, his father filled the office of assessor at the meetings of the twenty guilds. But, as it was discovered that he betrayed and sold their secrets for money, he was expelled in disgrace.

A still darker shadow rested upon the Günzer family in consequence of an incident connected with the assessor's brother This man – the uncle of the present Günzer – was accused of counterfeiting. He fled to the other side of the Rhine but was seized and brought back to Strassburg. Scarcely, however, had he reached the bridge, when he escaped from his guards, sprang over the railing into the river, and was drowned.

As for Günzer – who now played so important a part in the affairs of Strassburg – his parents left him in the most destitute circumstances. He was a boy of intelligence, but of most crafty character. An orphan, he would doubtless have speedily gone to ruin, if the ancient family of Zorn von Plobsheim and that of von Bernhold, which was closely connected with the von Plobsheim, had not kindly received him.

Günzer was treated precisely like a child of the house, educated and placed in the various institutions of learning. His great ability soon displayed itself, so that his patrons not only loaded him with favors, but Herr von Bernhold placed him on almost precisely the same footing as his oldest son.

At the time Turenne was celebrating his great success in Alsace, Herr von Bernhold was sheriff of Strassburg and, as even then, it was necessary to use every precaution to protect the city against the ever increasing power of Louis XIV, a young man with good legal and diplomatic ability was sent to the French court. Herr von Bernhold selected for this purpose Günzer, believing that his numerous and constant favors had bound him to his interests.

After Herr von Bernhold had supplied his protégé with the necessary authority from the government, and provided him liberally with means to defray the expenses of the journey and a long residence in Paris, he explained the diplomatic career he was to inaugurate with the Comte de Reuvigny.

Comte de Reuvigny, in consequence of Herr von Bernhold's recommendation, procured Günzer the acquaintance of several prominent individuals at the court, especially that of the Marquis de Louvois. The minister's keen eye instantly read Günzer's character and as he saw in the young man an admirable tool for his extensive plans, honored him with his special confidence. Matters went so far that Günzer was called «*le mignon connu de la France.*»

But Günzer seemed to have used his influence only in favor of his native city. Absolute confidence on the part of the magistrates rewarded his skill and zeal, and thus it happened that on his return to Strassburg, he was appointed first clerk to the city and afterwards to the council. Of course all foreign affairs, especially the business with France, were entrusted to the clever diplomat, the man honored by the favor of Louvois. What a web of treachery Günzer spun, by what vast sums he was bribed to aid by voice in the meetings of the magistrates, the fall of Strassburg and the delivery of this important German city to France, we already know. Besides Louvois had promised him in case of success the office of Syndicus and Director of affairs in Strassburg.

This was Günzer's conduct to the government and his native city – but how did he treat his benefactor and his family?

When Günzer, as a young man, found himself a member of the family of

A royal robber

Herr von Bernhold, and the latter – his benefactor, his second father – reposed the utmost confidence in him, and also afterwards when the old gentleman died and his son, with whom Günzer had been educated, became the head of the family, he was entrusted, among other things, with the legal documents of the families of von Benihold and von Zorn. The clever young man was also specially commissioned to examine the papers and legal documents belonging to the Plobsheim property, about which many discussions had arisen.

But the younger Herr von Bernhold also died suddenly and unexpectedly. His widow, a member of the von Zorn family, was inconsolable. Robbed of her natural protector in these troubled times, she turned, assured that Günzer was devoted to her whole family, to him. and chose him for her trustee and adviser.

Now that tnis man was dead, Frau von Bernhold a widow, the family without head or support, Günzer purloined the papers relating to the Plobsheim property, in order to obtain possession of it himself.

Those were bright, beautiful, summer days which Alma, the lovely daughter of Syndicus Frantz, spent in a visit at Plobsheim.

Both families had long been on intimate terms, and Hedwig and Alma considered it a duty, after the recent death of the younger Herr von Bernhold, to console the young, deeply mourning widow.

Hedwig could not leave her husband; but Alma had time to devote several weeks to her afflicted friend, so Hedwig had brought her to Plobsheim some time before, and she willingly filled the place of an affectionate comforter.

Alma's frank, simple nature, which had inherited from the Syndicus the great art of confining everything unlovely, painful, and perplexing within the narrowest limits, that room might be obtained for a free, broad life, seemed to have bccn created for this office.

Yet it did not escape the notice of the Syndicus' daughter, that a cloud of deep sadness often rested upon the little lady's head. But this cloud – Alma's feminine keenness instanth' perceived – was not caused by grief, but by an-

A royal robber

xiety, which Frau von Bernhold had hitherto concealed from her young friend.

It was Sunday. Frau von Bernhold and Alma were sitting at a window of the stately castle of Plobsheim, the center of the beautiful estate of which the young widow was now sole mistress.

This young widow was still a beautiful woman. Her limbs and figure were delicately moulded, her features possessed a winning sweetness, so that she could justly be called a very pretty woman. Moreover she possessed a gentle loving nature, had been a tender, faithful wife to her husband, and was a good mother to her children.

In intellect, energy and vitality, it is true, Frau von Bernhold was far surpassed by Alma, but as she had retained her purity of soul, the difference in years between the two was scarcely perceptible.

They sat side by side, busied with some piece of fancy-work, while the gentle breeze bore the fragrance of the flowers and the sounds of the bells, ringing for afternoon service, through the open window.

There was something infinitely pathetic in the merry playing, laughing and shouting of little ones in the deepest mourning – the thought of the irreparable loss they had sustained, and Vv'hich they did not even suspect. And yet the sight of them must have afforded the mother consolation ; they were the living images of her dead husband – while they were a constant admonition to bestow on the poor, fatherless little ones a double share of tenderness, rear them to be worthy of their father.

When the children smiled, waved their little hands, and cried «mother!» tears gushed from the widow's eyes. Mother! echoed in the young widow's heart; and with the sound a voice also cried: «They no longer have a father, they have only you; you their mother, to provide for their education, their defense against the wicked world, the maintenance of their imperiled rights.»

And this was what pressed like a mountain on Frau von Bernhold's soul.

Alma did not utter a word, but let the poor lady cry quietly.

Günzer, as he declared, had not yet found among the family papers the documents that secured to the Bernhold family undoubted possession of the beautiful estate of Plobsheim.

Old Herr Bernhold, Günzer' s benefactor and second father, had long since declared with the utmost certainty, that these papers must be in existence, must at least be found somewhere.

Everything depended upon the discovery of the documents, since the *Reunions-Kammern* demanded them. If they could not be shown, the worst might be expected from the French government, whose unjust decisions in Alsace were well-known.

Thus the whole means of existence of the mother and that of her children was at stake; for though the family possessed other property, the estate of Plobsheim was by far the large portion.

Alma listened to this communication with a throbbing heart. She, too, now felt great anxiety about the young widow's situation; but another thought oppressed her still more, the thought that the whole affair was in Günzer's hands.

Günzer – of whose treacherous designs towards Strassburg the Frantz family were morally certain, though no piece of rascality had been proved against him, who had treated Hugo von Zedlitz so shamefully – was a terror to Alma. To her pure, innocent, childlike soul, there was something fiendish about him.

Alma covdd not help giving a slight warning against Günzer.

«Are you sure of his honesty?» she asked at last.

«Certain of his devotion to our family,» the widow replied. «Günzer owes all he is and has to my dead father-in-law and my own father. My husband loaded him with favors.»

Alma sighed, but was silent; it seemed wrong to shake such well-founded confidence.

At the same moment they saw two horsemen turn from the main road into the avenue leading to the castle.

A royal robber

The two ladies looked intently at them and turned pale.

They were Günzer and his brother-in-law, Kampffer.

Both ladies' hearts throbbed wildly, they knew not why.

A second glance through the window showed them that Kampffer went on as if intending to pass round the castle, while Günzer came towards it.

Alma begged permission to withdraw to her own room, and Frau von Bernhold, anticipating a business inteview, made no objection.

A few minutes after, Günzer entered.

«You doubtless bring me good news!» said the young widow, after the first greetings had been exchanged, while a faint flush – a pale reflection of her former bloom – suffused her cheeks, and in contrast with her black dress, gave her a peculiar charm.

«*Good* news certainly,» replied Günzer cordially, «if you recieve it favorably.»

«Why should I not» – continued Frau von Bernhold, «in my desolate, sorrowful position I greatly need it. You know this very well, Herr Günzer. But sit down.»

«In what does your news consist,» the widow resumed, «I suppose something in relation to Plobsheim.»

«It has one relation to it,» replied Günzer with a peculiar smile and a courtesy Frau von Bernhold was not in the habit of noticing in his manner.

«*One* relation.»

«Yes.»

«And the other?»

«Permit me, madame, to speak of that later.»

«As you choose. But don't keep me on the rack. How stands the affair of the documents? Have you found them?. Since my husband's death, this matter has weighed upon me like a mountain, not for my own sake, Heaven knows, but that of my poor, fatherless children.»

A royal robber

Tears flowed from the eyes of the young widow.

Günzer cast a strange glance at her, a look of blended defiance and triumph.

«You must console yourself!» he said. «The fact cannot be altered, and it is useless to yield to sorrow.»

«Life has lost everything for me!» replied the widow sadly.

«You go too far,» rejoined Günzer. «Time brings solace for every grief. You are still young and beautiful, madame.»

«Günzer!»

«You may yet be happy.»

«And you say that, you knew my dear husband so well, who were educated with him?»

«Yes!» replied Günzer,. watching her. «He was indeed a good and very estimable man. But everything in life may be supplied.»

«Nothing will supply my husband's place,» said the widow in a low tone, while tears again filled her eyes.

«Time will teach you to think otherwise. No wave rises and falls, whose place may not be supplied.»

«That comparison may suit life and our position in it,» replied Frau von Bernhold. «but not a loving heart. However, let that pass, Herr Günzer, and calm my anxiety about the matter we have just mentioned.»

Günzer darted a piercing glance at the young widow, and then said curtly:

«It is in a very bad condition.»

Frau von Bernhold turned pale.

«What!» she said, scarcely able to control her voice, «didn't you say just now that you had good news?»

«If you would favorably receive the proposition I have to make.»

«I don't understand you ! Haven't you found the documents, which afford incontestable proofs of our right to Plobsheim?»

A royal robber

«No!»

«But, good Heavens! They must be there!»

«I have already searched for them for years!»

«And earned in return our sincere gratitude, but – have you examined everything?»

«Every nook and corner, every parchment!»

«Günzer!» exclaimed Frau von Bernhold in uncontrollable agitation, «you know how much depends upon the discovery of those papers.»

«I know!» he replied with icy composure. «Everything. If the title to the estate is not found, Plobsheim will be lost to you.»

«And I and my children?»

«There are means of defending yourself !»

«No, no,» cried the young widow, «there is still a just God, who will not suffer bold hands to rob a widow and her children.»

«France and her Chambers de. Reunion consider it no robbery. On the contrary! To secure legal possession of property, they require legal proofs of ownership»

«And they must be there! My father and father-in-law, as well as many members of the Bernhold and Zorn families, clearly remember having seen them with their own eyes.»

Günzer's face darkened, and he said as if wounded:

«Do you distrust me, madame! Or do you think me negligent in this important matter?»

«Certainly not!» cried Frau von Bernhold in alarm – Günzer was her sole support in the matter. «But you might, perhaps, have overlooked the papers. Perhaps they have been pushed aside – perhaps – –»

«Here are the keys to both chests!» said Günzer gravely. «Pray search them yourself, madame.»

A royal robber

«How could I? And —»

«Then choose some other legal adviser.»

«Günzer?»

«You do not trust me.»

«How can you say so? Will you desert me, the widow of the man with whom you were reared like a brother, desert me and his poor children, now, when an attempt is made to rob us of our property, the estate of Plobsheim, which we have owned for centuries?»

«No!» said Günzer' with a sudden touch of cordiality, beneath which, however, lurked something that produced an uncomfortable impression, «no, that I will not, but precisely the contrary.»

«Good Heavens!» exclaimed Frau von Bernhold joyously, «then you know of some expedient. Perhaps you have discovered a way to tear Plobshiem from the greedy hands of the *Reunions-Kammern*. If it requires sacrifice, I will gladly make them for my children.»

«I don't think the affair can be termed a sacrifice.»

«What affair?»

«Let me speak plainly.»

«Pray do so.»

«France is not to be trifled with.»

«Who does not know that.»

«Therefore the utmost exertions must be made to retain possession of the castle and estate of Plobsheim, together with the title and rights of nobility appertaining to it; for the person to whom Plobsheim is assigned receives the title and privileges of a nobleman, an owner of the *seigneurie de Plobsheim*.»

«That would be —»

«Madame, that is so! Unfortunately. But we have examples enough.»

«But pray —»

A royal robber

«Let us keep to the fact. We must always subject the feelings to calm reason, and not confound our own idea of right with that the law recognizes as right.»

«But –»

«Therefore the utmost exertions must be made to retain possession of Plobsheim. But this is difficult and dangerous. Difficult, because the title deeds are missing – dangerous, because the enmity of France threatens us in the background.»

«Louvois is your friend.»

«I too rely upon that.»

«And you will do your utmost for me and my children?»

«Yes – on one condition.»

«And that is?»

«Let us make common cause.»

Frau von Bernhold looked at him in astonishment.

«What do you mean?» she asked. «I don't understand.»

«Why – you are a widow –»

«Unhappily!»

«And I –»

Frau von Bernhold did not believe her ears.

«You have the kindness to act as my legal adviser,» she answered, turning deadly pale.

«Yes,» continued Günzer. «But I am also clerk of the city and council of Strassburg, a man who can show a very pretty property, and – is unmarried.»

«But what has that to do with our affair?»

«A great deal. I will pledge myself to retain possession of Plobsheim if – we make common cause – that is, if you will give me your hand as my wife.»

A royal robber

A loud cry escaped the widow's lips. Alma's warning darted through her mind. The turf was still fresh on the mound that covered her dear husband's corpse, and Günzer, the son of a dishonored man, the nephew of a base counterfeiter, who, raised from the dust by her family, dared – not only to sue for her hand, no it was now clear as daylight; the miserable wretch wooed her, to obtain possession of the Plobsheim estate.

This was too much for a simple, honest nature, too much for a lady like Frau von Bernhold, too much for a loving wife, whose bleeding heart still mourned for her lost husband, too much for a mother, who saw her children's rightful inheritance threatened by the rapacious greed of a scoundrel.

Proudly, but pale as death, she rose from her seat, and grasped the keys of the chests containing the family documents, which Günzer had laid on the table before her. Then, with a dignity usually foreign to the little lady's manner, she said:

«Herr Günzer, you are dismissed! I will select another legal adviser.»

Günzer had also risen. His face was livid, his eyes darted piercing glances, an expression of cold, diabolical scorn hovered around his lips. Yet his voice trembled as he cried: «Consider what you do!»

«I consider but one thing!» replied Frau von Bernhold, «that there is still a God of eternal justice.»

«And you really refuse my hand?»

«I have only a contemptuous yes in response to a question so insulting.»

«Consider your future and that of your children.»

«Widows and orphans are in God's hands.»

«You will repent this some day.»

«Never,» cried the widow proudly, «even if you, who thrived on the benefits of my family, intend some knavish trick against me and my children.»

With these words, Frau von Bernhold, trembling from head to foot, left the room, to give way to passionate tears.

XI.
The witch's kitchen.

«How much time yet, d'Auvaux?»

«Ten minutes.»

«The deuce! I thought the hour must have come.»

«Time creeps for those who wait, and flies for those who feast.»

«It will certainly fly only too quickly, for the person for whom we're brewing this broth.»

«I wasn't talking of such enjoyment.»

«And yet it is one.»

«Of course, Le Sage, you're right – a double one.»

«How so?»

«Why a confoundedly bitter one for the person who tastes the bitter drink, and a more consoling one to the individual – who offers it.»

«At any rate the latter is sure of his point.»

«I think we do honor to our art.»

«But the art does none to us.»

«Because we are fools.»

«Fools?»

«Of course! Don't we work for La Voisin instead of ourselves?»

«Well, she pays well.»

«What is that! She gives us miserable scraps, compared with the immense sums she pockets.»

«Let's rub the fur the other way, and make her pay better.»

«How will you do that?»

A royal robber

«We have her in our power.»

«And she has us in hers.»

«But the *poudre de succession* – isn't that our invention?»

«Not entirely; we got it from the crafty Italian Exili, the teacher of La Croix and the Marquise de Brinvilliers.»

«Don't mention those names.»

«Why?»

«Because – for very excellent reasons – I never like to think of the end of those people.»

«Why did they allow themselves to be caught? I think there is more craft under our skulls.»

«Pshaw! I wouldn't give a straw for that; the pitcher goes to the well until it breaks. The only thing that soothes me is, that we and La Voisin are screened by our distinguished customers; haven't we among them: Monsieur, the king's brother, the queen herself, the Marquis d'Esiat, Comtesse Soisson, Duc de Launzun, Prince Cardinal de Bouillon, Grand Almoner of France, Duc de Saint Aignan, and many other prominent personages. They will beware of compromising such names.»

«Possibly! But I don't rely much upon it. *One* crow doesn't pick out another's eyes. If the king should some day find himself compelled to use vigorous measures.»

«We poor devils will be caught in the net – that's true – and the great rascals will slip out.»

«Don't let us think of such foolish things. For us it is written to enjoy life to the dregs. If the devil then leaves us in the lurch – why – the jest is done.»

«And I suppose my broth is now?»

«Yes – a minute more, and it will have cooked long enough.»

This conversation was carried on by two priests d'Auvaux and Lesage, who – in connection with Vigoureux and the famous fortune-teller La Voisin –

conducted the secret manufacture of poisons with such success, that all France trembled.

It was they who had aided La Voisin in performing the devil's mass, by means of which the Grand Almoner of France, the Prince Cardinal de Bouillon, accompanied by the Duc de Saint Aignan, had tried to discover Turenne's treasures.

During this conversation, they were in the laboratory where were prepared the terrible poisons, which in those days, amid the boundless immorality and corruption of the French court, found such extensive use, that even now it makes every honest man shudder to look back to that terrible time.

The surroundings harmonized with the occupation. It was a dark, gloomy, cellar-like room, a vaulted apartment in the lower story of a damp, dull house in the Faubourg St. Germain. Retorts and distilling apparatus of every description, alembics and crucibles of various shapes, mortars and other utensils, were piled along the walls and in the corners. On a wide hearth, surmounted by a massive chimney, a charcoal fire was burning, over which Lesage had been boiling a brown liquid for an hour.

Unsavory odors rose from it, and strove to escape from the room.

In a corner behind the hearth lay a dead cat, its stomach horribly swollen, and its stiff limbs stretched far apart. It had been used to try the effects of a newly invented poison.

Rabbits hopped to and fro. The poor creatures did not suspect that they were intended for similar experiments.

Exili, St. Croix, the Marquise de Brinvillier, La Voisin and the priests d'Auvaux and Lesage possessed, in the low condition of chemistry and medicine at that time, wonderful knowledge and skill in the preparation of poisons.

The reports of the experts of those days cannot express sufficient admiration for the nature and preparation of these deadly potions, which certainly far surpassed all the knowledge and experience of the pharmacology of that period.

The Saint Croix poisons – they say – defied all attempts to apply to them the laws of chemistry. The poisonous material was so concealed that it could not be perceived, and so subtle that it evaded all the skill of the physicians. All rules hitherto known prove useless, and all experience unavailing. To be sure, the doctors themselves, owing to the number of those in high position who were implicated, were not disposed to discover the poison. The hens, doves, and dogs, that drank some of Saint Croix's poisoned water, died a short time after, it is true, but on opening them every part of their bodies was found in a perfectly natural condition, with the exception of some clotted blood in the heart.

Saint Croix's powder – found after his death in a little box – when administered to a cat, caused constant vomiting and speedy death; but here also no one portion of its body was found to be affected by the venom.

The poisons these terrible persons prepared, no longer exist to be examined by the chemists of our days. Undoubtedly the principal ingredient would be found to be arsenic. But it is a terrible sign of the want of morality of those times, that their preparation, concealment and use, could rise to the dignity of an art. Exili and Saint Croix are said to have really made the manufacture of poison a science. La Voisin's assistants, d'Auvaux and Lesage, followed in the footsteps of these worthy men.

Both at this moment were occupied in preparing a new poison. Lesage had been boiling a brown liquid over a charcoal fire for an hour, till it became a thick mass.

Now – at the close of the conversation – he took the vessel from the fire and extinguished the coals.

«There,» said he, «let it cool.»

At this moment one of the rabbits hopped nimbly up and stopped at the hearth.

A repulsive smile flitted across Lesage's face.

«So you introduce yourself,» said he, turning to the little creature with a touch of rude humor, «very well, you shall have the honor of trying this liquor first.»

A royal robber

«It ought to die in violent convulsions within fifteen minutes,» said d'Auvaux quietly, «otherwise the potion will be too weak for a man.»

«You forget,» rejoined Lesage, «that it isn't to kill at once. Death is not to be expected until after a week or fortnight and – take notice – without any startling symptoms.»

«Exili's receipts; number 35!» replied d'Auvaux, nodding.

At that moment an odd, rattling noise was heard.

«La Voisin!» said Lesage, «that is her signal.»

«Let her come in!» replied d'Auvaux, «I wish she was obliged to swallow one of the drinks we brew for her, and which she sells for such immense sums. Then we could be independent and receive the money undiminished, directly from the customer's hands.»

La Voisin entered. She was dressed richly, but with the exaggeration of ornament peculiar to persons who have risen from a low origin, and her by no means plain features wore a very crafty expression. Her color, complexion, and plumpness implied ample enjoyment of material pleasures.

«Disagreeable news!» she said, entering and closing the door behind her. «The king and court are about to leave Versailles.»

«Well, what of that,» replied d'Auvaux. «They are only going to spend a short time at some pleasure castle.»

«If that were so, who would think it worth mentioning,» replied La Voisin. «But the king is going farther.»

Lesage shrugged his shoulders. «The king, or the Duchesse de Fontanges.»

«This time it is the king,» Madame Voisin answered.

«And where is he going?» asked d'Auvaux.

«To Reims, Thionville, Metz, Nancy.»

«Aha!» said Lesage, laughing. «Do you notice anything?»

«What?» inquired d'Auvaux.

A royal robber

«His Majesty seems to want to remain in the vicinity of the Strassburg cathedral.»

«It may be so!» replied the fortune-teller. «The Duc de St. Aignan, who called on me yesterday to consult the cards about a certain matter of business, told me in confidence that the court would remain some time at Colmar.»

«At Colmar?» repeated Lesage and d'Auvaux.

«I don't believe it. What should the pleasure-loving duchesse want in that old nest?»

«But if the king has a special object.»

«And the Duchesse de Fontanges does not desire it?»

«Pshaw!» observed La Voisin, who meantime had seated herself on an old chair. «Things no longer stand on the old footing.»

«With the duchesse?» asked d'Auvaux with an expression of the utmost incredulity.

«With the Duchesse de Fontanges!» replied the lady.

«You are mistaken, madame,» d'Auvaux answered confidently. «The rule of the Duchesse de Fontanges is firmer than ever. Don't you know the latest fashion?»

«To wear the hair à la Fontanges!» said La Voisin, shrugging her shoulders.

JWhat sort of a story is that?» asked Lesage, who meantime had been holding his sauce-pan of brown liquid in a vessel of water, to cool it.

«Last week,» replied d'Auvaux, «a grand hunting party was given, which was attended by the whole court. There is no end of pleasure excursions and amusements of every kind, since the beautiful marble statue from Limagne became the object of the king's devotion.»

Lesage laughed loudly exclaiming:

«D'Auvaux is turning moralist.»

«So is the devil,» replied d'Auvaux, «the contry will soon be unable to bear the expense.»

«What is that to us,» observed.Lesage scornfully, «we get our living from the court and distinguished persons, not the common people. But we were talking of a new fashion?»

«Yes!» cried d'Auvaux. «On this hunting party, the wind disordered the duchesse's hair and she fastened it as well as she could with a ribbon. As this arrangement happened to be uncommonly pretty and wonderfully becoming to the duchesse, the following day all the ladies of the court – princesses, duchesses, marchionesses, down to the most insignificant maid of honor – appeared with a similar ribbon in their hair.»

«And this style of coiffure is now the fashion?» asked Lesage.

«Yes,» said La Voisin, «and is being adopted throughout Europe, under the name of the coiffure à la Fontanges. But does that prove anything in regard to the security of the duchesse's position? Abbé Choisy told me, when he visited me a short time ago, that the Duchesse de Fontanges was beautiful as an angel, but silly as a goose. And he is right! Her position has turned her brain. For some time she has shown an arrogance that will prove her ruin. She passes the queen without any salutation, and has treated Madame de Montespan with such hauteur as to make the latter her mortal enemy.»

«All this affords no ground to anticipate her fall!» said d'Auvaux, «the king loves her to madness.»

«Loved!» corrected La Voisin.

«Only last week he ordered a charming suite of apartments to be furnished for her, the walls of the salon hung with tapestry representing his victories. The witty flatterer Saint Aignan instantly wrote some lines which greatly delighted the king and duchesse.»

«Have you finished, d'Auvaux?» asked La Voisin.

«At your service.»

«Then I'll tell you why I – for my part – believe that the earth is shaking under the feet of the beautiful Duchess de Fontanges.»

A royal robber

«I am all ears for – if she falls, we must know to whom we are to look in future. So madame, your reasons!»

«I have already mentioned that yesterday –»

«The Duc de Saint Aignan visited you to consult the cards.»

«And what do you suppose he wanted to ascertain?»

«How should I know?»

«Whether a certain person, who now occupies a very prominent position, would remain long at the helm.»

«The deuce!» exclaimed d'Auvaux with an expression of the greatest astonishment. «Why if the case stands so, if Saint Aignan asks Fate that question –»

«It is evident that he, who is so closely associated with the king and duchesse, already has a suspicion from what quarter the wind is beginning to blow.»

«Well, and what did the cards say?»

«What my small share of wisdom whispered. The queen of hearts was followed – after four other cards – by the ace of clubs.»

«Excellent, excellent!» cried d'Auvaux, «the powerful favorite, after a certain time – it may be four days, four weeks or four months – is to be supplanted.»

«Cold!» here remarked Lesage.

«Who?» asked d'Auvaux in surprise, «the Duchesse de Fontanges?»

«Nonsense,» replied Lesage, «my broth.»

«Then we'll try it!» replied d'Auvaux quietly, seizing one of the rabbits by the ears – «here!»

Lesage took it and poured a few drops of the brown liquid down its throat.

La Voisin smiled. «May it do it much good,» she observed.

D'Auvaux still held the poor creature firmly.

A royal robber

The three gloomy fiends watched it in silence with eager expectation the point in question was to ascertain the effect of the poison.

It was intended for human beings, and not to produce death immediately, therefore, according to Exili's estimate, it should kill a rabbit in twenty minutes.

After a few moments the little creature grew restless, the eyes dilated, and singular movements of the neck began.

Lavoisin again laughed loudly. «The rogue is coquetting like a school girl just fledged,» she observed.

«No, it is swallowing,» observed Lesage gayly, «like a courtier to whom the king has just given a pill that does not want go down and yet must.»

«They often burn the throat as much as my potion,» said Lesage, calmly watching the contortions of pain made by the poor little animal.

Convulsions were already commencing, burning pains and cramps in the stomach.

«It takes effect too quickly,» said d'Auvaux, «the poison is too strong. Convulsions ought not to take place in a rabbit, in less than ten minutes at the earliest.»

«They may at the end of five,» replied Lesage.

«No!» said d'Anvaux. «Exili expressly says in regard to the trial: in a half-grown rabbit, not before ten minutes.»

«What will you bet I'm not right in saying five?» cried Lesage eagerly.

«Three bottles of sack.»

«Done!»

Lesage went to an old cupboard, drew out a roll of dirty papers, opened them, and following the lines with his fingers, read a few words. Then he looked up triumphantly, pointed to a passage, and exclaimed:

«What's this?»

A royal robber

D'Auvaux and La Voisin looked at the page.

«Five!» cried the latter gayly, «Lesage has won.»

«Yes,» observed d'Auvaux, «a man may be mistaken, I'll pay.»

«And I'll help drink the wine,» observed La Voisin.

«We'll have as pleasant an hour as we three have ever spent together. I feel ready for anything. But the sack must be good and strong.»

«Watch!» said d'Auvaux, «our candidate for death is vomiting.»

«Is there any blood?»

«No!»

«It will come!»

«Hop! hop! that's what I call convulsions!» exclaimed La Voisin. «It's absurd that we are obliged to try our poisons on animals, human beings would give unerring symptoms.»

«But we should be obliged to wait a week or forties night!» observed Lesage, «and our potion must be delivered to-night.»

«True!» replied La Voisin, «the customer is in a great hurry.»

«The customer?»

«I don't know who he is.»

«But he belongs to the court?»

La Voisin laid her finger on her lip, and cast a significant glance at d'Auvaux.

«I understand!» said the latter. «Government business.»

«What is it to me?»

«Doesn't Monsieur Louvois go away early to-morrow morning?» asked Lesage.

«So they say.»

A royal robber

Lesage hummed a song.

The rabbit was in its last convulsions. Blood oozed from the mouth and nose. Its sufferings appeared to be terrible.

«And the payment?»

«As I have already told you, d'Auvaux, princely,» replied the fortune-teller. «This man doesn't haggle over such things.»

«I believe so,» cried Lesage laughing. «It costs him nothing.»

«Only divide honestly,» said d'Auvaux, with a meaning glance at Lesage, which the latter answered by a look at La Voisin.

«As usual!» replied La Voisin.

«Done!» exclaimed Lesage at the same moment.

«The rabbit is dead.»

He took up the little creature and tossed it beside the dead cat.

«The poison is all right.»

«If it isn't too strong.»

«Then a smaller dose must be used.»

«But I must know exactly how many drops to a glass of wine,» said La Voisin – «death is not to ensue for a week or fortnight.»

«Without any extraordinary symptoms?»

«Yes. That is the express condition.»

«Man, woman, or child?»

«Man!»

«How old?»

«About sixty.»

«Strong?»

«Not very!»

A royal robber

«Then five drops will do it.»

«Very well.»

«And when shall we get our money?»

«You shall have it to-night, when we drink your three bottle of sack in the secret room in my house,» replied La Voisin, with a repulsive glance at her companions. «I will provide a supper of which Monseigneur Louvois himself need not be ashamed.»

«But three bottles won't be enough.»

«Then I'll add three more,» replied La Voisin.

Lesage and d'Auvaux laughed.

«We have worked, now we will feast.»

«As people make their way honestly in the world.»

«One thing more before we part!» said d'Auvaux, turning to La Voisin, as Lesage pushed. back the bolt. «Why did you seem so disturbed about the news, that the court would leave Versailles for some time?»

«As if we should not as good as lie fallow in consequence.»

«Then we'll rest a short time on our laurels. Besides you won't lack fortune-telling, prophesies of the future, etc.»

«Trumpery,» replied La Voisin. «But, before I forget it: Madame de Montespan is beguiling the weary hours in a singular way.»

«Probably by prayers; that's usually the end of votaries of pleasure.»

«Possibly! But –»

«Well?»

«The lonely woman is now seeking – the philosopher's stone.»

«She ought to have done that before the Duchesse de Fontanges took the helm.»

«Jesting aside,» said La Voisin, and her eyes expressed as much as her words,

A royal robber

«she is pursuing the study of alchemy.»

«Who says so!»

«She informed me by a confidential servant and asks – for some chemicals.»

«Aha!» exclaimed Lesage with a malicious smile.

«But there must be no poisonous substances among them.»

«I understand!» said Lesage, «I'll give her what is necessary.»

«Then bring it this evening; the servant is coming for it to- day.»

«It shall be done.»

The three left the room.

XII.
The duchesse de Fontanges

Fourteen miles from Strassburg and ninety-six from Paris is the little city of Colmar.

Under the French monarchy, Colmar (Columbaria) was only a farm which gradually increased to a village. The Emperor Charlemagne established here a workhouse for women, while the Emperor Friedrich II raised it to the rank of a city, which increased rapidly in size.

Soon after 1282 Colmar entered the ranks of the free German cities and re-tained its position until in 1673, Louis XIV took violent possession of it, de-molished its fortifications, and destroyed its freedom.

Since that time Colmar had ceased to flourish, but now a new star seemed to have risen on ancient Columbaria, for the inhabitants themselves scarcely realized it – Louis XIV and his court had spent several days within its walls.

The venerable Rathaus had been transformed into a royal palace.

The modest little city and its inhabitants really did not know what had hap-pened to them, but as it rained gold, and every service was liberally rewar-ded, they cheerfully submitted Lodgings and provisions reached fabulous prices and yet the most necessary food could scarcely be procured. Princes and noblemen, marchionesses and duchesses were often obliged – for want of better things – to satisfy their hunger -with milk and cheese. Lodgings and beds were inferior to those occupied in Versailles and Paris by their lowest servants. But – after the first painful surprise, the French tempera-ment came to their aid. With but few exceptions, all viewed the matter from its comic side.

At the close of every day the most aristocratic ladies glided out of the hou-ses in the simple costumes of Colmar burgher women and girls which they had borrowed from their servants, and the gentlemen of course did the same. True, they did not also put on the plebeian virtues of the worthy citi-zens of Colmar, and Versailles and Paris might perhaps have marveled if they had witnessed what Colmar saw at this time.

The whole visit of the court was really an idyl of rural life composed of countless amusing episodes. The affair was new and piquant. Even the king was said not to have remained entirely aloof from the romance.

But Louis XIV and his ministers Louvois and Colbert were not the men to undertake a journey like this for a mere whim or pastoral romance. Beneath the glittering cloak of this original and truly French caprice, the great serious drama of the time went on.

Never had the intercourse between the French court and the neighboring city of Strassburg been more constant, or at the same time so little likely to arouse anxiety.

France had most positively denied any knowledge of the conspiracy connected with the Franciscan monastery, throwing the whole responsibility on the monks, and their superior.

True, the latter with his followers had instantly crossed the frontier and sought the protection of France, but the affair must be allowed to remain as it was for the present. Any farther steps – in opposition to so powerful a neighbor – would be dangerous and unwise.

Louis XIV now seemed to intend to soothe the excitement prevailing in Strassburg as speedily as possible, for he and his ministers were overflowing with friendly sentiments.

This was especially the case when the court came into the immediate vicinity of Strassburg. Assurances of the utmost friendship were lavished on the citizens. France desired nothing but the welfare and prosperity of the city; and it was only because it was so completely left in the lurch by emperor and empire that Louis XIV desired to take it under his protection.

The French ambassador had plenty of occupation in transmitting these professions of friendship, orally and in writing, to the magistrates of Strassburg. The partisans of France, the timid and time-serving magistrates, were radiant with delight; the warnings of the other party, who saw in these maneuvers only a diplomatic snare, fell on empty air.

A royal robber

Nay, the government of Strassburg even resolved to send deputies to convey a greeting to the king of France during his stay in Colmar.

Syndicus Frantz, Günzer as «*le mignon connu de la France,*» and several other members of the magistracy were chosen.

Frantz positively declined; but Günzer exerted all his influence to induce the Syndicus to accept the honor. The king expressed a desire to see Syndicus Frantz at the head of the embassy.

Under these circumstances, a refusal from the Syndicus would have been a violation of diplomatic custom, nay – an act of cowardice. Frantz therefore consented, though with a heavy heart. The brave man opposed a quiet resolution to the fears of his wifa and child, the warnings of Hugo, but in the silence of the night set his house in order, made every needful preparation in case he did not return – or died.

Thus the day arrived which His Majesty had graciously appointed to receive the ambassadors sent from Strassburg to greet him.

The embassy was a pompous one, and – like all such city affairs – arranged in the style of the Middle Ages.

The ambassadors traveled in five clumsy state-coaches.

In the first sat two heralds, attired in the colors of the city, with the armorial bearings of Strassburg on their breasts and backs, and white wands in their hands.

The four following coaches contained the magistrates: Dominikus Dietrich, Johann Leonhard Fröreisen, Johann Störr, Günzer and Syndicus Frantz.

Frantz drove alone with Hugo von Zedlitz, who would not be denied the privilege of accompanying – the worthy man, the father of his beloved Alma, as his private secretary. Hugo clearly perceived the Syndicus' dangerous situation.

It was still early – that is, early for people whose real life begins at night, and who measure the morning according to the position of the noon-day sun – when Saint Aignan called on the Duchesse de Fontanges.

A royal robber

Only the king had the right to enter her apartment unannounced at this hour.

The duchesse was in a bewitching morning-dress. A robe of white India muslin, so light and delicate that it floated around the beautiful figure like an airy cloud, revealing the luster of the white satin dress beneath, but partially concealed her matchless symmetry of form.

Laces of priceless value encircled her throat, wrists, and bust, fastened coquettishly here and there by clasps of pearls.

The complexion of this singular woman was like white marble, alabaster, while the magnificent red hair surrounded her as if with a halo of gold.

Angeline de Fontanges was beautiful as a queen; but proud as one, and this pride, blended with her peculiar cold manner and want of sprightliness, gave her of late – since it constantly increased – a somewhat harsh, imperious, repellant air.

This was felt by no one more keenly than Saint Aignan. It was he, who – aided by Madame de Montespan – had brought the insignificant little Angeline to the court of France and paved the way for her to reach her present power. It was he, who had at first stood by her side to counsel and protect her, she had given him her entire confidence, been guided by him, served him and his wishes against the king, nay even, in some bright hours, bestowed upon him the gift of her heart. True, this was not wholly discontinued, but Angeline's inate vanity, fostered by the royal luxury that surrounded her, so increased her pride and love of authority that she strove to rule Saint Aignan like all the rest.

But Saint Aignan had brooight her to the court, in order, through her, to rule the king. He did so still, externally wearing the chains of the lovely Duchesse de Fontanges with the patience of a crafty courtier, but irritated by the pride and imperiousness of a creature whom he had raised and to whom he was greatly superior in intellect, a certain coldness had come between them.

Although passion may blaze fiercely in the breast of a libertine, it is of no long duration.

A royal robber

Saint Aignan's keen eye had for some time perceived something else, something that always produces an effect upon every courtier; he fancied that the king shared his feelings.

The duchesse undoubtedly now stood at the height of her power; the luxury with which Louis XIV surrounded her was truly royal – the king still loved her, but – since the night when he had found Gauthier in her presence and arrested him, a worm had gnawed the flower of his love.

Louis XIV doubtless saw with pleasure that the object of his love looked down with royal pride on all the world save himself; nay he even secretly rejoiced in the humiliations she inflicted upon the queen, but in the depths of his heart – so contradictory men often are – did not forgive Angeline these insults to majesty.

No symptoms of all this escaped Saint Aignan's keen, watchful eyes. He knew his lord and king thoroughly, knew his great and feeble traits of character, his truly royal generosity where he loved, and his destructive fury when rage took possession of him, but above all else he knew – his inconstancy in love. It was not intellect but mere physical beauty, the novelty and peculiarity of her loveliness, that charmed the king in Angeline.

But Saint Aignan knew how feeble was such a bond to a Louis XIV. He saw how, like a good general, the king, in the midst of his love, was storing in his heart an arsenal of defensive weapons, in order at a fitting moment, that is when satiety overtook him, to be duly prepared for a back stroke.

Thus Saint Aignan now had a double task, and this was to sustain and uphold Angeline's influence over the king – behind which he himself stood – as long as possible; but on the other hand, carefully watch the barometer of royal favor towards the Duchesse de Fontanges, in order as soon as it perceptibly fell, to withdraw from the person who was sure to be speedily out of favor.

The sun of the royal favor was still shining upon Angeline with all its power and brilliancy, keeping the little clouds of single instances of disapproval far below the horizon. And indeed the charming object of the king's love made the utmost use of this favor. One brilliant entertainment, one pleasure followed another wtih dizzy, intoxicating haste.

True, there were many thoughts in Angeline's mind that needed stifling; the pangs of conscience, the memory of a mother who had gone to her grave in grief and shame at her daughter's fall, and above all things, the recollection of Gauthier.

Did she even know whether he was alive or dead? If the repose of the grave did not yet surround the victim, then – oh! the thought was terrible – he was buried alive in the Bastille. Buried alive on account of his love for her – for her, who, in reward for her treachery to him, was revelling in royal luxury, wealth, power and splendor.

This was the cause of the perpetual entertainments, the whirl of pleasure and amusement which devoured millions and yet – could not deaden her conscience.

Saint Aignan had just entered the apartments of the Duchesse de Fontanges.

Angeline in her white, airy, négligé attire looked like a fairy rising from a lily.

The nobleman greeted her with this compliment, and taking her little hand, pressed a light kiss upon it.

The duchesse – accustomed to such homage – received both with a proud smile. She already considered herself the real queen of France. But this imprudent pride and arrogance were the first symptoms that made Saint Aignan fear her fall. He knew what the real queen thought of them, and that – deeply insulted – she with her whole party, the party of the highest nobility were laboring to prejudice Angeline de Fontanges in the eyes of the king.

He did not fail to give the duchesse many hints of this, but they were rarely understood. Usually, according to his habit, they were veiled by anecdotes.

To-day he pursued the same course. In order to make the duchesse think of her own position, he turned the conversation with consummate skill to the beautiful, gentle, and unfortunate la Vallière, one of the first of her predecessors. The new *coiffure à la Fontanges* served to introduce the subject.

They had spoken of her and several whimsical fashions, when Saint Aignan suddenly exclaimed;

«But I'll wager, fair duchesse, that you don't yet know the oddest of all feminine fashions.»

«And this is? –» asked Angelina.

«When the Marquise de Montespan was about to become a mother, she invented a new costume, dressed herself precisely like a man, with the exception of a petticoat, over the belt of which the shirt was puffed in such a manner as to conceal her figure.»

«Pshaw!» cried the duchesse, «that couldn't have been a pretty style.»

«And yet it was instantly adopted by all the ladies of the court. Strangely enough, from that moment all the courtiers deserted the poor Duchesse de la Vallière.»

«Why?»

«Because,» said Saint Aignan, with apparent carelessness, but in a very peculiar tone, «because the favor bestowed upon Madame de Montespan foretold La Vallière's fall. All went over to the side of the marquise, and this was solely because poor La Vallière, striving solely to please the king, never thought of making friends.»

«Was it not enough that the king was her friend,» cried the Duchesse de Fontanges proudly, raising her beautiful head as if a heavy crown rested upon it.

«That did not seem to be the opinion of the Maréchal de Grammont.»

«How so?» asked Angeline with a little pout.

«Why?» replied Saint Aignan gayly, «when the Duchesse de la Vallière complained to him of her sudden fall, he answered: 'Deuce take it, my friend, while you had reason to laugh, you ought to have made others laugh, too; then when you now have cause to weep, others would at least help you.'»

The Duchesse de Fontanges smiled scornfully and then, gazing at her image in the mirror, said, that «La Valiere was a foolish child. People should understand how to bind His Majesty with stronger chains, and forever.»

A royal robber

The Duc de Saint Aignan, who stood before Angeline – the latter was reclining in a costly arm-chair – holding his plumed hat in his hand, smiled craftily, as he bowed and answered:

«A task that cannot be difficult for a lady so beautiful and intellectual as Madame la Duchesse.»

«A stool!» said Angeline.

A page placed one about four feet from the duchesse's chair and – Saint Aignan bowed and accepted it.

The conversation now turned upon the approaching event of the day: the audience given the embassy from Strassburg; but Angeline did not care for politics, she wanted amusement, even now, besides she was mortally tired of Colmar.

«Help tne pass away the time! St. Aignan,» she exclaimed with a yawn, «tell me one of your thousand anecdotes. You can be entertaining when you choose.»

The duc bit his lips but bowed and smiled.

Hours passed in lively conversation with Saint Aignan, who as usual was full of witticisms and anecdotes.

Far more serious was the manner in which these hours were spent by others.

XIII.
An audience

The great audience took place in the hall of the ancient Rathaus, whose walls had been hung with costly tapestry and furnished as handsomely as the hort time and long distance from Paris would permit. Everywhere glittered the royal arms of France, only from the center of the ceiling – as if in mockery – looked down the escutcheon of Austria, carved in wood.

Louis XIV had appeared with his whole court, since he desired to awe the ambassadors from Strassburg by every means in his power. All shone in velvet and silk, glittered with gold, silver and jewels, and all this splendor was surpassed by the galaxy of beautiful women, who never failed to surround the most gallant sovereign of the age.

Louis XIV had taken his seat upon a lofty throne. Around him stood the princes of the blood, as well as his ministers Louvois and Colbert.

These, however, were only stars of the first magnitude; they were surrounded by the other nobles of France and dignitaries of the kingdom, nor were authors and artists in every department lacking.

Louis XIV liked to have his surroundings harmonize with the epithet of «great,» bestowed upon him by his century.

And now, preceded by the two heralds, appears before this brilliant assembly, the simple citizens of Strassburg: Ammeister Dominikus Dietrich, Syndicus Frantz, Günzer and the magistrates Fröreisen and Hecker.

Their plain, black costume formed a striking contrast to the ladies and gentleman of the court, glittering in garments of every hue, adorned with the most superb embroidery of gold and silver and ornaments of flashing jewels – but no less marked was the difference in their demeanor.

None of these hearts felt any emotion of fear, yet all these men were pale, except Günzer, who, familiar with the court and its life, remained unawed by the imposing aspect Louis XIV and his brilliant train, could not fail to present to the others.

A royal robber

Yet the innate dignity of Ammeister Dietrich and Syndicus Frantz was clearly apparent; they advanced with calm, grave, measured steps and, after bowing low before the king, held their heads steadily and proudly erect as beseems a free man – even when he stands in the presence of kings and emperors.

But Louis XIV was unusually gracious to-day.

He listened with a smile to the salutation addressed to him by Günzer, in the name of the magistrates of Strassburg. The crafty speaker knew how to utter them in such a way that they appeared to express far greater devotion than had been intended.

The same gracious reception was bestowed upon the costly gift, which Ammeister Dietrich, in the name of the city, as a token of respect and neighborly kindness laid at the feet of the king of France.

Louis XIV uttered the most friendly thanks, and never – according to his assurances – had the throne of France been occupied by a monarch who bore such good will to Strassburg as himself.

The king's words flowed like honey and evidently produced a marked effect upon all the ambassadors – except Syndicus Frantz. While the heads of the others were bowed lower and lower in gratitude and reverence, he alone remained erect with a cold, grave expression upon his features.

This could not escape the eagle eye of Louis XIV – besides, he was also fully aware of the Syndicus' views. He therefore suddenly paused and then said in his slow, impressive manner:

«And you do not agree with our views, Syndicus Frantz?»

«No, your Majesty» replied Syndicus Frantz, quietly but firmly.

«And why not?» asked the king, with a look that would have made any one else tremble. «We do not wish to force the good city of Strassburg to anything, although according to natural boundaries and the claims of the *Reunions-Kammern*, it belongs to France. According to our opinion, however, the worthy citizens of Strassburg ought to be wise enough to place themselves under the protecting wings of our power. Is not this your view, Syndicus?»

A royal robber

«No, your Majesty!» replied Frantz again.

A death-like stillness prevaded the hall.

Günzer, Dietrich, and the others stood in terror.

«Then express your opinion,» said the king, after a short pause, «and do so frankly, we desire and expect perfect sincerity.»

Frantz stood with his figure drawn up to its full height, but a death-like pallor overspread his face, the great moment, as he had anticipated had come.

Syndicus Frantz now began:

«Your Majesty!» he cried – and his voice sounded so full and sonorous that all present started. «Your Majesty, Strassburg, the ancient, free, German city, has sent us here to offer a friendly and reverent greeting to her distinguished neighbor, the King of France, Louis XIV, whom the world calls great.

«Surely no mortal man will deny the greatness of Louis XIV when he looks at France and beholds the progress this great and beautiful country has made under your Majesty's government. France rules sea and land, prospers by commerce and manufactures, surpasses all the other kingdoms of Europe by the luster Louis XIV has fostered, in the realms of poetry and art.

«Corneille and Racine divide the scepter of tragedy boasting of being the representatives of modern elegance, the successors of the Greeks. Molière produces his masterpieces. La Fontaine writes his fables, Bossuet his history, Fenelon his Télémaque. Boileau will cease to write when Louis XIV ceases to live, since he will then have no campaign in Holland, no passage of the Rhine to record.

«And not only by poesy, the arts, and sciences, but also by a wise fostering of manufactures your Majesty has understood how to make France superior to all the countries that surround her. Not a year passes unmarked by the creation of new factories. Forty-four thousand looms are in motion in the kingdom, French cloth and silk, carpets, and hangings, laces and mirrors surpass those of all the world.

«And – what shall I say of your Majesty's armies. Here my lips are silent where the names of Condé, Turenne, Luxemburg, Catinat and Baudone speak, and – history asserts her prerogative.

«Your Majesty, I willing and loudly proclaim that the man who would not call Louis XIV the great, would call down disgrace upon himself.

«Therefore Strassburg sends us, and this homage we cheerfully lay at your Majesty's feet.

«But, Sire, permit us, citizens of Strassburg, to also have the pleasure of calling Louis XIV the just.

«Strassburg is an ancient, free, German city. She honors the king of France as her distinguished and powerful neighbor; but in this very power she places her trust – that it will not be abused.»

Louis XIV sat motionless, not a muscle of his face moved.

«Strassburg,» continued Syndicus Frantz, «Strassburg is German and wishes to remain German. Strassburg is a free city, and desires and will guard her freedom, and – we are sure of this: that Louis XIV, who is called 'the great,' will show this greatness, the nobility of his nature, by protecting Strassburg's freedom and independence, and honoring the loyalty with which she clings to the German empire.

«But if your Majesty asks: why does the German empire leave Strassburg so isolated, I have a reply, which it is true also contains a heavy accusation against German princes. The aristocracy of the empire are thus careless of Strassburg's interests, because the point in question concerns only a free city, and not a princely house.

«But it is not princely to uphold themselves and their power by the oppression of the middle classes, by the destruction of the freedom of individual cities, by the arbitrary abolition of their well-earned rights! It is not princely, I say, and in direct opposition to real greatness. This is the conviction of the citizens of Strassburg and this, sire, is surely your Majesty's opinion. A great heart can only have noble feelings, as a lofty soul can only act in a generous, high-minded manner.»

Louvois face here grew crimson with anger. Louis XIV still sat motionless, only from time to time his eyes darted furious glances at the bold speaker.

Syndicus Frantz noticed neither; carried away by his subject, he continued to delineate with bold strokes the perfidious policy of the time, without, however, directly mentioning the King of France. Then, suddenly turning to the latter, he cried:

«To pursue such a policy is not worthy of Louis XIV! He knows that the people hate the conflictsof ambition and selfishness, that history – that eternal tribunal of the world – condemns them. Your Majesty's keen eyes will see through the veil of mist that dims the sight of so many men, will penetrate it and perceive that the consequences of this wretched policy of ambition and selfishness may easily form illusions; that they may lead to complications and wars, which must drench the world with blood and ruin, and might be capable of shattering all existing relations.

«The German is peaceful – the German values nothing more than an honorable and lasting peace. His heart is large and full of love for mankind. Therefore he hates neither France nor the French nation. Does not envy it what it is and has. But the German heart also throbs for its most sacred possessions: its honor and native land. If the attack on these should exhaust his patience, evil consequences might ensue and even to the powerful. It will and must be so, when the policy of the strong is that of ambition and selfishness.

«But no, no, I repeat it, Louis XIV cannot pursue *such a policy*, his heart is too generous, his soul too noble; he, whom history adorns with the name of «the great» will, cannot fail to, act nobly.

«And it will be noble to honor in the ancient free German city – that desires to remain German – nationality, freedom and independence.

«In this sense, sire, the citizens of Strassburg greet Louis XIV as their distinguished neighbor and rely upon his justice and the protection of their rights.»

Syndicus Frantz paused. A death-like stillness prevailed. Günzer and his companions stood pale, rigid motionless.

303

A royal robber

The king did not move; but those nearest heard the grinding of his teeth, the deep, heavy breathing which, forcibly repressed, with difficulty escaped his lips.

All eyes were fixed upon him. But Louis XIV had already regained his composure. Life on and by a throne is one scene of dissimulation from the cradle to the grave.

Gently – nay, even with a smile – he bent his head, then said slowly, putting a jnarked emphasis upon each syllable:

«We love sincerity and respect the opinion of every individual. Let the ambassadors from Strassburg present to their city our greeting and the assurances of our favor. The fate of Strassburg lies very near our lieart. We will not lose sight of it.»

With these words, the king rose, making a sign to Louvois.

The marquis instantly approached, followed by five pages, each of whom bore a gold chain on a velvet cushion.

With flattering words the minister stated that His Majesty desired to honor the ambassadors, and in them the good city of Strassburg, by presenting each with a gold chain.

Then, at Louvois' signal, Günzer, Dietrich, and the two others advanced, receiving with low bows the gift Monseigneur Louvois presented under the eyes of the king.

But when Louvois requested Syndicus Frantz to come nearer, the latter quietly, but firmly, refused the gift, saying with a smile, that chains were chains whether forged of gold or iron. A free man ought to wear none save those of the love that bound him to his native land.

A death-like pallor glided over the countenance of the king, but Louvois said with a scornful laugh:

«Consistency is a virtue! Your Majesty surely will not dismiss this worthy republican without any token of your favor; so as he has such a horror of chains, which ought never to bind him in life, your Majesty will perhaps allow me to offer him the cup of honor.»

«Yes!» said the king, in a curt, cold tone, yet there was a slight tremor in his voice as he uttered the short word.

Louvois motioned towards the corner of the hall; two pages approached, one bearing a gold cup, the other a gold flagon, on salvers of the same metal.

Louvois filled the cup.

Frantz could not refuse the wine without offering the king a direct insult.

Bowing to the monarch, he raised the cup to his lips.

But at the same instant the Syndicus perceived the Bishop of Strassburg standing behind Louvois.

The sight pierced him like a dagger. He merely sipped the wine and after swallowing a single mouthful returned it to Louvois.

The king left the hall. The audience was over. Courtiers and ambassadors withdrew.

At the door of the Rathaus stood Hugo von Zedlitz, waiting anxiously for the Syndicus.

He started at the pallor of the worthy man, who had become his second father.

«It is nothing,» said Frantz, «I am only a little excited. Let us get on to our lodgings.»

But on the way the Syndicus grew still paler.

«What is the matter, father?» Hugo again asked anxiously.

«It will pass away,» said Frantz, «the excitement has made me ill, I feel some pain and am very thirsty.»

They reached the lodgings of the Strassburg ambassadors, and the Syndicus asked for some meat and bread and a mug of wine.

But, good Heavens, where under present circumstances were wine and meat to be procured in the little city of Colmar for anyone not belonging to the highest rank of nobility?

Even for gold, Hugo von Zedlitz could obtain nothing except a mug of milk which was very greasy.

Necessity has no law, Syndicus Frantz was tortured by a terrible thirst. He drained the milk with long, eager draughts.

XIV.
Darkness and sorrow.

Deep stillness pervaded Syndicus Frantz's sleeping room. Although broad day, the window curtains were drawn, so that a gloomy darkness filled the spacious apartment, while the low, monotonous ticking of the clock increased the uncomfortable air of mystery. The bed-curtains were also so nearly closed that only a narrow space afforded a glimpse of the person sleeping within, and this was Syndicus Frantz himself.

Frantz had returned from the audience at Colmar seriously ill.

It was no acute disease that attacked him, but a strange languor confined him to his bed.

Medical science in those days was at a very low ebb, and as the Syndicus' family physician was a plain, good-natured man, but by no means a remarkably skillful doctor, the cause of the sickness remained a mystery. The first symptoms were burning pains and cramps in the stomach, followed by vomiting, thirst, and severe suffering, but gradually these symptoms passed away and then came remarkable weakness and desire to sleep, both of which had so increased during the week since his return, that the physician was wholly at a loss, while Hedwig, Alma and Hugo, and a large number of the citizens, were in the greatest anxiety.

This was the case with Wenck; but some other thought also oppressed him. Wenck seemed completely transformed, som.ething evidently weighed heavily on his mind; he was more silent than ever, and instead of his favorite: «Who knows what good it may do!» only shook his head gloomily.

Some dark, terrible thought – that was evident – must be haunting him, but he did not express it to anyone, even Hugo von Zedlitz.

Frantz still lay wholly destitute of strength, in a sort of lethargy. The physician talked of apoplexy and gave little hope. Hedwig, Alma and Hugo were frantic with grief.

The sad news of the Syndicus' critical condition soon spread through the city, where it excited the more interest, as at the same time news arousing still greater terror reached the citizens, news that instantly showed what Strassburg had already lost by Frantz's absence from the meetings of the magistrates. The Günzer faction, which now that the patriots had lost their leader, won their game, had passed and were about to carry into immediate execution, a resolution that filled the whole city with terror and confusion.

Louis XIV, before leaving Colmar with his court, desired to again express through Louvois to the magistracy of Strassburg his friendly feelings and the assurances of his royal favor, but requested in return equal courtesy from the magistrates of Strassburg. But the token of this courtesy was to be given by the destruction and removal of the tete de pont facing towards Kehl. France would allow only a small intrenchment there, for that was all the treaty of Nymwegen granted the city.

But what did this mean except relinquishing of onfe of the most important bulwarks of Strassburg, and to expose the city to a hostile attack from this direction?

Never would this proposal have been accepted if Syndicus Frantz could have taken his seat in the council of magistrates. But none knew better than Louvois that Frantz was lying at death's door and Günzer had entire control of the government.

The moment was admirably chosen.

The gentlemen to whom Louis XIV had given the gold chains were enthusiastic in their admiration of the «great king,» his friendly intentions, magnanimity and good wishes, things that ought not to be repelled; while Günzer won others, the timid, by conjuring the magistrates for Heaven's sake to avoid everything that could arouse the distrust of the French government. The king and Louvois now seemed so well disposed towards Strassburg, that they must not be repulsed on any account.

Wenck foamed with rage, the guilds hurried to their assembly rooms, fiery speeches were made, deputies hastily chosen and sent to the government; Hugo von Zedlitz endeavored to rouse the higher class of citizens and all the patriots to an immediate protest – in vain. In the higher circles, timidity or corruption frustrated any step of this nature, and besides all was too late; for while the people were meeting, making speeches, writing and getting signatures to the intended protest, the best and strongest bulwark of Strassburg had already fallen.

Hugo brought the terrible news to Alma and Hedwig, who sitting beside the unconscious Syndicus, gazed with redoubled despair at the beloved husband and father, now hovering on the verge of the grave.

This was not the only grief Alma endured; besides her sorrow for her sick father, the terror, anxiety and doubt with which she regarded her native city and her own future, she was also saddened by the terrible blow which now fell upon her widowed friend, Frau von Bernhold.

After the day on which Günzer had had the presumption to sue in such an unseemly manner for the hand of his aristocratic benefactress, the widow who still wept for her scarcely buried husband, he had not appeared again at Plobsheim.

Although this state of affairs was very agreeable to Frau von Bernhold, the threatening words, «you will repent it some day!» still rang in her ears, and made her the more anxious because she herself knew noth ing about the family papers, while Günzer, to whom this business had been entrusted for years, was thoroughly familiar with them.

Frau von Bernhold was more anxious about her children's future than her own fate. Yet she persuaded herself that it was impossible for Günzer – who owed everything he was and had to her family – could abuse the confidence reposed in him. She ascribed his indelicate proposal for her hand to his well-known avarice. When he had grown calm, he would surely regret his conduct.

«Evil» – she had said to Alma – «is not in man but on him. It always seems to me like the soiled garment of his originally pure soul. He can lay it aside if he seriously desires to do so and then the white robe of virtue and honesty is always at hand. Every discord in and among men will finally vanish in the harmonious chorus of the universe.»

But Alma was no longer with her; the Syndicus' illness had called her home,

A royal robber

and in loneliness all our cares grow heavier.

What did it avail that the beautiful estate of Plobsheim extended before her in all its summer loveliness? Her oppressed and troubled heart had no appreciation of the beauties of nature, to which the little lady was usually so keenly sensitive. It seemed as if a black veil rested upon everything; her garden, the castle, nay the world and mankind.

Only one thing afforded her comfort and support: religion. As a flower beaten by a thunder storm seeks to raise itself under the warm rays of the sun, the sorrowful widow looked up to God, relying upon Him, trusting Him, placing her fate in His hands.

So she sat this morning at one of the windows of the castle, gazing – after solacing herself with a heartfelt prayer – thoughtfully over the rich landscape. She had resolved, since Günzer no longer came to her, to entrust the Plobsheim business to another attorney and for that purpose intended to go to Strassburg the following morning, in order with the newly chosen legal adviser, to herself carefully search the family documents in her city house once more for the important title-deeds and then, still in her own person, apply to the *Reunions-Kammern*, if necessary, to the king himself.

She could gladly have set out that very day, but – what is this, what is moving along the road to Castle Plobsheim?

The whirling cloud of dust almost conceals the road.

Frau Bernhold gazes more intently.

They are horsemen.

But what are they doing here?

The widow rises to see the approaching figures more clearly.

They are certainly horsemen and – and French troops into the bargain. Twenty or thirty men.

Strange!

What do French joldiers want here in time of peace?

A royal robber

This is no road to a French garrison.

But what is this? Are not two men in civilian's dress riding at the head of the troops?

The terrible clouds of dust conceal everything.

A pause ensues.

Yes, there are two civilians.

Suddenly the widow totters and turns deadly pale, she had received a mortal blow.

Trembling in every limb and pressing the child she holds in her arms to her heart, she passed her hand across her eyes to see more distinctly.

Merciful God! No! It cannot be, and yet – the two men in civilian's dress are Günzer and his brother-in-law, Kampffer.

What do they want here at Plobsheim accompanied by French troops? Now the men turn into the avenue leading to the castle, the horses' hoofs ring on the pavement of the courtyard. Günzer and Kampffer dismount and the troopers halt behind them.

But what does Günzer mean? He goes to the bell to summon the servants.

«What does this mean? Who has the right to command here?» exclaims Frau von Bernhold.

She wants to go down – but her limbs refuse their service. She stands as if spell-bound.

Hark, how loudly and imperiously the bell sounds.

The servants hurry to the courtyard, flock from the castle, the grounds, the stable and stand motionless with astonishment.

Five and twenty mounted French soldiers with drawn swords!

And here too was Herr Günzer from Strassburg, looking sternly, gravely and haughtily around him.

Hush! he is going to speak!

A royal robber

And Günzer draws from his pocket a parchment provided with huge seals and read aloud ia a solemn tone:

«In the name of his glorious Majesty, Louis XIV, King of France, and the *Reunions-Kammern*, be it hereby announced that, after having received proof that the investiture of the families of von Bernhold and von Zorn with the Seignurie of Plobsheim is extinct, the said estate has now passed into the pos-session of the Seigneurs Günzer and Kampffer, Syndicuses of the Lower Alsatian nobilty, by virtue of the document given us and signed by His Majesty. All members of the families of von Bernhold and von Zorn are therefore commanded to instantly leave the castle and estate of Plobsheim, and all individuals belonging to their service to take the oath of allegiance to the above mentioned Seigneurs, Günzer and Kampffer, as the owners of the estate.»

At these words a piercing shriek rang from one of the windows of the castle, accompanied by the cries and sobs of children.

Frau von Bernhold had fallen senseless on the floor.

But the French dragoons in the court-yard rode forward several steps their shining swords flashing brightly in the sunlight.

Seigneur Günzer received from the trembling servants the oath of allegiance to himself and his brother-in-law as the owners of Plobsheim.

Günzer had actually laid before the *Reunions-Kammer* forged documents, according to which the time for which the families of von Bernhold and von Zorn were entitled to possess Plobsheim had expired. At the recommend-dation of Louvois, he and his brother-in-law therefore received it without ceremony, and the transfer was instantly recorded by the proper magistrate.

As the sun was setting, a pale woman – holding a little child in her arms and with two others beside her – walked down the avenue leading from the castle to the highway.

It was Frau von Bernhold and her children.

Günzer, unheeding her entreaties, tears, and sorrow, had pitilessly turned her out of the castle of her ancestors.

A royal robber

Part VI.
The fall of Strassburg

A royal robber

A royal robber

I.
The secret of the bridge.

Francois Michel le Tellier, Marquis de Louvois, had just entered his private room.

It was an unusually large apartment, furnished with royal luxury, yet the impression produced was a gloomy one.

Hangings of stamped leather, with bouquets of gilt flowers, covered the walls. Ancient pictures in exquisitely carved, black frames, beautiful Venetian mirrors, and marble tables resting on gilded goats' hoofs appeared in every direction. , The huge arm-chairs that stood around were of such beautiful and artistic workmanship, that the heart of an antiquary of our days would have throbbed high with pleasure at the sight.

Over the doors were superb bas-reliefs by Bacon the younger. But the principal ornaments were cups and flagons of wrought gold and silver, and magnificent weapons arranged in artistic groups upon the walls. The latter decoration was the one on which the minister of war specially prided himself, since some of these weapons reminded him of the campaigns of Flanders and Franche-Comté, as well as many other victories.

Grave, gloomy magnificence and strength characterized the spacious apartment and the impression was greatly heightened by the silence that pervaded it, although twenty noblemen were in the room.

All stood in silence, holding their gold-laced hats in their hands.

And besides these, admitted to the sanctuary, three hundred other nobles were waiting in the minister's ante-room.

At the head of the line, which seemed to be formed of statues, was, in accordance with the spirit of the times, a representative of the church. He was a tall, pale, emaciated monk, who might have served admirably as a model for a pious murderer. Surely such a thin figure, 5'ellowish complexion, haircloth robe, long, bony figure and crafty look, gave him a wonderful resemblance to one of the huge spiders that weave their- almost invisible nets in dark places, and crouching in a corner, greedily' watch for their prey.

His features expressed the mindless, soulless nature that stifles all fresh life In the Catholic church. He was an image of the pious Inaction that always leads to wickedness, and so willingly puts rascality In the place of Industrious life and labor.

When Father Medardus, Louvois' confessor, passed women, even the ladies of the court, he never seemed to look at them. And yet he did, but as the faces of those who were to be condemned on the Last Day, and like a fiend entrusted with the delightful commission of persecuting and torturing them with all the torments of hell throughout eternity.

This diabolical thought afforded him such delight, that he used every effort to make a beginning on earth; and the Huguenots offered the best opportunity for this purpose. The morning and evening prayer of the worthy priest to his penitent, the marquis, was there fore for a renewal of the old persecutions of the heretics. In this Father Medardus walked hand in hand with La Chaise, the king's confessor. They were already paving the way for the sad and terrible per secution of all who were not Catholics, which afterwards, under the bigoted Madame de Maintenon, was to become an eternal brand of disgrace upon the reign of Louis XIV.

Quite different was the appearance of the young man, who stood beside the priest. He was a handsome nobleman, Monsieur de Chamille, the bearer of an ancient name. His features expressed intellect, courage, and eager ambition. Pride, as well as youthful freshness and gayety, was enthroned upon them.

The younger man relied not a little upon himself, but as he had a clear head and was ambitious, he early perceived that even the finest painting does not arouse enthusiasm unless placed in a good light.

His next neighbor – the manager of the royal theater – knew nothing of all this. It was the Comte de Rhulières, a short, stout, well preserved man, the embodiment of quiet comfort, which nestles with calm satisfaction in the position it has won. He was not at all wearied by the minister's delay; he was thinking with a smile of Donna Antonia Tordesillas, the charming, new Spanish ballet dancer whom he had engaged, and the *Blanquette aux champignons* and *Mayonnaise de poisson* that would await him to-day at dinner.

The grave, aristocratic man beside him was really vexed by the quiet enjoyment of the fat, little manager, whom he – as Councillor of *Reunions-Kammern* of Alsace – thoroughly despised General procurator Fortounais therefore closed his eyes and allowed the important matters which he was to report to the minister to pass in review before his mind.

A strange medley prevailed throughout the remainder of the party: officers, officials in the war department, secretaries from the different divisions of this department with piles of papers, councilors of the crown and courtiers.

And now he entered – the man of his time – the dreaded Minister of War of Louis XIV, François Michel le Tellier, Marquis de Louvois.

All bowed low, as if before the king.

Louvois advanced with his figure drawn up to its full height. The head covered by the plumed hat scarcely bowed.

A deep stillness pervaded the room.

The minister took his seat; the by-standers raised their backs a little, but all remained in a somewhat stooping posture.

Louvois' eyes glided over the group with a cold, arrogant, scornful glance. His proud heart enjoyed the slavish humility shown him.

But even the powerful of the earth have to show some consideration – opposite to the minister stood a representative of the church, his confessor.

The throne and the church are onh' strong and unconquerable when they walk hand in hand.

Father Medardus – Louvois secretly hated and despised him – stood it is true with his head bowed lowest, his hypocritical face expressed humility, submission, and piety, but- he was a Jesuit. The marquis knew him thoroughly. His power was the power of the church, invisible, ruling over the minds and souls of men, but therefore all the more dangerous; it extended to Rome, and what was impossible to Rome?

A royal robber

The pope had already seen emperors and kings at his feet – what would ministers be to him if he were angered, even though they appeared all-powerful?

And did not Louvois need the church in order to rule? It would be an easy matter for it to oppose any of his acts.

«Reverend Father!» said the minister, In a gentler tone than he was in the habit of using to his inferiors, «what business brings you here? The ear of your penitent is ever open to holy Mother Church.»

«May jour Excellency be blessed in your going out and your coming in,» replied the priest, with clasped hands, making a low bow. «Monseigneur Louvois is the powerful prop of the church and the throne! France prospers more than ever under the scepter of His Most Christian Majesty Louis XIV and the strong hand of your Excellency.»

«The fame and greatness of His Majesty's government and the welfare of the church are my sole aim!» replied the minister. «If I can do any thing for either, speak, Reverend Father!»

The Jesuit knew Louvois' peculiarities; the minister was no friend to circumlocution, as statesman and courtier he had no time to lose.

«I have two petitions to lay at monseigneur's feet.»

«And they are»

«May it please His Majesty's government to at least restrain the ever-increasing luxury of the nation by a law?»

«Is it so great?» asked Louvois gloomily, for both he and the king loved it and knew why they fostered it in nobility and people; to the people it was a plaything that served to soothe them, to the nobility a drain, which kept them weak and submissive.

«Yes!» replied Father Medardus, in a mild, gentle tone, with a second bow, «it is leading the Christians of France to destruction.»

«It seems to me that it is a consequence of the universal prosperity.»

«That is the worm, which is already gnawing the delicate flower.»

318

A royal robber

«It is considered, with reason, a token of increased culture. It should not be carried to excess, but it is the garb every nation assumes in escaping from barbarism; – as such, I would not like to oppose it. No one can hold aloof from custom; it is a sort of universal language without which we are not understood. Thus, Holy Father, His Majesty looks at the matter, and thus do I regard it.»

«It was different in former days, customs were more simple and – the people more pious. Even in the sixteenth century it often happened that a princess gave a prince shirts made by her own hands.»

«Oh! yes!» cried Louvois, «and the middle classes were in the habit of sleeping naked. I think we ought to be glad that we have escaped from this state of barbarism. Besides it was the church that first introduced luxury – by music, sculpture, incense, gay robes, and costly vessels for the altar.»

«For the honor of God!» exclaimed the Jesuit unctuously. «The Church strove to introduce art and with it the sense of beauty. But this is not luxury.»

«What is luxury?» cried Louvois, angered by this new interference on the part of the priest with the affairs of government. «Each individual and class, each nation and period, declare everything a luxury with which they think they can dispense. You, Father Medardus, are certainly so holy a man that you despise all earthly things. But – all men cannot be saints. We still have some reports of Charlemagne's possessions; one account of the linen mentions only two sheets, a handkerchief, and a table-cloth. In Homer's time, kings ate only meat, bread and wine. Shall the household of His Majesty, Louis XIV, be arranged accordingly?»

«Your Excellency likes to jest!» murmured the Jesuit humbly, while the upper part of his body assumed an almost horizontal position, «the church does not desire to touch the annointed head of majesty, although in truth the court ought to set a good example; but where the people –»

«The court? What is done by the court is required to keep up His Majesty's state. The famous Earl of Warwick daily entertained thirty thousand persons. Ambassadors under James I, of England were attended by a suite of

A royal robber

five hundred followers, among whom were three hundred nobles. The Duke of Medina-Cœli spends four hundred and ninety thousand reals a year in wages, to his servants. But enough – and among the people? Why, luxury here is a proof of increasing industry and prosperity. My holy father – woe betide the monarchy In which too great simplicity, and thereby a comparative equality of dress, louses, mode of life and manners, gains ground. I do not like such equality. Where this takes place – we are on a fair way to equality of thought, comparisons, blossoms, whose poisonous fruit might be universal equality, that is: the fall of the throne.»

«Holy Virgin!» groaned the priest, crossing himself, «the church does not seek to touch such things. The keen eyes of a statesman like monseigneur –»

«Holy Father, your second petition,» interrupted Louvois. «Time is scantly measured to a statesman who stands at the head of a monarchy like France.»

«Monseigneur,» whispered the Jesuit, looking significantly at the minister.

Louvois understood him.

«Come nearer!» said he, and a wave of the hand sufficed to make the rest of the group retire.

Father Medardus, with crafty look and hypocritical air, drew nearer.

The man was cunning as a fox. He had not presented the first petition to the minister with any hope of seeing it granted; on the contrary he knew beforehand that Louvois would never consent. But this was precisely what he desired. If the minister refused the first request of the representative of the Catholic church, he could not, would not dare to hastily and positively reject the second and – only en the second was Father Medardus' heart fixed.

«Well Holy Father!» said Louvois; but it was with difficulty that he could repress his contempt. He knew his man, who – like a pike, had all his religion and passion; cup, sponge, cross, lance, nails and crown of thorns in his head, and his booty in his stomach.

The Jesuit uttered his request. Louvois had already guessed what would come: it was a renewed demand that His Majesty's government should at last take some decided step against the heretics, the Huguenots.

A royal robber

«And in what way, Holy Father, do you think this should be done?» asked the minister craftily. «The king swore to observe the Edict of Nantes when he ascended the throne.»

The priest's sunken eyes now began to glitter with a baleful light, as drawing up his tall, thin figure, he replied : «From the point of view of the divine right of kings, it is shown that every law, every gift, every promise may be revoked at will and conscience imposes it upon rulers as a duty: to force all heretics into the arms of Holy Mother Church.»

Louvois listened quietly; he was no enemy to such thoughts, out of secret hatred to Colbert, his colleague in the ministry, who, although himself a Catholic, was always a defender of the edict of Nantes and the Huguenots – of course only so far as the maintenance of the compact and protection against unjust persecution were concerned.

But Father Medardus – growing more and more animated and passionate – exhausted himself in explanations of his subject. He was rich in proposals of methods to intimidate the Protestants.

«Oh!» he exclaimed, and his thin, sallow face gradually became suffused with a crimson flush, which made his long features resemble those of a painted corpse – «oh! there is nothing easier than to recall these heretics to Mother Church. Let the Huguenots be forbidden to buy or sell meat on Catholic fast days, to bury their dead by daylight. Let them be excluded from guilds and trades, removed from all public offices, forbidden to rent property belonging to the church, deprived of all the patronage hitherto exercised. Physicians, apothecaries and nurses must be Catholics – children born of marriages contracted between a Catholic and a Protestant must be considered illegitimate, and all bastards given to the Catholic church. Let their courts of law be abolished; the Protestant churches – under pretense of dilapidation or some other excuse – be gradually torn down. Do not allow these accursed heretics, the Huguenots, to emigrate, declare any sale made within a year before a removal null and void, prohibit them from atttending any religious service outside of their own dwellings, or to teach Greek, Hebrew, philosophy or theology; declare that, since children seven years old are in possession of their reason and capable of making a choice in matters pertaining to

A royal robber

their souls, Huguenot children of that age have the right to decide whether they will remain with their Protestant parents or not. In the latter case, let them be reared as Catholics, in case of, stubbornness let them be soundly flogged –»

Here Father Medardus paused a moment; he had worked himself into such a state of excitement that his breath failed. His eyes were starting from their sockets, his sallow cheeks burned, and a white froth appeared in the corners of his mouth, while his long, bony fingers twitched convulsively, as if eager to seize and torture the victims of his fanaticism.

Even Louvois – a man with a heart of stone and iron – trembled; it seemed to him a trifle to overthrow long established rights, steal hardly earned property, and trample .domestic relations under foot; but he did all this quietly, with calm deliberation, not with fury bordering on the blood-thirstiness of a beast of prey.

But Father Medardus gave him no time for consideration. Bowing low, he said:

«If Monseigneur – we are all human – if Monseigneur, my distinguished penitent, should have anything on his conscience, holy Mother Church, in return for such service, would offer complete absolution, open tlie path to Heaven.»

A dark shadow flitted across Louvois' face but he controlled himself.

Father Medardus continued to whisper:

«Monseigneur might –»

«What?»

«If he would lend the arm of worldly power to the affairs of the church –»

«Well.»

«Greatly increase his authority and influence.»

The minister started. The serpent had touched the right chord – this was his vulnerable spot.

A royal robber

«Your excellency hitherto» – the serpent continued to hiss – «has exercised little influence on religious affairs. If within a short time –»

«Speak out!»

«If within a short time the rich Huguenots – of course without any mention of religion –»

«Well?»

«Should be obliged to lodge dragoons.»

A sudden flash of light darted through Louvois' soul.

«Dragoons!» he exclaimed under his breath – «for what purpose?»

«Only,» continued the priest cunningly, «only on the pretext that this had become necessary for the maintenance of the army.»

«But if the Catholics are spared –»

«Every intelligent person will perceive for what this measure is designed, and what must be done to avoid having soldiers quartered upon him. Thus Monseigneur as Minister of War, will have an influence in church matters at a single blow. When this kind of conversion is once in train –»

«Hush, holy father!» cried Louvois, starting up in violent agitation – «His Majesty will never consent.»

«An effort must be made to turn His Majesty's heart more to the church –»

Louvois shook his head. «So long as the duchesse –»

«Things will change!» whispered the priest, «and then His Majesty must have a pious soul at his side.»

Louvois was silent, but paced up and down the room with hurried steps.

The priest's eyes followed him; Medardus' soul was full of exultation. He saw that although he had not yet conquered, much of what he had said lingered in the minister's mind.

This was enough for the crafty Jesuit. Therefore, when Louvois suddenly paused before him and with a slight bend of the head, remarked:

A royal robber

«Holy Father, as a good, Catholic Christian, we will heed the warnings of the church.» Father Medardus bowed low, uttered his benediction, and withdrew.

Louvois paced silently up and down the room, while a breathless silence prevailed.

At last the minister raised his head. Young Chamilli's heart throbbed proudly and hopefully it was his turn – the next moment might bring the fulfillment of his ambitious plans.

Then, the youth turned pale as death, Louvois seated himself again and ordered the little fat manager, Comte de Rhulières to approach. Rhulières tripped forward with low bows, smiling brightly, in spite of the grave face of the dreaded minister. This man, happy in his narrow sphere, was not easily disheartened.

«Have the Spanish actors arrived?» asked the minister, in a curt, distant tone.

«Yes, Your Excellency!» replied de Rhulieres, «and they are admirable.»

«Any remarkably good members of the company?»

«Donna Antonia Tordesillas is an angel in beauty, a goddess in her performances –»

«And doubtless a queen in the kitchen» interrupted the minister with keen sarcasm – «I wish her, however, to do her best to please His Majesty. The day after the first performance I will speak to her.»

The manager's face had grown somewhat longer, but he bowed respectfully and, with a smile still lingering around the corners of his mouth, asked:

«What piece does Your Excellency desire to have given at the first performance?»

«The famous comedy, 'El Embaxador de sisismo,' by Lope de Vega,» said Louvois, and a wave of the hand dismissed the manager.

Chamilli uttered a sigh of relief.

Now his turn would probably come.

But the minister passed him by again. The invitation to come forward was addressed to General procurator Forbonnais, Councilor of the *Reunions-Kammern* of Alsace.

The dignified man approached with a firm step and a low bow.

«Have you called upon Colbert, the chief of your department?» asked the marquis.

«I shall go to him, in accordance with my duty,» replied Forbonnais quietly, «after I have shown my fidelity to the first and greatest man in the kingdom, Monseigneur Louvois; to him first belong my activity and my life.»

An almost imperceptible smile flitted over the marquis' stern features. Le Telliers' pride was doubly flattered, since Forbonnais' duties really had nothing to do with the Minister of War. General procurator Forbonnais had just arived from Alsace, his first visit ought to have been paid to Colbert – he came to Louvois.

Louvois was still the most powerful minister, but court favor is a frail and dangerous ladder; he, who desires to mount it, ought to trust only the firm, stout rounds.

«How stands the affair of Plobsheim?» asked the minister.

«As Monseigneur commanded,» replied Forbonnais.

«Since the rights of the families von Zorn and von Bernhold have expired and Herr von Günzer, supported by your Excellency, applied for this fief of France, it was given to him and the Sieur Kampffer.

«The estate and castle are in his hands, the transfer registered and the matter thus settled forever.»

«And the families of von Zorn and von Bernhold?»

«Will make a great outcry; but that will do them no good.»

«It is of no consequence either; both families are opposed to France. With the loss of Plobsheim their influence will be destroyed. Besides His Majesty says: *'tel est notre plaisir!'* And Günzer, have you nothing to tell me from him?»

A royal robber

«Yes, Monseigneur; but I don't know whether I ought here –»

«What? what?» cried Louvois scarcely concealing the great interest he took in the communication.

«It is not much after all –»

«Speak, speak!»

«He wishes your Excellency to know that more than half the paid soldiers are lying seriously ill. Besides the time of the Frankfort fair is approaching and many citizens will set out this week to visit the ancient city.»

Forbonnais was silent.

Louvois' soul was full of exultation; but not a muscle of his grave, cold face quivered. On the contrary, he seemed to feel unconquerable scorn, as he now asked whether this was all Günzer had confided.

Forbonnais assented.

«Then we will pass on to other matters,» said the minister.

Forbonnais advanced nearer, and a long, mysterious conversation ensued. The Councilor reported in detail what he intended afterwards to communicate to Colbert.

The position occupied by Louvois and Colbert towards each other – although they were externally on the best of terms – was secretly, on account of their rivalry, a hostile one.

Colbert was the son of a wine dealer in Reims, Le Tellier, Louvois' father, took him in 1668 into his service, which, however, Colbert soon exchanged for that of Cardinal Mazarin, who made the talented young man his intendant.

From this time Colbert hiad a share in the financial affairs of France, became in 1654 secretary to the young queen, and was at last recommended with Louvois to the king as minister by the dying Mazarin.

The rivalry between the two immediately began, but was strictly concealed, as outwardly they were absolutely necessary to each other, Louvois was great in war, Colbert in finance; both – by war and finance – raised Louis XIV to the height of power which gave him fame and splendor. Thus both were indispensable to the king as well as each other, only – neither wished to allow the other a superior influence over His Majesty and the government.

It was the old struggle for supremacy. And the moles worked cleverly.

Louvois was now again digging his subterranean mole-tracks. To be sure he thus gained a great deal unobserved; but Colbert's great services to France sustained him. He left the state a revenue of 116 millions and a progress in art, science and manufactures, which flattery ascribed to Louis XIV, the «Great.»

The secret conversation between Forbonnais and Le Tellier, during which the former had delivered what was apparently a very important letter from Günzer, was now over.

Once more Chamilli hoped – and again in vain.

The audience had continued two hours, and the Chevalier de Camilli still stood in the background.

Officers, employees in the War Department, with their piles of papers, councilors, courtiers, who had various secret reports to make – some regarding the most notorious scandals of the day – had been dismissed.

Now the last – retreating towards the door with low bows – left the apartment.

Young Chamilli stood as if crushed. How many scornful glances had fallen upon him – almost every one who had departed had given him a sarcastic smile – how his chest had heaved each time the powerful minister uttered another name than his, signed to another to approach.

And no glance from Louvois had fallen upon him! None was vouchsafed now and yet he was alone with the minister, who paced slowly and thoughtfully up and down the room.

Suddenly he paused before him.

A royal robber

Chamilli trembled, but Louvois' eyes did not rest disapprovingly upon him.

«Young man,» he began; «I have kept you waiting a long time and apparently overlooked you. Do you know why?»

«Monseigneur, in his wisdom, undoubtedly has excellent reasons for it,» replied the young chevalier, with a low bow.

«Yes!» said Louvois, «those I undoubtedy have and they are of a twofold nature. In the first place I detained you to give you a proof of my confidence. You are to have an important secret commission; but it also occurred to me to give you in the commencement of your career a lesson upon which your whole success depends. Machiavelli's policy rests upon the great principle of always subordinating the lesser advantage to the greater. So – in your situation, ardent selfconscious youth, overweening self-conceit must bend to the higher welfare of the state. Always remember, young man, these hours which made you so clearly feel your own insignificance; then you will never lack the self-denial, and submission to guidance, so necessary to a diplomatic career.»

There was a touch of sarcasm in the last words, even though they were perhaps well-meant; satirical manner was one of the characteristics of the statesman.

Young Chamilli was clever enough to understand this manner and, on being requested to give an account of his last mission, did so with calmness and modesty.

He had really accomplished all that could be expected, and the minister declared himself satisfied, an event that rarely happened.

Chamilli's expectations of higher and more important duties again rose. The minister had just told him that he was to have an important secret commission. During the last few days rumors had been in circulation at the court about great political events, which were close at hand.

Louvois' keen eyes doubtless read this expectation in the features of the young man, who had just entered the school of dissimulation and was anything but a master in the art.

A royal robber

Again a scornful smile flitted over his stern, gloomy features, as he continued:

«Chevalier! You have justified the confidence I reposed in you. As a reward you shall now receive a new, and extremely important mission.»

«I am at your service, Monseigneur!» cried the young man eagerly, his eyes sparkling with joy. «I will risk my life to satisfy Your Excellency.»

«Very well!» continued Louvois quietly, with a peculiar smile, «then listen.»

Chamilli drew himself up in attitude of eager attention.

«Go,» began the minister slowly, placing a strong emphasis upon each word, «go this very evening to Basle in Switzerland. You will remain there three days. On the fourth, punctually at two o'clock, station yourself, provided with paper, pen and ink, on the bridge that crosses the Rhine. Watch and write down with the utmost care everything that passes before your eyes for two hours. Precisely at four o'clock, take post-horses, travel day and night, and bring me your observations. At whatever hour you may arrive, report yourself to me at once. Do you understand?»

Chamilli assented, though this commission made him ready to sink into the earth.

So this was the hoped for higher diplomatic employment. Could not an ordinary clerk be used for such a purpose?

But Louvois, the all powerful minister, had commanded, and was it not possible that on the bridge of Basle, Heaven knows what complications might arise? Important – yes, the matter must be of great importance, that was proved by the closing words: «At whatever hour you may arrive, report yourself to me at once.»

«And,» Louvois now added gravely, «you will answer to me with your life for the most absolute secrecy in regard to this commission and everything relating to it.»

«I will,» replied the chevalier, bowing.

«Then may God be with you,» replied Le Tellier, and he dismissed the young man by a wave of the hand.

It was on the fourth day after this conversation, at precisely two o'clock in the afternoon, that le Chevalier de Chamilli stepped upon the bridge at Basle.

On leaving Paris, he had laid aside his court dress and donned the coslume of a simple citizen – the style adopted by the artists and authors of those days. And in fact the attire was very becoming to the young man; it gave him an air of originality well suited to an artist.

The servant who accompanied him on the journey was also obliged to exchange his livery for a plain coat.

The gay, French blood flowed in his veins and Chamilli at last laughed at himself and his commission. Curiosity to see what would happen on the bridge at Basle outweighed wounded pride, and as provided with paper, pen and ink he now assumed his strange' post, the whole affair seemed extremely comical.

However, there was no time to think of himself and his situation; the passing was sufficiently constant to claim his whole attention. A corner was quickly chosen, the little inkstand placed on a beam, the paper taken from his pocket and the pen from a small tin case and – the oddest of all records began.

Peasant women returning from market with their empty baskets; and a traveler in a blue coat on horseback crossed the bridge.

Chamilli wrote: peasant women, etc., a traveler in a blue coat, with long riding boots, a dog-whip in his hand.

Then came an old peasant, a ragged beggar, a porter.

The perspiration ran down the young diplomat's forehead. He was, according to the minister's commands, to watch and write down with the utmost care everything that passed before his eyes for two hours.

Young Chamilli wiped the perspiration from his brow. His strange reporting was making him very warm. Shaking his head, he took up the pen again; but

A royal robber

the slight frown on his brow instantly relaxed, an extremely pretty girl in burgher dress was passing him.

The eyes of the two young people met, and both flushed crimson.

Chamilli wrote a pretty burgher maiden, simple in dress and appearance, is passing by with a little open basket on her arm – but here a gap occurred in the record; the mutual look and blush took place.

Again came market women, peasants, a shepherd with a flock of sheep.

A thief, with his hands bound behind his back, was also led across by bailiffs.

Then came more citizens passing to and fro – wagons of all kinds, a party of gipsies, gamblers, drunkards, singing merry songs in their glee.

Chamilli perspired furiously; he was secretly very angry at being obliged to write down such trifles – at being entrusted with such a commission. His excitable nature rebelled against the minister, and his heart throbbed passionately.

Suddenly he smilingly laid his hand upon his beating heart; two joiners were carrying a new coffin – the quiet lodging of a now quiet man – across the bridge.

And Chamilli gayly noted down the joiners and the coffin. The clocks in Basle were striking three.

At the same moment, a man in a yellow vest and yellow breeches stopped in the middle of the bridge, then approached the river, leaned over the parapet, gazed down into the water and with a large cane gave three distinct raps on the floor.

Fool! thought Chamilli, and fuming over his childish task, wrote down the occurrence. If it had not been Monseigneur Louvois who had given him the commission, he would have thought himself the fool. As it was, by Heaven, he was on the point of throwing the paper into the water.

But see! Ah! – this was some little compensation for the tiresome work, the pretty burgher maiden came back.

A royal robber

She had probably been to some garden near the bridge, for her little basket was now filled with autumn, roses; but still brighter than these was the crimson flush on her cheeks as soon as she perceived tho young man.

It is strange how suddenly a mutual kindness, a mutual attraction, flames up in young hearts without any acquaintance, without the exchange of a single word.

So it was here, and the fact was announced by the mutual blushes; the glance with which the young people looked at each other, revealed to them the strange emotion which had so suddenly and unexpectedly taken possession of their hearts. Was it accident or design? As the girl passed the handsome young man – whom she probably took for an artist, one of the most beautiful roses fell at Chamilli's feet. Of course the young Frenchman's passionate heart glowed with redoubled ardor. The rose was a frank confession of love to the hot blooded chevalier a confession that found full confirmation in the happy smile that flitted over the girl's features as – looking back – she saw him hastily raise the flower and press it joyously to his lips.

At this moment the young man had completely forgotten his commission, the bridge, even Louvois and his own ambitious hopes for the future.

«Follow her!» cried a voice in his heart, «follow the lovely creature!»

And he was actually on the point of throwing pen and paper, together with the childish, useless reports he had been writing and over which he had been angrily fretting, into the water, when – his carriage drove up and almost at the same moment the clock in the city struck four.

Oh! accursed recollection – «Precisely at four o'clock take post-horses, travel day and night and bring me your observations. At whatever hour you may arrive, report yourself to me at once,» Louvois had said with a grave face and stern glance. No jest was concealed behind those words, but grave earnest to which the thought of the Bastile lent a gloomy background. It brought the chevalier back to his senses.

He cast one more glance after the pretty girl who again turned towards him, then, cursing himself and all diplomatic commissions, the young man threw himself into the carriage. The horses started and dashed away like the wind towards Paris.

But the return was even more unpleasant to Monsieur de Chamilli than the journey to Basle had been.

What in the name of Heaven and all the saints had he to report to the minister?

Nothing! nothing of any importance had happened on the bridge during the two hours. What did his notes contain; they were a mere record of market women, beggars, citizens, a shepherd, an old clergyman with his pupils, a fellow in a yellow vest and breeches who acted like a fool. Ah! and a confoundedly pretty girl, with whom he might have had a delightful flirtation and from whom he was obliged to run away.

Chamilli struck his forehead angrily.

And what would the minister say to such trifles. Oh! surely, surely, he had expected more – different things!

Might not this deprive the young nian of Louvois' favor and thus ruin his future without any fault of his own – for – he was sure of this – nothing had escaped his notice.

Two days after leaving the bridge he arrived in Paris. It was midnight, but the door of the minister's apartments instantly opened to him.

Louvois hastily advanced to meet him.

«The paper!» were his only words. Chamilli, in great embarrassment, delivered it.

The Marquis de Louvois, sat down and read the contents with eager attention. Suddenly, as he reached the place where mention was made of the man in yellow vest and breeches, who had rapped three times with his stick, he started up in delight.

«The victory is ours!» he exclaimed. «To the king!»

Chamilli was obliged to follow.

His Majesty was asleep. Louvois ordered him to be awaked and entered.

A royal robber

Chamilli, fairly beside himself with amazement, waited in the ante-room. He now heard that four couriers had been awaiting his arrival for several hours.

Fifteen minutes after, the doors of the royal sleeping room opened and the minister, greatly excited, come out. He held four despatches in his hand. The couriers advanced one by one – each received a despatch and a sealed order which must be opened at the first station he reached.

A sign – and all hurried away.

«We are satisfied Chamilli!» said the minister. «Now rest alter your fatiguing journey. Your diplomatic career, if you continue to be equally faithful, will be a prosperous one. You can take with you the assurances of His Majesty's favor and mine. To give you an opportuinty of seeing the pretty girl again.» Louvois added smiling – «you shall return to Basle in a week on a more peaceful mission.»

With these words the minister dismissed the surprised and overjoyed young man.

A royal robber

II.
The gardener's wife.

Entering Strassburg at the present day through the ancient «Weissturmtor,» one perceives on the inner side of this gate, which dates from the time of the Reformation, a face carved in stone with a broad thick tongue stretched far out of the mouth.

This place was at the time of our story and still remains – the quarter of the Strassburg gardeners.

At the time of which we are writing, this gardeners' quarter and the gardeners' guild were in their prime. Many of the now ancient and dilapidated houses were still new and looked pleasantly forth from among the gardens that surrounded them. At the end of this quarter stood a one story house, to which were attached several fields of vegetables and a small, well-kept flower garden. All this was the property of a young gardener named Geiger, who had been married two years, and who was called on account of his skill in the culture of flowers «Flower Geiger,» a nickname which pleased the man all the better because he felt that it honored his profession.

Geiger's wife was a stout, muscular woman, neither beautiful nor ugly; strong and hardy as was natural in her profession, for she was a gardener's daughter. She had no children, and therefore could devote herself entirely to her business; but this consisted chiefly in selling flowers and vegetables – while her husband was working in the fields and garden.

She did not do a bad business, for she was cunning and extremely avaricious. To earn money, everything was right to her. Her avarice had become such a proverb among the neighbors and members of the guild, that when they wanted to speak of another miserly woman they said in their rude way: «Yes, she'd sell clothes and soul like Geiger's wife.»

But to-day the usually industrious woman did not go to work. Her husband had gone to his field out; side the city early in the morning – a large basketful of flower-pots and plants in blossom stood on a stone bench before the house, ready for her to carry about the city, as she did almost daily during the summer -and autumn whether it was market day or not, but the basket was untouched, the flowers still waited to be carried away, though the sun already stood high in the heavens.

The gardener's wife was pacing restlessly up and down as people do when expecting someone.

She often went to the end of the little garden and looked out into the street.

The woman was dressed to go out and, though she only wore the simple costume adopted by all the women and the girls of the gardener's guild, looked very neat.

She looked very pretty, this gardener's wife, with the bright eyes and red cheeks that gave her sunburnt face an expression of exuberant health.

She pulled her skirt a little farther down on the sides with both hands. And the bodice required a little adjusting too.

Now her figure looked slighter.

Then she tightened her garter, smiling at the handsome calf reflected in the water.

Now the other garter needed tightening.

From whom did she receive these handsome garters.

Her husband?

Oh! no, a plain gardener doesn't buy such dainty things.

Wasn't that a G. wrought in pearls that appeared in the center of one?

Again the woman smiled as she fastened above her knee the second garter with the pearl G.

Her husband – who usually felt great respect for his wife's tongue – had once asked her where she got the «things» and what the G. meant?

«From a friend,» she answered with her arms akimbo, «and the G means God preserve us from a stupid, inquisitive man.» Since that time the gardener had asked no more questions of the kind.

A royal robber

The garters were now firm and the woman stood up.

Not a soul was in sight.

The basket of flowers had been standing on the bench three hours – for three hours the woman had been ready to go out – what was lacking?

She generally did not waste a minute, and if kept waiting while engaged in business made her customers pay well for it.

She must undoubtedly have been well paid for the delay this morning; or she wouldn't have had so pleasant a face over it.

Even now, as if for consolation, she drew several ducats out of her' pocket, eyed them lovingly and after a few moments, put them back again.

Still no one came.

But stop. Was not somebody approaching up the street?

Yes.

But the person was not the man she expected – he wore neither a yellow vest nor yellow breeches and carried no cane.

The figure was small, the head rested stiffly between high shoulders.

«Ah, it's he,» said the gardener's wife in a contemptuous tone – «what does he want here?»

Wenck was coming up the street.

«Curse the luck!» she added, «and just now. I wish the tailor was in Jericho. I must get rid of him as quick as I can. If Herr Günzer should know, or if –»

Wenck was just entering the garden, the woman hurried towards him.

«Good-morning, Frau Geiger!» cried the little tailor pleasantly.

«Good-morning!» she replied, by no means in the same tone

«I should like a pretty bouquet,» replied Wenck and it was evident he was very much delighted.

«Bouquet?» said the gardener's wife, «I haven't time to make one now.»

A royal robber

«That isn't necessary.»

«Shall I get it by witchcraft?»

«Why so? You have several in your basket.»

«They are engaged.»

«All?»

«All three.»

«And what does one of them cost?»

The woman named an extravagant price.

Wenck looked at her with a comical expression, but, as he knew her disposition, said no more but laid a larger sum than she asked on the stone bench beside the basket.

This produced its effect.

«There, take one, I shall make nothing by it, for they are rare now and only to be had from hot-houses,» said Frau Geiger in a somewhat more amicable tone, hastily pocketing the money.

Wenck obeyed and selected one of the bouquets.

«Ah!» said he, «if you only knew for whom and for what festival the flowers were intended.»

«How shall I?»

«Guess?»

«A wedding?»

«Pshaw!»

«A christening?»

«No.»

«Then I don't know.»

«The celebration of a recovery.»

A royal robber

«And who has got well?»

«Who? One of the noblest and best men in all Strassburg.»

«Do you know whom I mean?» continued the little tailor loquaciously.

«No!»

«Well – Syndicus Frantz.»

«What!» exclaimed the woman in surprise – «has he got well?»

«Yes!» cried Wenck, his little eyes sparkling with joy. «With God's help the noble man has escaped death. Well, who knows what good it may do! Today – though still pale and weak – he attends the council for the first time, and I must show him my heartfelt joy.»

«It was said that he would never recover.»

«Of course, and there were many evil-minded people, in and out of Strassburg, who desired it. But our Lord has preserved to Strassburg her best citizen.»

«Why!» cried the gardener's wife, scornfully, «matters are not quite so bad as that. There are other able men here.»

«None better than the Syndicus, Heaven knows! The poor man was in a bad way and his family too. For weeks he hovered on the verge of the grave, and mother and daughter – and somebody else – never left his bedside. Oh! my dear woman, you might have learned there what true love is. They nursed him day and night, and night and day without giving themselves a moment's rest.»

The gardener's wife looked restlessly around.

«And he had an evil dish!» said the tailor with marked emphasis.

«I must go!» said the woman. «I really must go, I have something to do in the city.»

But the gardener's wife now became very uneasy. She fancied she saw another figure hastily approaching.

A royal robber

She could no longer control her restlessness. «Fare well!» she said again, this time in a very snappish tone. «Here is the best way out.» She opened a gate opposite to the one by which Wenck had entered the garden and which led through the gardener's quarter into the center of the city, and at the same time pushed the little tailor out in by no means the most gentle manner.

«May Satan take him!» she muttered. «If I had known the bouquet was for Syndicus Frantz, he certainly wouldn't have got it.»

As Wenck left the garden, she carefully locked the gate through which he had passed and hurried in the opposite direction.

The man she had just perceived in the distance was advancing so rapidly that his pace resembled a run rather than a walk.

«It is he!» cried Frau Geiger in evident agitation.

Yes! The man hurrying towards her wore a yellow vest, yellow breeches and carried a stout cane.

When he saw the woman waiting at the garden gate, he suddenly stopped, tossed the cane three times into the air as if in sport, caught it again and then rapidly approached her.

Frau Geiger – without saying a word – took the cane.

The woman now walked forward, followed by her companion.

He was bathed in perspiration – covered with dust.

It was evident that he had been running a long distance.

In fact as soon as he reached the house, he sank down on a wooden bench, almost fainting. Brandy and water, bread and cheese stood ready for him. Wiping the perspiration from his forehead with his shirt sleeve, he seized the glass and emptied the contents at a single draught.

No word had yet been exchanged between the two, but the gardener's wife held out her hand to the man. as if she expected to receive something.

«Here!» said the latter at last, drew from under his vest a small leather pouch suspended by a leather strap, and gave it to the woman.

A royal robber

She snatched it eagerly, pulled her handkerchief from her shoulders, slipped her head through the strap, let the pouch slide down under her bodice, fastened the handkerchief again, and running to the basket of flowers, which had been ready several hours, lifted it on her head.

When it was firmly placed on her head, she hurried off towards the city without troubling herself in the least about the man sitting in the house.

But the man, who had already made a four hours journey and traversed, almost at a run, the distance from the spot where a French courier on a horse covered with foam, had handed him the leather pouch, fell asleep from weariness as soon as he had finished his breakfast.

Meantime the gardener's wife hurried as fast as her feet could carry her to Herr Günzer's house.

On reaching here, she hastily ascended the steps, opened a door and stood in the private apartment of the master of the dwelling.

«Ha!» cried Günzer, who was pacing up and down, evidently in the greatest agitation and had been waiting for his visitor a long time – «at last, at last! Has he come?»

«I ran instantly like a weasel as your Excellency commanded, with the basket which had already been ready several hours,» said Frau Geiger, removing the basket with Günzer's aid and setting it on the floor.

«And the pouch, the pouch!»

The woman removed her handkerchief and drew the pouch from her bosom.

Günzer eagerly seized it; he could scarcely wait for her to draw her head out of the strap by which it was suspended.

He now took a key, which he wore fastened by a cord around his own neck and unfastened the lock of the leather bag.

If Günzer – sentenced to death – had been standing on the scaffold and expected to find his pardon in the pouch, his movements could not have been more rapid.

A royal robber

His hands trembled as he unlocked it and drew out a despatch fastened by a large seal.

It was Louvois' seal, the paper was addressed to the Sieur Günzer of Plobsheim.

The man devoured the lines with sparkling eyes – at each word his brow cleared and instead of an anxious, troubled look his face at last wore an expression of the utmost triumph.

The gardener's wife, who seemed to be perfectly at home here, had meantime sat down in a chair and watched him intently.

The neck handkerchief still lay en the floor beside the basket; but the provoking garters with the pearl G. would not stay fastened to-day.

As Günzer finished the letter, the woman was just tightening one. His eyes glittered, his head burned, he took a step forward but hastily turned as if an iron hand had seized and snatched him back.

«Madman!» he murmured, «let childish follies alone. Have you not more important things to do?»

Hastening to a drawer in his writing-table, he took out a handful of ducats, went back and threw them into the lap of the delighted woman.

«That's a token of gratitude for your services, Anna!» he said, «but they are not yet over and – you must do still more for me.»

The woman's whole face was one broad, radiant smile of delight. Günzer had never been so liberal as to-day, why should she not declare herself ready for any farther services?

She did so.

«I require an oath, Anna,» said Günzer.

«An oath?» repeated the woman. «About what?»

«That you will conceal from all the world – even your husband – to the hour of your death, the secret services you have performed and will still render.»

«From that simpleton,» cried the woman laughing, «I should have plenty to do if I bothered about everything he needn't know.»

«But from every one else.»

«You have already seen, Herr Günzer, that I know how to rule my tongue.»

«Anna!» said Günzer, putting his arm affectionately around her waist, «these are secrets of a nature –»

«What do I care for your secrets. I don't want to know them. If I can earn something by –»

«Why I think you might be satisfied to-day.»

«Good gracious! So I am.»

«But if you want to earn more in the same way –»

«Give me the oath, Herr Günzer!» she cried, raising her right hand.

Günzer made her vow secrecy with a terrible oath.

«And now,» he said, «listen. Have you put the flowers in your basket as I told you?»

«Of course, there are twelve little pots of plants and three bouquets.»

«One, two, three, six – nine – twelve. Yes. But there are only two bouquets.»

«Then one must have dropped out of the basket.»

«Make two out of one as quick as you can.»

The gardener's wife did so, bending low over the basket. The neck handkerchief still lay on the ground and Günzer saw something more beautiful than flowers.

The bouquet was now divided into two smaller ones, and the gardener's wife stood erect.

«Now then, Anna, quick!» cried Günzer, with an energy unusual to him. «The greatest haste is necessary. Twelve flower-pots and three bouquets make fifteen. Here are the addresses of fifteen of the most prominent magistrates. Go – as fast as your feet can carry you, but in such a way as to attract no attention – to each of these gentlemen, ask to see him in person and give each – do you understand me?»

«Certainly!»

«One of the flower-pots or bouquets,» saying – «pay close attention.»

«I'm listening!»

«Herr Günzer sends it. Greeting and happiness in the country! Do you understand?»

«Zooks!» cried the gardener's wife laughing, «since when have you taken me for a child? I'm to give each of the fifteen gentlemen a flower-pot, saying: 'Herr Günzer sends it. Greeting and happiness in the country,'»

«Bravo!» cried Günzer, clasping the woman in his arms and giving her a hearty kiss, which she quietly received.

«And now go, as fast as your feet can carry you,» said Günzer, helping her to raise the basket. «For a week, Anna, we must not see each other. At the end of that time, bring me some flowers, then I shall want very beautiful ones, so give me plenty of time to choose, and –»

«Farewell, Herr Günzer!» cried the gardener's wife, already on her way out of the room. «In a week!» Günzer clasped his head with both hands. Heavens! how his thoughts surged through his brains.

As soon as the fifteen receive the flowers, each, according to agreement, will send to his friends. In an hour, if Anna does not delay, we can meet at the appointed place. But the deuce – the woman – yet what have I to do with her, now, when the moment of victory, won by years of toil, is approaching? Forward quickly, the die is cast. General Montclar and Colonel von Alsfeld are on their way; at midnight – hurrah, at midnight Strassburg will be mine, and I, I will lay it at the feet of His Majesty, Louis XIV, King of France.

III.
Hannibal ante portas.

It was the evening of the same day. The interior of the house occupied by Syndicus Frantz had assumed a fest'al appearance, especially in the story in which the family lived.

The worthy Syndicus' room was charmingly decorated and was just receiving from Hedwig and Alma the final touch, which consisted of a transparency surrounded by garlands, which in simple but earnest words expressed sincere gratitude for the recovery of the beloved husband and father.

This was Hugo's work; but the rest of the decorations had proceeded from the hearts and hands of the mother and daughter.

The principal object with every woman – and this was beautifully shown in Hedwig and Alma – should be to keep their feelings truthful in every incident of life.

To-day, for the first time since his sickness, Syndicus Frantz had attended the council of magistrates, and Hedwig, Alma and Hugo were expecting his return.

«Here, Hugo,» said Alma, casting such a happy radiant glance at her lover, that the latter longed to embrace her, «let us fasten the last garland here. It will look well on the high back of the chair. Then when father sits down in it, it will seem as if the dear flowers were taking him in their arms.»

«You are right!» replied Hugo, as he aided Alma to carrry her idea into execution, «only I pity the flowers.»

«Pity them? Why?»

«On account of the jealousy they will feel when you throw your arms around your father's neck, then the fairest and sweetest of the flowers will embrace him.»

«Flatterer!» replied Alma with a slight blush, yet giving him such a frank affectionate glance that Hugo could no longer restrain himself and, bending over the back of the chair, impressed a tender kiss on her cheek.

With his arm thrown around Alma, Hugo gazed with satisfaction at the completed task, while Alma, leaning her head upon his shoulder, followed the direction of his glance with a happy smile. Then the young man turned, and looking deep into her eyes, said:

«How beautifully this common feeling, thought and labor unites us. How delightful it will be, Alma, when we belong to each other entirely for life.»

«Yes, it will be beautiful, inexpressibly beautiful,» she said softly, while her cheeks were suffused with that timid flush of girlish confusion which far surpasses ‹every other charry›, and seems to exert a magical influence not only over ardent youth, but the grave man in his prime, nay even the gray-beard. «It will be beautiful, and yet the thought of this future often makes me anxious –»

«Makes you anxious?»

«Because I see no tokens that it will ever become *the present*. Do not the political storms daily increase? Where is the prospect of the happy time for which father said we must wait?»

«It will come.»

«And storms lie behind it also.»

«Storms? Oh dearest!» cried Hugo, gravely and tenderly drawing the beloved form closer to his heart, «when we are once united, a loving married pair, let the storms come. Then rely on me and our love. Remain frank, trusting, happy and brave as you are now, and we will conquer everything that assails us from without; nay, the darker and fiercer grows the tempest, the lighter and happier will be our hearts.»

«And how easy and sweet the duty of a good housekeeper. and wife will be to me,» replied Alma, her eyes radiant with joy. «How I will always meet you, dear good brave heart, with gentleness and love, that our life may be like a beautiful melody, a long musical accord, in which the dissonances of the outside world will vanish.»

A royal robber

The father entered and was received with delight. Hedwig saw at the first glance with pleasure that the attendance at the council of magistrates had left no cloud on her husband's brow. And she saw aright.

The French minister had been questioned in regard to some disquieting rumors about the movements of French troops in Alsace and especially the massing of large numbers at Breisach and Freiburg, but the explanations received and laid before the magistrates to-day were so perfectly satisfactory that even the anti-French party declared themselves entirely content. General Montclar merely intended to review the army and this had been arranged to take place not very far from the frontiers of Strassburg.

Moreover, the spies, who had been sent out, brought the decisive message that the French troops would be instantly recalled to their respective garrisons.

The French ambassador's letter to the council was full of the warmest expressions of the peaceful, friendly disposition of France.

Thus the Syndicus. had returned home somewhat soothed and, as he did not wish to cloud the joy of his family, his firm will banished from his mind the last trace of anxiety.

Friends and relatives had arrived at his house and all united around a simple, but excellent supper at which universal gayety prevailed.

Alma appeared happier than all the others. Hugo thought he had never before seen her in such a joyous mood. Alma's simple nature possessed a peculiar charm. The most insignificant event was made as charming as a fairy tale, by the manner in which she related it.

This was particularly the case this evening. Her happy mood lent a new charm to all her good qualities, her bright, quick intellect and clear mind.

Hugo often looked at her in astonishment, he perceived so many new and beautiful traits of character to-day, though he had known her so long.

The gay mood of the company remained unaltered and unshadowed all the evening and until far into the night.

A royal robber

All present were sincerely happy and when, towards twelve o'clock, the friends and acquaintances – out of consideration for the invalid – wished to take leave, he himself begged them to stay.

They did so gladly. Hedwig brought out some bottles of fine old sack, and thus, amid jest and laughter, the mirth and pleasure reached a point it had long lacked.

As the glass clinked merrily and the worthy people assembled in the room gayly shook hands, the clock in the neighboring cathedral struck the hour of twelve.

«Midnight!» exclaimed several, «it is time –»

Then suddenly all were silent.

«What was that?» asked the Syndicus.

«It seems to me as if I heard the sound of distant firing,» replied Hugo, opening the window.

«Perhaps a fire has broken out in the city,» exclaimed Alma in alarm. "How I pity the poor people it will ruin.»

All ran for their wraps.

«But what?»

«Don't you hear anything?» said the Syndicus, who had suddenly grown deadly pale as if some terrible thought had darted through his mind, «another gun, another, heavy firing –»

«What is it?» all exclaimed.

"For God's sake, what does it mean?"

«What does it mean?» cried the Syndicus, drawing his tall figure up to its full height, while his eyes flashed like those of an angry lion, «what does it mean?» he repeated, in a trembling voice, and while the glass he held in his hand fell shattered on the floor, added with an exclamation of pain «it means treachery!»

«Treachery?» repeated the whole party, turning pale.

348

A royal robber

«Yes, yes, treachery,» cried the Syndicus again, «this is the cause of the most exaggerated assurances of the friendship of France at the meeting of magistrates today. That is why – oh! God, it is Montclar, returning from the review of his army.»

Suddenly the bells in the churches and towers along the wall began to peal loudly, then came one, two, three heavy reports.

«The alarm cannon on the walls!» cried all, running for caps and canes, shawls and overcoats.

Hugo now returned panting for breath; as he could discover nothing from the window, he had rushed down into the street. But there also nobody knew what this nocturnal firing meant.

«Only this much is certain!» cried Hugo, no less pale than the Syndicus, «that the firing is at or near the Rhine redoubt.»

«And what do you think of it, my boy?» asked the Syndicus.

«May God withdraw the sun from this court of France,» Hugo burst forth, grinding his teeth, «for all signs must deceive if this is not a shameless breach of peace, a fierce attack, after the most solemn assurances of good will, under cover of night and darkness.»

«That is so!» cried the Syndicus, «my coat, my official cap!»

«What are you going to do, father?» exclaimed mother and daughter in one breath.

«My duty as usual. I'll go and –»

«But consider, you have just been so ill,» pleaded Hedwig and Alma.

«The times are sicker than I, they are suffering from rascality!» cried the old man, pushing them away, «my coat, my cap!»

Hedwig and Alma pleaded, the firing still echoed in the distance – the alarm bells pealed loudly, the reports of the cannon sounded in the intervals, the signal horns also echoed on the night air, summoning the citizens and members of the guilds.

A royal robber

The Syndicus was ready to hurry off, Hugo also stood prepared, the guests had already hastened to their homes.

«Now, let us go!» cried the Syndicus, with an energy that would have done honor to a younger man, «let us go and may God protect you and our good city.»

But at the same moment, the door flew wide open and Wenck – armed to the teeth – rushed in, his café crimson with fury; his eyes were almost starting from their sockets, the veins on his forehead were swollen, his head – as usual in moments of excitement – seemed sunk still lower between his shoulders.

«Heaven and Hell!» he cried, forgetting all consideration in his indescribable rage, «this is a fine business. There are the consequences when traitors sit in the council of magistrates and direct the affairs of government. It would have been better to demolish all the fortifications, as they did the one on the Rhine, while the Syndicus was ill. Now we have it.»

«What?»

«What has happened?»

«The fortification on the Rhine? Didn't I say so?»

«What about it?» cried all in a breath.

«What about it, Herr Syndicus?» cried the little tailor, stretching out both clenched fists, «it has gone to the devil. The French have attacked and captured it!»

All trembled as if they had been stabbed to the heart.

«The French? Captured? In the night? In the midst of peace?» cried Hedwig.

«Oh! why were we such simpletons as to believe their assurances!» exclaimmed Wenck.

«And are you sure, Wenck,» the Syndicus now asked hastily, «that the fortifications on the Rhine have been attacked and catpured by the French?»

«Unfortunately ! Unfortunately!»

A royal robber

«Then to our posts,» cried the old man, «now is the time to act.»

And with these words the Syndicus, Hugo von Zedlitz and Wenck hurried away.

But what indescribable confusion and excitement prevailed in the city!

Everyone was rushing to and fro in the darkness.

Nobody knew exactly what had happened.

«The French!»

«The French are here»

«The Rhine fortification is captured!»

«The whole city is surrounded!»

«Up citizens, the enemy! the enemy!»

«To the walls!»

«To arms!»

«Down with the traitors!»

«Down with Frischman, the hypocrite, the liar, the French hound!»

«Down with the traitors in the council!»

«Mount the cannon on the walls!»

«Up, citizens, up, up!»

«Death and damnation to the traitors!»

Such were the shrieks and shouts that echoed through the night – and still the firing continued, the bells rang from the steeples, cannon thundered from the walls, and the signal horns sounded in the streets.

All were running to and fro, the magistrates to the Rathaus, the citizens armed and unarmed, to the guild-rooms and walls, the few soldiers capable of duty to the gates to increase the number of defenders, women with dishevelled hair, only half dressed in their haste, rushing to the corners of the streets, to hear and see what was going on.

A royal robber

And to add to the confusion, darkness brooded over the city, only interrupted here and there by the flaring of lights.

But the worst feature of all was the universal lack of order and management.

A large number of the magistrates had lost their wits. Commander von Jenneggen was not to be found, the soldiers, half of whom were sick, had only one officer capable of service, some of the officers and principal men of the armed citizens and guilds were absent from the places of meeting or did not know what was to be done, and quarreled because one wanted this, the other that.

Who was to command?

How and by whom were the long lines of walls and numerous fortifications of the city to be garrisoned? This was not possible, even If all the soldiers and citizens could have been assembled and – a large number of the latter had gone to the Frankfort fair.

The key of the arsenal was loudly demanded, that guns might be mounted on the walls.

Was it in Jenneggen's possession or the principal magistrate's? Nobody knew. . .

And the magistrate himself? Part of the citizens wanted him to give counsel, help, explanations, orders – others raged against him, charged him with being the sole cause of the trouble, or shrieked that he had betrayed the city.

Crowds rushed toward the Rathhaus, shrieking, raging, swearing.

And in fact, the state of affairs among the magistrates was not much better. Here also confusion, disorder, irresolution and the darkest passions prevailled. Only a small number of the magistrates retained their presence of mind, at their head were Syndicus Frantz and Dominikus Dietrich.

Günzer had rushed to Frischmann to demand an explanation of this attack from the French ambassadors in the name of the Senate. He now returned with the statement that Frischmann protested by all that was sacred, that he knew as little about the matter as the worshipful senate itself.

A royal robber

And he told no falsehood, Monseigneur Louvois had not considered it necessary to inform the ambassador, or he had only received directions, in case any inquiries were made about the assembling and movements of troops, to give the magistrates of Strassburg the warmest and most soothing assurances of friendship.

He did so and meantime – the four couriers Louvois had despatched after Chamilli's return from Basle, had also done their duty: the order for the capture of Strassburg had been given.

General Montclar, who commanded the troops in Alsace instantly assembled – under the pretext of reviewing his army – thirty or thirty-five thousand men. The review was really held, only Colonel von Alsfeld instantly set out with a large division, and strangely enough moved in the direction of Strassburg, noiselessly occupying that very evening some woods in the immediate vicinity, where stores had already been placed.

No one had the least suspicion of it, but at midnight Alsfeld emerged from his concealment and rushed with all his troops on the Rhine fortification, which by Louvois' desire and advice was feebly garrisoned and half demolished. Of course, after a short struggle, it fell into his hands.

The post was taken and all the garrison, who did not succeed in flying to the city, were prisoners.

Such was the state of affairs now.

But was this all? Must not attacks from other quarters be hourly expected, perhaps a general assault upon the city? And was it possible that such a crying injustice, such an unexampled act of villainy could proceed from the French government? Or, was the whole matter a misunderstanding, an undue exercise of military authority on the part of Colonel von Alsfeld for General Montclar?

This must first be ascertained.

But now, after the first panic and cry of *Hannibal ante portas*, the most able citizens took the lead.

The alarm bells still pealed, the trumpets still sounded, shouts echoed on the air and crowds rushed to and fro, but Wenck, Hugo von Zedlitz and other brave men had already, though with great difficulty, brought order out of the confusion in the armed guilds.

Citizens and militia hurried to the walls to be prepared for battle in case of further attacks.

The resolute and patriotic party among the magistrates had also speedily conquered and restored order.

More than sixty citizens, with their servants, guarded the Rathhaus – Frischmann, whom the crowd in their rage, threatened to murder, received similar protection, the senate remained in permanent session, and cannon were brought to the walls from every direction. At the same time messengers were sent to Colonel von Alsfeld and repeatedly despatched to Frischmann, to learn the meaning of such an insolent assault, such an unexpected violation of the peace, how it happened that, after all the assurances of the king and the heavy security given by the city for its neutrality, the peace had been so shamefully broken.

Couriers, bearing despatches containing urgent appeals for aid, were instantly sent to the emperor and Reichstag at Regensburg.

Meantime the citizens waited in unutterable anxiety and excitement.

Frischmann renewed his assurances of being in no way connected with what had occurred. But Colonel von Alsfeld – after the manner of Louvois, perhaps even by his direction – added mockery to his disgraceful act of violence. «General Montclar,» he replied in smooth words, «had thought it well to pursue this course, because he had learned that imperial troops were to occupy the pass. The city was thus rendered a positive service.»

A second messenger returned without having effected anything, but bearing a message that fell upon the patriots like a thunderbolt.

Colonel von Alsfeld had been shown that there were no imperial troops within fifty miles and the feeble garrison of Phillippsburg could not venture upon such an undertaking. In reply, the colonel laughed and excused his conduct on the, pretext of an order received from General Montclar, which he had too blindly obeyed. However – and this was the thunderbolt – the most worthy magistrates need only to wait until morning, when General Montclar would arrive in person and could give more explicit information.

«*Hannibal ante portas!*» cried Syndicus Frantz, turning deadly pale, while his gloomy eyes rested upon Günzer. «*Hannibal ante portas!* Will the traitors among us open the gates to him?»

A terrible storm arose, when suddenly news arrived that Louvois was in Breisach, the king on the way to Strassburg.

All were silent – they sat pale and rigid as marble statues, but in the eyes of Syndicus Frantz glittered a tear – it fell upon the corpse of the ancient republic of Strassburg.

IV.
A sad day.

The night through which Strassburg had just passed had been a terrible one – terrible especially in consequence of the excitement of the entire population. Thousands stood in the darkness on the walls, listening anxiously, expecting every moment that some new attack would take place.

Morning came and with it amarmy of thirty thousand men, commanded by General Montclar, appeared before the city.

The magistrates, as was natural, had remained in council. The terrible situation of the city had allayed the storm. Günzer and his party behaved as if they were frantic with indignation at the unwarrantable conduct of France; Syndicus Frantz and the patriots sat with gloomy brows, determined to take the utmost risks. They could still rely upon the majority of the citizens and guilds. If the city only held out bravely till help came from Phillippsburg or elsewhere. Strassburg had never yet been captured, Strassburg had withstood Charles the Bold, Heinrich II, the numerous army of France and Sweden during the Thirty Years War and thus saved freedom and independence, why should she not conquer now? Though assailed by a powerful army – was it to be supposed that Louis XIV would carry his arbitrary will so far as to commit open robbery upon the German empire, venture to brsak the peace by armed force, trampled every right under foot and perhaps rouse all Europe to war?

Ammeister Dominikus Dietrich and Syndicus Frantz now took matters in hand and strangely enough this time Günzer joined them.

The first consideration was to arm men enough to keep communication with the outside country open and enable the inhabitants to enter the city.

For this purpose several thousand men capable of bearing arms had already been secured.

To the surprise of the Syndicus – who since Günzer's rascally trick against the von Zorn family had despised as well as hated him – the latter joined in this movement also and with such apparent zeal as to perplex many.

For greater security a second courier had been dispatched to the Emperor and Reichstag.

Moreover the last cannon in the arsenal had been distributed to the citizens to mount on the walls of the city, and the guns there were also given to arm those who might hasten to her relief.

With the first dawn of morning. Colonel von Alsfeld had advanced towards the city from the Rhine. Fifteen minutes loiter came the news that bodies of troops were approaching from other directions.

Soon the western side was also enclosed and by noon, the whole city.

Günzer secretly exulted; he had known all this before. The fatal words «too late» now characterized the measures of the magistrates, which he approved. Before the peasants, summoned from the neighboring country, could come to the city's aid, every avenue of approach would be closed by French troops and all communication cut off. But the worst feature was that Strassburg was so closely invested that all the couriers to the emperor and Reichstag, though they had used various disguises, would be taken and their despatches delivered to Montclar.

To be sure none of this was known within the city. Günzer had shuffled the cards in such a way that the game could not be lost.

The Senate now attempted to obtain farther explanation from Montclar by means of a letter. The reply was awaited wjth mortal anxiety. At last it came: the French general flatly refused the magistrates' request, but according to a royal command, asked to treat with the council by means of deputies.

Haughty – in a half imperious, half mocking tone – the general explained to the deputies that the city had been ceded to the king by the treaty of Westphalia, and his right was confirmed by that of Nymwegen. Although His Majesty, Louis XIV, had not hitherto considered it advisable to assert his claim, it now suited his interests to do so, as he had received the unexpected news that a considerable body of imperial troops had been transferred to the city and passes of the Rhine.

A royal robber

Montclar, with the air of a patron, added that he had desired to inform the city – to which he had aways been friendly – of the condition of affairs in time, that it might not by reckless obstinacy plunge into misfortune and ruin. The Minister of War, Monseigneur Louvois, would arrive on the following day and it would then depend upon the citizens themselves whether by submission they retained their rights and form of government, or by resistance exposed themselves to the peril of being treated as enemies and rebels!

At these words the older men among the deputies were seized with indignation, especially Syndicus Frantz, who stood at their head.

With his figure drawn up to its full height, steadfast and grave – as beseemed a German – he answered the French general v,rith great dignity that they appealed tp the long maintained independence of their little free state, whose existence, by the law of nations, was as unassailable as that of any other recognized government; that they also appealed to the words of the Westphalian treaty of peace, which established its permanence, that the city upto the time of the treaty of Nymwegen had always dealt with France as a sovereign power, and even at the present time France had an accredited ambassador to her, and finally, it was not becoming in France to give the treaty a one-sided interpretation.

General Montclar, who certainly had nor expected such a grave, dignified and resolute bearing on the part of the deputies, listened to the Syndicus in surprise, with an air of gloomy pride.

Montclar scarcely suppressed his anger, only the mask of cold scorn and military brutality enabled him to conceal it. Arrayed with this he now curtly declared, that he had nothing to do with any treaties, his duty was merely to execute the commands imposed upon him. The council had to consider the answer it was to give the minister the next morning, but he could tell the minister's reply in advance: it would be submission or utter destruction of the city.

With these words, he proudly turned his back upon the deputies.

The return of the deputies was awaited by the citizens with the utmost anxiety. Crowds thronged around the gates of the city. Everywhere only pale, troubled, careworn faces were seen. When the deputies – themselves gloomy and depressed – returned, every one beset them with questions, all wished to know the fate that threatened the beloved city. But the majority of the magistrates, who were themselves extremely perplexed by the condition of affairs, now lost their presence of mind. All classes of the population were instantly informed of Montclar's answer; public prayers were ordered, the whole great council with its three hundred judges was summoned and Commander von Jenneggen received orders to prepare to make the best possible resistance.

Jenneggen instantly appeared before the magistrates, but his report was also extremely discouraging.

«He was ready to do his duty and obey the commands of the most puissant and worthy council,» he said, «only the possibility of a real effective defense was very remote, nay utterly unimaginable. It need only be considered that Strassburg had fourteen irregular bastions, which must all be defended, while he was not in condition to garrison one, since of the five hundred soldiers under his command only one-half were fit for duty and but one officer was capable of service.

The despondency of the magistrates had now reached the point for which Günzer had been waiting with secret impatience. When therefore Syndicus Frantz rose, and with ardent zeal, with the power and strength of an eloquence that springs from the depth of the soul, implored the fathers of the city not to lose courage now; when he pointed to the strength which the population of a city like Strassburg can always develope when animated by a bold, manly, patriotic spirit, when he advised that men, youths, children and gray-beards should be summoned to arms, when he called attention to the fact that aid might yet come from without, and the walls of Strassburg were supplied with a large number of the best cannon, to serve which – in case of necessity – there would be no insurmountable impediment then, then Günzer suddenly stepped forward, played the anxious patriot, sorely concerned about the destiny of beloved, beautiful Strassburg, and in his turn, with fervid eloquence entreated all present, for Heaven's sake, not to enter into

A royal robber

these well-meant but fool-hardy ideas of Syndicus Frantz.

«Oh! men of the city, do not allow yourselves to be blinded!» he exclaimed as if overwhelmed with grief, and tears filled his eyes. «You have just heard how weak we unhappily are and – before our walls stands an army of forty thousand men accustomed to victory! One shot from our walls and the signal will be given – General Montclar will order his troops to storm the city! Then woe to us and Strassburg. Then our beloved city- will be given to the flames – your houses will fall in ashes, pillage will rob every man of his last grain of corn, your wives and daughters will be ruined and streams of blood – hear me, fathers of the city – streams of the blood of our citizens will cry to Heaven for vengeance on those who misled you and the people.

«I vote for a sensible negotiation with the crown of France, and above all that the mad crowds of citizens, who now have possession of the walls and guns of the city, be refused ammunition of every description on any grounds you may think proper.»

«Yes, yes, yes!» was shouted on every side.

What did it avail that Frantz and a few others of his Stamp battled with all their strength, enthusiasm, and logic against the phantoms of terror and selfcreated images of horror?

Their voices were drowned and they were finally outvoted by an immense majority. Ammeister Dominikus Dietrich and all the discreet ones were on Günzer's side.

The proposal to negotiate with Monseigneur Louvois and withhold all ammunition from the citizens, that no incautious, hare-brained man should bring misfortune, was carried.

Syndicus Frantz and the few who shared his views protested against this resolution in voices trembling with grief and agitation.

Günzer bit his lips till they bled.

«Now the simpletons are caught in the snare!» he whispered to Hecker, one of the purchased magistrates, who sat beside him.

A royal robber

«Thank God!» the latter murmured; but at the same time turning deadly pale – Syndicus Frantz was appealing to the great council.

At last the conflict resulted in the support of the resolution just formed, by the determination to commit the final decision – in regard to the negotiations with Louvois – to the great council of the three hundred as the representatives of the whole body of citizens, as was natural in so important a case.

V.
The capitulation.

The night of the 28th and 29th of September of the year 1681 – one of the most terrible to Strassburg – was passed in anxiety, terror, and tribulation, but quietly.

Neither the magistrates nor the citizens had left their posts, since no one knew whether General Montclar might not make another treacherous attack upon the city. But everything remained quiet, and morning slowly dawned conveying fresh cares to men already exhausted by the night of watching.

The thought of this decision weighed heavily upon all minds; there were but two possibilities in it: either subjection to the crown of France and with it the total resignation of the beloved ancient independence and freedom, the sacrifice of the republican form of government which, by history, birth and habit, had been interwoven with their very natures, separation from tfie beloved native land, or a terrible, almost hopeless struggle, which might end in the total destruction of the city, its transformation into dust and ashes, the sacrifice of property and life. To be sure it was possible – at least this was the hope cherished by the braver portions of the citizens – that the couriers sent out – they had been despatched to the neighboring fortress of Philipps-burg and the nearest German princes, as well as the Congress at Frankfort – would soon return with help: but this hope was as faint as the one that Lou-vois and Louis XIV would shrink from a deed of actual violence.

The terrible examples, which had occurred in the Netherlands and Palati-nate, were still too fresh in the hearts of all for them to believe in any hu-man feeling, the slightest respect for international law on the part of the ru-ler of France and his ministers and generals.

Moreover, the majority of the citizens preserved true loyalty to Germany, saw in the French only enemies of their native land and oppressors of free-dom, and were ready, under all circumstances to make any sacrifice for the preservation of their independence. Should the citizens of Strassburg, who looked back with pride to the republican freedom and independence preserved for four hundred years, in whom this pride had become a portion of their flesh and blood, so lightly resign their precious privileges?

The robbers had now come like the thief in the night, and – the traitors shamefully bound the hands of the imperilled party by giving, as if in mockery, the brave citizens cannon which they rendered useless by refusing ammunition.

Wenck and Hugo von Zedlitz, as well as a large portion of the guilds – were enraged by this conduct on the part of the magistrates. All demanded to have the arsenals broken open. But in the consultation which had taken place during the night upon the walls among themselves, Hugo von Zedlitz had opposed this act of self-help for the moment; a deputation, with Wenck at its head, had been sent to the magistrates to urge with the greatest energy the distribution of the necessary ammunition.

The deputies had been at the Rathaus since four in the morning – hours had passed, and the citizens still waited vainly for their return.

Meantime, the guilds stationed on the walls had given the chief command to Hugo von Zedlitz.

The most important matter for Hugo was to obtain a survey of the situation of affairs and ascertain what stations the enemy had occupied near the city. It was also necessary to know whether any help was approaching from the distance.

For this purpose, while awaiting the return of the deputation, Hugo went up to the top of the cathedral.

In spite of his youth and strength, the ascent was to-day a difficult one. He had neither slept nor eaten a mouthful of food for two days and nights.

The first rays of the rising sun were just illuminating the steeples as Hugo reached the top of the cathedral.

How beautiful, how like Paradise was the fair country outspread before him.

Wherever he looked he beheld long lines of tents – the abodes of soldiers summoned to capture beautiful Strassburg – or give her up to fire and

A royal robber

sword, death and ruin.

Oh! Hugo felt as if a thousand swords were piercing his heart.

And no help from without! No possibility that even the peasants who lived outside of Strassburg could reach the city.

Every road was occupied by large bodies of troops, every pass and village guarded.

No help! No imperial troops! Not a single German banner in sight!

Hugo felt as if his eager eyes must summon armies to the city's aid.

It seemed as if he must shriek aloud to the German Empire, «Come, German brothers! Come to the help of your oppressed countrymen. They are ready to defend themselves so far as lies in their power – protect their own property – to fight until death, but it will be useless without your assistance, since they cannot cope with the vastly superior numbers of the foe, nay are robbed of almost all means of defense.»

Hugo von Zedlitz clasped both hands over his brow as if he could no longer trust his own brain, where mad thoughts were brooding – for it was madness in the German empire, emperor, princes and people to let this happen, to look on with careless indifference, to see the avaricious King of France rob Germany of one of its best, most beautiful and important provinces – a great, wealthy province, a true pearl of the empire.

And not a banner, not the tiniest German flag – as far as the eye could reach.

Hugo stood with both hands clasped behind his back, gazing into vacancy.

Great souls in supreme moments feel a grief so mighty that only great souls can understand it. Hugo's heart was not bleeding only for Strassburg, but for all Germany, which he saw humiliated, trampled in the dust jeered and dismembered by the arrogant foe.

Yonder – where a bridge spanned the Ill – stood the village of Ilkirch. It was Montclar's headquarters and here Louvois was to arrive – and the fate of Strassburg be decided.

A royal robber

This recollection darted like a falcon on Hugo's sorrowful thoughts and tore them to pieces.

Anger filled his heart and the old courage rose as if on eagle's wings.

His arms fell and his hand clutched his sword-hilt; he drew himself up proudly and his eyes flashed upon Illkirch as if his glances could destroy the servants of the crowned robber.

Hugo felt his heart still throbbing with love for his native land and – he knew – thousands of citizens were standing below on the walls who thought as he did, who had appointed him their leader; who were willing to try – cost what it might – to hold the city until perhaps aid could come, or the bold robber – shamed by the resistance – should withdraw.

If this did not succeed – why, it was settled among them to at least save the honor of Strassburg and Germany, and – defend the city to the last man.

Hugo von Zedlitz was restored to himelf and the object that brought him to the cathedral.

His keen eye now calmly surveyed the wide expanse of country, whose every tree and bush he knew. He hastily estimated the strength of the enemy, noted the positions and estimated the greater or lesser danger that threatened each bastion of Strassburg.

Then – with one more glance into the distance to see if no aid were near, one more sad sigh – Hugo turned to go.

But what? Did he see right? Was God sending an angel to him? In his returning agitation it seemed so, for at this moment, a lovely girl, followed by an older woman, appeared on the platform of the cathedral.

Hugo looked up. Oh! Heavens! It was Alma and her mother.

«Alma!» cried Hugo, hurrying towards her with extended arms, «Alma, mother, how do you come here? At this time, *this* hour?»

«We have come to look for you!» replied the Syndicus' daughter with a sad smile, while a momentary flush crimsoned her fair face.

«Our anxiety and fear for my husband and you,» added the mother, «would not allow us to remain at home – you have eaten nothing for two days and nights –»

«It is true!» said Hugo, «since that happy evening when we celebrated our dear father's recovery.»

«And which was so terribly interrupted – Who would have thought of it –»

«But it is of no consequence!» Hugo interrupted. «Who has time to think of anything except the defense of the city. If only father –»

«We saw him in the city,» replied Alma, «he is not to be recognized; his energy has redoubled his strength; he works, talks and struggles against the Günzer party like a mere youth.»

«But the refreshment will do him good. He who desires to struggle bravely, be it mentally or physically, must keep up his strength.»

«That is why we hurried to find *you* –»

«And heard on the walls that you were here, noting the position of the enemy –»

«And here are food and drink!» said Alma eagerly, as she drew out the provisions and Hedwig took a flask of wine from her pocket – «and now eat.»

«You kind souls!» exclaimed Hugo gratefully.

«Not a word, my son!» said the Syndicus' wife, «at such times each person has a share of duty to perform. All the brave girls and women in Strassburg are doing the same as ourselves.»

«Ah! then I have fresh hope!» cried Hugo joyously.

All three now sat down a moment on a stone bench, while the young man hastily eat the food so unexpectedly brought. There certainly was no time to lose, he was already expected below; nay his presence might be necessary.

Even while taking the hasty meal his thoughts were busied with his brothers and companions inarms. He asked whether the deputies from the guilds had returned and the ammunition had been delivered; but only learned that the Syndicus was still laboring in behalf of the measure, yet anxiety and dread of precipitation had such power over the magistrates that they would hear no reason.

Hugo hastily swallowed the last mouthful.

«I must go down!» he exclaimed, «I must go to the magistrates, to entreat them to trust the citizens! The guilds are faithful and well disposed; they are ready to risk money and life 'to save the city.»

«Then go where your duty calls you!» said Alma. «I am proud of you and wish to continue to be so.»

«And you» asked Hugo in surprise.

«We will have our share in the sacred struggle.»

«You? How?»

«The warder of the tower is old and feeble,» said Hedwig; «but his son and assistant is a young vigorous man. Such men are now worth more than money. Therefore the son shall go to take his place among the defenders of the city –»

«And we!» cried Alma with eager interest, «we will remain here all day and lend the old man our eyes and hands. If we see aid approaching, we will wave white handkerchiefs which we brought with us, but should we perceive any suspicious movement on the part of the enemy towards the city, we will sound the alarm bell there by giving you a warning, the old warder can then announce the direction from which the danger is approaching by hanging the red flag out towards the neighborhood concerned.»

«Admirable!» cried Hugo, «then good angels will surely watch over us and our city.»

«But when darkness comes,» Hedwig continued, «we will go down and bring food to father and you. I also told the maid-servant to carry to the walls every noon a basket filled with meat, bread and wine to strengthen those who are weak from want of food. I am sure the example will be imitated and then this want will be relieved.»

«Oh! Strassburg! Strassburg!» cried Hugo enthusiastically, «you are not lost

A royal robber

while such women dwell within your walls.»

Then embracing Alma and her mother, he said :

«Now I go down and boldly bid defiance to fate. If the emperor and empire have deserted us, we will not shrink back, but hold out to the last man, and defend the city to our latest breath.»

«May God protect her and us!» cried the mother.

But Alma threw herself into her lover's arms, pressed an ardent kiss on Hugo's lips and said:

«Heaven be with you. I am yours – in life and death.»

Then she turned away – and motioned to Hugo to go.

When Hugo reached the street, every one was in motion.

He asked some one, who was hurrying by, the cause; and learned that the French Minister of War, the Marquis of Louvois, had reached the headquarters at Illkirch and instantly demanded that a deputation of magistrates should be sent to him, as he had communications to make in the name of His Majesty, Louis XIV.

The deputation was actually about to set forth for Illkirch.

Hugo hurried to the walls. His first question was to ask Wenck what the magistrates had said about the ammunition?

The little tailor laughed aloud in his rage, and replied. «What have they decided? That no determination can be made until the return of the deputation from Illkirch.»

«What?» cried Hugo turning pale, «not yet?»

«Patience, young hot-head,» said Wenck, while his face actually turned green and yellow with anger. «Patience! the ammunition will come – only that scoundrel Günzer won't deliver it to us, but the accursed French. Well, who knows what good it may do!»

Not far from Strassburg, in the open country, lie the villages of Illkirch and Grafenstaden. Even at the present day, in the former may be seen the ever memorable building where the negotiation of 1681 was conducted, although now ruined and robbed of the beautiful window from which Monseigneur Louvois gazed at his prey wuth triumphant eyes.

A small number of horsemen were now approaching the house.

It was the deputation of magistrates from Strassburg.

At their head rode a trumpeter and two heralds arrayed in the colors of the city.

These were followed at a short distance by eight grave pale-faced men attired in black, who rode silently along and whose dignified appearance made the spectators forget the skill which, in the eyes of practised horsemen, they might lack in this knightly art. They are the magistrates, von Zedlitz, Dominikus Dietrich, Hecker, Fröreisen, Richshoffer, Stör, Frantz and Günzer, Sieur of Plobsheim.

When the little party approached the house at Illkirch, the guard presented arms and received them with a salute.

The trumpeter blew a loud blast, the heralds – holding their white wands – stopped, and the magistrates silently dismounted. Their features expressed the utmost gravity.

Two officers had received them at the door and now conducted them to a wide, spacious apartment in the upper story.

Here they were requested to wait for his Excellency. And in fact – it was probably a quarter of an hour before Monseigneur condescended to allow the sun of his favor to rise before their eyes.

This was an extremely painful delay – especially to Frantz and Dietrich – and seemed prolonged to hours.

No one uttered a word; but every heart throbbed heavily; perhaps it was the iron finger of conscience, which, in this decisive hour, knocked loudly at one and another.

At last the door opened and the Marquis de Louvois entered, followed by General Montclar and his whole staff.

A royal robber

Louvois' head was covered, but on perceiving the low bows of the Strassburg magistrates, he slightly raided his hat.

The minister sat down – the negotiation began, but it was very similar to the interview with General Montclar the day before.

The objections and replies of the magistrates were also the same. Syndicus Frantz spoke with the warmth and eloquence peculiar to him, but Louvois hastily cut him short.

«It is well, gentlemen!» he harshly exclaimed, «Spare your words. I did not come here to discuss the question but to perform the will of my master and king. The city, by the treaty of Westphalia, was ceded to France, and the treaty of Nymwegen confirmed the right of His Majesty, Louis XIV.»

«Pardon me, Your Excellency!» interrupted Syndicus Frantz with a courage that made his companions tremble, «pardon me, Your Excellency, but that is *not* so. The Westphalian treaty runs as follows!...»

Frantz drew a parchment from his pocket and read:

«France receives the consent of the empire to retain possession of Metz, Toul, and Verdun, which she has held since 1552 as well as the provinces of Upper and Lower Alsace, the Sundgau, Breisach, and Hagenau, with the exception that the bishops of Strassburg, *the city of Strassburg*, and ten other free cities in Alsace, four abbots, the Counts of Lützelstein, Hanau, Fleckenstein, and Oberstein, and the knights of the empire residing there, are to retain their fealty to the German empire.

«The treaty of Nymwegen, as Your Excellency knows, made no alteration in this respect. The Westphalian treaty was confirmed, and for that very reason no mention is made of Strassburg.»

Frantz was silent.

Louvois' eyes blazed with anger.

«Enough!» he thundered – «The *Chambres de Réunion* have already decided –»

«Which they cannot do!» replied Frantz steadily. «Neither the *Chambres de Réunion* nor His Majesty of France have the power to interpret and explain the treaty of Westphalia. To make a valid interpretation of this treaty requires the consent of all the powers that signed it.»

«Doubtless this is your opinion, Syndicus!» exclaimed Louvois with bitter scorn. «It is a pity that France does not require this wise counsel. As I said before, the *Chambres de Réunion* have decided and that settles the matter. Take notice, gentlemen,» he added, turning to the other deputies, «take notice that General Montclar has already made known His Majesty's views to the magistrates of Strassburg, so they have had time for reflection and I require prompt decision. If no assenting answer is received by seven o'clock this evening, I shall pay further attention and – treat the citizens of Stassburg not only as ordinary enemies, but – *rebels*.

«There can be no question of consideration after the capture of the city. If therefore the citizens accept the proffered favor of His Most Christian Majesty, Louis XIV of France, all their privileges, forth civil and ecclesiastical, will be secured to them.»

With these words Louvois rose and, with a scornful farewell, left the room.

What excitement and despair the return of the deputation occasioned throughout the city.

Ammeister Dominikus Deitrich, Syndicus Frantz and Hugo von Zedlitz, had the utmost difficulty in maintaining order, though aided by three sensible, far sighted men. The guilds shrieked for ammunition; hundreds loudly shouted: «Down with the traitors among the magistrates.»

«Down with the traitors! Down with the French!»

Such were the shouts that echoed from the walls; amid such outcries, throngs of people consisting of men, women and children, rushed though the streets to the Rathaus.

But no help came.

How often Hugo's eyes wandered to the cathedral, the white flags would not wave.

Not one banner, not one little flag belonging to the imperial troops appeared.

But Hugo had most difficulty in soothing Wenck.

The jovial, little tailor had become a tiger. His eyes glittered like lightning. He fairly thirsted for French blood, especially since from one of the towers built along the wall, he had discovered a regiment of French cuirassiers near the city.

«Hack them all in pieces!» he cried again and again. «Who knows what good it may do.»

Yet Hugo, the Syndicus and others at last succeeded in restoring the city to order at this infinitely important moment of her destiny.

Even the guilds – down to the one most eager for the fray, the tailor's guild, headed by Wenck – allowed themselves to be persuaded to wait for the decision of the great council of three hundred.

Confidence returned with the assembling of the three hundred; for all the citizens were represented in the great council. What it decided must be considered as the legal result of the public will.

But hour and hour passed audi – no decision was reached.

Frantz and his adherents struggled to have the French demands refused and the city defended. Ammeister Dietrich and the timid ones saw unless the city desired to plunge into ruin, but one means of escape, that of yielding to inevitable destiny. But Günzer in his craft, assailed the assembly in its most sensitive point, the pocket, painted in vivid colors the horrible consequence of the conquest and pillage of the city, and calculated in terrible figures what the expenses of the war would be to the community and each individual.

A request was sent by a mounted messenger to Monseigneur Louvois for an extension of the time of giving the answer until noon of the following day.

Louvois granted the petition.

But the state of affairs did not change, the discussions consultations, enumerations of the dangers on one side and the other, questions of votes, lasted all night.

A royal robber

From hour to hour, news was sent to the guilds on the walls regarding the state of affairs in the council. Nay, the council even asked their views and opinions.

The verdict was almost unanimous for the defense of the city.

Then news suddenly arrived which crushed the last hope, news that all the couriers sent out by the magistrates with despatches appealing for help had been captured by the French.

Now aid was no longer to be expected and resistance became madness and folly.

The iron die of fate fell – the great majority of the council voted for capitulation. The tailor's guild alone rejected every agreement and wanted to defend themselves unto death.

Frantz and his party submitted to the decidedly expressed will of the people. Reason told them what even love for their native city now dictated, that under such circumstances only a surrender could save Strassburg from total destruction.

Hugo von Zedlitz also submitted with a sigh to the inevitable – he would rather have been buried under the ruins of the walls.

The various articles of the act of capitulation were now written and the paper, after receiving the approval of the magistrates and citizens, sent to the Marquis de Louvois, who showed great pleasure at the sight of the document.

By virtue of this capitulation the French army fifteen thousand strong, occupied the city of Strassburg on the 30th of September, 1681.

The inhabitants gazed at the entering troops in silence.

All remained quiet – one alone could not endure this disgrace, this blow. It was Wenck. Though grinding his teeth and clenching his hands, he controlled himself for some time, but when he suddenly saw a regiment of his hated enemies, the French cuirassiers march by, he could bear it no longer.

As if pursued by the furies, Wenck hurried home, snatched his gun from the wall, filled his pockets with powder and lead, and returned with flying feet.

«Where are the scoundrels!» he shouted, foaming with rage.

«What scoundrels?» people asked in astonishment.

«Why, the French cuirassiers!» cried Wenclc, his eyes flaming with anger.

«They are encamped on the Barfüsserplatz.»

«Good!» said the little tailor, darting onward like an arrow.

Now he reached the square, caught sight of them, and with the shout

«Down with the tyrant's slaves – long live freedom. Long live Strassburg! Follow me, citizens!» two shots from the double barrelled gun crashed on the air, the bullets whistled by and four cuirassiers fell wounded on the ground.

«Madman!» cried Hugo von Zedlitz, dragging him back among the crowd.

«Madman! What can one do against a crowd; away from here and save yourself!»

«One?» cried Wenck with burning brain. «If they had all thought as I do, our dear, beautiful Strassburg would still be free, gut I've shot four of the dogs. God grant that they may be dead! Who knows what good it may do !»

«Away!» cried Hugo, who saw a party of cuirassiers rushing forward. «Away,» and he dragged Wenck off by force. In a few bounds they reached the corner of the street, but the pursuers had seen them, several bullets hissed through the air and Wenck lay dead on the ground. A French bullet had pierced his heart.

VI.
Dreams and illusions.

So Strassburg was in the hands of the French.

On the following day, the first of October, the council of three hundred assembled and the capitulation was read. As it secured all their privileges and the exercise of the Protestant religion, they expressed themselves satisfied. The city authorities were occupied several days in arranging quarters for the troops. In the letter, in which Louvois announced to his king with joyful satisfaction the capitulation of Strassburg, he requested a speedy ratification, as he was in haste to take possession of the fortifications between the city and the Rhine. On the morning of October ist he ordered engineers to draw plans, that Vauban, who was to arrive the next day, might be able to carry his projected fortification into execution as soon as possible. On the 4th of October Vauban commenced his task; to the works already in existence, which he found in the best condition, he added the citadel, not only to make the place unassailable, but also to hold the inhabitants in check; besides at this time a canal was dug to procure building materials.

Paris exulted. The king and his whole court left the capital to go to Strassburg and receive the homage of his new subjects.

But sad thoughts were filling the heart of Louis XIV. Fierce storms had passed over him of late, and dark shadows rising from another quarter clouded his joy at the fall of Strassburg.

It was just after the return from Colmar that the Duchesse de Fontanges – who was now, at least according to appearances, at the summit of power – received through her maid news which produced a deep impression upon her.

Since Gauthier's arrest in her room and imprisonment in the Bastile, it had been impossible for her to gain the smallest information about the fate of the unfortunate companion of her childhood.

Only once she had ventured to implore the king's pardon for him, but this once had sufficed. The outburst of anger from her royal lover forever sealed her lips.

But there was no depth or energy In Marie Angeline's character. Her innate vanity and love of splendor smothered all deeper feelings and, in the constant intoxication of pleasure that surrounded her, she only too easily forgot everything serious in life, everything that affected her unpleasantly.

The memory of the scene in her sleeping room, however, as well as that of Gauthier, haunted her like ghosts.

The Bastille was in the habit of keeping silence in regard to everything that passed within its walls. It was a gigantic grave to all those whose unhappy fate led them to it. It stood like a terrible secret in the midst of gay, thoughtless Paris, the gloomy building with its moats, bastions and eight huge towers – in which so many were buried alive forever.

But money and influence can make even the thickest walls speak, and there was some one in France who was interested in Gauthier's fate. Angeline's former relations to this young man and the story of his encounter with the king in her apartment formed the vulnerable point in the armor of the haughty Duchesse de Fontanges.

This was the spot where she might be mortally wounded, she and – the king.

Was it not always possible to ruin the hated beauty by this story?

Who could tell?

There was one who bitterly hated the haughty Angeline, desired nothing more ardently than her fall, one who had made the fall of the Duchesse de Fontanges, whose elevation had been the cause of her own ruin, the one task of her life. And this person was – the Marquise de Montespan.

The court of Louis XIV was the school of love and hate. The marquise had not passed through this school in vain; nor had she sighed her time away in torturing loneliness during her exile at Tonnay-Charente. She had secretly come to Paris long ago, in order to watch the course of affairs in which she was interested. And indeed she – who had herself woven so many court intrigues – possessed an eagle eye in such matters. – But she also possessed something peculiar to those days – superstition, and this weakness led her to the famous fortune-teller, La Voisin.

She must learn through this woman the future fate of her hated and now victorious rival.

«The rule of the Duchesse de Fontanges will be short,» replied the mysterious cards, «but only the hand that raised can ruin her.»

The marquise secretly exulted.

The answer was certainly mysterious. Who had raised this little Duchesse de Fontanges? Undoubtedly she, the marquise; yet one might also say the king, the Duc de Saint Aignan had a share, and Gauthier too, who had been used as a means.

How was the affair to be commenced?

The marquise's cunning aided her to a master-piece in the art of intrigue. She said to herself : La Voisin's prediction must prove true if I use the four hands that combined to raise the Duchesse de Fontanges – to ruin her.

Darkness and silence concealed the Marquise de Montespan's farther negotiations with La Voisin. In the first place her money opened the lips of the Bastille. She learned precisely how Gauthier fared, and as the Duchesse de Fontanges' maid was secretly employed by the Marquise de Montespan, the haughty Angeline – at a hint from the former – learned the news which we have said, deeply moved her.

It was the tidings that Gauthier lived, but was condemned to death. The sentence would be executed in a few days.

This blow fell upon Angeline with too crushing a weight not to rouse her from her frivolity. Her heart was neither bad nor unfeeling, only, like her whole nature, it lacked depth.

Condemned to death? They are terrible words, especially when conscience says that we are to blame for the horrible sentence.

Startled from the giddy whirl of pleasure, the delirium of luxury and spleen-dor, this news almost crushed her to the earth.

In her excited imagination she already saw the terrible deed done.

Angeline was frantic with grief. Pain, sorrow, and the pangs of conscience had hitherto had little place in the book of her life. The former fate had spared her, the latter she had spared herself. But – this time her conscience was no courtier: it did not bend, was not silent, but cried loudly: «You are his murderess!»

In vain the proud, beautiful duchesse strove to recall her former frivolity – it was useless.

Vainly, in her anguish and despair, she strove to plunge into a still madder whirl of pleasure and excitement – it was useless. The pallid ghost of Loches again rose before her soul.

Angeline would gladly have implored Gauthier's forgiveness on her knees, and yet – so weak was her character – that she did not venture to appeal to the king. The fear of her royal lover's anger, the dread of imperiling her position again, won the victory over the better and nobler emotions of her heart.

Her maid now gave a fresh proof of her kind feeling towards the young duchesse. She listened affectionately, tenderly endeavored to console Angeline, and suggested a plan to save the unfortunate prisoner.

«Money,» she said, «money can do anything in the world.»

«I will joyfully pay the price of a principality,» cried Angeline, «if I can save him. I will scatter money, jewels, only help me rescue him from death.»

«And would you have courage to visit him in secret?»

«It would be my most ardent desire to beseech him on my knees to forgive the wrong I have done him; but the king –»

«He will know nothing about it.»

«And the Bastille?»

«Will open to you in the quiet night. You have the key in your own hands.»

A royal robber

«I?»

«Your gold.»

«Take it, take all you need.»

«It will be a great deal.»

«No matter. His Majesty's kindness to me is inexhaustible. But through whom?»

«Through the Duc de Saint Aignan.»

«Through the Duc de Saint Aignan. No, that won't do. He hates Gauthier.»

"But he loves – you, and therefore will do all in his power for you if we ask him.»

«It is too dangerous.»

«Let me arrange the matter. The duc has nothing to fear from the prisoner.»

«No,» said Angeline with a sorrowful smile, «and Saint Aignan is certainly my best and most reliable friend.»

«Then consent, Madame la Duehesse, and trust me, as you have so often done.»

«As if you did not possess my entire confidence. I think I have given you plenty of proofs of it.»

«For which I shall be eternally grateful,» said the maid, kissing her mistress' hand – «so it is settled?»

«Yes,» replied the Duchess de Fontanges, «but I entreat you to use the utmost caution. The king must not on any account have the slightest suspicion of it.»

«He lives only for politics just now. Rely upon me, Madame la Duchesse.»

The second night after this exciting day, an ordinary hired carriage stopped in one of the little streets of Paris not far from the royal palace.

A man in citizen's dress sat within. It was Saint Aignan.

A royal robber

He sat resting his head on his hand and his elbow on his knee, absorbed in thought.

Saint Aignan paused a moment.

He seemed to be listening for something; but all was still.

The narrow, dark little street where his carriage stood was deserted.

The Duc sank back on the cushions.

«Yes,» he continued. «The little Duchesse de Fontanges will form no exception to her predecessors, she will fare like the beautiful brilliant days of the tropic zone – sunlight and brightness will be suddenly followed by the gloom of night. It is a pity about her. She's confoundedly handsome and – though otherwise cold as marble – a volcano in love.

«But the ground is undermined – the king is beginning to grow weary of her. Beauty without intellect or wit can bind no one long, far less such a spoiled child as Louis XIV. Such a palate requires spicy food. Devil take me if my keen nose isn't on the right scent, if – if – His Most Christian Majesty hasn't for sometime cast an eye on the clever and virtuous governess of his children, the Duc de Maine and Comte de Toulouse. The worthy widow Scarrous seems very devout, to be sure, but – that is something new and piquant, let us try piety awhile. His Majesty, out of gratitude, has bestowed upon her the beautiful estate of Maintenon, made her a marquise too. I really believe this new Marquise de Maintenon will soon be Madame de Maintenant.»

The Duc sat up and then exclaimed in an undertone:

«Watch» the wind has changed – he is a fool who tries to steer against it. And, faith, Saint Aignan will never deserve that title.

«This little Duchesse de Fontanges has of ten by her boundless pride insulted me, as well as the queen and all the nobility – let us play for revenge and so that we shall win the game. The short-sighted creature – deluded by my apparent love and submission, gives herself into my hands. Poor thing –» and the duc laughed lightly – «your sentimentality puts the rope around your own neck.»

A royal robber

At this moment the clock struck ten.

«Ten,» said the duc – «now she will be here directly and – my letter will be placed in the king's hands.»

Saint Aignan was silent and alighting from the carriage, went to the corner of the street to watch.

A few minutes after, two muffled female figures approached. They were the Duchesse de Fontanges and her maid.

Both entered the carriage, followed by the due, then at a sign, the vehicle proceeded to the Bastille.

A cold shiver ran through Angeline's frame as she entered the gloomy walls of this terrible prison, over which already centuries, with their storms, sighs, and crimes, had passed.

The fate of the builder of the Bastile must be considered a dark omen of the deeds of horror which the tyranny of the rulers of France caused to be executed here for centuries. It was Hugo Aubriot, Intendant of the finances at the French court, who – at the king's command – erected the Bastile, and afterwards, on the charge of being a heretic, breathed out his life there, the first prisoner within its walls.

Angeline drew her cloak closer around her, and involuntarily pressed her hand upon her heart, to feel whether it was still beating.

Such terrible dread suddenly took possession of her, that if it had been possible to return, she would have done so.

They were standing before a door heavily bound with iron and closed by three huge locks. It was the door of Gauthier's prison.

The Duchesse de Fontanges pressed a purse full of gold into the warder's hand, but her own trembled so violently that the money almost slipped from her grasp.

The jailer took the bunch of keys from his side. The locks were opened – three bolts creaked – the door swung back.

Darkness and silence pervaded the damp, narrow apartment.

A royal robber

The atmosphere that met the young duchesse almost stifled her. Her senses failed, an icy weight oppressed her heart – she was on the verge of fainting. Fortunately at that moment Saint Aignan offered her his arm, her foot sought the threshold, the jailer led the way with a lamp.

The feeble light of the lamp, which the jailer held aloft to give its faint rays more space, flickered unsteadily in the dark room, and dimly illuminated the damp, gloomy walls.

It was some seconds ere Angeline's and Saint Aignan's eyes could penetrate the dusk.

«He's asleep,» said the jailer, and with these words he pointed towards a corner of the dungeon.

The duchesse approached; but a sudden horror seized upon her as she saw a human form, emaciated almost to a skeleton, lying on a heap of mouldy straw.

With a terrible pang in her heart, she involuntarily put out both hands and retreated.

Horror and repugnance suddenly took possession of the spoiled child of fortune. Her whole nervous system trembled. She deeply repented the step she had taken.

Nothing escaped Saint Aignan's keen eyes.

He too trembled, but from other motives.

If the duchesse withdrew too soon, his game might be lost. Hastily forming his resolution, he approached Angeline and whispered:

«Don't you wish to speak to the unfortunate man?»

A flush of shame crimsoned the lady's pale face. The presence of the due, by whose secret mediation she had taken a step so dangerous to him and herself, urged her onward.

But her terror was not yet conquered – and pointing to the motionless form, she asked with trembling lips:

A royal robber

«And this is – Gauthier de Montferrand?»

«Yes,» said the jailer in a curt cold tone.

«Then – wake him,» said Angeline de Fontanges, «and – leave us – alone a moment.»

The jailer, who had already been bribed; and had himself made all the necessary preparations for Gauthier's flight, put the lamp on a stone table and attempted to obey the command.

«Wake!» he cried rudely, «wake, somebody wants to speak to you!»

And he shook the motionless form.

But at the same moment he stopped, laid his hand on the man's brow, clasped his wrist, looked into his face and at last said, quietly, turning away:

«He'll never wake again – he's dead.»

A piercing shriek escaped Angeline's lips.

«He's dead!» she repeated and her senses failed.

Tottering, she clung to St. Aignan for support.,

«Dead!» repeated the jailer, secretly rejoicing that he had earned so much money without being compelled to aid the fugitive's escape.

«Too late!» groaned the duchesse, while her hands fell feebly by her side as if she had heard her death sentence.

She stood silently with closed eyes in the presence of fate, like a criminal.

«Calm yourself!» said Saint Aignan, «perhaps it is better so.»

But these words suddenly opened Angeline's whole heart; a terrible anguish, the sense of infinite remorse overwhelmed her, and – covering her face with her hands – tears gushed from her eyes.

«Oh! God! oh, God! so I am really his murderess!» she exclaimed. And utterly forgetting herself, she sank down beside Gauthier's corpse, seized his cold, rigid hand and pressed it to her heart.

The fierce surges of sorrow had washed from her soul everything that had occurred since her departure from Limagne. Only the memories of her childhood remained, but – all these memories pierced her heart like daggers.

She saw herself at home; she saw her dear faithful mother, the good Père Hilaire; she saw by her side Gauthier, the loyal playmate who had loved her so truly, seen everything with her eyes, she saw the fair days which she had spent so happily in her innocent childhood – and now?

With the most caressing words she implored Gauthier to wake. She shook him, she shrieked to God to recall the unfortunate man to life.

Then she again sank down beside the cold, lifeless corpse and in the most pathetic words implored the dead man's pardon for all the misery, all the suffering, all the horrors she had caused him.

«Oh! forgive me, forgive me, Gauthier! Forgive your murderess!» she cried in heart-rending tones – «forgive her for sacrificing your beautiful young life, sacrificing it *thus!* Oh! hear me, Gauthier, hear me! open your eyes once more to see my repentance.

«Gauthier! Merciful God! He is dead! dead! he no longer hears' or sees his Angeline, he no longer sees her writhing in the dust to implore his forgiveness for having broken his kind, faithful heart!

«Yes, I have broken it! It was I who crushed your beautiful life, and – I cannot restore it to you.»

Suddenly, close beside her, there was a cry of: «The king!» – and with the words the gloomy room grew bright as day.

The duchesse shrank as if a thunderbolt had fallen. She could not regain her self-command.

What was the king doing here? What, whom did he seek?

The king! It required the exertion of all her mental powers to recall herself to reality.

But – to be found thus! She uttered a cry of terror.

Louis XIV stood at the entrance with a grave, stern face, at his side, a little in the rear, were four torchbearers, and still farther back, strangely enough, several nuns.

«You here, madame?» said the king with icy, terrible coldness, «we did not expect to find you here.»

«Your Majesty!» replied the Duchesse de Fontanges, in a voice trembling with grief. «Your Majesty sees that I am with the dead.»

«And I once found the living man with you.»

«I came here to bid farewell to a dying playmate – a dear *relative*.»

«A dying man, but one who – if he had not died – would no longer be here! However, we will let that pass, madame! I honor and respect this grief, this truly Christian devotion to another's fate –»

«Sire!☼

«And that you may see, madame, that I am not wicked enough to interfere with your natural sorrow, your pious mood, or efface this deep and sacred impression, I have requested the holy Abbess of the convent of Port Royal, in the suburb of Saint Jacques, to take you under her protection.

And the king, turning to the sisters, added: «Do your duty, Abbess,» and preceded by the torchbearers and followed by Saint Aignan, left the dungeon.

The duchesse uttered a piercing shriek and sank fainting into the arms of the nuns.

VII.
A withered rose.

A death-like stillness brooded over the convent of Port Royal in the suburb of Saint Jacques. It was the abode of «penitents,» and many a repentant heart indeed looked back from here into the darkness, shuddered and – bled in secret.

A death-like stillness and the peace of a church-yard pervaded the spot.

And was not this convent of Port Royal indeed a church-yard? Only the grave-stones wandered about as still, pale, shadowy forms, garbed in the robes of nuns. But beneath each of these moving grave-stones was a heart that had burnt out into dust and ashes.

The cells of the convent of Port Royal were graves – only one apartment in the spacious building formed a strange contrast to the terrible simplicity and poverty of the other rooms.

This was a large chamber, whose high, narrow windows opened upon the inner court-yard.

The floors of the cells were composed of hard, cold stones, and those who trod them had bare feet, for they were «penitents.»

The floor of this apartment was covered with a soft, rich carpet, such as had probably never been seen in any convent before.

The cells of the convent of Port Royal contained wooden beds, which were often strewn with thorns and thistles, for those who used them were «penitents.»

In the room just mentioned was a costly couch, richly adorned with silk and lace.

Throughout the spacious convent earthen vessels were used for food and drink. The occupant of this chamber was served in silver dishes.

The walls of the cells were bare; embroidered hangings covered those of the room.

A royal robber

In a word, it was richly furnished, and three times a week the duc de la Feuillade drove up to visit the occupant, and in the name of His Majesty, the King, inquire for her health.

But indeed her state of health was bad enough.

A pale, emaciated figure lay on the superb couch in the magnificently furnished chamber. It was Marie Angeline, once Mademoiselle de Fontanges, afterwards the all-powerful duchesse, radiant in beauty, power and splendor, the object of the devotion of His Majesty, Louis XIV, King of France.

But where was the beauty of the poor child, who had not yet reached her twentieth year?

What had become of the color in her cheeks, the freshness of her complexion, the roundness of her limbs?

Was this pale, drooping figure, with the haggard cheeks and dim eyes red with weeping the haughty duchesse, who but a short time before had ruled the heart of the King of France and with it his whole court, who had passed the queen without a salutation before whom bowed dukes and duchesses, princes and princesses, for whose favor the whole court, the highest nobility, vied with each other?

How crushed, how broken she lay – this early withered rose!

How incredibly rapid had been her decline. But a fortnight before, the abbess, accompanied by two sisters had brought her senseless to the convent one dark night – attended only by a single maid.

The very first night her maid had given the duchesse, who was passing from one fainting fit to another, a brown liquid, which really revived her and threw her into a sleep that lasted nearly twenty-four hours.

But on awakening from the sleep Angeline's features were strangely altered. Her usually dazzlingly fair Complexion had assumed a sickly yellow hue. Her nerves were so relaxed, her mental powers so enfeebled, her mind so stupefied, that she spent whole days without tears, gazing rigidly into vacancy as if her thoughts were far away. Her arms hung loosely by her side, her feet seemed paralyzed, dizziness bewildered her, the pupils of her eyes were contracted to an almost invisible size, and her pulse was nearly imperceptible.

She did not utter a word. Her silence seemed the echo of the death-like stillness that pervaded the whole convent of «penitents.»

This condition, however, was soon followed by other alarming symptoms: terrible headaches, rapid emaciation, and loss of physical and mental power.

The maid no longer left her mistress bed-side. She took so warm an interest in her that she even counseled her not to summon a physician, since in these evil, corrupt days nobody was to be trusted, especially by those who had powerful enemies.

But the illness daily increased, she grew weaker and weaker, and soon felt – that she was dying.

And strangely enough, with this conviction, her mind grew calmer, especially in regard to Gauthier.

«I shall atone for the sin I have committed against him by my own death!» she thought.

But the misfortune that had so suddenly overtaken her, also tore the bandage from her eyes.

Her fall was terrible, and when she now found herself lying crushed in the abyss – buried alive in the gloom and solitude of a convent – the dream she had once had in Limagne, and which the good Père Hilaire had interpreted as a warning sent by God, returned to her memory.

Her tears streamed forth again, but – this time they were precious pearls, for they flowed from sincere repentance for her former life.

Oh! Thou Merciful God! A last ray of sunlight illumined the darkness of her soul – Père Hilaire stood by her bedside.

He had followed the course of her life and remained near her, because he knew how it must end. Besides, Gauthier's fate had detain him in Paris. But what could the poor old priest do for the unfortunate man?

To kneel before the king and implore pardon for Gauthier would have instantly placed him also in the Bastille. Yet Père Hilaire was not intimidated, he tried in every possible way to alleviate Gauthier's fate, but in vain. The king's anger had spoken, and this was the sentence of inexorable Minos.

Angeline's last visit to Gauthier, of which he heard, as well as the poor girl's fate, had reconciled him to his long blinded pupil.

He requested the favor of giving his former charge the last consolations of the church – and it was granted.

Louis XIV, the «great» king, was now very complaisant – he felt infinitely relieved, that the rose chains which had bound him to the Duchesse de Fontanges had been so easily stripped off, and – had another conquest in view, that of the clever Marquise de Maintenon.

Angeline – feeling the approach of death – had thrice besought the king, as a last favor, to let her, who had loved him so fondly, so unutterably, see his dear face once more.

But the king would not listen. Even the thought of being obliged to visit a dying person was extremely painful and unpleasant to him, and Louis XIV did not like to meet with anything *unpleasant* in his life.

He did not come.

Then Angeline sent the fourth time.

This time also the monarch refused; but his confessor – doubtless in the hope that the sight of the dying girl would have a good influence upon the mind of the too worldly monarch – at last induced him to pay the visit.

Louis XIV had therefore promised to come to the convent of Port Royal that morning.

A death-like stillness pervaded the convent of the penitents, and a death-like stillness also brooded over the room occupied by the dying girl.

Angeline, amid burning tears of deep, heartfelt repentance, had made her confession to Père Hilaire and received absolution.

The priest had prayed fervently with her – no Latin, no church prayers, but such as were prompted by his fatherly love for his erring daughter.

A royal robber

Angeline was lying silent – the mental exertion had exhausted her last strength but a peaceful smile flitted over her features, the reflection of the peace that had filled her soul during the last hour. ,

Only Père Hilaire was present, and he was praying silently over his breviary.

The maid was standing In the corridor, awaiting His Majesty's arrival with a throbbing heart. One could not say that peace pervaded her soul. Half an hour before she had concealed with almost anxious haste a silver goblet, from which she often gave the invalid something to drink.

She was agitated, very much agitated and – excitement also pervaded the usually quiet convent – all were expecting the visit of His Majesty, the King.

At last he appeared. Like his suite, he was attired in mourning.

There was something majestic in his grave, dignified bearing, and majesty was also enthroned upon the handsome face.

His head, as usual, was covered with a huge peruke, but not – and this was very significant – by the broad brimmed hat with three floating white plumes.

Louis XIV removed it as he approached the dying girl.

His train had of course entered with bared heads.

Only one of the king's constant attendants was absent – the duc de Saint Aignan. He had begged to be excused on the plea of sudden illness.

The king gently approached; but when he saw the face, which but a short time before he had so passionately loved, which had bloomed before him in health and beauty so radiant that it seemed as if they could never fade, he turned pale.

The change in Angeline's features was so great, that it was difficult for Louis to recognize the former object of his love. Her pallor, her haggard cheeks, her sad, dim eyes, which still beamed with love, moved him so powerfully, that – tears filled his own.

Then an indescribably gentle, angelic smile flitted over the features of the dying girl and, making a great effort to raise herself, she said, extending her little emaciated hand to the king:

«Oh! now I can die content, since my last moments have seen the tears of my king.»

«Don't talk so, Madame la Duchesse,» replied the king, in a low, tremulous tone, «you will not die, and when you are well again –»

«Not so, Sire,» murmured Angeline, «I already feel death's cold breath. But just because I know – that I shall not survive this day – I earnestly entreated Your Majesty – for the favor –»

«Don't tax your strength!»

«Of a visit.»

«Which was willingly granted.»

The dying girl cast a long affectionate glance at the king.

«Sire!» she said, «I have loved Your Majesty – infinitely – and – Gauthier de Montferrand – I swear in this solemn hour before the omniscient God – was only my friend – my relative – the playmate of my childhood.»

«Let this pass,» said Louis with a somewhat clouded brow. «God himself has decided. Peace to his ashes!»

«And – Sire – if I have ever angered – offended –»

«What folly, Madame la Duchesse! We are all human, and have our passions. Ask any favor, and we will show you how highly we still prize you.»

Tears filled Angeline's eyes. A heavy sigh escaped her lips, then she said:

«For myself – I have but one favor to implore and – that is – the mercy – of God. But will Your Majesty remember my old mother – Père Hilaire – and – my good Barbezieux –» she looked at the maid, who was supporting her on the pillows.

«We will!» said the king in a firm, grave tone.

Suddenly death approached and threw his dark veil over the dying girl's eyes. She moaned – her fingers plucked strangely at the silk coverlid.

A royal robber

«Then I shall die in peace,» faltered Angeline, as her head fell gently back.

«We will go!» said the king, «this excitement is too much for the poor girl,» and making the sign of the cross over the dying form, he turned and left the room with his train.

Again a death-like silence prevailed. Earthly majesty had left the room – the majesty of death had entered.

Père Hilaire murmured in an undertone the Latin prayers prescribed by the church.

Angeline's eyes grew fixed and glassy. Her fingers still played with the coverlid.

«Gauthier!» she murmured faintly, «Gauthier – don't hurry – me – so – I'm – coming – oh! – the mountain – the cloud – woe, woe, betide me! It is growing dark.»

«Not yet!» said the old priest., no longer able to restrain his tears, bending over Angeline, «God is gracious and merciful! God is love, and love is light and happiness!»

«Love!» said the dying girl almost Inaudibly, «yes – love – is light – and happiness.»

«Amen!» said the priest.

«Amen!» whispered Angeline.

Then the faint notes of an organ echoed through the air, followed by a soft, yet melancholy chant.

The nuns were imploring God to grant the dying girl an easy passage to eternity.

And her death *was* easy. He kissed Angeline on the brow – a loud moan – a convulsive quiver then – a stretching of the limbs, and Marie Angeline, Duchesse de Fontanges – was no more!

VIII.
The rule of Nemesis.

All Paris was in a state of feverish excitement; but not about the death of the charming young Duchesse de Fontanges; the latter had speedily been forgotten at court, while the people actually rejoiced over the ruin of one whose pride, vanity, and love of pleasure had lured the king to the most unprecedented expenses.

Besides the nation was accustomed to the rise and fall of the objects of the king's love, and the Parisians with true French frivolity, laughingly asked each other: «Well, who will take the helm now?»

Angeline de Fontanges had bloomed and charmed the eye for a few spring days, like a beautiful fragrant rose, and then, overtaken by a sudden storm, quickly withered. The rush of new events effaced her memory, as the storms of nature blow rose leaves away.

Her pride and vanity had made her think only of herself; why should others now think of her?

Besides the news of more important things, which nearly concerned the court and a large number of the citizens of Paris, had arrived at the same time as the tidings of the duchesse's death – things which made the worthy Parisian's hair stand on end, and filled them with that thrill of pleasurable horror, which the discovery of a great crime exerts upon the majority of mankind.

All Paris – as has already been mentioned – was in a state of feverish excitement, for as the cases of secret poisoning had lately reached a truly alarming number, a court for the discovery of such crimes – the *Chambre ardente* – had not only been appointed by the king himself – but had actually detected and arrested the prepetrator in the person of La Voisin, the fortune-teller, and her confederates.

What noble names were compromised; what victims had succumbed to this band of criminals, to whom belonged La Voisin's assistant Vigoureaux, and

A royal robber

– the world heard it with horror – the priests, Lesage and d'Auvaux.

The most horrible things were whispered abroad; but – the *Chambre ardente* remained silent, like the terrible subterranean chambers of torture. Yet it was ascertained that several persons belonging to the court had been brought before the tribunal, among them the Duchesse de Bouillon and Marshal de Luxembourg.

Something was also said to have been discovered in regard to the Marquise de Montespan, and the names of Saint Aignan and his relative, the Cardinal, were mixed into the affair. The two latter were charged with a blasphemous raising of the devil, which they had undertaken with La Voisin's aid, and who was asserted to have brought the duc and cardinal boundless wealth.

Saint Aignan laughed at the story, made all sorts of jokes about it, and continued to be the king's prime favorite. The Comtesse de Soissons, in whom His Majesty had always lelt much interest, yielded to his wish and withdrew to Brussels for the benefit of her health. The Duchesse de Bouillon and Franz Heinrich de Montmorency-Bouteville, duke, peer and Marshal of France, who bore the name of Montmorency united with that of the imperial House of Luxembourg – were acquitted.

The good Parisians laughed and made jokes over it.

Of course the state of the case was far different with La Voisin and her accomplices. Here Nemesis did not shrink from grasping her victims with a firm hold and leading them to well-merited punishment.

To-day – on the day of the death of the poor Duchesse de Fontanges, who it was darkly rumored had also been poisoned – all Paris was violently excited by the announcement of the sentence of the *Chambre ardente*.

The verdict of the court was: that La Voisin should be burned alive, Vigoureux hanged, and the two priests, Lesage and d'Auvaux, suffocated.

The news made a deep impression upon all the citizens of Paris. They thanked God for this decision Qi the court whose execution they might hope would not only cause the destruction of the whole band of murderers, but forever prevent the recurrence of such crimes.

A royal robber

Of course the only subject discussed in the court and city was this cause célèbre, but – at the court as well as in the city – many hearts throbbed and trembled, counting the seconds up to the time of the execution of the criminals, because each moment they had cause to dread the betrayal of their own crimes by these their accomplices.

But their terror did not seem to be justified. Vigoureux had first been tried. She had either remained silent throughout the examinations or stoutly denied all accusations; but when she was condemned she sent word to Monseigneur Louvois, that she would disclose the most important things, if he would spare her life.

Louvois replied:

«Pshaw! Torture will loosen her tongue.»

But the powerful Minister of France was mistaken. When Vigoureux received the marquis' answer, she replied quietly:

«Very well, then the wise gentleman will learn nothing.»

And in fact – such energy did this corrupt woman possess – Vigoureux endured all degrees of horrible torture without uttering a word. She was thrown naked on her back upon a table with her hands and feet fastened to the floor and the table was raised upward by screws till all her joints were nearly wrenched asunder and blood started from under the nails, the mouth, eyes, ear and nose.

Vigoureux did not utter a word.

Matches were burned under her arms and on her body. She writhed – as much as her bands permitted – like a worm, but – did not utter a word of confession. She was burned with hot pincers – and was silent but her eyes shot basilisk glances.

The resoluteness was the more amazing, as the doctor more than once declared that the horrible torture must be stopped, or the criminal would die.

What terrible delusion of mind, dishonoring to all humanity! What hardness of the heart! What mistaken legal ideas! The judges appointed to mete out

A royal robber

justice and punish human crimes humanely, become while condemning murder – murderers themselves, and those who were tortured were not always murderers, but often *innocent people.*

On reaching the Place de Grêve the following day Vigoureux sent for the magistrates.

The latter hurried to the spot, hoping at last to obtain some confessions from this condemned woman; but Vigoureux with one foot already on the steps of the scaffold, said the following words:

«Gentlemen, be kind enough to tell the Marquis de Louvois that I am his most humble servant, and – have kept my promise to him; perhaps he would not have done so to me!»

Then she turned to the executioner, exclaiming:

«Now, my friend, do your duty!»

She went up the steps of the scaffold and aided the executioner in his business, as well as her tortured body would permit.

A few moments after a dark life was ended.

When the story of Vigoureux's death, with all the circumstances attending it, was related to La Voisin, the latter said:

«I recognize her true character in that; she was a brave girl, but she made a mistake; I shall tell everything that concerns me.»

But her course was of no more avail than that of her fellow-criminal. When the former was stretched upon the rack, she confessed many things, but – her tormentors wanted to know more, and as she could tell nothing farther, poured combustible fluids over her and ignited them. To escape hearing her horrible shrieks of agony, a gag was placed in her mouth.

Thus the fury of her judges made her endure every extremity of torture.

Nemesis, the gloomy goddess of vengeance, triumphantly swung her dark rod.

A royal robber

The next day – after witnessing the strangling of the two accomplices, the priests, Lesage and d'Auvaux – she was dragged to the place of execution. Here, when placed on a pile of wood, an attempt was made to cover her with straw, but La Voisin in her horrible death agony pushed executioners and straw away several times – till her strength failed.

The straw and wood were now quickly lighted, and the flames blazed above the unhappy wretch.

When the heap of wood fell the ashes were scattered in all directions.

The world was delivered from four horrible wretches.

Strassburg had fallen – Louvois summoned his sovereign to make a formal entry and receive the homage of the conquered city.

Though Louis XIV had expected the summons it was doubly welcome at this moment.

The very next day, the king, attended by his whole court, set out for Alsace.

IX.
The consecration of the robbery.

A wonderfully beautiful October day smiled upon the earth. The sky was so blue and clear, that it recalled the memory of Italy, and the sun shone so brightly that the heart of every worthy human being would have swelled with delight, if – yes, if men did not often make the Paradise of earth a hell to each other.

There stood the city, illumined by the sunlight, while deep sorrow and mourning filled the hearts of a larger portion of its inhabitants.

The bells rang solemnly, the houses were richly adorned, flags waved from the cathedral ; but only a few of the citizens of Strassburg could endure to-day to raise their eyes to the superb edifice, for there – high above the flags of the city – floated the proud banner of France. The streets and squares were crowded with gaily dressed people but only a few were natives of Strassburg; the majority had flocked in from the country, from Alsace and the neighboring provinces of France. Louvois had even secretly directed that all French cities and parishes in the vicinity must send a certain number of their inhabitants.

Thus to-day Strassburg presented an animated scene, although most of the citizens remained quietly in their houses. Nay, the throngs even wore a joyful appearance, as the numerous French subjects certainly had plenty of cause to consider the day one of true rejoicing and victory. To-day . . . to-day the ceremonious entry of the King of France into Strassburg and the occupation of this important place were to occur.

But each individual Frenchman seemed to himself a conqueror, and gazed proudly at the beautiful city, which was henceforth to be incorporated with France. And the proud presumption of the French was also increased by a new rumor of victory, which spread like an alarm of fire. It was the news that on the very day of the fall of Strassburg, the key of Germany, the king's troops had captured the fortress of Casale, called the key of Italy. This capture seemed the first step towards paving the way for Louis XIV to obtain the mastery of Italy. The French exulted, the fame of the «great king» flew from lip to lip; his subjects already saw a road opened to a universal monarchy with the ruler of France at its head, the world belonged to French and Frenchmen.

Thousands of people surged through the streets, especially around the house of the new French governor of the city, the *Marquis de Chamilli* one shout of «Long live the king; long live the conqueror of Strassburg and Casale!» followed another.

But every such shout was a dagger in the hearts of the Strassburg patriots, and many now envied the poor little tailor Wenck, who – sleeping in Mother Earth – no longer saw or heard what was passing here.

Syndicus Frantz and his family suffered most deeply.

Terrible tidings constantly assailed them: now that the fate of the city was decided and Catholic France had obtained the mastery, the long ripening fruit of treason fell into the hands of the government. A number of the first families – principally belonging to the magistracy – loudly and publicly declared their willingness to serve France in any way, and – wished to join the Catholic church.

At the head of these cowardly and doubly bribed apostates were the names of Günzer, Stosser, Zedlitz, Obrecht, Hecker, Frischmann, etc. Of course the most brilliant rewards were bestowed upon such noble deeds. Günzer had already – while retaining possession of his former offices with their revenues – been appointed Syndicus General of the city and Kanzlei Director. A new and lucrative post was created for Hecker, that of a royal Stadtrichter (*une charge de Lieutenant prêteur royal*).

A few days before, Prince Franz Egon of Fürstenberg, bishop of Strassburg, had entered the city with truly royal pomp.

Franz Egon, the holy man, came from Zabern, which since the Reformation had been the residence of the bishop of Strassburg, in triumph back to the old bishopric, to resume possesion of the superb cathedral.

He came – not as a modest announcer of the gospel of love – but a haughty conqueror, armed with worldly and ecclesiastical power, firmly resolved if possible to crush out the last trace of Protestantism in Strassburg.

In the eight equipages, among others, were Prince Wilhelm, Count Maximilian, and Philip Eberhard von Löwenstein, Count Salm, Count Felix of Fürstenberg, and Barons Roswurn Lerchenfeld, Elsenheim, von Wangen, and finally the Prince Bishop's civil and ecclesiastical officers.

Thus Franz Egon, amid the thunder of cannon and ringing of bells, entered Strassburg between lines of French troops and heralded by the blare of trumpets, but – amid total silence on the part of the people, only the inhabitants of the surrounding country, and the lowest classes of citizens, had added their contingent to the mute and sullen crowd.

But the cathedral, whose possession had been so long striven for by such shameful means, was to be occupied immediately.

The bishop's triumphal procession moved directly towards the superb monument of the immortal Erwin von Steinbach, the pride of Strassburg, the ancient cathedral.

Here, at the principal entrance, saluted by the troops and greeted by twenty-one salvos of artillery, the new French governor, the Marquis de Chamilli, received the prince of the church, delivering the cathedral to him in the name of His Majesty, Louis XIV, king of France.

When this great moment was over, Prince Franz Egon went to the palace of his sister, the Margravine of Baden, which had been superbly fitted up for him. A captain of the royal troops, with sixty men, formed his body guard by Louvois' express command.

Scarcely had the holy man alighted from his carriage, when Lieutenant General Baron de Visat, commander of the fifteen thousand French troops in Strassburg, paid his respects, with all the French nobles who had arrived. The magistrates also sent a delegation, which was of course composed of men like Günzer, Stosser, Obrecht, and others of similar views, who – traitors to their religion and country – heartily congratulated the victorious bishop upon the possession of the cathedral.

A royal robber

The cathedral was superbly decorated and adorned with banners, the bishop's train imposing in its splendor. But – it was also necessary to display the mediaeval magnificence of the Catholic church, the blameworthiness of Protestant heresy.

Banners waved, incense floated on the air, choirs sang, maidens attired in white preceded the train, while in the midst of the ecclesiastical dignitaries, surrounded by the whole chapter, attended by the assistant bishops, the Prince of Nassau, the grand vicar of the purple robed canons, the Prince Bishop Franz Egon of Furstenberg entered the cathedral, in order, first of all, to perform the great act of exorcism, that is to expel the demon of heresy from the sacred place. Then followed the joyous ceremonial of a new conescration and the first masses at the seven hastily erected altars.

The majority of the citizens of Strassburg naturally remained absent from these ceremonies, only the apostates, with cowardly servility and the desire to be seen, pressed forward with redoubled zeal, as well as a few of the lowest class, who were anxious to witness the spectacle.

But who could describe the sorrow and mourning which during these hours oppressed so many loyal Protestant hearts?

All Stassburg felt a common sorrow but, – it was a deep anguish of the soul, anguish which the German nation inherited, and which has now lasted for almost two centuries.

Sharp was the contrast between the grave, repressed sorrow of the citizens and the enthusiasm displayed by the conquerors.

The fifteen thousand men under Lieutenant General Baron de Visat's command already stood formed in two lines in the streets, but behind the ranks a vast crowd surged to and fro, while others were endeavoring to obtain a good position to see the king pass.

Strassburg – good old German , Strassburg – had to-day for the first time assumed the character of a French city, since on every side nothing was heard but that language, nothing was seen but *French faces* – only the cry: *Vive le Roi! Vive le vainqueur de Strasbourg et Cassale!* rang on the air.

A royal robber

Every honest patriot felt that he was standing by the grave of the old freedom, and the present festival – was a funeral.

Hours elapsed and the king did not appear.

The impatience of the crowd increased every moment.

One mounted messenger after another was sent towards Vitry, from whence the king would approach with his train ; but even on the frontier nothing was to be seen of the triumphal procession.

At last – it was nearly eleven o'clock – rockets appeared in the distance.

Couriers, covered with sweat and dust, darted to the city, bringing news to the magistrates that His Majesty was approaching. A new thrill ran through the throng, all the bells in the city began to ring and the cannon thundered from the walls.

At last! At last! The city was gained and Louis XIV entered.

«Vive le Roi!» thundered on the air.

«Vive le vainqueur de Strasbourg et Casale!» was the answering shout.

Immense bodies of troops formed the vanguard of the procession, followed by an endless succession of the various officers of the court, constantly interrupted by mounted divisions of cuirassiers, trumpeters, heralds and officials of lower rank.

All glittered with a pomp that could scarcely be described, a splendor whose brilliancy was increased by the superb weather.

And this magnificence became greater in proportion to the vicinity of His Majesty, until at last the king's equipage, drawn by eight horses, appeared with the scarcely less costly carriages of the various members of the royal family.

His Majesty, Louis XIV, King of France, was accompanied by Her Majesty the Queen, the dauphin and dauphiness, monsieur and madame, and all the lords and ladies of the court and kingdom.

Then came all the equipages, horses and servants belonging to the courtiers, together with the pages and officials of the royal household, and finally more bodies of troops.

In fact this imposing procession lasted nearly two hours.

And the bells still rang, the cannon thundered, the trumpets blared, the shouts of the crowds rent the air. But in many houses the windows – even while the procession was passing – remained closed – closed like the hearts, which the King of France alienated still farther by the order that, during his stay in Strassburg no Protestant should be permitted to visit the cathedral, and the citizens should be forbidden, on pain of the most severe punishment, to hold any communication whatever with the outside world. This was a fine indication of the manner in which promises made at the time of the capitulation would be kept.

One man of God, however, received the *other* at the door of the cathedral: Prince Franz Egon of Fürstenberg, Bishop of Strassburg, welcomed His Most Christian Majesty.

There stood the shameless wretch, greeting the usurper of Strassburg, Louis XIV as follows: «Blessed be God the Father, God the Son, and God the Holy Ghost, for this hour! After being reinstated by the strong omnipotent arm of Your Majesty, the greatest king of the earth, in the possession of this church, from which my predecessors were driven by the violence of the heretics, I may well say with old Simeon: 'Lord, now lettest Thou Thy servant depart in peace, for mine eye have seen Thy salvation.'»

Such were the words of the shameless traitor to his native city and country, the German prince, Franz Egon of Fürstenberg, Bishop of Strassburg, as he extended the crucifix for Louis XIV, King of France, to kiss. Then, according to custom, he offered His Majesty the holy water the folding doors flew wide open, the organ sounded, the king and his train entered the magnificent edifice, and the *Te Deum laudamus* began.

Before the high altar knelt Louis XIV, King of France, thanking God – for having prospered his robbery of Strassburg.

X.
Joy and sorrow.

The king had left Strassburg, but the bells still rang, the cannon still thundered to escort His Majesty to the boundaries of the now French city.

But the impression made by Louis XIV on the better portion of the inhabitants was very unfavorable, and greatly increased the universal anxiety regarding the future.

His first act showed distrust and love of tyranny. The king, as soon as he arrived, mounted his horse, in order – accompanied by Louvois and Vauban – to visit the citadel the latter had planned.

His Majesty ordered the work to be executed as rapidly as possible, as well as the building of the two redoubts Louvois had directed to be erected within the city to hold the inhabitants in check, if they chanced to be rebellious.

Moreover, on the same day, Louis XIV orderied that eighty pieces of the captured artillery – among them the ancient Maise, dear to the hearts of the citizens – should be taken to Breisach to be recast, while at the same time the citizens, on account of some free speaking, received fresh and strict commands to deliver up their guns, nay even their swords and pistols.

Strassburg received these first fruits of the new rule in sullen, angry silence. But what resistance could the inhabitants make? Fifteen thousand Frenchmen held them in check and watched the grave of their four centuries of freedom.

But the patriots – so far as was possible – had proudly and firmly closed their eyes and ears to all the brilliant festivals of the last week. Even the houses in many streets were shut, and many hundreds of windows remained closed by curtains, while usurping royalty was displaying its magnificence and splendor without.

Ah! the pain in the hearts of the patriots was far too great, the grief of the Frantz family was indescribable.

A royal robber

To deep sorrow over the fall of Strassburg was united secret rebellion, indignation at the manner in which the treacherous deed had been effected and the traitors themselves, as well as sincere mourning for the death of the worthy Wenck.

Hugo von Zedlitz and the Syndlcus had had him buried quietly, and followed his body to the grave. Never was grief more sincere than theirs, but in these troublous times they locked it deep in their hearts.

And must not fresh anxieties be added to these cares? The new government had already proved faithless to its pledge in many instances, who was to prevent its violation of the eighth article of the capitulation with its promise of a universal amnesty? And were not Frantz and his family, as well as Hugo von Zedlitz, seriously compromised in regard to the new government? Had they not cause to expect the worst from Günzer, their mortal enemy, who now held the highest place among the magistrates, whom he directed by virtue of his position, nay who was commissioned by the French government to watch the magistrates and citizens and report any hostile feeling.

And how was such a loyal German as the Syndicus to abjure allegiance to Germany and swear fealty to France? How could Hugo von Zedlitz do this?

Syndicus Frantz had therefore, ever since the inevitable capitulation, remainned absent from the meetings of the magistrates and had not appeared to take the oath. Hugo, by his advice, remained in concealment, at least for the present.

With deep sorrow Hedwig and Alma beheld the man to whom their hearts clung as the best and most faithful husband and father, aging rapidly since his last illness and especially since the fall of his beloved Strassburg. His brown hair, which of late had only been sparsely tinged with gray, had now become white, his erect frame bowed ; his grave, dignified features had assumed a look of still greater earnestness, nay a somewhat stern, harsh expression, which was usually utterly foreign to his gentle, kindly nature.

Besides the Syndicus of late had talked very little – even to his own family. Locked in his room all day, he worked busily with closed curtains and, only came down to his meals. What he did no one knew, only Hedwig perceived that letters came and went by a mysterious, disguised messenger.

But the most troubled member of the Frantz family was Alma. Her bright hopes were all crushed – the deepest gloom rested upon her heart and future.

Alma would not have been her father's daughter, if her trouble had showed itself in any way except greater quietness, grave, silent earnestness.

Hedwig respected in both, what she sympathized with only too keenly.

Thus the house – standing so near the cathedral and therefore surrounded by noise and tumult – had become as silent as a grave. Deep solemnity rested upon it, and to-day – the day when the king intended to leave Strassburg again – to day a greater shade of mystery was added.

Frantz had asked his wife and daughter to put on their black holiday dresses at the time of the monarch's departure.

Both looked at the old gentleman in surprise, but, – accustomed to obedience and respecting the resigned gravity with which he had spoken, instantly assented. But still more surprising was the request to instantly pack up everything that would be necessary for an absence of several weeks.

So afternoon had come and His Majesty Louis XIV, King of France and now master of Alsace and Strassburg, had quitted the city with the same pomp with which a few days before he had entered.

The bells were still pealing, the cannon still thundering to accompany His Majesty to the frontier.

In the Syndicus' house, on the contrary, a deathlike silence prevailed. He himself was locked into his own room ; the mother and daughter were changing their dresses, after fulfilling the old gentleman's wish and packing up everything the family would need for an absence of several weeks.

Hedwig and Alma – each coming from her chamber – entered the sitting-room at the same moment.

Both were deadly pale, but the pallor and black silk dress made Alma so beautiful, that even the most critical eye would scarcely have wished her to look otherwise. There was a lofty expression on the lovely but now grave features, while from the beautiful blue eyes looked forth sad, quiet resignation, a deeply agitated mind, and the thick, fair hair, whose braids framed her head, lent the tall, slight, girlish figure a gentle grace. The whole effect was enhanced by the plain black dress, which gave the child a pathetic charm. Alma was attired as she would have been for some religious festival.

The bells were still ringing and the cannon still thundering as she entered with her mother.

«So my father's wish is fulfilled!» she said in a quiet, gentle tone, as she perceived her mother also in holiday dress; «but what is to be done now?»

«Do I know, my child?» replied Hedwig. «But whatever your father desires, let us obey without opposition. We know how kind are his intentions, know his wise, thoughtful mind, and must respect his deep grief by quiet compliance.»

«I trust him entirely!» said Alma calmly.

«And your father deserves this confidence,» replied the mother, «nay, it will strengthen him in his bitter conflicts. If we are not to be ruined amid the calamities of life, we must have by our side hearts that not only understand and feel with us, but also know the depths of our natures and devote themselves to us, even when all the rest of the world desert us.»

«Well!» said Alma, with a melancholy smile, but an expression of the sweetest filial devotion, as she clung to her mother and kissed her, «such a heart you have in me.»

Hedwig returned the caress; but in doing so saw the tears, which involuntarily sprang to her child's eyes.

But she was silent. She knew what the tears meant; but there was no room for discussion here; the Syndicus had said at the time of the happy betrothal: «On the day that makes us free again you, my children, shall become man and wife!» But where was this freedom now – was it not forever lost? Was not the personal liberty of the father and lover at stake? Was not the future – at least for the moment – veiled in darkness and gloom?»

A royal robber

«Have confidence here also, my child,» said the mother. «The Eternal Father has never deserted any of his children, who turned with love and trust to his heart. Rely, too, on yourself and your own heart. In times of conflict the wise must know how to bear the inevitable with strength and dignity; if they do this, faith in a fairer future will support them.»

«I will do so, mother!» replied Alma, and Hedwig knew her daughter did not lack the strength of character necessary to keep this promise.

At this momnet the Syndicus entered, also in holiday dress.

The wife and daughter went to meet him.

«Children!» said the Syndicus with gentle earnestness, as he held out a hand to each, while to their surprise something like a smile flitted over his features. «Children, God still lives and does not desert those who do not abandon Him. Come, let us act. I love not idle sorrow that leads to nothing and only consumes our strength.»

«But what is to be done?» asked Hedwig in surprise.

«Come!» replied the old gentleman, «and you will see and hear.»

He led the way; but his figure was less bowed than it had been of late. «He must be sustained by some bold resolve!» thought Hedwig. And in truth she knew her husband.

The Syndicus led the v/ay upstairs to his study, from which opened another room, only to be reached by passing through the study itself.

When they gained the top, the Syndicus opened the floor and allowed the ladies to enter. But what was the astonishment of Hedwig and Alma to perceive a party of intimate friends. Both men and women were present; but only people of the same views as those held by the Frantz family. Hugo von Zedlitz, Frau von Bernhold – the pretty little widow whom Günzer had so shamefully robbed of her estate of Plobsheim – and the venerable pastor, to whose sermons Hedwig and Alma had so often listened in the beautiful cathedral now forever closed to them, appeared.

The latter was in his ecclesiastical dress and Hugo in holiday attire.

A royal robber

Heavens, what did this mean? A feeling of joyful surprise thrilled the hearts of the mother and daughter, suffusing the latter's face with a crimson flush. Hugo greeted her tenderly, but the deep, though gentle gravity did not vanish from his features.

It was the same with the others.

When the quiet greetings, which revealed the sorrow in every heart, were over, the Syndicus said:

«Dear friends! Grave times demand grave measures. I will not tear open the deep, never to be healed wounds in my heart and yours. Strassburg's freedom, preserved, for four hundred, years, has vanished; Strassburg no longer belongs to the German empire, it is now – though by treachery and unprecedented violence – the property of France. As an honest man, a good citizen and loyal German, I battled against this shameful deed to the last. Fate has conquered us, we must submit to the inevitable, but that is not saying that loyal Germans must bow beneath the French yoke. I at least – cannot! That is why I have given up my office, that is why to day with my family I leave the city of rny birth, the city which has grown dear to my soul. I leave it with a bleeding heart, but – I cannot do otherwise – may God help me.»

There was a universal movement; but no one ventured to speak a word.

«But I cannot quit my beloved city without having finished one last act of my political labor!» continued Syndicus Frantz. «I did so by secretly writing, during the last few days, a short account of the causes which led to the fall of the city and its transfer to the French government. We owe such a statement and defense to the better classes of magistrates and citizens, to our own honor, to Germany, the emperor and empire, as well as posterity. Here it is, I shall have it printed and laid on the altar of my native land.

«But with this document my activity in the now *French* city of Strassburg is over. I am and wish to remain a German. But if the alarm bells peal again, if the emperor again unfurls the old banner, if through all .Germany the cry resounds: 'Up, German brothers, on to the Rhine! Avenge the disgrace and wrong done you and our German native land by the robbery of Alsace and Strassburg, then, then, my friends, old Frantz will not be absent; then I will return to you, dear beloved Strassburg and help regain your freedom, though I should shed my old blood before your ramparts.»

Frantz had spoken with ardent enthusiasm; now, in spite of his age, he stood with his figure drawn up to its full height, his eyes sparkled, his cheeks glowed, and raising both hands to Heaven as if to conjure it to speedily bring about such an awakening of the German nation, such a restoration of its honor, tears gushed from his eyes.

Filled with the solemnity of the moment, and obeying the impulse of their own hearts, all the men present, raising their hands as if to take an oath, exclaimed:

«Yes, yes, we will be here too, we, too, will fight to regain for our dear native city its old freedom and allegiance.»

And all with glowing hearts, and tears of mingled sorrow and holy anger, clasped hands and shook them upon the solemn oath.

«Be it so!» Syndicus Frantz now continued. «And with this vow and the resolve to quit Strassburg with my family, the day of freedom has returned for me and mine. Long ago I purchased a modest little estate in one of the loveliest valleys of the Rhine – *on German soil.* Thither I go to-day with my relatives. An attorney here will arrange my business in Strassburg and send us the remnants of our property. It will be enough to enlarge the little estate sufficiently to enable us all – with our modest wishes – to live on, and by, if free in God's free nature, far from the pettinesses of men.

«But ere this happens, I have one pleasant duty to perform.» Turning with open arms to Hugo and Alma, he exclaimed: «Come to my heart, my children! I promised that on the day that made us free again, you should become man and wife. True, he added sadly, I then thought of a far different freedom. God has willed otherwise; we mortals must bow before Him and His often veiled wisdom. But we need not therefore allow ourselves to be made slaves. Freedom and loyalty to Germany is the breath of life to us. Away with chains, and let us live free Germans in our German native land. The day of our removal from here is also the day that makes us free again, that is: your wedding day, the day on which the blessing of God, our blessing, and love will unite you as husband and wife.»

At these words Alma's friend, young Frau von Bernhold, her beautiful face wet with tears, approached and placed a myrtle wreath on the young girl's luxuriant hair. The father opened the door of the adjoining room, which had been transformed into a simple chapel.

Upon a plain desk lay the Bible. Candles burned on either side. As the bridal pair entered, led by the old pastpr and followed by parents and guests, a deep silence prevailed, amid which was heard without the solemn pealing of the bells, blending with the dull roar of the cannon.

Solemn and earnest were the words now spoken by the old pastor; profoundly earnest, yet pervaded with tender warmth: a marriage address beside the grave of freedom. «But freedom,» said the venerable old man, «is the true Messiah of humanity, and will therefore rise from every grave.»

«When he ended the bells and cannon were silent. His Majesty, Louis XIV, King of France, had left the possessions of Strassburg behind him; the robbery of the city had been completed and secured. But in the quiet little room, surrounded by a few faithful friends, bidding them farewell with tearful eyes, two deeply agitated but infinitely happy human beings were clasped in each others arms.

At the same hour, by Hugo von Zedlitz' directions, some unknown hand secretly placed a clay statue of honest little Wenck on the gable roof of his house. It stood there – a memento of the leal, patriotic soul – until very recently. But although it finally fell a victim to Time, and long years seemed to sanction the possession of Strassburg by France – Germany and the German nation ought and must never forget one thing and that is:

The seizure of Strassburg in 1681.